Praise for
Bernard Cornwell's
THE NATHANIEL STARBUCK
CHRONICLES

"The most entertaining military historical novels. . . . Always based on fact, always interesting . . . always entertaining."
—*Kirkus Reviews*

"[A] wonderful series . . . believable, three-dimensional characters . . . a rollicking treat for Cornwell's many fans." —*Publishers Weekly*

"Highly successful." —*The Times* (London)

"Fast-paced and exciting. . . . Cornwell—
and Starbuck—don't disappoint."
—*Birmingham News*

"A top-class read by a master of historical drama.
Nate Starbuck is on the march, and on his way to fame."
—*Irish Press*

About the Author

BERNARD CORNWELL is a native of England, where he worked as a journalist in newspapers and television. In addition to *Rebel, Copperhead, Battle Flag,* and *The Bloody Ground,* the four novels in the Nathaniel Starbuck Chronicles, he also wrote the bestselling Sharpe series, featuring the adventures of Captain Richard Sharpe of the British Army in the wars against Napoleon, which has been dramatized for television by *Masterpiece Theatre*; the Warlord Chronicles, about Arthurian England; *Stonehenge: 2000 B.C., a Novel;* and *The Archer's Tale.* A resident of the United States for fifteen years, Bernard Cornwell now lives with his American wife on Cape Cod.

BOOKS BY BERNARD CORNWELL

~ The Sharpe Novels ~
(in chronological order)

Sharpe's Tiger
*Richard Sharpe and the Siege
of Seringapatam, 1799*

Sharpe's Triumph
*Richard Sharpe and the Battle
of Assaye, September 1803*

Sharpe's Fortress
*Richard Sharpe and the Siege
of Gawilghur, December 1803*

Sharpe's Trafalgar
*Richard Sharpe and the Battle
of Trafalgar, 21 October 1805*

Sharpe's Rifles
*Richard Sharpe and the French
Invasion of Galicia, January 1809*

Sharpe's Eagle
*Richard Sharpe and the
Talavera Campaign, July 1809*

Sharpe's Gold
*Richard Sharpe and the Destruction
of Almeida, August 1810*

Sharpe's Battle
*Richard Sharpe and the Battle
of Fuentes de Onoro, May 1811*

Sharpe's Company
*Richard Sharpe and the Siege
of Badajoz, January to April 1812*

Sharpe's Sword
*Richard Sharpe and the Salamanca
Campaign, June and July 1812*

Sharpe's Enemy
*Richard Sharpe and the Defense
of Portugal, Christmas 1812*

Sharpe's Honor
Richard Sharpe and the Vitoria
Campaign, February to June 1813

Sharpe's Regiment
Richard Sharpe and the Invasion
of France, June to November 1813

Sharpe's Siege
Richard Sharpe and the
Winter Campaign, 1814

Sharpe's Revenge
Richard Sharpe and
the Peace of 1814

Sharpe's Waterloo
Richard Sharpe and the Waterloo
Campaign, 15 June to 18 June 1815

Sharpe's Devil
Richard Sharpe and
the Emperor, 1820–21

~ The Nathaniel Starbuck Chronicles ~

Rebel
(Book One)

Copperhead
(Book Two)

Battle Flag
(Book Three)

The Bloody Ground
(Book Four)

~ Other Novels ~

Stonehenge: 2000 B.C., a Novel

The Archer's Tale

Redcoat

Bernard Cornwell

THE BLOODY GROUND

THE

NATHANIEL STARBUCK

CHRONICLES

~ BOOK FOUR ~

HARPER ● PERENNIAL

NEW YORK ● LONDON ● TORONTO ● SYDNE

A hardcover edition of this book was published in 1996 by HarperCollins Publishers.

HarperCollins books may be purchased for educational, business, or sales promotional use. For information please write: Special Markets Department, HarperCollins Publishers Inc., 10 East 53rd Street, New York, NY 10022.

First Perennial edition published 2001.

Designed by David Lane

Library of Congress Cataloging-in-Publication Data
Cornwell, Bernard.
        The bloody ground / by Bernard Cornwell.— 1st Perennial ed.
        p. cm—(The Nathaniel Starbuck chronicles ; bk. 4)
        ISBN 0-06-093719-X
        1. Starbuck, Nathaniel (Fictitious character)—Fiction. 2. United States—History—Civil War, 1861–1865—Fiction. 3. Antietam, Battle of, Md., 1862—Fiction. I. Title.

PR6053.O75 B56 2001
823'.914—dc21
                                                                2001021408

12 13 14 15 WB/RRD 20 19 18

For Zachary Arnold, may he
never know the horrors of war

The Battle of Antietam
September 17, 1862

V I R G I N I A
(NOW WEST VIRGINIA)

M A

POTOMAC RIVER

SHEPHERDSTOWN

To
**HARPER'S
FERRY**

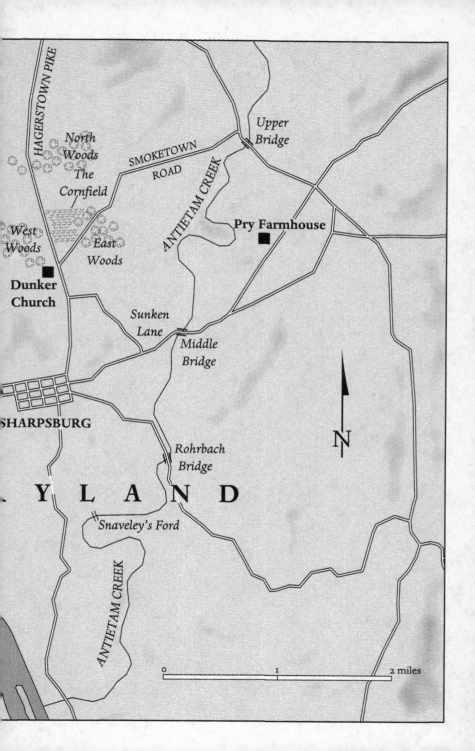

~ PART ONE ~

IT RAINED. IT HAD RAINED ALL DAY. AT FIRST IT HAD BEEN a quick, warm rain gusted by fitful southern winds, but in the late afternoon the wind had turned east and the rain became malevolent. It pelted down; a stinging, slashing, heavy rain fit to float an ark. It drummed on the armies' inadequate tents; it flooded the abandoned Yankee earthworks at Centreville; and it washed the shallow dirt off the grave mounds beside the Bull Run so that an army of fish-white corpses, scarcely a day or two buried, surfaced like the dead on Judgment Day. The Virginia dirt was red, and the water that poured in ever-widening muddy streams toward the Chesapeake Bay took on the color of the soil so that it seemed as if the whole tidewater was being drenched in blood. It was the first day of September 1862. The sun would not set on Washington till thirty-four minutes after six, yet by half past three the gas mantles had been lit in the White House, Pennsylvania Avenue was a foot deep in mud, and the open sewers of Swampoodle were overflowing. In the capitol the rain slashed through the beams and scaffolding of the half-finished dome to pour onto the newly arrived wounded from the North's defeat at Manassas, who lay in misery on the rotunda's marble floor.

Twenty miles west of Washington more fugitives from John Pope's beaten army trudged toward the safety of the capital. Rebels tried to bar their road, but rain turned the confrontation into confusion. Infantrymen huddled for shelter under soaking trees, artillerymen cursed their rain-soaked powder charges, cavalrymen tried to calm horses terrified by the bolts of lightning that raked from the heavy clouds. Major Nathaniel Starbuck, commander of the Faulconer Legion of Swynyard's Brigade of Jackson's Corps of the Army of Northern Virginia, was trying to keep a cartridge dry as he poured its powder into his rifle. He tried to protect the cartridge with his hat, but the hat was drenched and the powder that he shook from the wax paper was suspiciously lumpy. He shoved the crumpled paper onto the powder, spat the bullet into the rifle's muzzle, then rammed the charge hard down. He pulled back the hammer, fished a percussion cap from the box at his belt and fitted it onto the rifle's cone, then took aim through the silver sheeting of the rain. His regiment was at the edge of a dripping wood, facing north across a rain-beaten cornfield toward another stand of trees where the Yankees sheltered. There was no target in Starbuck's sights, but he pulled the trigger anyway. The hammer thumped onto the percussion cap that exploded to puff its little wisp of smoke, but the powder in the rifle's breech obstinately refused to catch the fire. Starbuck swore. He eased back the hammer, prised the shattered percussion cap off the cone, and put another in its place. He tried again, but still the rifle would not fire. "Might as well throw rocks at the bastards," he said to no one in particular. A rifle fired from the far trees, but the bullet's passage through the leaves over Starbuck's head was drowned by the thrashing rain. Starbuck crouched with his useless rifle and wondered what the hell he was supposed to do now.

What he was supposed to do now was cross the cornfield and drive the Yankees out of the farther trees, but the Yankees had at least one regiment and a pair of field guns in that far wood and Starbuck's combat-shrunken regiment had already been bloodied by those two guns. At first, as the Legion had waded into the tangle of rain-drenched cornstalks, Starbuck had thought the guns' noise was merely thunder; then he had seen that his left-hand companies were being shredded and broken and he had noticed the Yankee gunners handspiking their weapons about to take the rest of the Legion in the flank. He had ordered his men to fire on the guns, but only a handful of rifles had powder dry enough to fire, and so he had yelled at the survivors to go back before the artillery fired again and then he had listened to the Northerners jeering at his defeated men. Now, twenty minutes later, he was still trying to find a way across or around the cornfield, but the ground to the left was an open space commanded by the enemy guns while the woods to the right were filled with still more Yankees.

The Legion plainly did not care if the Yankees stayed or went, for rain was their enemy now, not the North. Starbuck, as he walked toward the left-hand end of his line, noticed how the men took care not to catch his eye. They were praying he would not order another attack, for none of them wanted to stir out of the trees and go back into the water-logged corn. All they wanted was for the rain to stop and for a chance to make fires and a time to sleep. Above all to sleep. In the last month they had marched the length and breadth of Virginia's northern counties; they had fought; they had beaten the enemy; they had marched and fought again; and now they were weary with marching and fighting. Their uniforms were rags, their boots were in tatters, their rations were mouldy, and they were bone tired, and so far as Starbuck's men were concerned the Yankees could keep the rain-soaked wood beyond the cornfield. They just wanted to rest. Some of them were sleeping now, despite the rain. They lay like the dead at the wood's edge, their mouths open to the rain, and their beards and moustaches lank and dripping. Other men, truly dead, lay as though asleep in the bloodied corn.

"I thought we were winning this damned war," Captain Ethan Davies greeted Starbuck.

"If it doesn't stop raining," Starbuck said, "we'll let the damned navy come and win it for us. Can you see the guns?"

"They're still there." Davies jerked his head toward the dark wood.

"Bastards," Starbuck said. He was angry with himself for not having seen the guns before ordering the first attack. The two cannon had been concealed behind a breastwork of branches, but he still cursed himself for not having suspected the ambush. The small Yankee victory galled him and the gall was worsened by an uncertainty whether the attack had really been necessary, for no one else seemed to be fighting. An occasional gun sounded somewhere in the bleak, wet gloom, and sometimes a rattle of musketry sounded over the crashing rain, but those sounds had nothing to do with Starbuck and he had received no further orders from Colonel Swynyard since the first urgent command to cross the cornfield. Perhaps, Starbuck hoped, the whole battle had been soaked into stalemate. Perhaps no one cared anymore. The enemy had been going back to Washington anyway so why not just let them go? "How do you know the guns haven't gone?" he asked Davies.

"They tell us from time to time," Davies answered laconically.

"Maybe they have gone," Starbuck said, but no sooner had he spoken than one of the Yankee field guns fired. It had been loaded with canister, a tin cylinder crammed with musket balls that shredded apart at the gun's muzzle to scatter its missiles like a giant charge of buckshot, and the balls ripped through the trees above Starbuck. The gun had been aimed fractionally too high and its fire wounded no one, but the blast of metal cascaded a deluge of water and leaves onto Starbuck's miserable infantrymen. Starbuck, crouching low beside Davies, shivered from the unwanted shower. "Bastards," he said again, but the useless curse was drowned by a crack of thunder that split the sky and rumbled into silence. "There was a time," Starbuck said sourly, "when I thought guns sounded like thunder. Now I think thunder sounds like guns." He considered that thought for a second. "How often did you ever hear a cannon in peacetime?"

"Never," Davies said. His spectacles were mottled with rainwater. "Except maybe on the Fourth."

"The Fourth and Evacuation Day," Starbuck said.

"Evacuation Day?" Davies asked, never having heard of it.

"March seventeenth," Starbuck said. "It's the day we kicked the English out of Boston. There are cannon and fireworks in Boston Garden." Starbuck was a Bostonian, a northerner who fought for the rebel

South against his own kind. He did not fight out of political conviction, but rather because the accidents of youth had stranded him in the South when the war began and now, a year and a half later, he was a major in the Confederate army. He was barely older than most of the boys he led, and younger than many, but a year and a half of battles had put a grim maturity into his lean, dark face. By rights, he sometimes reflected wonderingly, he should still be studying for the ministry at Yale's Divinity School, but instead he was crouched in a soaking wet uniform beside a soaking wet cornfield plotting how to kill some soaking wet Yankees who had managed to kill some of his men. "How many dry charges can you muster?" he asked Davies.

"A dozen," Davies answered dubiously, "maybe."

"Load 'em up and wait here. When I give the order I want you to kill those damn gunners. I'll fetch you some help." He slapped Davies's back and ran back into the trees, then worked his way further west until he reached A Company and Captain Truslow, a short, thick-set, and indefatigable man whom Starbuck had promoted from sergeant to captain just weeks before. "Any dry cartridges?" Starbuck asked as he dropped beside the captain.

"Plenty." Truslow spat tobacco juice into a puddle. "Been holding our fire till you needed it."

"Full of tricks, aren't you?" Starbuck said, pleased.

"Full of sense," Truslow said dourly.

"I want one volley into the gunners. You and Davies kill the gunners and I'll take the rest of the Legion over the field."

Truslow nodded. He was a taciturn man, a widower, and as hard as the hill farm he had left to fight against the Northern invaders.

"Wait for my order," Starbuck added, then backed into the trees again, though there was small respite from the rain under the thick leaf cover that had long before been soaked by the downpour. It seemed impossible for rain to go on this venomously for this long, but there seemed to be no diminution to the cloudburst that beat on the trees with its sustained and demonic force. Lightning flickered to the south, then a crash of thunder sounded so loud overhead that Starbuck flinched from the noise. A slash of pain whipped across his face and he staggered back, dropped to his knees, and clapped a hand to his left cheek. When he took his hand away he saw that his palm was covered in blood. For a moment he just stared helplessly at the blood being diluted and washed off his hand, then, when he tried to stand, he discovered that he was too weak. He was shaking and he thought he was going to vomit, then he feared his bowels would empty. He was making a pathetic mewing noise, like a wounded kitten. One part of his mind knew that he was not in any trouble, that the wound was slight, that he could see and think and breathe, but still he could not control the shaking, though he did manage to stop the stupid kitten noise and take in a deep breath of humid air. He took another breath, wiped more blood from his cheek, and forced himself to stand. The thunder, he realized, had not been thunder at all, but a blast of canister from the second Yankee gun, and one of the canister's musket balls had driven a splinter from a tree trunk that had razored his face to the cheekbone. An inch higher and he would have lost an eye, but instead the wound was clean and trivial, though it had still left Starbuck quivering and frightened. Alone in the trees he leaned for an instant on the scarred trunk and closed his eyes. Get me out of here alive, he prayed, do that and I'll never sin again.

He felt ashamed of himself. He had reacted to the scratch as though it had been a mortal wound, but still he felt bowel-threatening spasms of fear as he walked east toward his right-hand companies. Those companies were the least loyal, the companies that resented being commanded by a renegade Yankee, and those were the companies he would have to provoke out of their miserable shelters into the open cornfield. Their reluctance to attack was not just a question of loyalty, but also the natural instinct of wet, tired, and miserable men to crouch motionless rather than offer themselves to enemy rifles. "Bayonets!" Starbuck shouted as he passed behind the line of men. "Fix bayonets!" He was warning them that they would have to advance again and he heard grumbling coming from some of the soldiers, but he ignored their sullen defiance, for he did not know if he was in a fit state to confront it. He feared his voice would crack like a child's if he turned on them. He wondered what in God's name was happening to him. One small scratch and he was reduced to shivering helplessness! He told himself it was just the rain that had soaked his tiredness into pure misery. Like his men he needed a rest, just as he needed time to reshape the Legion and to scatter the troublemakers into different companies, but the speed of the campaign in northern Virginia was denying Lee's army the luxury of time.

The campaign had started when the North's John Pope had begun a ponderous advance on Richmond, the capital of the Confederacy. That advance had been checked, then destroyed at the second battle to be fought on the banks of the Bull Run, and now Lee's army was pushing the remaining Yankees back toward the Potomac River. With any luck, Starbuck thought, the Yankees would cross into Maryland and the Confederate army would be given the days it so desperately needed to draw breath and to find boots and coats for men who looked more like a rabble of vagabond tramps than an army. Yet the vagabonds had done all that their country had demanded of them. They had blunted and destroyed the Yankees' latest attempt to capture Richmond and now they were driving the larger Northern army out of the Confederacy altogether.

He found Lieutenant Waggoner at the right-hand end of the line. Peter Waggoner was a good man, a pious soldier who lived with a rifle in one hand and a Bible in the other, and if any of his company showed cowardice they would be hit by one of those two formidable weapons. Lieutenant Coffman, a mere boy, was crouching beside Waggoner and Starbuck sent him to fetch the captains of the other right-flank companies. Waggoner frowned at Starbuck. "Are you all right, sir?"

"A scratch, just a scratch," Starbuck said. He licked his cheek, tasting salty blood.

"You're awful pale," Waggoner said.

"This rain's the first decent wash I've had in two weeks," Starbuck said. The shaking had stopped, but he nevertheless felt like an actor as he grinned at Waggoner. He was pretending not to be frightened and pretending that all was well, but his mind was as skittish as an unbroken colt. He turned away from the Lieutenant and peered into the eastern trees, searching for the rest of Swynyard's Brigade. "Is anyone still there?" he asked Waggoner.

"Haxall's men. They ain't doing nothing."

"Keeping dry, eh?"

"Never known rain like it," Waggoner grumbled. "It never rains when you want it. Never in spring. Always rains just before harvest or when you're cutting hay." A rifle fired from the Yankee wood and the bullet thudded into a maple behind Waggoner. The big man frowned resentfully toward the Yankees almost as though he felt the bullet was a discourtesy. "You got any idea where we are?" he asked Starbuck.

"Somewhere near the Flatlick," Starbuck said, "wherever the hell that is." He only knew that the Flatlick ran somewhere in Northern Virginia. They had pitched the Yankees out of their entrenchments in Centreville and were now trying to capture a ford the Northerners were using for their retreat, though Starbuck had seen neither stream nor road all day. Colonel Swynyard had told him that the stream was called the Flatlick Branch, though the Colonel had not been really sure of that. "You ever heard of the Flatlick?" Starbuck now asked Waggoner.

"Never heard of it," Waggoner said. Waggoner, like most of the Legion, came from the middle part of Virginia and had no knowledge of these approaches to Washington.

It took Starbuck a half hour to arrange the attack. It should have taken only minutes, but the rain made everyone slow and Captain Moxey inevitably argued that the attack was a waste of time because it was bound to fail like the first. Moxey was a young, bitter man who resented Starbuck's promotion. He was unpopular with most of the Legion, but on this rainy afternoon he was only saying what most of the men believed. They did not want to fight. They were too wet and cold and tired to fight, and even Starbuck was tempted to give in to the lethargy, but he sensed, despite his fear, that if a man yielded to terror once then he would yield again and again until he had no courage left. Soldiering, Starbuck had learned, was not about being comfortable, and commanding a regiment was not about giving men what they wanted, but about forcing them to do what they had never believed possible. Soldiering was about winning, and no victory ever came from sheltering at a wood's edge in the slathering rain. "We're going," he told Moxey flatly. "Those are our orders, and we're damned well going." Moxey shrugged as if to suggest that Starbuck was being a fool.

It took still more time for the four right-flank companies to ready themselves. They fixed bayonets, then shuffled to the corn's edge, where a vast puddle was churning with water flooding from between the furrows. The Yankee guns had fired sporadically during the long moments when Starbuck had been preparing the Legion, each shot sending a blistering cloud of canister into the Southern-held trees as a means of dissuading the Confederates from any thoughts of hostility. The cannon fire left a sulphurous cloud of gunsmoke that drifted in the rain like mist. It was getting darker and darker, an unnaturally early twilight brought on by the sodden gray clouds. Starbuck positioned himself at the left-hand side of the attackers, closest to the Yankee guns, drew his bayonet, and slotted it onto his rifle's muzzle. He wore no sword and carried no badges of rank, while his revolver, which might betray him to the Yankees as a Confederate officer, was holstered at his back where the enemy could not see it. He made sure the bayonet was firm on the rifle, then cupped his hands. "Davies! Truslow!" he shouted, wondering how any voice could cut through the pelting rain and gusting wind.

"Hear you!" Truslow called back.

Starbuck hesitated. Once he shouted the next command he committed himself to battle and he was suddenly assailed with another racking bout of shivering. The fear was sapping him, but he forced himself to draw breath and shout the order. "Fire!"

The volley sounded feeble, a mere crackle of rifles like the snapping of cornstalks, but Starbuck, to his surprise, found himself on his feet and shoving forward into the corn. "Come on!" he shouted at the men nearest him as he struggled through the stiff, tangling stalks. "Come on!" He knew he had to lead this attack and he could only hope that the Legion was following him. He heard some men crashing through the crop near him and Peter Waggoner was roaring encouragement from the right flank, but Starbuck could also hear the sergeants shouting at the laggards to get up and go forward. Those shouts told him that some men were still cowering in the shelter of the trees, but he dared not turn round to see how many were following him in case those followers should think that he was giving up the advance. The attack was ragged, but it was launched now and Starbuck forced himself blindly on, expecting a bullet at any second. One of his men raised a feeble rebel yell, but no one else took it up. They were all too tired and wet to shrill the defiant call.

A bullet flickered through the bent corn tops, shedding water from the drooping cobs as it whipped across the field. The cannon were silent and Starbuck had a terror that the two guns were being slewed round to enfilade his attack. He shouted again, urging his men on, but the attack could only go at a slow walking pace, for the field was too muddy and the corn too entangling to let the men run. Other than the one rifle shot, the Yankees were silent and Starbuck knew they must be holding their fire until the ragged gray attackers were at point-blank range. He wanted to cringe from that expected volley, he wanted to drop into the wet stalks and hug the earth and wait for the war to pass. He was too terrified to shout or think or do anything except plunge blindly on toward the dark trees that were now just thirty paces away. It seemed stupid to die for a ford across the Flatlick, but the stupidity of the endeavor did not explain his fear. Instead it was something deeper, something he tried not to admit to himself because he suspected it was pure unalloyed cowardice, but the thought of how his enemies in the Legion would laugh at him if they saw his fear kept him going forward.

He slipped in a puddle, flailed for balance, and thrust on. Waggoner was still roaring defiance to his right, but the other men were just trudging through the soaking stalks. Starbuck's uniform was as wet as if he had just waded through a river. He felt he would never be dry or warm again. The drenched heavy clothes made each pace an effort. He tried to shout a battle cry, but the challenge emerged like a strangulated sob. If it had not been raining he would have suspected he was weeping, and still the Yankees did not fire and now the enemy wood was close, very close, and the terror of the last few yards gave him a maniacal energy that hurled him through the last clinging stalks, through another vast puddle and right into the trees.

Where he found that the enemy was gone. "Oh, Jesus Christ!" Starbuck exclaimed, not sure if it was a profanity or a prayer. "Jesus Christ," he said again, staring in sheer relief at the empty wood. He stopped, panting, and stared about him, but the wood really was empty. The enemy had vanished, leaving nothing behind except a few scraps of damp cartridge paper and two sets of deep wheel ruts showing where they had pushed their two guns back out of the trees.

Starbuck called his remaining companies across the cornfield, then walked gingerly through the timber until he reached the far side and could stare over a wide stretch of rain-swept pastureland to where a stream was flooding its banks. There was no enemy in sight, only a big house half obscured by trees on a far rise of land. A fork of lightning whipped down to silhouette the house, then a surge of rain blotted the building like a sea fog. The house had looked like a mansion to Starbuck, a mocking reminder of the comfortable life that a man might expect if his country was not riven by war.

"What now?" Moxey asked him.

"Your men can stand picket," Starbuck said. "Coffman? Go and find the Colonel, tell him we're across the cornfield." There were the dead to bury and the wounded to patch up.

The intermittent sounds of battle died utterly, leaving the field to rain and thunder and the cold east wind. Night fell. A few feeble fires flickered in the depths of woods, but most men lacked the skill to make fires in such rain, so instead they shivered and wondered just what they had done and why and where the enemy was and whether the next day would bring them warmth, food, and rest.

Colonel Swynyard, lean, ravaged, and ragged bearded, found Starbuck after nightfall. "No trouble crossing the cornfield, Nate?" the Colonel asked.

"No, sir, no trouble. No trouble at all."

"Good man." The Colonel held his hands toward Starbuck's fire. "I'll hold prayers in a few minutes. I don't suppose you'll come?"

"No, sir," Starbuck answered, just as he had answered every other evening that the Colonel had invited him to prayers.

"Then I'll pray for you, Nate," the Colonel responded, just as he had every other time. "I surely will."

Starbuck just wanted sleep. Just sleep. Nothing but sleep. But a prayer, he thought, might help. Something had to help, for he feared, God how he feared, that he was becoming a coward.

Starbuck took off his soaking clothes, unable to bear their chafing any longer, and hung them to take what drying warmth they could from the remains of his fire, then he wrapped himself in the clammy embrace of his blanket and slept despite the rain, but the sleep was a wicked imitation of rest for it was a waking sleep in which his dreams were mingled with rain and dripping trees and thunder and the spectral figure of his father, the Reverend Elial Starbuck, who mocked his son's timidity. "Always knew you were rotten, Nathaniel," his father said in the dream, "rotten all the way through, rotten like decayed timber. No backbone, boy, that's your trouble," and then his father capered unscathed away through a gunfire that left Starbuck dreaming that he was clinging to damp soil. Sally was in his dream too, yet she was no comfort for she did not recognize him, but just walked past him into nothingness, and then he was woken as someone shook his shoulder.

At first he thought the shaking was a part of his dream, then he feared the Yankees must be attacking and rolled quickly out of his wet blanket and reached toward his rifle. "It's all right, Major, ain't the Yankees, just me. There's a man for you." It was Lucifer who had woken him. "Man for you," Lucifer said again, "a real smart man." Lucifer was a boy who had become Starbuck's servant; an escaped slave with a high opinion of himself and an impish helping of sardonic humor. He had never revealed his true name and instead insisted on being called Lucifer. "You want coffee?" he asked.

"Is there any?"

"I can steal some."

"Then get thieving," Starbuck said. He stood, every muscle aching, and picked up his rifle that he remembered was still loaded with its useless charge of damp powder. He felt his clothes and found them still damp and saw that the fire had long gone out. "What time is it?" he called after Lucifer, but the boy was gone.

"Just after half past five," a stranger answered and Starbuck stepped naked out of the trees to see a cloaked figure on horseback. The man clicked shut his watch's lid and drew back his cloak to slip the timepiece into a fob of his uniform jacket. Starbuck glimpsed a braided smart coat that had never been blackened by powder nor soaked in blood, then the scarlet lined cloak fell back into place. "Maitland," the mounted man introduced himself, "Lieutenant-Colonel Ned Maitland." He blinked a couple of times at Starbuck's nakedness, but made no comment. "I've come from Richmond with orders for you," Maitland added.

"For me?" Starbuck asked dully. He was still not awake properly and was trying to work out why anyone in Richmond should send him orders. He did not need orders, he needed rest.

"You are Major Starbuck?" Maitland asked.

"Yes."

"Good to meet you, Major," Maitland said and leaned out of his saddle to offer Starbuck his hand. Starbuck thought the gesture inappropriate and was reluctant to take the offered hand, but it seemed churlish to refuse and so he stepped over to the horse and clasped the Colonel's hand. The Colonel withdrew his hand quickly, as though fearing that Starbuck might have soiled it, then pulled his glove back on. He was hiding his reaction to Starbuck who, Maitland thought, looked an atrocious mess. His body was white and skinny while his face and hands were burned dark by the sun. A clot of blood scarred Starbuck's cheek, and his black hair hung long and lank. Maitland was proud of his own appearance and took care to keep himself smart. He was a young man for a Lieutenant-Colonel, maybe thirty, and boasted a thick, brown beard and carefully curled mustaches that he oiled with a scented lotion. "Was that your mess boy?" He jerked his head in the direction Lucifer had disappeared.

"Yes." Starbuck had fetched his damp clothes and was pulling them on.

"Don't you know blacks ain't supposed to carry guns?" Maitland observed.

"Ain't supposed to shoot Yankees either, but he killed a couple at Bull Run," Starbuck answered ungraciously. He had already struggled with Lucifer over the Colt revolver the boy insisted on wearing and

Starbuck had no energy to refight the battle with some supercilious colonel come from Richmond. "What orders?" he asked Maitland.

Colonel Maitland did not answer. Instead he was staring through the dawn's wan light toward the mansion beyond the stream. "Chantilly," he said wistfully. "I do believe it's Chantilly."

"What?" Starbuck asked, pulling on his shirt and fumbling with its remaining bone buttons.

"That house. It's called Chantilly. A real nice place. I've danced a few nights under that roof, and no doubt will again when we've seen the Yankees off. Where will I find Colonel Swynyard?"

"On his knees, probably," Starbuck answered. "Are you going to give me those orders?"

"Aren't you supposed to call me 'sir'?" Maitland enquired courteously, though with an undercurrent of impatience because of Starbuck's antagonism.

"When hell freezes over," Starbuck said curtly, surprised at the belligerence that seemed to be an ever more salient part of his character.

Maitland chose not to make an issue of the matter. "I'm to hand you the orders in the presence of Colonel Swynyard," he said, then waited while Starbuck pissed against a tree. "You look kind of young to be a major," he remarked as Starbuck buttoned his pants.

"You look kind of young to be a colonel," Starbuck responded surlily. "And my age, Colonel, only matters to me and the fellow who carves my tombstone. If I ever get a stone. Most soldiers don't, not unless they do their fighting from behind a desk in Richmond." After delivering that insult to a man who looked like a desk soldier, Starbuck stooped to tie the laces of the boots he had collected off a dead Yankee at Cedar Mountain. The rain had stopped, but the air was still heavy with moisture and the grass thick with water. Some of the Legion had drifted out of the trees to stare at the elegant Lieutenant Colonel who endured their scrutiny patiently as he waited for Starbuck to collect his coat. Lucifer had come back with a handful of beans that Starbuck told him to take to Colonel Swynyard's bivouac. He pulled his wet hat onto his unruly black hair, then gestured to Maitland. "This way," he said.

Starbuck deliberately forced the elegant Maitland to dismount by leading him through the thickest part of the timber where the leaves and brush soaked the Colonel's silk-lined cloak. Maitland made no protest, nor did Starbuck speak until the two men had reached Swynyard's tent where, as Starbuck had predicted, the Colonel was at his prayers. The tent's flaps were brailed back and the Colonel was kneeling on the tent boards with an open Bible on his cot's blanket. "He found God three weeks ago," Starbuck told Maitland in a voice loud enough to disturb the Colonel, "and he's been bending God's ears ever since." The three weeks had worked a miracle on Swynyard, turning a drink-sodden wretch into a fine soldier who now, dressed in shirtsleeves and gray pants, turned his one good eye toward the men who had disturbed his morning prayers.

"God will forgive you for interrupting me," he said magnani-mously, climbing to his feet and tugging his suspenders over his lean shoulders. Maitland gave an involuntary shudder at the sight of Swyn-yard, who seemed even more unkempt than Starbuck. Swynyard was a thin, scarred man with a ragged beard, yellow teeth, and three missing fingers from his left hand.

"Bites his nails," Starbuck explained, seeing Maitland staring at the three stumps.

Maitland grimaced, then stepped forward with an outstretched hand. Swynyard seemed surprised at the offered gesture, but responded willingly enough, then nodded at Starbuck. "Good morning, Nate."

Starbuck ignored the greeting, jerking his head toward Maitland instead. "Man's called Lieutenant-Colonel Maitland. Got orders for me, but says he has to see you first."

"You've seen me," Swynyard said to Maitland, "so give Nate his orders."

Instead Maitland led his horse to a nearby tree and tied its reins to a drooping branch. He unbuckled a saddlebag and took out a packet of papers. "You remember me, Colonel?" he called over his shoulder as he rebuckled the bag.

"Alas, no." Swynyard sounded suspicious, wary of someone from his old, pre-Christian life. "Should I remember you?"

"Your pa sold some slaves to my pa. Twenty years back."

Swynyard, relieved that one of his old sins was not being revisited on him, relaxed. "You must have been a boy, Colonel."

"I was, but I remember your pa telling my pa that the slaves were good workers. They weren't. They were no damn good."

"In the trade," Swynyard said, "they always say that slaves are no better than their masters." Swynyard had spoken equably, though the words made it clear he had taken as great a dislike to Maitland as Starbuck had. There was an assumption of privilege about Maitland that grated on both men, or perhaps the irritation came from the incursion into their lives of a man who so obviously spent his time far from the bullets.

"Lucifer's bringing some coffee, Colonel," Starbuck said to Swynyard.

The Colonel hospitably fetched a pair of camp chairs from his tent and invited Maitland to sit. He offered Starbuck an upturned crate and set another as a table. "So where are these orders, Colonel?" he asked Maitland.

"Got 'em right here," Maitland said, putting the papers on the crate and covering them with his hat to stop either Swynyard or Starbuck from plucking them up. He took off his damp cloak to reveal a uniform that was immaculately cut and decorated with a double line of brass buttons polished to a high gloss. The twin gold stars on each of his shoulders seemed bright enough to be made of gold, while the braiding on his sleeves appeared to be fashioned from gold thread. Starbuck's coat was threadbare, had no gold or brass or even cloth marks of rank, but only white salt marks where sweat had dried into the material's weave. Maitland brushed the chair seat then twitched up his pants with their elegant yellow stripes before sitting. He lifted the hat, put the sealed papers aside, and handed another single sheet to Swynyard. "I am reporting to you as ordered, Colonel," he said very formally.

Swynyard unfolded the sheet, read it, blinked, then read it again. He looked up at Maitland, then back to the paper. "You done any fighting, Colonel?" he asked in what struck Starbuck as a bitter voice.

"I was with Johnston for a time."

"That ain't what I asked you," Swynyard said flatly.

"I've seen fighting, Colonel," Maitland said stiffly.

"Done any?" Swynyard demanded fiercely. "I mean have you been in the rifle line? Have you shot your piece, then stood to reload with a line of Yankees taking a bead on you? Have you done that, Colonel?"

Maitland glanced at Starbuck before answering and Starbuck, puzzled by the conversation, caught a look of guilt in Maitland's eye. "I've seen battle," Maitland insisted to Swynyard.

"From a staff officer's horse," Swynyard said caustically. "It ain't the same, Colonel." He sounded sad as he spoke, then he leaned forward and plucked the sealed papers off the crate and tossed them onto Starbuck's lap. "If I weren't a saved man," he said, "if I hadn't been washed in the redeeming blood of Christ, I'd be tempted to swear right now. And I do believe God would forgive me if I did. I'm sorry, Nate, more sorry than I can tell you."

Starbuck tore open the seal and unfolded the papers. The first sheet was a pass authorizing him to travel to Richmond. The second was an order requiring him to report to a Colonel Holborrow at Richmond's Camp Lee, where Major Starbuck was to take over the command of the 2nd Special Battalion. "Son of a bitch," Starbuck said softly.

Swynyard took Nate's orders, read them quickly, then handed them back. "They're taking you away, Nate, and giving the Legion to Mister Maitland." He pronounced the newcomer's name bitterly.

Maitland ignored Swynyard's tone. Instead he took out a silver case and selected a cigar that he lit with a lucifer before staring serenely into the wet trees where the men of Swynyard's Brigade were coaxing fires and hacking at hardtack with blunt bayonets. "I doubt we'll get more rain," he said airily.

Starbuck read the orders again. He had commanded the Legion for just a few weeks and had been given that command by Major General Thomas Jackson himself, but now he was ordered to hand his men over to this popinjay from Richmond and take over an unknown battalion instead. "Why?" he asked, but no one answered. "Jesus!" he swore.

"It ain't right!" Swynyard added his protest. "A regiment is a delicate thing, Colonel," he explained to Maitland. "It ain't just the Yankees who can tear a regiment to bits, but the regiment's own officers. The

Legion's had a bad stretch, but Nate here was turning it into a decent unit again. It don't make sense to change commanders now."

Maitland just shrugged. He was a handsome man who carried his privilege with a calm self-confidence. If he felt any sympathy for Starbuck, he did not betray it, but just let the protests flow past him.

"It weakens my brigade!" Swynyard said angrily. "Why?"

Maitland offered an airy gesture with his cigar. "I'm just the messenger, Colonel, just the messenger."

For a second it looked as though Swynyard would swear at Maitland, then he conquered the impulse and shook his head instead. "Why?" he asked again. "This brigade fought magnificently! Doesn't anyone care what we did last week?"

It seemed no one did, or no one for whom Maitland spoke. Swynyard momentarily closed his eyes, then looked at Starbuck. "I'm sorry, Nate, real sorry."

"Son of a bitch," Starbuck said of no one in particular. The gall of the moment was particularly bitter, for he was a northerner who fought for the South and the Faulconer Legion was his home and his refuge. He looked down at the orders. "What's the Second Special Battalion?" he asked Maitland.

For a second it looked as though Maitland would not answer, then the elegant Colonel gave Starbuck a half smile. "I believe they're more commonly known as the Yellowlegs," he said with his irritating tone of private amusement.

Starbuck swore and raised his eyes to the clouded heavens. The Yellowlegs had gained their nickname and lost their reputation during the week of springtime battles in which Lee had finally turned McClellan's Northern army away from Richmond. Jackson's men had come from the Shenandoah Valley to help Lee and among them were the 66th Virginia, a newly raised regiment that saw its first and, so far, last action near Malvern Hill. They had run away, not from a hard fight, but from the very first shells that fell near them. Their nickname, the Yellowlegs, supposedly described the state of their pants after they pissed themselves in fright. "Pissed in unison," Truslow had told Starbuck on hearing the story, "and made a whole new swamp." Later it was determined that the regiment had been too hastily raised, too skimpily trained, and too badly officered, and so its rifles had been given to men willing to fight and its men taken away to be retrained. "So who's this Colonel Holborrow?" Swynyard asked Maitland.

"He's in charge of training the punishment battalions," Maitland answered airily. "Wasn't there one at the battle last week?"

"Hell, yes," Starbuck answered. "And it was no damn good." The punishment battalion at the previous week's battle had been a makeshift collection of defaulters, stragglers, and shirkers, and it had collapsed within minutes. "Hell!" Starbuck said. Now, it seemed, the 66th Virginia had been renamed as a punishment battalion, which suggested its morale was no higher than when it had first earned its nickname and, if the performance of the 1st Punishment Battalion was anything to go by, no better trained either.

Lucifer put two mugs of coffee on the makeshift table and then, after a glance at Starbuck's distraught face, backed far enough away so that the three officers would think he was out of earshot.

"This is madness!" Swynyard had found a new energy to protest. "Who sent the order?"

"The War Department," Maitland answered, "of course."

"Who in the War Department?" Swynyard insisted.

"You can read the signature, can't you, Colonel?"

The name on the order meant nothing to either Starbuck or to Swynyard, but Griffin Swynyard had a shrewd idea where the papers might have come from. "Is General Faulconer posted to the War Department?" he asked Maitland.

Maitland took the cigar from his mouth, spat a speck of leaf from his lips, then shrugged as if the question were irrelevant. "General Faulconer's been made Deputy Secretary of War, yes," he answered. "Can't let a good man idle away just because Tom Jackson took a dislike to him."

"And General Faulconer made you the Legion's commanding officer," Swynyard said.

"I guess the general put in a good word for me," Maitland said. "The Legion's a Virginia regiment, Colonel, and the general reckoned it ought to be led by a Virginian. So here I am." He smiled at Swynyard.

"Son of a bitch," Starbuck said. "Faulconer. I should have known." General Washington Faulconer had been the Legion's founder and the brigade's commander until Jackson had dismissed him for incompetence. Faulconer had fled the army convinced that Starbuck and Swynyard had been responsible for his disgrace, but instead of retreating to his country house and nursing his hurt, he had gone to Richmond and used his connection and wealth to gain a government appointment. Now, safe in the Confederate capital, Faulconer was reaching out to take his revenge on the two men he saw as his bitterest enemies. To Swynyard he had bequeathed a man of equal rank who would doubtless be an irritant, but Faulconer was trying to destroy Starbuck altogether.

"He'd have doubtless liked to get rid of me too," Swynyard said. He had led Starbuck away from the tent and was walking him up and down out of Maitland's hearing. "But Faulconer knows who my cousin is." Swynyard's cousin was the editor of Richmond's *Examiner*, the most powerful of the five daily papers published in the Confederate capital, and that relationship had doubtless kept Washington Faulconer from trying to take an overt revenge on Swynyard, but Starbuck was much easier meat. "But there's something else, Nate," the colonel went on, "another reason why Maitland took your job."

"Because he's a Virginian," Starbuck said bitterly.

Swynyard shook his head. "I guess Maitland shook your hand, yes?"

"Yes. So?"

"He was trying to see if you're a Freemason, Nate. And you're not."

"What the hell difference does that make?"

"A lot," Swynyard said bluntly. "There are a lot of Masons in this army, and in the Yankee army too, and Masons look after each other. Faulconer's a Mason, so's Maitland, and so am I, for that matter. The Masons have served me well enough, but they've done for you, Nate. The Yellowlegs!" The colonel shook his head at the awful prospect.

"I ain't good for much else, Colonel," Starbuck admitted.

"What does that mean?" Swynyard demanded.

Starbuck hesitated, ashamed to admit a truth, but needing to tell someone about his fears. "I reckon I'm turning into a coward. It was all

I could do to cross that cornfield yesterday and I'm not sure I could do it again. I guess I've used up what courage I ever had. Maybe a battalion of cowards deserve a coward as their commander."

Swynyard shook his head. "Courage isn't like a bottle of whiskey, Nate. You don't empty it once and for all. You're just learning your trade. The first time in battle a boy reckons he can beat anything, but after a while he learns that battle is bigger than all of us. Being brave isn't ignorance, it's overcoming knowledge, Nate. You'll be all right the next time. And remember, the enemy's in just the same funk that you are. It's only in the newspapers that we're all heroes. In truth we're most of us frightened witless." He paused and stirred the damp leaves with the toe of a boot from which the sole was gaping. "And the Yellowlegs ain't cowards," he went on. "Something went wrong with them, that's for sure, but there'll be as many brave men there as in any other battalion. I reckon they just need good leadership."

Starbuck grimaced, hoping Swynyard told the truth, but still unwilling to leave the Legion. "Maybe I should go and see Jackson?" he suggested.

"To get those orders reversed?" Swynyard asked, then shook his head in answer. "Old Jack don't take kindly to men questioning orders, Nate, not unless the orders are plumb crazy, and that order ain't plumb crazy. It's perverse, that's all. Besides," he smiled, trying to cheer Starbuck, "you'll be back. Maitland won't survive."

"If he wears all that gold into battle," Starbuck said vengefully, "the Yankees will pick him off in a second."

"He won't be that foolish," Swynyard said, "but he won't stay long. I know the Maitlands, and they were always high kind of folk. Kept carriages, big houses, and acres of good land. They breed pretty daughters, haughty men, and fine horses, that's the Maitlands. Not unlike the Faulconers. And Mister Maitland hasn't come to us because he wants to command the Legion, Nate, he's come here because he has to tuck one proper battlefield command under his belt before he can become a general. Mister Maitland has his eye on his career, and he knows he has to spend a month with muddy boots if he's ever going to rise high. He'll go soon enough and you can come back."

"Not if Faulconer has anything to do with it."

"So prove him wrong," Swynyard said energetically. "Make the Yellowlegs into a fine regiment, Nate. If anyone can do it, you can."

"I sometimes wonder why I fight for this damn country," Starbuck said bitterly.

Swynyard smiled. "Nothing to stop you going back North, Nate, nothing at all. Just keep walking north and you'll get home. Is that what you want?"

"Hell, no."

"So prove Faulconer wrong. He reckons that a punishment battalion will be the end of you, so prove him wrong."

"Damn his bastard soul," Starbuck said.

"That's God's work, Nate. Your's is to fight. So do it well. And I'll put in a request that your men are sent to my brigade."

"What chance is there of that?"

"I'm a Mason, remember," Swynyard said with a grin, "and I've still got a favor or two to call in. We'll get you back among friends."

Maitland stood up as the two ragged officers walked back to the tent. He had drunk one of the two cups of coffee and started on the second. "You'll introduce me to the Legion's officers, Starbuck?" he said.

"I'll do that for you, Colonel," Starbuck said. He might resent this man displacing him, but he would not put difficulties in Maitland's way because the Legion would have to fight the Yankees whoever commanded them and Starbuck did not want their morale hurt more than was necessary. "I'll talk you up to them," he promised grudgingly.

"But I don't think you should stay after that," Maitland suggested confidently. "No man can serve two masters, isn't that what the good book says? So the sooner you're gone, Starbuck, the better for the men."

"Better for you, you mean," Starbuck said.

"That, too," Maitland agreed calmly.

Starbuck was losing the Legion and had been consigned to a battalion of the damned, which meant he was being destroyed and would somehow have to survive.

LUCIFER WAS NOT HAPPY. "RICHMOND," HE TOLD STAR-
buck soon after they had arrived in the city, "is not to my taste."

"Then go away," Starbuck retorted grumpily.

"I am considering it," Lucifer said. He was liable to pompousness
when he perceived that his dignity was under assault, and that dignity
was very easily offended. He was only a boy, fifteen at the very most,
and he would have been small for his age even if he were two years
younger, but he had crammed a lot of living into those few years and
was possessed of a self-assurance that fascinated Starbuck quite as much
as the mystery of the boy's past. Lucifer never spoke directly about that
past, nor did Starbuck ask about it, for he had learned that every query
merely prompted a different version. It was plain the boy was a contraband, an escaped slave, and Starbuck suspected Lucifer had been trying
to reach the sanctuary of the north when he had been apprehended by
Jackson's army at Manassas, but Lucifer's life before that moment, like
his real name, remained all mystery, just as it was a mystery why he had
elected to stay with Starbuck after his recapture.

"He likes you, that's why," Sally Truslow told Starbuck. "He knows you'll give him plenty of rope and he's mischievous enough to want rope. Then one day he'll grow up and you won't ever see him again."

Starbuck and Lucifer had walked from the rain-soaked battlefield to the railhead at Fredericksburg, then taken the Richmond, Fredericksburg, and Potomac Railroad to the capital. Starbuck's travel pass gave him admission to one of the passenger cars while Lucifer traveled in a boxcar with the other Negroes. The train had puffed and jerked and clanked and shuddered and thus crept south until, at dawn, Starbuck had been woken by the cry of a Richmond milkmaid. The Richmond, Fredericksburg, and Potomac depot was in the heart of the city and the rails ran right down the center of Broad Street, and Starbuck found it a strange experience to see the familiar city through the soot-smutted window of a slow-moving railcar. Newspaper boys ran alongside the train offering copies of the *Examiner* or *Sentinel*, while on the sidewalk pedestrians edged past the carts and wagons that had been herded to the street's sides by the train's slow, clangorous passage. Starbuck stared bleary-eyed through the window, noticing gloomily how many doors were hung with black, how many women were in mourning, how many cripples begged on the sidewalk, and how many men had crêpe armbands.

Starbuck had convinced himself that he would not call on Sally. He told himself that she was no longer his woman. She had found a lover, Starbuck's good friend Patrick Lassan, a French cavalryman who was ostensibly observing the war on behalf of the French army but who really rode with Jeb Stuart. Starbuck told himself that Sally was no longer his business and he was still telling himself that truth when he knocked on the blue painted door beside the tailor's shop on the corner of Fourth and Grace. Sally had been glad to see him. She was already up, already busy, and she ordered her slaves to bring Starbuck a breakfast of coffee and bread. "It's bad bread," she said, "but there ain't any good bread. Nor any good coffee, for that matter. Hell, I'm using acorns, wheat berries, and chicory for coffee. Nothing's good now except the cigars and business." Sally's business was to be Madame Royall, Richmond's most expensive medium, who offered expensive seances to reunite the living with the dead. "It's all tricks," she said scornfully, "I just tell 'em what they want to hear and the more I charge the more they believe me." She shrugged. "Dull business, Nate, but better than working nights." She meant the brothel on Marshall Street where Sally had first discovered her business acumen.

"I can imagine."

"I doubt that you can, Nate," Sally said good humoredly, then gave him a long searching look. "You're thin. Look worn out like a mule. That a bullet cut on your face?"

"Tree splinter."

"The girls will love it, Nate. Not that you ever needed help in that department, but tell them it's a bullet and they'll all want to pet you. And you got a slave too?"

"I pay him when I can," Starbuck said defensively.

"Then you're a damn fool," she said fondly. "Bad as Delaney." Belvedere Delaney was a lawyer officially attached to the War Department, but his duties left him plenty of time for running his various businesses, which included Richmond's most exclusive brothel as well as the crêpe-curtained premises where Sally manufactured conversations with the dead. Sally had first met Delaney by being one of his employees in the brothel, and not just any employee, but the most sought-after girl in Richmond. She was Captain Truslow's only child and had been raised to hard work and small reward on Truslow's hill farm, but she had fled the farm and embraced the city, a transition made easy by her striking looks. Sally had a deceptively soft face, a mass of golden hair, and a quick spirit to liven her attractiveness, but there was far more to Sally Truslow than nature's accident of beauty. She knew how to work and knew how to profit from that work, and these days she was Delaney's business partner rather than his employee. "Delaney's a fool," she said tartly. "He lets his house boy twist him round his little finger, and you're probably just as bad. So let's have a look at your boy. I want to know you're being looked after." And thus Lucifer was summoned up to the parlor where he quickly charmed Sally who recognized in the boy someone who, like herself, was working up from rock bottom. "But why are you carrying a gun, boy?" she demanded of Lucifer.

" 'Cos I'm in the army, miss."

"The hell you are. You get caught with a gun in this town, boy, and they'll skin your backside and then send you down the river. You're damn lucky to have survived this long. Take it off. Now."

Lucifer, who had resisted every former effort to disarm him, meekly unbuckled the gunbelt. It was plain that Lucifer was awestruck by Sally, and he made not even the smallest complaint as she told him to hide the revolver in Starbuck's baggage and then dismissed him to the kitchen. "Tell them to feed you up," she said.

"Yes, miss."

"He's got white blood," Sally said when Lucifer had gone.

"I guess."

"Hell, it's obvious." She poured herself more of the strange-tasting coffee, then listened as Starbuck told her why he was in Richmond. She spat derisively when Washington Faulconer's name was mentioned. "The city was full of rumor about why he'd left the army," she said, "but he rode right over the rumor. Arrived here bold as brass and just claimed Jackson was jealous of him. Jealous! But your General Jackson, Nate, he makes enemies like a louse makes itches and there are plenty of men here ready to sympathize with Faulconer. He got office soon enough. I guess you're right and the Masons looked after him. Delaney will know, he's a Mason. So what do you do now?"

Starbuck shrugged. "I have to report to Camp Lee. To a Colonel Holborrow." He was not looking forward to the moment. He was unsure of his ability to lead the worst battalion in the South's army, and he already missed the companionship of the Legion.

"I know Holborrow," Sally said, "not personally," she added hastily, "but he's pretty considerable in town." Starbuck was not surprised at her knowledge, for Sally kept an ear very close to the ground to snap up every trifle of gossip that she could turn into a mystical revelation in her seances. "He's got money," she went on, "God knows how, 'cos he wasn't nothing but a penitentiary governor in Georgia before the war. A prison man, right? Now he's in charge of training and equipping the replacements at Camp Lee, but he spends most of his time down in Screamersville."

"The brothels?"

"Them and the cockpit."

"He gambles?" Starbuck asked.

Sally shook her head at Starbuck's naïveté. "He don't go there to admire the birds' feathers," she said tartly. "What the hell did they teach you at Yale?"

Starbuck laughed, then perched his muddy boots on a tapestry-covered ottoman that stood on an Oriental rug. Everything in the room was in the best of taste; understated but expensive. Napoleon's bust glowered on the mantel, leatherbound books stood ranked in glass-fronted cases, while exquisite pieces of porcelain were displayed on shelves. "You live well, Sally," Starbuck said.

"You know any merit in living badly?" she asked. "And you can get your boots off the furniture while you think about the answer."

"I was thinking of going to sleep," Starbuck said, not moving.

"Hell, Nate Starbuck," Sally said, "are you reckoning on staying here?"

He shook his head. "I thought I might let you buy me lunch at the Spotswood, then walk with me to Camp Lee."

Sally waited until he had moved the offending boots from the ottoman. "Now why," she asked, "would I want to do that?"

Starbuck smiled. "Because, Sally, if I've got to take a pack of skulking cowards to war, then they need to know I'm a lucky man. And how much luckier can a man be than to show up with someone like you on his arm?"

"Glad to see the Yankees haven't shot your glib tongue out," she said, disguising her pleasure at the compliment. "But are you reckoning on going into the Spotswood looking like that?"

"Got nothing else to wear." He frowned at his disheveled uniform. "Hell, if it's good enough for fighting battles it's good enough for the Spotswood Hotel." Six hours later a well-fed Starbuck walked with Sally and Lucifer west out of the city. Sally wore a bonnet and shawl over a simple blue dress that was nowhere near plain enough to hide her beauty. She carried a fringed parasol against the sun, which had at last appeared from the clouds and was sucking up the remnants of the rain-

storm into drifting patches of mist. They walked past the State Penitentiary, crossed the head of Hollywood Cemetery where the freshly
turned earth lay in grim rows like the battalions of the dead, and skirted
the municipal waterworks, until at last they could see Camp Lee on its
wide bluff above the river and canal. Starbuck had visited the camp earlier in the year and remembered it as a grim, makeshift place. It had
once been the Richmond Central Fairgrounds, but the onset of war had
turned it into a giant dumping ground for the battalions that had flocked
to the defense of Richmond. Those battalions were now on Virginia's
northern border and the camp was a dirty stretch of muddy ground
where conscripts received a rudimentary training and where stragglers
were sent to be assigned to new battalions. At the war's beginning the
camp had been a favorite place for Richmonders to come and watch the
troops being drilled, but that novelty had worn off and these days few
people visited the dank, derelict-looking barracks where old moldering
tents stood in rows and tarpaper huts flapped in the breeze. The gallows
of the camp jail still topped the hill, and round the jail was clustered an
array of wooden huts where most of the camp's present occupants
seemed to be billeted. Two sergeants playing horseshoes confirmed to
Starbuck that the huts were the Special Battalion's quarters and he
walked slowly uphill toward the flat crest where a half dozen companies
were being drilled. A few lackluster work parties were patching the
decrepit buildings among which, like a palace among hovels, stood the
house that the sergeants had said was Holborrow's headquarters. The
house was a fine two-story building with a wide verandah all around
and slave quarters and kitchens in its backyard. Two flagpoles stood in
front of the house, one with the Confederate's stars and bars and the
other flying a blue flag crested with the coat of arms of Georgia.

Starbuck paused to watch the companies being drilled. There
seemed small point to the activity, for the men were proficient enough,
though every tiny fault was enough to force the sergeant in charge to a
barrage of obscene abuse. The sergeant was a tall, gangling man with an
unnaturally long neck and a voice that could have carried clean across
the river to Manchester. The troops had no weapons, but were simply
being marched, halted, turned, and marched again. Some were in gray

coats, but most wore the increasingly common butternut brown that was easier to produce. At least half the men, Starbuck noted with alarm, had no boots, but were marching barefoot.

Sally put her arm into Starbuck's elbow as they walked closer to the headquarters, where a group of four officers was stretched out in camp chairs on the verandah. One of the idling officers trained a telescope toward Starbuck and Sally. "You're being admired," Starbuck said.

"That was the point of me wasting an afternoon, wasn't it?"

"Yes," Starbuck said proudly.

Sally paused again to watch the troops on the parade ground who, so far as the screaming sergeant allowed, returned her inspection. "They're your men?" she asked.

"All mine."

"The pick of a bad bunch, eh?"

"They look all right to me," Starbuck said. He was already trying to imbue himself with a loyalty toward these despised troops.

"They can kill Yankees, can't they?" Sally said, sensing Starbuck's apprehension. She brushed at the ingrained dirt on his uniform sleeve, not because she believed the dirt could be swept off, but because she knew he needed the small consolation of touch. Then her hand paused. "What's that?" she asked.

Starbuck turned to see that Sally was gazing at a punishment horse that had been erected between two of the huts. The horse was a long beam that was mounted edgewise on a pair of tall trestles, and the punishment consisted of a man being forced to straddle the beam's edge and stay there while his own weight turned his groin into a mass of pain. A prisoner was on the horse with his hands bound and his legs tied to prevent him dismounting, while an armed guard stood beside the steps that were used to mount the instrument. "A punishment," Starbuck explained, "called a horse. Hurts like hell, I'm told."

"That's the point of punishment, ain't it?" Sally said. She had taken her share of beatings as a child and the experience had thickened her skin.

The man beneath the horse appeared to ask a question of the straddling man. The prisoner shook his head and the man yanked down on his bound ankles so that the man screamed.

"Shit," Starbuck said.

"Ain't that a part of it?" Sally demanded.

"No."

Sally looked at the distaste on Starbuck's face. "You going soft, Nate?"

"I don't mind punishing soldiers, but not torture. Besides, think of them." He nodded toward the companies on the parade ground who were mutely watching the horse. "A regiment's a fragile thing," he said, echoing Swynyard's words to Maitland. "It works best when the men are fighting the enemy, not each other." He flinched as the guard tugged on the prisoner's ankles again. "Hell," he said, reluctant to intervene, but also unwilling to watch any more brutality. He strode toward the horse.

The guard who had tugged on the prisoner's ankles was a sergeant who turned and watched Starbuck's approach. Starbuck wore no badges of rank and had a rifle slung on his left shoulder, both of which suggested he was a private soldier, but he carried himself confidently and had a woman and servant, which suggested he might be an officer and the sergeant was consequently wary. "What's he done?" Starbuck demanded.

"Being punished," the sergeant said. He was a squat, bearded man. He was chewing tobacco and paused to spit a stream of yellowish spittle onto the grass. "Sergeant Case's orders," he added as though that should be sufficient explanation.

"I know he's being punished," Starbuck said, "but I asked what he had done."

"Being punished," the sergeant said obstinately.

Starbuck moved so he could see the drawn face of the prisoner. "What did you do?" he asked the man.

Before the prisoner could give any answer the drill sergeant abandoned the companies on the parade ground and marched toward the horse. "No one talks to prisoners under punishment!" he screamed in a terrifying voice. "You know that, Sergeant Webber! Punishment is punishment. Punishment is what will turn this lily-livered rabble of squirrel shit into soldiers." He slammed to a halt two paces from Starbuck. "You have questions," he said forcefully, "you ask them to me."

"And who are you?" Starbuck asked.

The tall sergeant looked surprised, as though his fame must have been obvious. He gave no immediate answer, but instead inspected Starbuck for clues to his status. The presence of Sally and Lucifer must have convinced him that Starbuck was an officer, though Starbuck's age suggested he was not an officer who needed to be placated. "Sergeant Case," he snapped. Case's long neck and small head would have looked risible on any other man, and his ridiculous appearance was not helped by a wispy beard and a thin broken nose, but there was a malevolence in the sergeant's dark eyes that turned amusement into fear. The eyes were flat, hard, and merciless. Starbuck noted too that Case's gangly body was deceptive; it was not a weak, thin frame, but lean and muscled. He was uniformed immaculately, every button polished, every crease hot-pressed, and every badge shining. Sergeant Case looked just as Starbuck had imagined soldiers ought to look like before he discovered that, at least in the Confederacy, they were generally ragged as hell. "Sergeant Case," Case said again, leaning closer to Starbuck, "and I," he stressed that word, "am in charge here."

"So what did the prisoner do?" Starbuck asked.

"Do?" Case asked dramatically. "Do? What he did is of no business to you. Not one scrap."

"What battalion is he?" Starbuck demanded, nodding toward the prisoner.

"He could belong to the Coldstream bloody Guards," Case shouted, "and it still ain't your business."

Starbuck looked up at the prisoner. The man's face was white with pain and rigid with the effort needed not to show that pain. "Battalion, soldier?" Starbuck snapped.

The man grimaced, then managed to say a single word. "Punishment."

"Then you are my business," Starbuck said. He took his folding knife out of a pocket, unsnapped the blade, and sawed at the rope binding the prisoner's ankles. The motion made the prisoner whimper, but it provoked Sergeant Case to leap forward threateningly.

Starbuck paused and looked up into Case's eyes. "I'm an officer,

Sergeant," he said, "and if you lay a damned hand on me I'll make sure you spend the rest of today on this horse. You won't walk for a god-damn week. Maybe not for a goddamn month."

Sergeant Case stepped back as Starbuck cut through the last strands of hemp and put a hand under one of the prisoner's boots. "Ready?" he called, then heaved up hard, throwing the prisoner off the beam. The man thumped onto the damp ground where he lay still as Starbuck crouched and sliced through the rope about his wrists. "So what did he do?" Starbuck asked Sergeant Case.

"Son of a bitch!" Case said, though whether of Starbuck or the pris-oner it was impossible to tell, then he turned abruptly and strode away with his companion.

The prisoner groaned and tried to stand, but the pain in his crotch was too savage. He crawled to one of the horse's supporting trestles and dragged himself to a sitting position, then just clung to the timber. His eyes watered and his breath came in small, stuttering gasps. Even Sally flinched at his evident pain. "Guns," he finally said.

"Guns?" Starbuck asked him. "What about them?"

"Son of a bitch is stealing guns," the freed prisoner said, then was forced to stop because of the pain. He clutched his groin, held a deep breath, than shook his head in an effort to banish the dreadful agony. "You asked why I was on the horse? Because of guns. I was on a detail to unload rifles. We got twenty boxes of them. Good ones. But Holborrow made us put them in crates marked CONDEMNED and then gave us mus-kets instead. Richmond muskets. Hell," he spat, then momentarily closed his eyes as a spasm of pain made him grimace. "I don't want to go shooting no Yankees with buck and ball, not if they've got minie balls. That's why I argued with that son of a bitch Sergeant Case."

"So where are the rifles now?" Starbuck asked.

"Hell knows. Sold, probably. Holborrow don't care so long as we never go to war. We're not supposed to fight, see? Just get supplies that the son of a bitch sells." The man frowned up at Starbuck. "Who are you?" he asked.

"Potter!" A new and angry voice yelled from the headquarters building. "Potter, you son of a bitch! You bastard! You lunkheaded piece of dog shit. You black-assed fool!" The speaker was a tall, lean officer in a braided gray coat who stumped toward Starbuck with the help of a silver-tipped cane. Sergeant Case marched behind the officer, who had a neat blond goatee beard and a narrow mustache that had been carefully waxed into stiff points. He shoved the cane hard into the turf to aid each step and in between he brandished it toward the astonished Starbuck. "Where the hell have you been, Potter?" the officer demanded. "Just where the hell have you been, boy?"

"He's talking to you?" Sally asked Starbuck in bemusement.

"Hell, boy, are you drunk?" The limping officer bellowed. "Potter, you black-ass lunkhead piece of leper shit, are you drunk?"

Starbuck was about to deny being either Potter or drunk, then a mischievous impulse welled up inside him. "Don't say a word," he said quietly to Sally and Lucifer, then shook his head. "I ain't drunk," he said as the officer came close.

"Is this how you repay a kindness?" the officer demanded fiercely. He had the stars of a colonel on his shoulders. "My apologies, ma'am," the colonel touched his free hand to the brim of his hat, "but I can't abide tardiness. Can't abide it. Are you drunk, Potter?" The colonel stepped close to Starbuck and thrust his goatee up toward the younger man's clean-shaven chin. "Let me smell your breath, Potter, let me smell your breath. Breathe, man, breathe!" He sniffed, then stepped back. "You don't smell drunk," the colonel said dubiously, "so why the hell, forgive me, ma'am, did you throw Private Rothwell off the horse. Answer me!"

"It was upsetting the lady," Starbuck said.

The major looked at Sally again and this time he registered that she was a startlingly pretty young woman. "Holborrow, ma'am," he said, snatching off his brimmed hat to reveal a head of carefully waved gold hair, "Colonel Charles Holborrow at your service." He gaped at Sally for a second. "I should have known," he said, his voice suddenly softening, "that you come from Georgia. Ain't girls anywhere in the world as pretty as Georgia girls, and that's a plain straight fact. 'Pon my precious soul, ma'am, it's a fact. The Reverend Potter did say as how his son was married and was bringing his good lady here, but he never did say just how pretty you are." Holborrow shamelessly leered down to judge Sally's figure before grasping her hand and giving it a firm kiss. "Sure pleased to meet you, Mrs. Potter," he said, still holding on to her hand.

"Pleasure's all mine, Colonel." Sally pretended to be flattered by Holborrow's admiration and left her hand in his.

Holborrow leaned his cane against his hip so he could fold his other hand over Sally's. "And you were upset by the punishment, ma'am, is that it?" he inquired solicitously, massaging Sally's hand between his.

"Reckon I was, sir," Sally said humbly, then sniffed.

"Right upsetting for a lady," Holborrow agreed. "But you have to understand, ma'am, that this lunkhead prisoner struck Sergeant Case. Struck him! A serious military offense, ma'am, and your husband here had no business interfering. None at all. Ain't that the case, Sergeant Case?"

"Sir!" Case snapped, evidently his way of articulating an affirmative to officers.

Holborrow let go of Sally's hand to step closer to Starbuck. "Sergeant Case, boy, is from North Carolina, but he spent the last fourteen years in the British army. Ain't that the case, Case?"

"Sir!" Case snapped.

"Which regiment, Case?" Holborrow asked, still staring into Starbuck's eyes.

"Seventh, sir, Royal Fusiliers, sir!"

"And while you were still sucking the milk from your mother's titties, Potter, forgive me, ma'am, Sergeant Case was fighting! Fighting, boy! Ain't that the case, Case?"

"Battle of the Alma, sir! Siege of Sevastopol," Case snapped, and Starbuck got the impression that he was listening to a much practiced dialogue.

"But Sergeant Case is a patriot, Potter!" Holborrow continued, "and when the Yankees broke the Union by attacking us, Sergeant Case left Her Majesty's service to fight for Jeff Davis and liberty. He was sent here, Potter, to turn the Yellowlegs into a proper regiment instead of a bunch of schoolgirls. Ain't that the case, Case?"

"Sir!"

"And you," Holborrow spat at Potter, "dare to countermand a man like Sergeant Case! You should be ashamed of yourself, boy. Ashamed! Sergeant Case has forgotten more about soldiering than you ever learned or ever will learn. And if Sergeant Case says a man deserves punishment, then punished he shall be!" Holborrow stepped back and took Sally's hand into his again. "But seeing as how you're a ray of Georgia sunshine, ma'am, I'll spare you from seeing any more unpleasantness this afternoon. I think your husband has learned his lesson, so thank you, Sergeant Case." Holborrow nodded to the sergeant, who scowled at Starbuck, then marched stiffly back to the parade ground. Holborrow ordered the freed prisoner to make himself scarce, and then, his grip still enfolding Sally's hand, he turned back to Starbuck. "So where have you been, boy? Your father wrote that you'd left Atlanta ten days back. Letter got here, but you didn't! Ten days! It don't take ten days from Atlanta to Richmond, boy. You been drinking again?"

"It was my fault," Sally said in a frightened little voice. "I had the fever, sir. Real bad, sir."

Lucifer giggled at Sally's invention and Holborrow's head snapped round. "You snigger once more, boy, and I'll whip the flesh clean off your black bones. Is he your nigger?" he asked Starbuck.

"Yes," Starbuck said, wondering how the hell he would back out of this deception.

"Yes, sir," Holborrow said, correcting him. "You forgetting I'm a Colonel, Potter?"

"Yes, sir. I mean no, sir."

Holborrow, still holding Sally's hand, shook his head at Starbuck's apparent confusion. "So how is your father?" he asked Starbuck.

Starbuck shrugged. "I guess," he began, then shrugged again, suddenly bereft of imagination.

"He's mending," Sally said. She was enjoying the play-acting much more than Starbuck who, though he had started it, was now regretting the deception. "Thank the Lord," Sally said as she finally extricated her fingers from Holborrow's grasp, "but he is surely mending."

"Praise the Lord," Holborrow said. "But you've been a burden to him, boy, a burden," he snarled at Starbuck, "and you'll forgive my bluntness, Mrs. Potter, but when a man's son is a burden it's right he should be told plain."

"It sure is," Sally agreed firmly.

"We was expecting you a week ago!" Holborrow snarled at Starbuck, then gave Sally a yellow-toothed smile. "Got a room all set up for you, ma'am. Bed, washstand, clothes press. The reverend wanted you comfortable. Not to be pampered, he said, but comfortable."

"You're too kind, sir," Sally said, "but I'm sleeping with my cousin Alice in the city."

Holborrow looked disappointed, but Sally had spoken firmly and he did not contest the issue. "Your cousin's gain is our loss, ma'am," he said, "but you'll stay for a lemonade and maybe partake of a peach? I'm partial to a fine peach, as all Georgians ought to be."

"Pleasure, sir."

Holborrow glanced at Lucifer, who was carrying Starbuck's shabby bag. "Get to the kitchen, boy. Move your black ass! Go!" Holborrow turned to Starbuck again. "Hope you've got a decent uniform in that bag, boy, because the one you're wearing is a disgrace. A dis-grace. And where the hell are your lieutenant's bars?" He gestured at Starbuck's shoulders. "You sell your bars for liquor, boy?"

"Lost them," Starbuck said hopelessly.

"You are a sad man, Potter, a sad man," Holborrow said, shaking his head. "When your father wrote and asked my help he had the grace to tell me as much. He said you were a sore disappointment, a reproach to the good name of Potter, so I can't say as how I wasn't warned about you, but get drunk with me, boy, and I'll kick your son of a bitch ass blue, forgive me, ma'am."

"Forgiven, Colonel," Sally said.

"Your father now," Holborrow continued to lecture Starbuck, "he never drinks. Every day we had an execution the Reverend would come to the penitentiary to pray with the bastards, forgive me, ma'am, but he never touched a drop of the ardent. Not a drop! Even after the bastards, forgive me, ma'am, were strung up and kicking away and the rest of us felt the need for a restorative libation, your father would stick to lemonade, but he often said that he feared you'd end up on that same scaffold, boy, with him saying a prayer on one side of you and me ready to push the stool out from under your feet on the other. So he's sent you here, Potter, to learn discipline!" This last word was shouted into Starbuck's face. "Now, ma'am," he turned his attention back to Sally, "give me your pretty little hand and we'll divide ourselves a peach, and after that, ma'am, if you'll permit me, I'll give you a ride back to the city in my carriage. It's not the best day for walking. A mite too hot and a pretty lady like you should be in a carriage, don't that sound good?"

"You're too kind, Colonel," Sally said. She had thrust her left hand, which was conspicuously lacking a wedding ring, into a fold of her shawl. "I ain't never ridden in a carriage," she added in a pitiful voice.

"We must accustom you to luxury," Holborrow said lasciviously, "like a pretty little Georgia girl should be." He led her to the house and put his free arm around her waist at the bottom of the steps. "I've been riding in a carriage ever since a Yankee bullet took away the use of my right leg. I must tell you the tale. But for now, ma'am, allow me to assist you up the stairs. There's a loose board or two," Holborrow half lifted Sally up the verandah's stairs, "and you just sit yourself down, ma'am, next to Captain Dennison."

The four officers, all captains, had stood to greet Sally. Captain Dennison proved to be a thin clean-shaven man whose face was horribly scarred by some skin disease that had caused his cheeks and forehead to be foul with livid sores. He pulled a wicker chair forward and brushed at its cushion with his hand. Holborrow gestured at Starbuck. "This here's Lieutenant Matthew Potter, so he ain't a rumor after all." The four captains laughed at Holborrow's witticism, while the colonel ushered Sally forward with his right arm still firmly planted about her slender waist. "And this his wife. I'm sorry, my dear, but I don't have the advantage of your name."

"Emily," Sally said.

"And a prettier name I never did hear, upon my soul, but I never did. You sit down, ma'am. This here is Captain Dennison, Captain Cartwright, Captain Peel, and Captain Lippincott. You make yourself at home and I'll settle your husband. You don't mind if I put him to work straight off? He should have been at work a week ago."

Holborrow limped ahead of Starbuck into a gloomy hall where a tangle of gray officers' coats hung on a bentwood stand. "Why a good woman like that would marry a no-good son of a bitch like you, Potter," the colonel grumbled, "the good Lord only knows. Come in here, boy. If your wife ain't staying then you don't need a bedroom. You can put a cot in here and sleep by your work. This here was Major Maitland's office, but then the son of a bitch got himself promoted and given a real battalion, so now we're waiting for a Yankee son of a bitch called Starbuck. And when he gets here, Potter, I don't want him pestering me about unfinished paperwork. You understand me? So get those papers straight!"

Starbuck said nothing, but just gazed at the pile of untidy papers. So Maitland had originally been assigned to the Yellowlegs? That was intriguing, but the bastard had evidently persuaded his lodge brothers to pull strings and so Maitland had been promoted and given command of the Legion and Starbuck had got the punishment battalion.

"Are you dozing, boy?" Holborrow thrust his face into Starbuck's.

"What am I to do, sir?" Starbuck asked plaintively.

"Tidy it up. Just tidy it. You're supposed to be the adjutant of the Second Special Battalion, ain't you? Now get on with it, boy, while I entertain your wife." Holborrow stumped out of the room, banging the door shut behind him. Then the door suddenly opened again and the colonel's narrow face peered round the edge. "I'll send you some lemonade, Potter, but no liquor, you hear me?"

"Yes, sir."

"No liquor for you, Potter, not while you're under my orders."

The door slammed shut again, so hard that the whole house seemed to shudder, then Starbuck let out a long breath and sank into a leather-upholstered chair that stood at a desk littered with a mess of papers. What the hell, he wondered, had he got himself into? He was tempted to end the deception right now except that there was a possible profit in it. He was certain that if he announced himself as Major Starbuck then he would learn nothing, for Holborrow would take care to cover up any deficiencies in the training and equipment of the Special Battalion, while the despised Lieutenant Potter was clearly a man from whom nothing needed to be hidden. Besides, Starbuck thought, there was no elegant way out of the deception now. Better to play the tomfoolery through while he spied on Holborrow's work, then he would go back into the city and find Belvedere Delaney, who would make sure Starbuck had a fine time and a warm bed for the next few nights.

He began to sift through the heaps of paper. There were receipts for food, receipts for ammunition, and urgent letters asking for the receipts to be signed and returned to the relevant departments. There were pay books, lists, amendments to lists, and prison rosters from all the military jails in Richmond. Not every man in the Special Battalion was from the Yellowlegs; at least a fifth had been drafted in from the prisons, thus leavening the cowards with crooks. Under the prison rosters Starbuck found a letter addressed to Major Edward Maitland from the Richmond State Armory acknowledging that the Special Battalion was to be equipped with rifles and requesting that the twenty boxes of muskets be returned forthwith. There was a grudging tone to the letter, suggesting that Maitland had used his influence to have the despised muskets replaced with modern weapons and Starbuck, knowing he would have to fight the battle all over again, sighed. He put the letter aside to find, beneath it, yet another letter, this one addressed to Chas. Holborrow and signed by the Reverend Simeon Potter of Decatur, Georgia. Starbuck leaned back to read it.

The Reverend Potter, it seemed, had the superintendence of the prison chaplaincies in the State of Georgia and had written to his old acquaintance—he seemed no more than an acquaintance and scarcely a friend—Charles Holborrow, to beg his help in the matter of his second son, Matthew. The letter, written in deliberate strokes in a dark black ink, irresistibly reminded Starbuck of his own father's handwriting. Matthew, the letter said, had been a sore trial to his dear mother, a disgrace to his family's name, and a shame to his Christian upbringing. Though educated at the finest academies in the south and enrolled in Savannah Medical School, Matthew Potter had insisted upon the paths of iniquity. "Ardent liquor has been his downfall," the Reverend Potter wrote, "and now we hear he has taken a wife, poor girl, and, furthermore, has been ejected from his regiment because of continual drunkenness. I had apprenticed him to a cousin of ours in Mississippi, hoping that hard work would prove his salvation, but instead of entering upon his duties he insisted upon engaging in Hardcastle's Battalion, but even as a soldier, it seems, he could not be trusted. It pains me to write thus, but in begging your help I owe you a duty of truthfulness, a duty thrice burdened by my faith in Christ Jesus, to Whom I daily pray for Matthew's repentance. I also recall a service I was once able to perform on your behalf, a service you will doubtless recollect clearly, and in recompense for that favor I would ask that you find employment for my son who is no longer welcome under my roof." Starbuck grinned. Lieutenant Matthew Potter, it was clear, was a ton of tribulation and Starbuck wondered what service the Reverend Simeon Potter had rendered to make it worth Holborrow's while to accept the Lieutenant. That favor had been subtly emphasized in the Reverend Potter's letter, suggesting that Holborrow's debt to the preacher was considerable. "I believe there to be good in Matthew," the letter finished, "and his commanding officer commended his behavior at Shiloh, but unless he can be weaned from liquor then I fear he is doomed to everlasting hellfire. My wife unites with me in sending our prayers for your kind aid in this sad business." A note, evidently in Holborrow's handwriting, had been penned at the bottom of the letter. "I'd be thankful if you could employ him." Maitland must have said yes, and Starbuck wondered how tangible Holborrow's thanks had been.

The door opened and a rebellious Lucifer brought in a tall glass of lemonade. "I was told to bring this, Lieutenant Potter," he said sourly, stressing the false name with a mocking pronunciation.

"You don't like it here, Lucifer?" Starbuck asked.

"He beats his people," Lucifer said, jerking his head toward the sound of Holborrow's voice. "You ain't thinking of staying here, are you?" he asked with alarm, seeing how comfortably Starbuck's boots rested on the edge of the major's desk.

"For a short while," Starbuck said. "I reckon I'll learn more as Lieutenant Potter than I ever could as Major Starbuck."

"And what if the real Mister Potter comes?"

Starbuck grinned. "Be one hell of a tangle, Lucifer."

Lucifer sniffed. "He ain't beating me!"

"I'll make sure he doesn't. And we won't be here long."

"You're crazy," Lucifer said. "I should have kept going north. I'd rather be preached at in a contraband camp than be living in a place like this." Lucifer sniffed his disgust and went back to the kitchens, leaving Starbuck to hunt through the rest of the papers. None of the battalion lists tallied exactly, but there seemed to be around a hundred and eighty men in the battalion. There were four captains—Dennison, Cartwright, Peel, and Lippincott—and eight sergeants, one of whom was the belligerent Case, who had joined the battalion just a month before.

Sally came to the office after a half hour. She closed the door behind her and laughed mischievously. "Hell, Nate, ain't this something?"

Starbuck stood and gestured at the mess in the room. "I'm beginning to feel sorry for Lieutenant Potter, whoever the hell Lieutenant Potter is," he said.

"You staying on here?" Sally asked.

"Maybe one night."

"In that case," Sally said, "I'm saying good-bye to my dearest husband and then the major's going to take me in his coach back to the city and I just know he's going to ask me to take supper with him. I'll say I'm too tired. You sure you want to stay?"

"I'd look an idiot telling him who I am now," Starbuck said. "Besides, there must be something to discover in all these papers."

"You discover how the hog's making his money," Sally said. "That'd be real useful." She stood on tiptoe and kissed his cheek. "Watch that Captain Dennison, Nate, he's a snake."

"He's the one with the pretty face, right?"

She grimaced. "I thought it had to be syphilis, but it ain't 'cos he ain't shaking or babbling like a loon. Must be nothing but a skin disease. I hope it hurts."

Starbuck grinned. "Begged you for a kiss, did he?" he guessed.

"I reckon he wants more than a kiss," she grimaced, then touched Starbuck's cheek. "Be good, Matthew Potter."

"And you, Emily Potter."

A few minutes later Starbuck heard the jingle of trace chains as the major's carriage was brought to the front of the house. There was the sound of good-byes being said, then the carriage clattered away.

And Starbuck suddenly felt lonely.

A hundred miles north of Starbuck, in a valley where corn grew tall between stands of thick trees, a fugitive crouched in a thicket and listened for sounds of pursuit. The fugitive was a tall, fleshy young man who was now severely hungry. He had lost his horse at the battle fought near Manassas four days before and, with the beast, he had lost a saddlebag of food and so he had gone hungry these four days, all but for some hardtack he had taken from a rebel corpse on the battlefield. Now, a dozen miles north of the battlefield and with his belly aching with hunger, the fugitive reluctantly gnawed at a cob of unripe corn and knew his bowels would punish him for the diet. He was tired of the war. He wanted a decent hotel, a hot bath, a soft bed, a good meal, and a bad woman. He could afford all those things for around his belly was a money belt filled with gold, and all he wanted to do was to get the hell away from this terrible countryside that the victorious rebels were scouring in search of fugitives from the Northern army. The rest of the Northern army had retreated toward Washington and the young man wanted to join them, but somehow he had got all turned about during the day of pouring rain and he guessed he had walked five miles west that day instead of north and now he was trying to work his way back northward.

He wore the blue coat of a Northern soldier, but he wore it unbuttoned and unbelted so that he could discard it at a moment's notice and pull on the gray coat that he had taken from the corpse that had yielded him the hardtack. The dead man's coat was a mite small, but the fugitive knew he could talk his way out of trouble if any rebel patrol did find and question him. He would be in more trouble if Northern soldiers found him for, though he had fought for the Yankees, he spoke with the raw accent of the Deep South, but deep in his pants pocket he had his papers that identified him as Captain William Blythe, second in command of Galloway's Horse, a unit of Northern cavalry composed of renegade Southerners. Galloway's Horse were supposed to be scouts who could ride the Southern trails with the same assurance as Jeb Stuart's confident men, but the fool Galloway had taken them right into the battle near Manassas where they had been shot to hell by a Confederate regiment. Billy Blythe knew that Galloway was dead and Blythe reckoned Galloway deserved to be dead for having got mixed up in a full battle. He also guessed that most of Galloway's men were probably dead and he did not care. He just needed to get away to the north and find himself another comfortable billet where he could stay alive until the war ended. On that day, Blythe reckoned, there would be rich pickings for Southerners who had stayed loyal to the Union and he did not intend to be denied those rewards.

But neither did he intend to land up in a Confederate prison. If capture was unavoidable he planned to discard the blue coat, don the gray, then talk his way out of trouble. Then he would find another way back north. It just took guile, planning, a little intelligence, and a helping of luck, and that should be enough to avoid the numerous folks in the Southern states who wanted nothing more than to put a rope around Billy Blythe's fleshy neck. One such rope had damn nearly done for him before the war's beginning, and it was only by the most outrageous daring that Billy had escaped the girl's family and fled north. Hell, he thought, it wasn't that he was a bad fellow. Billy Blythe had never thought of himself as a bad fellow. A bit wild, maybe, and a fellow who liked a good time, but not bad. Just faster witted than most others, and there was nothing like quick wits to provoke envy.

He scraped at the raw cob with his teeth and chewed on the tough corn. It tasted foul, and he could already feel a ferment in his belly, but he was half starving and needed strengthening if he was to keep going. Hell, he thought, but his life had gone all wrong these last few weeks! He should never have got mixed up with Major Galloway, nor with the Yankee army. He should be farther north, in New York say. Somewhere the guns did not sound. Somewhere there was money to be made and girls to impress.

A twig snapped in the woodland and Blythe went very still. At least he tried to go very still, but there was an uncontrollable shaking in his legs, his belly was rumbling from the fermenting corn, and he kept blinking as sweat trickled into the corners of his eyes. A voice sounded far away. Pray God the man was a Northerner, he thought, then wondered why the hell the Yankees were losing all the battles. Billy Blythe had wagered his whole future on a Northern victory, but every time the Federals met the men in gray they got beat. It just plain was not right! Now the Northerners had got whipped again and Billy Blythe was eating raw corn and was dressed in clothes still damp from the rainstorm of two days before.

A horse whinnied. It was hard to tell what direction the sound came from, at first it seemed to come from behind him, but then Billy heard the slow thump of hooves from in front of him and so, confused, and very cautiously, he raised his head out of the leaves until he could see across the corn. The shadows were harsh among the farther trees, but suddenly, in a slash of bright sunlight that cut across the dark, he saw the horsemen. Northerners! Blue coats. There were glints of reflected sunlight from saber scabbards, belt buckles, curb chains, carbine hooks, then a flash of white as a horse rolled its eye and sneezed. The ears of the other horses pricked forward. The wary cavalrymen had stopped at the corn's edge. There were a dozen or so troopers there, carbines at the ready, all watching across the crop toward Billy's left, and it was their watchfulness that kept Billy motionless. What was worrying them? He turned very slowly, but could see nothing. Were there rebels nearby? A bluebird flitted above the corn and Billy decided the bright feathers were a good omen and he was about to stand fully upright and shout toward the cavalrymen when suddenly their leader made a gesture with his hand and the troopers spurred their horses out into the corn. Billy stayed still. One of the cavalrymen had holstered his carbine and scraped his saber free of its scabbard, and that persuaded Billy that this was not a good time to attract the troopers' attention. One shout now and a volley of minie balls could be his answer and so he just watched as the horses advanced noisily through the stiff cornstalks.

A horse whinnied again, and this time the sound was definitely behind Billy and he turned softly, parted the screen of leaves, then peered hard through the dappled shadows of the woodland. He was holding his breath and wondering what the hell was going on, then sud-

denly he saw a movement down by the far end of the cornfield and he
blinked sweat away from his eyes and saw that there was a horse there.
A riderless, lonely horse. A horse all on its own. A horse that seemed to
be tethered. A horse with a saddle and bridle, but no rider. A horse, he
thought, for Billy Blythe and he wondered what would be the safest way
to attract the attention of the nervous Yankee troopers when suddenly a
blast of rifle fire ripped the warm afternoon to shreds.

Billy cried aloud with fear and dropped to his haunches. No one
heard his cry, for the Yankee horses were screaming terribly. There was
a great thrashing sound from the corn, then more rifles fired and suddenly the hateful rebel yell was sounding and a voice was roaring orders.
It had been an ambush. One riderless horse had been the bait that had
sucked the Yankees down the long narrow cornfield to where the rebels
had been hidden among the trees, and now the horsemen were either
dead, wounded, or desperately trying to gallop away. Two more rifles
cracked and Billy saw a blue-coated trooper arch his back, let go of his
reins, and fall backward off his galloping horse. Two more riderless
horses galloped north while a trooper was running desperately with his
scabbard held free of his legs. Two Northern horsemen seemed to have
made it safely into the shelter of the far trees, but otherwise there
seemed to be no survivors from the small Yankee patrol. It had taken
less than a minute.

"Fetch the horses!" a voice snarled. A Yankee in the corn was calling
for help, his voice desperate with pain. A horse was whinnying, then a
flat, hard shot abruptly ended the pathetic sound. Rebel voices laughed,
then Billy heard the scraping rattle as a rifle was reloaded. The rebels
were evidently collecting the horses; valuable prizes for an army already
short of good cavalry mounts, and Billy hoped they would be content
with that booty, but then the officer shouted again. "Look for any survivors! Careful now, but look good."

Billy swore. He thought about running, but he guessed he was too
weak to outrun a fit man and besides the noise he made would bring a
slew of the bastards chasing after him, so instead he feverishly stripped
off his blue coat and pulled on the threadbare gray jacket, and then he
pushed the betraying blue garment deep under the bushes where he

covered it with a thick layer of leaf mold. He buttoned the gray coat and buckled his belt about its waist and then he waited. Damn, he thought, damn and son of a bitch and damn again, but now he would have to play the rebel for a few weeks while he found another way to get back north.

Footsteps came nearer and Billy decided it was time to play his role. "Are you Southern boys?" he called aloud. The footsteps stopped. "The name's Billy Tumlin!" he called out, "Billy Tumlin from New Orleans." There was no future in using his real name, not when so many men in the Confederacy were eager to test a rope on Billy Blythe's gullet. "Are you boys Rebs?" he asked.

"Can't see you," a voice said flatly, neither friendly nor hostile, but then came the unmistakably hostile sound of a rifle being cocked.

"I'm standing up, boys," Billy said, "standing up real slow. Standing up right plumb in front of you." Billy stood and held his hands high to show he was not armed. Facing him were a pair of scruffy rebels with bayonet-tipped rifles. "Thank the good Lord above, boys," Billy said, "praise His holy name, amen."

The two faces showed only caution. "Who did you say you was?" one of the men asked.

"Captain Billy Tumlin, boys. From New Orleans, Louisiana. I've been on the run for weeks now and sure am pleased to see you. Mind if I lower my hands?" He began to lower his arms, but a twitch of a blackened rifle muzzle put them back up fast.

"On the run?" the second man asked.

"I was taken at New Orleans," Blythe explained in his broadest Southern accent, "and I've been a prisoner up north ever since. But I slipped away, see? And I'm kind of hungry, boys. Even a piece of hardtack would be welcome. Or some tobacco? Ain't seen good tobacco since the day I got captured."

An hour later Captain Billy Tumlin was introduced to Lieutenant Colonel Ned Maitland, whose men had discovered the fugitive. Maitland's regiment was bivouacking and the smoke from hundreds of small fires sifted into the early evening air. Maitland, a courtly and generous host, hospitably shared a leg of stringy chicken, some hard-boiled eggs, and a flask of cognac with the newly escaped prisoner. He seemed blessedly uninterested in Blythe's supposed experiences as a captive of the Northerners, preferring to discuss which prominent New Orleans families might be common acquaintances. Billy Blythe had spent just long enough in New Orleans to pass that test, especially when he figured that Maitland knew less about the city's society than he did himself.

"I guess," Maitland said after a while, "that you'd better report to brigade."

"I can't stay here?" Blythe suggested. Maitland would be a considerate commander, he reckoned, and the Legion would be serving close enough to the Yankees to give Blythe an easy chance to slip across the lines.

Maitland shook his head. He would have liked to keep Billy Tumlin in the Legion, for he considered most of his present officers to be well below the proper standard, but he had no authority to appoint a new captain. "I could use you," Maitland admitted, "I surely could. It looks like we'll all be moving north soon so there'll be plenty of fighting and I'm not exactly fixed right with good officers."

"You're invading the North?" Billy Blythe asked, horrified at the thought.

"There's nothing north of here but foreign soil," Maitland observed dryly, "but sadly I can't keep you in the Legion. Things have changed since you were captured, Captain. We don't elect or appoint officers anymore. Everything goes through the War Department in Richmond and I guess you'll have to report there. At least if you want wages, you will."

"Wages would help," Blythe agreed and so, an hour later, he found himself in the altogether less prepossessing company of the brigade commander. Colonel Griffin Swynyard's queries about Blythe's captivity were brief, but much sharper than Maitland's. "Where were you held?" he asked.

"Massachusetts," Blythe said.

"Where exactly?" Swynyard demanded.

Blythe was momentarily flustered. "Union," he finally said, reckoning that every state in the United and Confederate States had a town called Union. "Just outside, anyway," he added lamely.

"We must thank God for your escape," Swynyard said, and Blythe eagerly agreed, then realized he was actually expected to fall onto his knees to offer the thanks. He got down awkwardly and closed his eyes while Swynyard thanked Almighty God for the release of His servant Billy Tumlin from captivity, and after that Swynyard told Billy he would have the brigade major issue a travel pass permitting Captain Tumlin to report to the army headquarters.

"In Richmond?" Blythe asked, not unhappy at that thought. He had no enemies in Richmond that he knew of, for his foes were all further south, so Richmond would be a fine resting place for a short while. And at least in the Confederacy's capital he would be spared the bloodletting that would surely follow if Robert Lee took this hardscrabble army of ragged-uniformed men across the Potomac into the north's plump fields.

"They may send you to Richmond," Swynyard said, "or they might post you to a battalion here. Ain't my decision, Captain."

"Just so long as I can be useful," Billy Blythe said sanctimoniously. "That's all I pray for, Colonel, to be useful." Billy Blythe was doing what Billy Blythe did best. He was surviving.

"YOU DON'T SOUND LIKE A SOUTHERNER, POTTER," Captain Dennison said and the three other captains who shared the supper table stared accusingly at Starbuck.

"My ma was from Connecticut," Starbuck said.

"Sir," Dennison corrected Starbuck. Captain Dennison was more than a little drunk, indeed he had almost fallen asleep a moment before, but now he had jerked himself into wakefulness and was scowling at Starbuck down the length of the table. "I'm a captain," Dennison said, "and you're a shad-belly piece of ordure, otherwise known as a lieutenant. You call me sir."

"My ma was from Connecticut, sir," Starbuck said dutifully. He was playing his role as the hapless Potter, but he was no longer enjoying it. Impetuosity, if not downright foolishness, had trapped him in the deception and he knew that every moment he stayed in the role would make it more difficult to extricate himself with any dignity, but he still reckoned there were things to learn so long as the real Lieutenant Potter did not arrive at Camp Lee.

"So you picked up your momma's accent with her titty milk, did you, Potter?" Dennison asked.

"I reckon I must have done, sir."

Dennison leaned back in his chair. The sores on his face gleamed wetly in the flickering light of the bad candles set on the dinner table that bore the remains of a meal of fried chicken, fried rice, and beans. There were some of Colonel Holborrow's beloved peaches to end the meal, though Holborrow himself was not present. The colonel, having carried Sally to the city, had evidently stayed to make a night of it, leaving Starbuck to share this evening meal with the four captains. There were plenty of other officers in Camp Lee, but they ate elsewhere for no one, it seemed, wanted to be contaminated by this handful of officers who remained with the Yellowlegs.

And no wonder, Starbuck thought, for even the few hours he had spent in the camp had proved enough to confirm his worst expectations. The men of the 2nd Special Battalion were bored and dispirited, kept from desertion only by the ever-present provosts and by their fears of execution. The sergeants resented being posted to the battalion and so entertained themselves with petty acts of tyranny that the battalion officers, like Thomas Dennison and his companions, did nothing to alleviate. Sergeant Case appeared to run the battalion and those men who were in his favor prospered while the rest suffered.

Starbuck had talked with some of the men and they, thinking that he was a harmless lieutenant and, besides, the man who had dared to take Case's prisoner off the horse, were unguarded in what they said. Some, like Caton Rothwell, whom Starbuck had rescued, were keen to fight and were frustrated that Holborrow appeared to have no intention of sending the battalion north to join Lee's army. Rothwell was not one of the original Yellowlegs, but had been posted to the Special Battalion after being found guilty of deserting from his own regiment. "I went to help my family," he explained to Starbuck. "I just wanted a week's furlough," he added, "because my wife was in trouble."

"What trouble?" Starbuck had asked.

"Just trouble, Lieutenant," Rothwell said bluntly. He was a big, strong man who reminded Starbuck of Lieutenant Waggoner. Caton

Rothwell, Starbuck suspected, would be a good man to have alongside in a fight. Given fifty other such men, Starbuck knew, the battalion could be made as good as any in Lee's army, but most of the soldiers were near mutinous through boredom and the knowledge that they were the most despised unit in all the Confederate army. They were the Yellowlegs, the lowest of the low, and no one thing was more symptomatic of their status than the guns they had been issued. Those weapons were still in store, but Starbuck had found the key hanging behind the office door and had unlocked the armory shed to find it filled with crates of old smoothbore muskets. Starbuck had brushed the dust off one musket stock and lifted out the weapon. It felt clumsy, while the wooden shaft beneath the barrel had shrunk over the years so that the metal barrel hoops were loose. He peered at the lock and saw the word VIRGINIA stamped there, while behind the hammer was written RICHMOND, 1808. The gun must have been a flintlock originally and at some time updated by conversion to percussion cap, but despite the modernization it was still a horrible weapon. These old muskets, made for killing Redcoats, had no rifling inside the barrel, which meant that the bullet did not spin in its flight and so lacked the accuracy of a rifle. At fifty paces the big-bore 1808 musket might be as lethal as an Enfield rifle, but at any greater range it was hopelessly inaccurate. Starbuck had seen plenty of men carrying such antiquated guns into battle and had felt sorry for them, but he knew for a fact that thousands of modern rifles had been captured from the North during the summer's campaign, and it seemed perverse to arm his men with these museum pieces. Such antique weapons were a signal to the Special Battalion that they were on the army's hind teat, but that was probably a truth the men already knew. They were the soldiers no one else wanted.

Sergeant Case had seen the open armory door and come to investigate. His tall body filled the doorway and shadowed the dusty room. "You," he had said flatly when he saw Starbuck.

"Me," Starbuck agreed pleasantly enough.

"Got a habit of poking your nose where it don't belong, Lieutenant," Case said. His menacing presence loomed in the dusty shed while his flat, hard eyes stared at Starbuck like a predator sizing up its kill.

Starbuck had thrown the musket to the sergeant, thrown it hard enough to make Case step back a pace as he caught it. "You'd want to fight Yankees with one of those, Sergeant?" Starbuck asked.

Case twirled the musket in his big right hand as though it weighed no more than a cornstalk. "They won't be doing no fighting, Lieutenant. These men ain't fit to fight. And that's why you were sent to us." Case's small head jerked back and forth on the ludicrous neck as he spat his insults. "Because you ain't fit to fight. You're a bloody drunkard, Lieutenant, so don't give me any talk of fighting. You don't know what fighting is. I was a Royal Fusilier, boy, a proper soldier, boy, and I know soldiering and I know fighting, and I know you ain't up to it else you wouldn't be here." Case threw the musket hard back, stinging Starbuck's hands with the impact of the weapon. The tall sergeant stepped further inside the armory and thrust his broken-nosed face close to Starbuck. "And one other thing, boy. You pull rank on me one more time and I'll nail your hide to a tree and piss all over it. Now put that musket back where you found it, give me the armory key, and bugger off where you belong."

Not now, Starbuck had told himself, not now. This was not the time to put Case right, and so he had merely put the musket in its box, meekly handed Case the key, and walked away.

Now, at the supper table, Starbuck was again the butt of bullies only this time it was Thomas Dennison and his cronies who had their sport with a man they believed was a weakling. Captain Lippincott rolled a peach to Starbuck. "Reckon you'd prefer a brandy, Potter," Lippincott said.

"Reckon I would," Starbuck said.

"Sir," Dennison said immediately.

"Reckon I would, sir," Starbuck said humbly. He had to play the fool so long as he decided against revealing his identity, but it went hard on him. He told himself to stay calm and to play the failure for a short while yet.

Lippincott edged his brandy glass toward Starbuck, daring him to take it, but Starbuck did not move. "Of course there's one thing to be said for being a drunk," Lippincott said, taking the glass back, "it means you'll probably sleep away the days here. Better than sitting around doing nothing. Ain't that right, Potter?"

"Right," Starbuck agreed.

"Sir," Dennison said, then hiccuped.

"Sir," Starbuck said.

"I ain't saying I'm not grateful for being here," Lippincott went on gloomily, "but, hell, they could give us some entertainment."

"Plenty in Richmond," Dennison said airily.

"If you've got the money," Lippincott acknowledged, "which I ain't."

Dennison stretched back in his chair. "You'd rather be in a fighting regiment?" he asked Lippincott. "They could always transfer you. If that's what you want, Dan, I'll tell Holborrow you're eager to go." Lippincott, a sallow man with a fringe of beard, said nothing. Most of the Yellowlegs officers had been transferred, either to garrison duty or to the provosts, but a few had been posted to fighting battalions, a fate that plainly worried these remaining captains, though not Dennison, whose skin disease was sufficient to keep him out of harm's way. He gingerly touched one of the horrid sores on his face. "If the doctors could just cure this," he said in a tone that suggested he was confident that the disease was incurable, "I'd volunteer for a transfer."

"You are taking the medicine, Tom?" Lippincott asked.

"Of course I am," Dennison snapped. "Can't you smell it?"

Starbuck could indeed smell something medicinal, and the smell was oddly familiar; a thin rank odor that disturbed him, but which he could not quite place. "What medicine is it, sir?" he asked.

Dennison paused while he considered whether the question constituted impudence, then he shrugged. "Kerosene," he answered after a while.

Starbuck frowned. "Is it ringworm?" he asked, then added, "sir."

Dennison sneered. "One year at medical college and you know it all, is that it? You mind your own damn business, Potter, and I'll mind the advice of a proper doctor."

Lippincott looked back at the glistening sores and shuddered. "It's all right for you, Tom," he said resentfully, "but what if this Starbuck wants us to fight? Holborrow can't keep us here forever."

"Holborrow's a colonel," Dennison said, hiccuping again, "and Starbuck's a major, so Holborrow will get what he wants and Starbuck can go piss himself. And hell," he went on resentfully, "none of us should be serving under Starbuck. He's a goddamn Northerner and I ain't taking orders from any goddamn Northerner."

Cartwright, a plumpish man with a petulant face and fair curly hair, nodded agreement. "You should have taken over from Maitland, Tom," he told Dennison.

"I know that, you know that, Holborrow knows that," Dennison agreed then clumsily extracted a cigar from his pocket and lit it at the nearest candle. "And Mister Starbuck will have to learn it," he finished when the cigar was lit.

Peel, a thin young man who seemed the best of this unprepossessing bunch, wiped peach juice from his clean-shaven chin then shook his head. "Why did they send us Starbuck?" he asked no one in particular. "They must be wanting us to fight. Otherwise why send him to us?"

"Because he's an unwanted son of a bitch," Dennison snapped, "and they want to be rid of him."

"He's got a reputation," Starbuck said, enjoying himself, "sir."

Dennison's dark eyes inspected Starbuck through the flickering light of the guttering candles. "It don't take much of a reputation to impress a drunkard," he said dismissively, "and I don't recall anyone here inviting you to speak, Lieutenant."

"Sorry, sir," Starbuck said.

Dennison went on inspecting Starbuck and finally prodded his cigar toward him. "I will say one thing for you, Potter, you've got a pretty wife."

"Reckon I have, sir," Starbuck agreed.

"Pretty, pretty, pretty," Dennison said. "Pretty enough to turn a head or two. Too pretty for a lunkhead like you, don't you agree?"

"She's sure pretty," Starbuck said, "sir."

"And you're a drunk," Dennison observed, "and drunks ain't no good where it counts with a lady. Know what I mean, Potter? Drunks ain't up to it, are they?" Dennison, half drunk himself, laughed at his own wit. Starbuck held the Captain's eyes, but said nothing and Dennison mistook his silence for fear. "You know where your pretty wife is tonight, Potter?"

"With her cousin Alice, sir," Starbuck said.

"Or maybe she's dining with Colonel Holborrow?" Dennison suggested. "The Colonel sure had his hopes up. Put on his best uniform coat, shined his boots, and oiled his hair. I reckon he thought your Emily might appreciate a little entertainment. Maybe a cockfight?" The other captains laughed at this jest while Dennison sucked on his cigar. "And maybe," he went on, "your Emily's so desperate after being married to you that she'd even say yes to Holborrow. You reckon she's playing the mattress to Holborrow's quilt, Potter?" Starbuck said nothing and Dennison shook his head scornfully. "You're a weak passel of shit, Potter, you truly are. God knows what that girl sees in you, but I guess she needs her pretty little eyes fixing." He drew on his cigar again as he stared at Starbuck. "Reckon I just might call on the little lady myself. Would you object, Lieutenant Potter, if I paid my respects to your lady wife? My skin might just benefit from a lady's healing touch."

Peel looked embarrassed, but the other two captains smiled. Both were weak men and were enjoying this chance to see an apparently weaker man being mercilessly bullied. Starbuck leaned back in his chair, making it creak. "What do you reckon your chances are with her, sir?" he asked Dennison.

Dennison seemed surprised that the question had been asked, but he pretended to consider it anyway. "A good-looking girl like that? And a handsome fellow like me? Oh, pretty fair chances, I'd say, Lieutenant."

"Out of five," Starbuck insisted, "what do you reckon, sir? Two chances out of five? One chance? Three?"

Dennison frowned, not entirely sure whether the conversation was going entirely to his liking. "Pretty fair, I'd say," he repeated.

Starbuck shook his head ruefully. "Hell, sir, I know Emily, and Emily never did take overmuch to poxed sons of bitches like yourself, sir, begging your pardon, sir, and I can't reckon you've got more than one chance in five. Pretty good odds, though, seeing as how pretty she is, but how lucky are you? That's the question, sir, ain't it?" He smiled at Dennison who was not smiling back. None of the captains was smiling; instead they were watching Starbuck, who had drawn out his Adams revolver while he was talking and had used a fingernail to lever four of the five percussion caps off the gun's cones. He tipped the caps onto an empty plate then looked up at Dennison through the candle flames. "How lucky are you, sir?" Starbuck asked and leveled the revolver's blued barrel at Dennison's scared eyes as he thumbed the hammer to half cock so that the cylinder was free to turn. He spun the cylinder and not one of the captains moved as the gun sounded a series of tiny clicks that only stopped when the cylinder came to rest. Starbuck eased the cock all the way back. "One chance in five, Captain, sir," he said, "so let's see how good those odds are." He pulled the trigger and Dennison gave a tiny jump of alarm as the hammer fell onto an empty cone. "You didn't make it that time," Starbuck said, "sir."

"Potter!" Dennison shouted, then stilled his protest as Starbuck half cocked the gun and spun the cylinder a second time.

"Of course a gentleman like you wouldn't be content with a lady's first refusal, would you, sir?" Starbuck asked and eased the hammer all the way back once more. It made two tiny clicks as the pawl engaged. He could see that the cone under the hammer was empty, but none of the others around the table knew which of the chambers was primed. They would be able to see the bullets nestled inside the lower chambers, but not the cones at the cylinder's rear. Starbuck smiled. "So my Emily's refused you once, Captain," he said, "but you'd surely ask her a second time, wouldn't you? I mean you don't have the manners of a goat, so you're sure to ask her a second time." He straightened his arm as though bracing himself for the gun's recoil.

Cartwright fumbled for his own revolver, but Starbuck pointed the gun momentarily at the frightened face and Cartwright immediately subsided. Starbuck shifted the gun back to Dennison. "Second chance coming up, Captain, sir. Dear Emily, please lay yourself down and play mattress for me. Let's see how lucky you are the second time of asking, Captain." He pulled the trigger and once again Dennison shuddered as the dead click echoed loud in the room. Starbuck immediately spun the chamber a third time and straightened his arm.

"You're mad, Potter," Dennison said, suddenly seeming very sober.

"I'm sober too," Starbuck said and reached out with his left hand for Cartwright's brandy, which he drank in one go. "I'll be madder still when I'm drunk," he said, "so how many chances do you reckon you've got with my wife, Captain? Are you going to ask her three times for the favor of a ride?"

Dennison considered reaching for his own revolver, but it was buttoned in its holster and he knew he would have no chance to free the weapon before a bullet slashed through the candle flames and shattered his skull. He licked his lips. "I guess I don't have any chance, Lieutenant," he said.

"I guess you don't, Captain," Starbuck said, "and I guess you owe me an apology too."

Dennison grimaced at the thought. "You can go to hell, Potter," he said defiantly.

Starbuck pulled the trigger, then immediately half cocked the gun and spun the cylinder a fourth time. When it came to rest he pulled the cock back and this time he could see the single percussion cap was waiting under the hammer. He smiled. "Three times lucky, Captain, but how good is your luck? I'm waiting for that apology."

"I apologize, Lieutenant Potter," Dennison managed to say.

Starbuck eased the hammer down, thrust the Adams into its holster, and stood up. "Never start what you can't finish, Captain," he said, then leaned forward and picked up the half full bottle of brandy. "Reckon I can finish this, though, but in privacy. You all have a nice conversation now." He walked out of the room.

It was a humid, rainy night in Washington with no wind to take away the thick stench of the garbage dump that lay at the southern end of Seventeenth Street just a few yards from the hospital tents pitched on the ellipse. The sewage in Murder Bay added its own fetid smell to the air above the Northern capital that was more than usually crowded with soldiers. They were men who should have been marching in John

Pope's army toward Richmond, but instead they had been whipped backward by Robert Lee from the banks of the Bull Run and now they filled the tented camps inside Washington's ring of forts and thronged the capital's taverns.

One young cavalry officer hurried along Pennsylvania Avenue to the corner of Seventeenth Street, where he took off his wide-brimmed cavalryman's hat to peer up at the street lamp. At every corner in Washington the lamps had their street's name painted in black on the glass covering the mantel, an intelligent device, and once the young man was sure he was in the right place he walked up Seventeenth until he reached a three-story brick building that was thickly surrounded by trees. Gas lights showed where the building's narrow end abutted onto the sidewalk and where a flight of steps led to a door guarded by two blue-coated sentries, though when the young cavalryman presented himself at that door he was told to go back to the garden entrance on Pennsylvania Avenue. He retraced his steps and discovered a driveway that led through night-blackened trees to an imposing portico of six massive columns that protected and dwarfed a small doorway guarded by a quartet of blue-coated infantrymen. Gas lamps hissed yellow under the portico, lighting a carriage that waited for its owner.

A clock struck nine as the cavalryman was granted entrance into the hallway where yet another guard demanded his name. "Faulconer," the young man replied. "Captain Adam Faulconer." The guard consulted a list, ticked off Adam's name, then told him to put his scabbarded saber into an umbrella stand and afterward climb one flight of stairs, turn left at the stairhead, and walk to the very end of the corridor where he would find a door marked with the name of the man who had summoned him. The guard rattled off these directions, then went back to his copy of *The Evening Star*, which heralded Major General George McClellan's reappointment as commander of the Northern army.

Adam Faulconer mounted the stairs and walked down the long, gloomy corridor. This building was the War Department, the very center of the North's military effort, yet there was little sense of urgency in its darkened passages where Adam's footfalls echoed as forlornly as the steps of a man pacing a deserted sepulcher. Most of the fanlights above the office doors were dark, though one light showed at the corridor's far end and in its small glow Adam saw the name COL. THORNE painted in white letters against one of the door's black panels. He knocked and was summoned inside.

He found himself in a surprisingly large room with two tall windows that were shut against both the rain and the moths that beat against the panes. The walls of the room were covered with maps, and one large desk stood beside one window, while two smaller clerks' tables occupied the rest of the room. All the desks were covered in papers that had flowed onto the chairs and hardwood floor. Two cast-iron gasoliers hissed beneath the high ceiling, while a longcase clock ticked hollowly between the windows. The room's only occupant was a tall uniformed man who stood with a ramrod-straight back as he stared at the scatter of lit windows showing above the trees in the White House. "Faulconer, yes?" the man asked without turning from the window.

"Yes, sir."

"My name is Thorne. Lyman Thorne. Colonel Lyman Thorne." Thorne had a coarse, almost angry voice, very deep toned, and when he abruptly turned toward Adam he revealed a face that matched the voice perfectly, for Thorne was a gaunt, white-bearded man with fierce eyes and with deep lines carved into his sun-darkened cheeks. His most prominent feature was his white hair, which grew thick, long, and wildly enough to make Thorne appear like a bearded version of Andrew Jackson. The Colonel carried himself straight and proud, though when he moved he favored his right leg, which suggested that his other might have been injured. He gazed at Adam for an instant, then turned back to the window. "There have been celebrations in Washington these last two days," he growled.

"Yes, sir."

"McClellan is back! John Pope is dismissed and the Young Napoleon has been given charge of the army again, and thus Washington celebrates." Thorne spat into a brass cuspidor, then glared at Adam. "Do you celebrate this appointment, young Faulconer?"

Adam was taken aback by the question. "I haven't considered it, sir," he eventually admitted lamely.

"I do not celebrate, young Faulconer. My God, I do not. We gave McClellan a hundred thousand men, shipped him to the Virginia peninsula, and ordered him to take Richmond. And what did he do? He took counsel of his fears. He havered, that's what he did, he havered! He dithered while the rebels scraped together a handful of rapscallion soldiers and trounced him straight back out to sea. Yet now the ditherer is to be our commanding general again, and do you know why, young Faulconer?" This question, like the rest of Thorne's words, was directed at the windowpane rather than toward Adam.

"No, sir," Adam answered.

"Because there is no one else. Because in all this great republic we cannot find one better general than little George McClellan. Not one!" Thorne spat into the cuspidor again. "I admit he can train troops, but he doesn't know how to fight them. Doesn't know how to lead. The man's a humbug!" Thorne snarled the last word, then abruptly turned and glared at Adam once more. "Somewhere in the Republic there's a man who can beat Robert Lee, but on my soul we haven't found him yet. But we will, Faulconer, we will, and when we do we shall pulverize the so-called Confederacy into bone and blood. Bone and blood. But until we do find that man then it is our duty to mollycoddle the Young Napoleon. We have to pat him and soothe him, we have to tell him not to be frightened of ghosts and not to imagine enemies where there are none. In short, we have to wean him off Pinkerton. Do you know Pinkerton?"

"I know of him, sir."

"The less you know, the better," Thorne growled. "Pinkerton isn't even a soldier! But McClellan swears by him, and even as you and I stand here talking Pinkerton is being given command of all the army's intelligence once more. He had that same command in the peninsula, and what did he do with it? He summoned rebel soldiers out of thin air. He told the Young Napoleon that there were hundreds of thousands of men where there was nothing but a huddle of hungry rogues. Pinkerton will do the same again, Faulconer, mark my words. Within one week we shall be told that Lee has two hundred thousand men and that little McClellan dare not attack for fear of being beat. We shall haver again, we shall dither, and while we piss our collective pants Robert Lee will attack. Do you wonder that Europe laughs at us?"

"Do they, sir?" Adam, confused by the tirade, asked the question feebly.

"Oh they do, Faulconer, they do. American pride is being humbled by a rebellion we seem powerless to defeat and Europe takes pleasure in that. They pretend not, but if Robert Lee destroys McClellan then I daresay we'll see European troops in the South. The French would love to join in, but they won't jump till Britain decides, and Britain won't join the game until they know which side is winning. Which is why Lee will attack us, Faulconer. Look!" Thorne strode to a map of the eastern seaboard that hung behind his desk. "We've made three efforts to capture Richmond. Three! And all have been defeated. Lee now controls all of northern Virginia, so what's to stop him coming further north? Here, Faulconer, into Maryland, and maybe farther north still, into Pennsylvania." The Colonel demonstrated these threats by sweeping his hand across the map. "He'll grab our good harvest for his starving men and beat up little McClellan and so demonstrate to the Europeans that we can't even defend our own territory. By next spring, Faulconer, there could be a hundred thousand European troops marching for the Confederacy, and what will we do then? Treat for peace, of course, and so the Republic of Washington and Jefferson will have lasted a mere eighty years and North America, Faulconer, will be fatally weakened for the next eighty years." Thorne leaned over his desk and glared at Adam. "Lee cannot be allowed to win, Faulconer. He cannot," the colonel said in a grave voice, almost as if he were charging Adam with the personal responsibility for saving the Republic.

"No, sir," Adam said, and felt it was a weak response, but he was being swamped by the sheer force of Lyman Thorne's personality. Sweat trickled down Adam's face. The night was oppressive, and the rain had not diminished the humidity at all, while the gasoliers' flaring mantles only added to the room's stifling heat.

The colonel waved Adam toward a chair, then sat down himself and lit a cigar from a gas flame that burned from a tabletop gas jet connected to a long rubber extension cord that snaked down from the nearest gasolier. Once the cigar was lit he pushed the gas jet and papers aside, then leaned back and rubbed his face as though he was suddenly tired. "You're a scalawag, right?" he demanded.

"Yes, sir," Adam said. A scalawag was a Southerner who fought for the North, the opposite of a Copperhead.

"And three months ago," Thorne went on, "you were a rebel on Johnston's staff, am I right?"

"Yes, sir."

"And back then, Faulconer, our Young Napoleon was marching on Richmond. No, that is the wrong verb. He was crawling toward Richmond, while Detective Pinkerton," Thorne mocked the description with his tone, "was convincing little George that the rebels had two hundred thousand troops. You sent information that would have corrected that misapprehension, only the news never got through. Some clever bastard on the other side replaced your dispatch with one of their own devising and so Richmond survived. I almost stopped that clever bastard, Faulconer, indeed I broke a leg trying, but I failed." He grimaced, then sucked on his cigar. The smoke hung in the room like the lingering skein of a rifle shot.

"Back then, Faulconer," Thorne continued, "I was working for the Inspector General's Department. I did the jobs no one else wanted. Now I am more exalted, but still no more popular with this army than I was when I inspected their damned latrines or wondered why they needed so many clerks. But now, Faulconer, I have a measure of power. It is not mine, but belongs to my master and he lives in that house there." He jerked the cigar toward the White House. "You follow me?"

"I think so, sir."

"The president, Faulconer, believes as I do that this army is largely commanded by cretins. The army, of course, believes that the country is ruled by fools, and perhaps both are right, but for the moment, Faulconer, I'd put my money on the fools rather than the cretins. Officially I am a mere liaison officer between the fools and the cretins, but in reality, Faulconer, I am the president's creature in the army. My job is to prevent the cretins from being more than usually cretinous. I want your help."

Adam said nothing, not because he was reluctant to help, but because he was astonished by Thorne and his words. He was also cheered by them. The North, for all its power, seemed to be wallowing helplessly in the face of the rebellion's energy and that made no sense to Adam, but here, at last, was a man who had a vigor to match the enemy's defiance.

"Did you know, Faulconer, that your father has become Deputy Secretary of War for the Confederacy?" Thorne asked.

"No, sir, I didn't."

"Well, he is. In time, maybe, that will be useful, but not now." Thorne pulled a sheet of paper toward him and in so doing toppled another pile that spilt close to the gas jet. A corner of paper burst into flames that Thorne slapped out with the air of a man forever extinguishing such accidental fires. "You left the Confederacy three months ago and joined Galloway's Horse?" he asked, taking the facts from the paper he had selected.

"Yes, sir."

"He was a good man, Galloway. He had some bright ideas, which is why, of course, this army starved him of men and resources. But it was still a damn fool idea for Galloway to get mixed up in battle. You were supposed to be scouts, not shock troops. Galloway died, yes?"

"I'm afraid so, sir."

"And his second in command is missing, maybe dead, maybe captured. What was his name?"

"Blythe, sir," Adam said bitterly. He had never liked, much less trusted, Billy Blythe.

"So Galloway's Horse, so far as I can see, is a dead beast," Thorne said. "No employment for you there, Faulconer. Are you married?"

The sudden question surprised Adam. He shook his head. "No, sir."

"Quite right, too. A mistake to marry early." Thorne went silent for a moment. "I'm making you a major," he said abruptly, then waved Adam's embarrassed thanks to silence. "I'm not promoting you because you deserve it, I don't know if you do, but because if you work for me you'll be constantly harassed by brainless staff officers and the higher your rank the less obnoxious that harassment will be."

"Yes, sir," Adam said.

Thorne drew on his cigar and stared at Adam. He liked what he saw. Major Adam Faulconer was a young man, fair haired and bearded, with a square, trustworthy face. He was, Thorne knew, an instinctive Unionist and an honest man, but maybe, Thorne reflected, those were the wrong qualities for this job. Maybe he needed a rogue, but the choice had not belonged to Thorne. "So what are you to do, Faulconer? I shall tell you." He stood again and began pacing up and down behind his desk. "We have hundreds of sympathizers behind the enemy lines and most of them are no damn good. They see a rebel regiment march past and they're so overawed by the column's length that they report ten thousand men where in truth they've only seen a thousand. They send their messages and Detective Pinkerton multiplies their figure by three and Little George quakes in his fighting boots and begs Halleck to send him another army corps, and that, Faulconer, is how we've been conducting this war."

"Yes, sir," Adam said.

Thorne tugged up a window sash to let some of the cigar smoke out of the room. The city's sewage stench wafted in with a flutter of moths that flew suicidally toward the yellow-blue flames of the gas jets. Thorne turned back to Adam. "But I have a handful of agents of my own, and one of them *is* of particular value. He's a lazy man and I doubt that his allegiance to the North is anything other than a cynical calculation as to the war's outcome, but he has the possibility of revealing the rebel's strategy to us, everything! How many? Where? Why? The same kind of thing you tried to reveal on the peninsula. But he's also a timid man. His patriotism is not so strong that he fancies a hempen rope round his neck on a rebel gallows, and for that reason he is a cautious man. He will send us dispatches, but he will not use any means except those of his own devising. He won't risk his neck trying to ride through the lines, but said I could provide a courier who could run that risk, but he insisted it would have to be someone he could trust." Thorne paused to draw on his cigar, then jabbed it toward Adam. "He named you."

Adam said nothing. Instead he was trying to think of someone who matched Thorne's description, someone he obviously knew well in his native Virginia, but he could pluck no name or face out of his tangled memories. For a few wild seconds he wondered if it was his father, then he dismissed that thought. His father would never betray Virginia as Adam had done. "Might I ask—" Adam began.

"No," Thorne interrupted. "I'm not giving you his name. You don't need his name. If a message reaches you then you'll probably realize who he is, but it won't help you to know now. To be frank, Faulconer, I don't know what will help you. All I know is that one weak man in the Confederacy has told me he'll address his dispatches to you, but beyond that all is mystery." Thorne spread his arms in a gesture that expressed his own dissatisfaction with the clumsy and imprecise arrangements he was describing. "How my man will reach you, I don't know. How you will reach him, I cannot guess. He won't take risks, so you'll have to. All I can tell you is this. Just over a week ago I sent this man a message demanding that he find an excuse, any excuse, to attach himself to Lee's headquarters and I have no reason to think he will disobey. He won't like it, but he will do as I ask. He will stay close to Lee's headquarters and you will stay close to McClellan's. Little George will think you're a nuisance, but you'll have papers saying that you work for the Inspector General and are preparing a report on the efficacy of the army's signaling systems. If Little George does try to hobble you, tell me and I'll rescue you." For a moment Thorne faltered, suddenly beset by the hopelessness of what he tried to do. He had told Adam the truth, but he had not revealed how ramshackle the whole arrangement was. His man in Richmond had provided Adam's name weeks before, not in connection with this scheme, but as a messenger who could be trusted and now, in utter desperation, Thorne was recruiting Adam in the hope that somehow his reluctant Southern agent could discover Lee's strategy and communicate it to Adam. The chances of success were slender, but something had to be done to neutralize Pinkerton's defeatist intelligence and to ward off the dreadful prospect of a Southern victory that would invite the damned Europeans to come and dance on America's carcass.

"You've got a good horse?" Thorne asked Adam.

"Very good, sir."

"You'll need money. Here." He took a bag of coins from his desk drawer. "United States gold, Faulconer, enough to bribe rebels and maybe get you out of trouble. My guess, and it is only a guess, is that my man will send you a message saying where he will leave his dispatches. That place will be behind enemy lines, Faulconer, so you'll need a good horse and the ability to bribe any rebel scum who give you trouble. Tomorrow morning you go to the camp on Analostin Island to meet a Captain Bidwell. He'll tell you all you need to know about the signals system so that you can talk intelligently to Little George about telegraphs and wig-waggers. After that you follow Little George and wait for a message. Take the gold with you. That's all."

Adam, so summarily dismissed, hesitated. He had a score of questions, but Thorne's brusqueness discouraged him from asking any of them. The colonel had uncapped an inkwell and had begun writing, so Adam just went to the desk and lifted the heavy bag, and it was not until he had reached the hallway downstairs and was buckling on his sword belt that it occurred to him that Thorne had never once asked him whether he was willing to risk his life by riding behind the rebel lines.

But maybe Thorne had already known the answer. Adam was a patriot, and for his country that he loved so passionately, any risk was worth taking and so, at a spy's bidding, he would ride into treachery and pray for victory.

Starbuck carried the brandy back to the office, locked the door, and lay down with the fully loaded Adams beside him. He heard Holborrow return, and later he heard the four captains go to their beds upstairs, and sometime after that he slept, but he was wary of Captain Dennison's revenge and so his sleep was fitful, though he was dreaming by the time Camp Lee's bugles called a raucous reveille to startle him awake. The sight of the undrunk brandy bottle reminded him of the previous night's confrontation and he took care to strap his revolver about his waist before he went through the house to the backyard, where he pumped himself a bucket of water. A mutinous Lucifer glared at him from the kitchen door. "We'll be leaving here in an hour or so," Starbuck told him. "We're going back to the city."

"Heaven be praised."

"Bring me some coffee with the shaving water, would you? And bread?"

Back in Maitland's old office Starbuck went through the papers to glean whatever other information he could about the battalion. This, he had decided, was the day that he revealed his true identity, but not till he had bargained the knowledge he had gleaned for some advantage and to do that he needed a bargainer. He needed the lawyer, Belvedere Delaney, and so he spent the dawn hours writing Delaney a long letter. The letter enabled him to put his ideas into order. He decided he would have Lucifer deliver the letter, then he would wait at Sally's apartment. The letter took the best part of an hour, but at last it was done and he shouted for Lucifer. It was well after reveille, but no one else was stirring in the big house. It seemed that neither Holborrow nor the battalion's four captains were early risers.

The door opened behind Starbuck. "We can go," he said, without turning round.

"Sir?" A timid voice answered.

Starbuck whipped round. It was not Lucifer at the door, but instead a small anxious face surrounded by brown hair that hung in pretty long curls. Starbuck stared at the girl who stared back at him with something akin to terror in her eyes. "I was told—" she began, then faltered.

"Yes?" Starbuck said.

"I was told Lieutenant Potter was here. A sergeant told me." The girl faltered again. Starbuck could hear Holborrow shouting down the stairs for his slave to bring hot shaving water. "Come in," Starbuck said. "Please, come in. Can I take your cloak?"

"I don't want to cause no trouble," the girl said, "I truly don't."

"Give me your cloak. Sit, please. That chair will be fine. Might I have your name, ma'am?" Starbuck had almost called her miss, then saw the cheap wedding ring glinting on her left hand.

"I'm Martha Potter," she said very faintly. "I don't want to be no trouble, I really don't."

"You aren't, ma'am, you aren't," Starbuck said. He had suspected from the moment the brown curls had timidly appeared around the door that this was the real Mrs. Potter and he feared that the real Lieutenant Potter could not be far behind. That would be a nuisance, for Starbuck wanted to reveal his true identity in his own way and not have the dénouement forced on him by circumstance, but he hid his consternation as Martha timidly perched on the edge of a chair. She wore a homespun dress that had been turned so that the lower skirt had become the upper to save the material's wear and tear. The pale brown dress was neatly sewn, while her shawl, though threadbare, was scrupulously clean. "We were expecting you, ma'am," Starbuck said.

"You were?" Martha sounded surprised, as if no one had ever paid her the compliment of expectation before. "It's just—" she began, then stopped.

"Yes?" Starbuck tried to prompt her.

"He is here?" she asked eagerly. "My husband?"

"No, ma'am, he's not," Starbuck said and Martha began to cry. The tears were not demonstrative, nor loud, just a helpless silent weeping that embarrassed Starbuck. He fumbled in his coat pocket for a handkerchief, found none, and could see nothing suitable to mop up tears anywhere else in the office. "Some coffee, ma'am?" he suggested.

"I don't want to be no trouble," she said through her quiet sobs, which she tried to staunch with the tasseled edge of her shawl.

Lucifer arrived, ready to leave for Richmond. Starbuck waved him out of the room. "And bring us a pot of coffee, Lucifer," he called after the boy.

"Yes, Lieutenant Potter," Lucifer said from the hall.

The girl's head snapped up. "He . . ." she began, then stopped. "Did I?" she tried again, then sniffed back tears.

"Ma'am." Starbuck sat opposite her and leaned forward. "Do you know where your husband is?"

"No," she wailed the word. "No!"

He gradually eased the tale out of the waiflike girl. Lucifer brought the coffee, then squatted in the office corner, his presence a constant reminder of Starbuck's promise that they were supposed to be leaving this hateful place. Martha cuffed at her tears, sipped at the coffee, and told the sad tale of how she had been raised in Hamburg, Tennessee, a small river village a few miles north of the Mississippi border. "I'm an orphan, sir," she told Starbuck, "and was raised by my grandma, but she took queer last winter and died round Christmas." After that, Martha said, she had been put to work by a family in Corinth, Mississippi, "but I weren't never happy, sir. They treated me bad, real bad. The master, sir, he—" she faltered.

"I can guess," Starbuck said.

She sniffed, then told how, in May, the rebel forces had fallen back on the town and she had met Matthew Potter. "He spoke so nice, sir, so nice," she said, and marriage to Potter had seemed like a dream come true as well as an escape from her vile employer and so, within days of meeting him, Martha had stood in the parlor of a Baptist minister's house and married her soldier.

Then she discovered her new husband was a drunkard. "He didn't drink those first few days, sir, but that was because they locked all the liquor up. Then he found some and he didn't never look back. Not that he's a bad drunk, sir, not like some men. I mean he don't hit anyone when he's drunk, he just don't ever get sober. Colonel Hardcastle threw him out of the regiment for drunkenness, and I can't blame him, but Matthew's a good man really."

"But where is he, ma'am?" Starbuck asked.

"That's it, sir. I don't know." She began sobbing again, but managed to tell how, after Potter had been dismissed from the 3rd Mississippian Infantry Battalion, he had used Martha's small savings to take them back home to Georgia, where his father had refused to receive either Potter or his new wife. "We stayed in Atlanta awhile, sir, then his pa told us to get ourselves up here and see Colonel Holborrow. He sent us the money to come here, sir, which was real Christian of him, I thought. Then Matthew and me got here three days since and I ain't seen him once in all those days."

"So he's drunk in Richmond?" Starbuck suggested flatly.

"I guess, sir, yes."

"But where have you been staying?" Starbuck asked.

"At a Mrs. Miller's house, sir, in Charity Street, only Mrs. Miller says her rooms ain't charity, if you follow me, and if we don't pay her the rent by this morning she'll throw me out, sir, and so I came here. But I don't want to be no trouble." She looked as if she would cry again, but instead she frowned at Starbuck. "You ain't Colonel Holborrow, are you, sir?"

"No, I'm not, ma'am," Starbuck paused, then offered Martha what he hoped was a reassuring smile. He liked her, partly because she seemed so very fragile and timid, and partly, he guiltily confessed to himself, because there was an appealing prettiness under her mask of misery. There was also, he suspected, a streak of stubborn toughness that she would probably need to survive marriage to Matthew Potter. "I'm a friend of yours, ma'am," he told her. "You have to believe that. I've been pretending to be your husband and doing his work so that he wouldn't get into trouble. Can you understand that? But now we have to go and find him."

"Hallelujah," Lucifer murmured.

"You've been doing his work, sir?" Martha asked, incredulous that anyone would perform such a kindness for her wastrel husband.

"Yes," Starbuck said. "And now we're all going to walk out of here and go find your Matthew. And if anyone speaks to us, ma'am, then I beg you to keep silent. Do you promise to do that for me?"

"Yes, sir."

"Then let's go, shall we?" Starbuck handed Martha her thin cloak, collected his papers, paused to make certain no one was outside the door, then ushered Lucifer and Martha through the hall and across the verandah. It promised to be a hot, sunlit day. Starbuck hurried toward the nearest huts, hoping to make good his escape without being seen, but then a voice shouted at him from the house. "Potter!"

Martha uttered an exclamation and Starbuck had to remind her of the promise to say nothing. "And stay here," he went on, "both of you." Then he turned and walked back toward the house.

It was Captain Dennison who had called and who now jumped down the verandah steps. The captain looked as if he had just risen from his bed, for he was in his shirtsleeves and was pulling bright red suspenders over his shoulders as he hurried toward Starbuck. "I want you, Potter," he called.

"Looks like you found me," Starbuck said as he confronted the angry captain.

"You call me 'sir.'" Dennison was standing close to Starbuck now and the smell of the ointment the captain had smeared on his diseased face was almost overpowering. It was a peculiarly sour smell, not kerosene, and suddenly Starbuck placed it, and the memory of his time in the Richmond prison came flooding back in a wave of nausea. "You call me 'sir'!" Dennison said again, thrusting a finger hard into Starbuck's chest.

"Yes, sir."

Dennison grimaced. "You threatened me last night, Potter."

"Did I, sir?"

"Yes you damn well did. So either you come into the house, Potter, right now and apologize in front of the other officers, or else you face the consequences."

Starbuck pretended to consider the alternatives, then shrugged. "Guess I'll take the consequences, Captain, sir."

Dennison gave a grim smile. "You are a miserable fool, Potter, a fool. Very well. Do you know Bloody Run?"

"I can find it, sir."

"You find it at six o'clock tonight, Potter, and if you have trouble just ask anyone where the Richmond dueling grounds are. They're by the Bloody Run under the Chimborazo Hill at the other end of the city. Six o'clock. Bring a second if you can find anyone stupid enough to support you. Colonel Holborrow will be my second. And one other thing, Potter."

"Sir?"

"Try and be sober. I don't relish killing a drunk."

"Six o'clock, sir, sober," Starbuck said. "I look forward to it, sir. One thing, sir?"

Dennison turned back. "Yes?" He asked suspiciously.

"You issued the challenge, sir, so I get to choose weapons. Ain't that the way it's done?"

"So choose," Dennison said carelessly.

"Swords," Starbuck said instantly and with sufficient confidence to make Dennison blink with surprise. "Swords, Captain!" He called airily as he turned and walked away. The smell of the medicine had betrayed Dennison's secret and Starbuck was suddenly looking forward to the day.

Lieutenant-Colonel Swynyard stood at the river's edge and thanked his God that he had been spared to witness this moment. A small breeze rippled the water to splinter up a myriad of bright sparkles reflected from a sun that blazed in a cloudless summer sky. At least three bands were playing and in this place, on this day, there was only one tune that they would ever play, though the colonel thought it was a pity that they did not play in unison, but instead competed merrily as they celebrated the momentous event. Swynyard's maimed left hand beat against his sword scabbard in time to the closest band, then, almost unaware of it, he began to sing. "Dear mother," the colonel sang softly, "burst the tyrant's chain. Maryland! Virginia should not call in vain, Maryland!" His voice became louder as the emotion of the hour embraced him. "She meets her sister on the plain; *Sic semper*! 'tis the proud refrain that baffles minions back amain, Maryland, my Maryland."

A burst of clapping sounded from the nearest company of the Faulconer Legion and Swynyard, oblivious that he had raised his voice loud enough to be heard, blushed as he turned and acknowledged the ironic applause. There had been a time, and not long before either, when these men cursed the very sight of Griffin Swynyard, but they had been won over by Christ's grace, or rather by the workings of that grace inside Swynyard, and now the colonel knew that the men liked him and for that blessing he could have wept this day, except that he was already weeping for sheer joy at this moment.

For the Southern army of Robert Lee, which had fought again and again against the Northern invaders of its country, was crossing the Potomac.

They were going north.

The Confederacy was taking the war into the United States of America. For a year now the Yankees had marched on Southern soil, had stolen from Southern farms, and boasted of sacking the Southern capital, but now the invaded had become the invaders and a great dark line of men was crossing the ford beneath the battle flags of the South. "I hear the distant thunder-hum," Swynyard sang and this time the Legion sang with him, their voices swelling beside the river in wondrous harmony. "Maryland! The old line's bugle, fife and drum, Maryland! She is not dead, nor deaf, nor dumb; Huzzah! She spurns the northern scum! She breathes, she burns, she'll come, she'll come! Maryland, my Maryland!"

"They're in good voice, Swynyard, good voice!" The speaker was Colonel Ned Maitland, the Legion's new commander, who spurred his horse to Swynyard's side. Swynyard was on foot because his horse, the one luxury he possessed, was being rested. A man like Maitland might need three saddle horses and four pack-mules loaded with belongings to ensure his comfort on a campaign, but Swynyard had forsworn all such fripperies. He owned a horse because a brigade commander could not do his job without one, and he had inherited a tent and a servant from Thaddeus Bird, but the tent belonged to the army and the servant, a half-witted soldier called Hiram Ketley, would return to Bird's service when Bird was recovered from the wound he had taken at Cedar Mountain.

"What will you do, Maitland, when Bird comes back?" Swynyard asked, needling the self-satisfied Maitland, who rode to war with two tents, four slaves, a hip bath, and a canteen of silver cutlery with which to eat his scumbled vegetables.

"I hear he won't return," Maitland said.

"I hear he will. His wife wrote to Starbuck saying he was mending well, and when he does come back I'll have to give him the Legion. He's their proper commander."

Maitland waved the problem away. "There'll be plenty of other vacancies, Swynyard."

"You think I might be killed, eh? You reckon you'll be brigade commander? You look the part, Maitland, I'll say that for you. What did that uniform cost?"

"Plenty enough." Maitland was a placid man who rarely rose to Swynyard's baiting, perhaps because he knew that his connections in Richmond would ensure his smooth rise up the army's senior ranks. The trick of that rise, Maitland reckoned, was to have just enough battle experience beneath his belt to make it plausible; just enough and no more. He took a pair of field glasses from a saddlebag and trained them on the distant Maryland shore while Swynyard watched a squadron of Stuart's cavalrymen spur into the river. The troopers reached down with their hats to scoop up water that they flung at each other like children at play. The army was in a holiday mood.

"I wish the Legion still had a band," Swynyard said as the nearest musicians launched into "My Maryland" for the umpteenth time. "We did have one," he said, "but it got lost. At least, the instruments did."

"A lot of things seem to get lost from the Legion," Maitland said airily.

"What on earth does that mean?" Swynyard asked, trying to disguise his irritation at Maitland's condescension. Swynyard was not certain that Maitland intended to give the impression he did, but that impression was of a superior man who observed and disapproved of all he encountered.

"Officers, mainly," Maitland said. "Most of the officers seem to have come up from the ranks in the last few weeks."

"We were fighting," Swynyard said, "which meant officers got killed. Didn't you hear about it in Richmond?"

"A rumor of it reached us," Maitland said mildly, cleaning the lenses of his field glasses. "Even so, Swynyard, I reckon I need some better men."

"Fellows who know what knife and fork to use on their hardtack?" Swynyard guessed.

Maitland let the sarcasm sail past him. "I mean more confident fellows. Confidence is a great morale booster. Like young Moxey. Pity he's gone." Captain Moxey had gone to Richmond to serve as Washington Faulconer's aide.

"Moxey was useless," Swynyard said. "If I was going into battle, Maitland, I wouldn't want weak reeds like young Moxey, but men like Waggoner and Truslow."

"But they're hardly inspirational men," Maitland observed tartly.

"Victory's the best inspiration," Swynyard said, "and men like Truslow deliver it."

"Maybe," Maitland allowed, "but I'd have liked to have held onto Moxey. Or that Tumlin fellow."

Swynyard had to think for a second to place Tumlin, then remembered the man from Louisiana who claimed to have been a prisoner in the North since the fall of New Orleans. "You wanted him?" he asked, surprised.

"He seemed a decent fellow," Maitland said. "Eager to serve."

"You think so?" Swynyard asked. "I thought he was a bit plump for a fellow who'd spent five months in a Yankee prison, but maybe our erstwhile brethren can afford to feed their captives well. And I have to say I thought young Tumlin was a bit glib."

"He had confidence, yes," Maitland said. "I suppose you sent him back to Richmond?"

"Winchester," Swynyard said. Winchester, in the Shenandoah Valley, was the campaign's supply base and all unattached men were now being sent there to be reappointed. "At least he won't get wished onto poor Nate Starbuck," Swynyard added.

"Starbuck could count himself lucky if he had been," Maitland said, raising the glasses again toward the far riverbank. That bank was heavily

wooded, but beyond the trees Maitland could see enemy farmland bask-
ing in the strong sunlight.

"If Starbuck's lucky," Swynyard said, "he'll be back with this
brigade. I requested that his battalion be given to us if it's ordered to the
army. No one else will want them, that's for sure."

Maitland shuddered at the thought of seeing the Yellowlegs again.
His appointment to its command had been the nadir of his career and
only the most energetic string-pulling had rescued him. "I doubt we'll
see them," he said, unable to hide his relief. "They aren't ready to march
and won't be ready for months." Not ever, he reflected, if Colonel Holborrow had his way. "And why would we want them anyway?" he
added.

"Because we're Christians, Maitland, and turn away no man."

"Except Tumlin," Maitland retorted tartly. "Looks as if they're
ready for us, Swynyard."

A messenger was spurring toward the brigade. A horse-drawn
ambulance had just splashed into the ford accompanied by a cheer from
the closest troops. Robert Lee was inside the vehicle, put there by
injuries to his hands when he tried to quiet his frightened horse. A
wounded commander, Swynyard thought, was not a good omen, but he
put that pagan thought behind him as the messenger rode to Maitland
under the assumption that the elegant lieutenant-colonel was the
brigade commander. "He's the fellow you want," Maitland said, indicating Swynyard.

The messenger brought orders for Swynyard's brigade to cross the
river and Swynyard, in turn, gave the Legion the honor of leading the
brigade onto Northern soil. The colonel walked down the Legion's column of companies. "Remember boys," he shouted again and again, "no
looting! No roguery! Pay in scrip for whatever you want! Show them
we're a Christian country! Go now!"

Truslow's A Company waited until a battery of South Carolinian
guns had splashed into the ford, then followed onto the road and down
the muddy ramp into the water. The color party followed with the
Legion's single flag held aloft by young Lieutenant Coffman, who found

it a struggle to hold the big battle flag high against the wind while his slight body was buffeted by the Potomac's swirling current, which rose above his waist. He pushed on gamely, almost as though the whole war's outcome depended on him keeping the fringed silk out of the water. Many of the men were limping, not through wounds but because their ill-booted feet were blistered and to those men the river's cool water was like the balm of Gilead. Some men, though, refused to cross. Swynyard paused to talk with half a dozen such men who were led by a gaunt young corporal from D Company. The corporal's name was Burridge and he was a good soldier and a regular worshipper at the colonel's prayer meetings, but now, as respectful and stubborn as ever, Burridge insisted he must disobey Swynyard's orders. "Ain't our task to go north, Colonel," he said firmly.

"It's your task to obey a lawful order, Burridge."

"Not if it's against a man's conscience, colonel, and you know it. And it is lawful for us to defend our homes, but not to attack other folks' homes. If a Yankee comes south then I'll kill him for you, but I won't go north to do my slaughtering," Burridge declared and his companions nodded their support.

Swynyard ordered the men back to where the provosts were collecting other soldiers whose consciences could not abide carrying the war off their home soil. It grieved Swynyard to lose the six men, for they were among the best in the brigade, but it had been a confrontation he could never win and so he bid them farewell then followed the Legion into the river. Some of the men ducked their heads into the water to give their hair a brief washing, but most just pressed on toward the Northern bank, climbed onto Maryland soil, then crossed the bridge over the Chesapeake and Ohio Canal that lay just beyond the river. And thus they entered the enemy country.

It was a fine place of comfortable farms, good wooded land, and gentle hills; no different from the landscape they had left, only these hills and farms and woods were ruled by an enemy government. Here a different flag flew and that gave a piquancy to the otherwise unremarkable countryside. Not that most of the men in the five regiments in Swynyard's Brigade considered Maryland an enemy; rather they believed it was a slave state that had been forced to stay with the Union because of geography, and there were high hopes that this incursion of a Confederate army would draw a flock of recruits to the rebel's slashed cross flags. But however sympathetic Marylanders might be to the rebellion, it was still an enemy state and here and there some farms yet flew a defiant stars and stripes to show that this was Yankee territory.

But such stars and stripes were far outnumbered by rebel flags, most of them homemade things with faint colors and uncertain design, but they were hung to welcome Lee's army and when, at midafternoon, Swynyard's men marched through Buckeystown they were greeted by a small crowd that was hoarse from cheering the arrival of the rebels. Buckets of water or lemonade were placed beside the road and women carried trays of cookies along the weary columns. One or two of Buckeystown's houses, it was true, were shuttered closed, but most of the village welcomed the invasion. A Texan band played the inevitable "My Maryland" as the column passed, the tune becoming ever more ragged and the harmony more cacophonous as the bandsmen were supplied with cider, beer, and whiskey by the villagers.

The brigade trudged on, their broken boots kicking up a plume of white dust that drifted westward on the breeze. Once, a mile beyond Buckeystown, a sudden crackle of firing sounded far away to the east and some of the men touched the stocks of their worn rifles as if preparing for battle, but no more shots sounded. The countryside stretched warm away, bounteous and calm under the summer sun. God was in His heaven, all seemed well in the world, and Lee's rebel army was loose in the North.

Starbuck walked into Richmond where he left Lucifer, his small luggage, and the letter for Belvedere Delaney at Sally's house, then he led Martha Potter on a tour of Richmond's drinking dens. Alcohol was officially banned from the city, but the government might as well have tried to outlaw breathing for all the difference their high-mindedness had made.

Starbuck began with the more respectable houses close to the Byrd Street depot of the Richmond and Petersburg Railroad, where Martha had last seen her husband. Starbuck spared her the brothels, reckoning that no whore would have endured a drunk for three days. Instead they would have picked Matthew Potter clean on the first night and then pitched him into the street to be swept up by the provosts. Once sober the lieutenant would have been sent to Camp Lee and his failure to arrive suggested that he had discovered some liquor-sodden haven, or worse.

Starbuck worked his way down the hierarchy of liquor shops. The first places he searched had some pretensions to gentility, maybe a gilded mirror or a stretch of tobacco-soaked carpet, but gradually the furnishings, like the liquor, worsened. He knocked on a half dozen doors in Locust Alley, but found no sign of the missing lieutenant. He tried Martin Street, where the whores hung out of the upper windows and made Martha blush. "He didn't have the money to drink all these days, sir," she told Starbuck.

"He might have," Starbuck insisted.

"There weren't more than three dollars in my purse."

"Three dollars will take you a long way in this town, ma'am," Starbuck said, "and I daresay he had a coat? He had a pair of boots? A revolver?"

"All those, yes."

"Then he could sell those and be drunk for three months. Hell," he said, then apologized. "Forgive my language, ma'am, but that's where he is. The Hells. I think, ma'am, I'd better take you back to Miss Sally's."

"I'm coming with you," Martha insisted. For all her timidity she was a dogged girl and no amount of Starbuck's persuasion could convince her to abandon the search.

"Ma'am, it ain't safe in the Hells."

"But he might be injured."

He might be dead, Starbuck thought. "I must insist, ma'am."

"You can insist all you want, sir," Martha said stubbornly, "but I'm still coming. I'll just follow you if you won't escort me."

Starbuck took out his revolver and checked that all five cones were primed with percussion caps. "Ma'am," he said, "where I'm going ain't called the Hells for nothing. It's in Screamersville, down by Penitentiary

Bottom. Ugly names, ma'am, ugly place. Even the provosts don't go there under company strength."

Martha frowned. "They outlaws there?" she asked.

"In a manner, ma'am. Some deserters, a lot of thieves, and a lot of slaves. Only these slaves aren't under orders, ma'am, they're out of the Tredegar Iron Works and they're tougher than the stuff they roll in the mills."

"Hell," Martha said, "I ain't afraid of niggers."

"Then you should be, ma'am."

"I'm coming with you, Major."

He led her down the hill past Johnny Worsham's barn-like establishment where gambling tables crowded close to the stage on which a troupe of girls danced in between entertaining their clients upstairs. Two black men in bowler hats guarded the door and watched Starbuck with flat, cold stares. He led Martha over a wooden bridge that spanned a creek flooded with sewage and then into an alley that ran between damp brick walls. "You know the town pretty well, sir?" Martha asked, lifting her skirts as she stepped between the fetid rubbish that lay on the cobbles.

"I served a few weeks with the provosts here," Starbuck said. They had been miserable weeks that had ended with his imprisonment on suspicion of being a Northern spy. A gutless little officer called Gillespie had made Starbuck's life a hell in that prison, and that was one prospect of revenge that Starbuck treasured.

He stepped over a pile of garbage and turned into an unnamed street. The stench of the iron works hung heavy here and the sound of the furnaces roared to rival the foaming of the nearby river where it cascaded over the rapids. A dozen slaves lay in the smoke-dimmed sunlight with stone bottles of liquor, which they raised in an ironic salute as Starbuck passed. "Why ain't they at work?" Martha demanded.

"They work hard enough," Starbuck said. "You can't whip a man into working hard, ma'am. You have to give them some rope and once the slaves are trusted in the Iron Works they can come and go pretty much as they please. Long as they stay down here and don't go into the upper town, no one minds. This is their territory, not ours."

"Matthew wouldn't come here, would he?"

"Lots of soldiers do. There aren't any rules here, and the liquor's real cheap."

A mad preacher in an ankle-length black coat stood on a corner yelling the good news of Christ to a town that was not listening. A dwarf woman, drunk to the wind, reeled down the cobbles singing, but otherwise there were not many people in the streets. Midday was the witching hour for the Hells, the time when the sun shone brightest and Screamersville's denizens slept indoors as they prepared for the night's business. Starbuck chose a random tavern and plunged inside. A few soldiers slouched on benches, but none was Potter. One offered Martha a dollar if she would go upstairs with him, while another looked up at her, sighed with lust, and then vomited. "I told you," Starbuck said as he led her back into the street, "that this is no place for a lady."

"Hell, Major," Martha said sturdily, "no real lady would have married Matthew Potter. Besides, I've heard worse."

She did hear worse that day, but she stayed close to Starbuck as they searched the canalside shacks where most of the Hells business was done. The smell of the place was nauseating; a mix of coal smoke, vomit, sewage, and raw liquor. They were summarily ejected from one house by four black men who had been playing cards. A thin white woman sat in the room's corner with a bruised face. She spat when Starbuck entered and one of the men picked up a shotgun and rammed it into the stranger's face. "She don't want you here, mister," the black man said.

Starbuck took the hint and backed out into the alley. "I'm looking for a friend," he explained hurriedly.

"Not me, soldier, not them," the slave gestured at his companions, "not her, not no one in here." He paused and gave Martha a long speculative look. "She can come in, though."

"Not today," Starbuck said.

"He shouldn't talk uppity like that," Martha protested when the door was slammed on them. "And why's he got a gun? That ain't allowed!"

"Ma'am," Starbuck sighed, "I told you there weren't any rules here.

He'd love me to pick a fight and a minute later you'd have a dozen black folk beating me to pulp."

"It ain't right."

"The underside of Dixie, ma'am. Sweet liberty." He gently edged Martha into the entry of an alley to keep her out of the way of a furious woman who pursued a man onto the street and hurled insults after him. The row became general as neighbors joined in. "Social gravity," Starbuck said.

"What does that mean?"

"It means we all go downhill, ma'am, till we hit the bottom."

"Some of us didn't start very high up."

"But keep going up, ma'am, keep going up." Christ, Starbuck thought, but if it were not for the rebel army then he would probably be down in these same slums. He had fled New England for a woman, and for her he had become a thief, and only the outbreak of war had offered him a chance of escape. What would he have done without the war, he wondered. Become a clerk and sought the solace of cheap drink and women, probably. And what would he do when the war was over, he wondered.

"Are you married?" Martha suddenly asked him.

"No, ma'am." Starbuck pushed open a door to find a cockpit made of straw bales arranged in a circle. Three rats fled the pit's floor, which was stained with blood and feathers, as Starbuck flooded the hovel with daylight. A soldier lay asleep on the bales stacked for the spectators, but he was not the missing lieutenant.

"Matthew's real good looking," Martha said after she had inspected the sleeper, who was missing one eye and most of his teeth.

"Is that why you married him?" Starbuck asked, going back into the street.

"Marry in haste, my grandma always said, and repent at leisure," Martha said sadly.

"I've heard the advice," Starbuck said, and crossed the road to push open another shaky door. And there they discovered Matthew Potter.

Or rather Martha recognized the man sleeping on the wooden verandah that creaked under their weight as they stepped onto its thin boards. Rats scuttled from under the planks and ran along the canal's edge. "Matthew!" Martha called and knelt beside her husband, who was dressed in nothing but gray pants.

Potter did not wake up. He groaned and stirred in his sleep, but did not open his eyes.

"I wondered when some soul would come for him." A black woman appeared at the verandah door.

"Been here long, has he?" Starbuck asked her.

"So long I thought he'd take root. Likes his liquor, don't he?"

"I hear he's fond of it."

The woman wiped her nose with a corner of her apron, then grinned. "He's a nice boy, though. Speaks nice. Kind of took pity on him. Tried to feed him, even, but he didn't want food, just his guzzle."

"Sold you his shirt, did he?"

"And his coat, and his shoes. Just about every damned thing he had."

"His revolver?" Starbuck asked.

"He wouldn't have done that, sir. 'Gainst the law, isn't it?" She grinned at Starbuck, who grinned back. "He says he's from Georgia," the woman said, peering at the prostrate lieutenant.

"He is."

"A preacher's son, see? They're always the worst." The woman laughed. "He was dancing for a time, and he even spoke poetry. Such nice poetry, I could have listened to him all night except that he fell over. Is that his wife?"

"Yes."

"Born to trouble. I never did understand why good women marry bad men."

"Lucky for us they do, eh?"

She smiled. "You going to take him away?"

"I reckon."

"Well, he had a good time. He won't remember it, but he did. Sad to think he'll probably go down to a Yankee bullet, a nice boy like that."

"He won't wake up!" Martha wailed.

"He will," Starbuck promised, then he pulled her away from her husband and made her go inside the shack. "Wait there," he told her, and once he had shepherded her off the verandah and closed the door he put his hands under Potter's armpits and hauled him first to a sitting position and then upright. It was not difficult, for Potter, though tall, was frailly built and as thin as a rail. Starbuck leaned the Lieutenant against the shack's wall.

Potter stirred at last. "Time is it?" he asked. He was, as Martha had said, a good-looking man with fair lank hair and a week's growth of pale beard. His face was long and thin and had a delicacy, almost a look of noble suffering that, when Potter was sober, might have suggested spirituality or some artistic sensitivity, but now, in the throes of his monumental hangover, the lieutenant simply looked like a whipped and sick puppy. A young puppy too, Starbuck guessed; certainly not more than nineteen. The Lieutenant tried to raise his head. He blinked slackly at Starbuck. "How do ye do," he managed to say.

Starbuck thumped him in the belly. He thumped him real hard, grunting with the effort of the blow that made Potter open his eyes wide, then double over. He almost fell, but Starbuck shoved him back against the wall before stepping smartly to one side as Potter threw up. Starbuck skipped further aside to stop the stream of vomit from splashing onto his boots.

"Jesus," Potter complained and cuffed at his mouth. He groaned. "You do that?"

"Stand up, Lieutenant."

"Oh, Jesus. Sweet Jesus. Sweet Lord Jesus." Potter tried to straighten. "Oh, suffering Jesus," he moaned as a stab of pain rammed down from his head. He pushed a long hank of hair off his face. "Who are you?" he demanded. "Announce yourself."

"The best son of a bitch friend you ever had," Starbuck said. "Is anything left in your belly?"

"It hurts," Potter said, rubbing his yellow-white skin where Starbuck had hit him.

"Stand straight!" Starbuck barked.

"Soldier! Soldier!" Potter said as he made a feeble effort to stand to attention. "Jesus wants me for a soldier." He retched again. "Oh, my God."

Starbuck pushed him back onto the wall. "Stand up straight," he said.

"Discipline," Potter said as he tried to straighten up. "The cure for all that ails me."

Starbuck took a handful of Potter's long, fair hair and rammed it back against the shack's wall, thus forcing the Lieutenant to look into his eyes. "What's going to cure you, you son of a bitch," he said, "is looking after your wife."

"Martha? Is she here?" Potter immediately cheered up and looked left and right. "Don't see her."

"She's here. And she's been looking for you. Why the hell did you leave her?"

Potter frowned as he tried to remember his last few days. "I didn't precisely leave her," he finally said. "I wandered, true, and did misplace her for a time. I was in need of a drink, you understand, and met a friend. Do you notice how that happens? You go to a strange city, incur a thirst, and the very first person you meet is someone you were at school with. The workings of providence, I suppose. Would you mind, sir, very much letting go of my hair so that I can be sick again? Thank you." He managed to say the last two words before jackknifing forward and spewing up a last pathetic throatful of vomit. He moaned, closed his eyes, and slowly stood up again. "Rinsed out now," he said reassuringly as he looked at Starbuck. "Do I know you?"

"Major Starbuck."

"Ah! Starbuck! A famous name!" Potter said and Starbuck tensed himself for the usual attack on his father, a notorious enemy of the South, but Matthew Potter had a different Starbuck in mind. "First mate of the *Pequod*, aren't I right?"

"Think of me as Captain Ahab, Lieutenant," Starbuck said.

Potter gazed momentarily at Starbuck's legs. "Rather overendowed with pins, aren't you, for such a role? Or is one of those an ivory peg?" Potter giggled, then winced as another pain lashed at him. "Should I be pleased to meet you?"

"Yes, you damn well should. Now come on, you son of a bitch, we're going to fight a duel."

Potter stared with horror at Starbuck, then shook his head. "Not in my line of business, sir. Really not. Don't mind battle, but not pistols at dawn."

"It's swords at dusk. Now come on! Don't tread in that!" Too late. Potter placed a bare foot in his puddle of vomit, grimaced, then followed Starbuck into the tavern where an emotional Martha threw herself into her husband's enfeebled arms. Starbuck thought about offering to buy back the Lieutenant's shoes and shirt, then decided against wasting his money. Potter could be equipped from the thin stores at Camp Lee, and until then he could go barefoot and bare-chested.

He persuaded a now-remorseful Lieutenant out into the street. Martha led Potter by the hand while he tried to explain his conduct. "Not intentional, my most darling one, not with malice aforethought, as the lawyers would say. It was merely a whim, a notion, a gesture of amity for an old friend. Thomas Snyder. That is his name and Snyder will vouch for the purity of my motives. He is an artilleryman now, he told me, and has gone partly deaf. All those loud bangs, you see? Whatever, I merely kept him company. We were at school together and together we mastered McGuffey's readers, together we added and subtracted and divided, and together we got drunk, for which I apologize. It will not happen again until the next time. Oh God, do I really have to walk?"

"Yes," Starbuck said, "you do."

"I do dislike strong, noisy men," Potter said, but stumbled obediently behind Starbuck up the hill toward Main Street. "The army is filled with strong, noisy men. The life must attract them. You didn't, I suppose, bring anything to eat, my dearest chick?" he inquired of Martha.

"No, Matthew."

"Or a mouthful to drink, perhaps?"

"No, Matthew!"

"Water, dearest love, mere water. A moment, Captain Ahab!" Potter called, then pulled away from his wife and staggered over the street to a horse trough that was already occupied by a shaggy cab horse. Potter stood beside the horse and plunged his face into the water, scooped it over his hair, and then drank greedily.

"I'm so ashamed," Martha said to Starbuck.

"I like him," Starbuck said, realizing as he spoke that it was true. "I do like him."

Potter stood and belched. He apologized to the horse, patted its neck, and walked unsteadily back to his wife. "My father," he said to Starbuck, "always maintains that self-knowledge is the harbinger of self-improvement, but I'm not entirely persuaded of that truth. Do I improve myself by knowing I am eternally thirsty, overeducated, and sadly fallible? I think not. Would you both excuse me for another trifling moment?" He walked to the nearest wall, unbuttoned his pants, and pissed noisily onto the brick. "Oh, dear God," he said, raising his eyes, "in one end and out the other."

"So ashamed," Martha whispered.

"Did you say ashamed, sweet love of my benighted life?" Potter called loudly from the wall. "Ashamed? Do not the poets piss? Does not an anointed king empty his royal bladder? Did not George Washington micturate? Was our dear Lord spared the need to sprinkle?"

"Matthew!" Martha protested, shocked. "He was perfect!"

"And that, sweetest one, was a perfect piss." He turned back to them, buttoning his trousers, then waved imperiously at Starbuck. "Onward, Captain Ahab! Death to Moby Dick! God hunt us all if we do not hunt Moby Dick to his death! Onward, dear souls!"

Sally, as she had promised, was waiting outside Mitchell and Tyler's jewelry store on Main Street and with her, as Starbuck had hoped, was Belvedere Delaney. The lawyer was dressed in one of the expensive uniforms he bought from Shaffer's, but no amount of tailoring could disguise Delaney's unmilitary soul. He was a short, plump, kindly man whose talents were making money and taking amusement from other men's weaknesses. Officially he was a captain in the legal office of the Confederate War Department, an appointment that seemed to require no duties except to take the pay and to wear a uniform when it was convenient. Today he sported a major's stars. "You've been promoted?" Starbuck asked, gladly greeting his old friend.

"I deemed the rank appropriate," Delaney answered grandly. "No one else seems to have the power to promote or demote me, so I assumed the rank as one more fitting for my dignity. In time, just like a gas balloon, I shall rise to the dizziest of heights. Dear Nate, you look dreadful! Scarred, dirty, used up. Is this what soldiering does to one?"

"Yes," Starbuck said, then introduced the barechested Lieutenant Potter, who seemed rather frightened by Delaney. Martha nervously shook the lawyer's hand, then fell back to cling to her disreputable husband.

"Here," Sally said to Starbuck as they began to walk eastward along Main, "you need this," and she held out one of Patrick Lassan's sabers.

Starbuck buckled the sword belt round his waist. "Did you find anything?" he asked Delaney.

"Of course I didn't find anything," the lawyer said testily. "I am not a detective bureau, I am merely an attorney." Delaney paused to raise his peaked cap to a passing acquaintance. "But it's quite obvious," he went on, "what Holborrow is doing. He is using the Special Battalion as a milch cow. He feeds it scraps and it yields him money. He doesn't want it to go to war, because that would mean he loses the income."

"What does that mean?" Starbuck asked.

Delaney sighed. "It's obvious, isn't it? The government issues the Special Battalion boots, so Holborrow sells the boots to another regiment, then complains to the government that the boots were faulty. In time he will receive more boots that will also be sold. The same for rifles, canteens, coats, and anything else he can gouge out of the system. He's doing it quite cleverly, for the system hasn't discovered him, but I'm sure that's his game. Are you really going to fight a duel?"

"Son of a bitch challenged me," Starbuck said belligerently, then, unable to hide his disappointment, glanced back at the lawyer. "So you can't help me?" he asked. Starbuck, in the careful letter he had written to Delaney that morning, had described his suspicions that Holborrow had purloined the rifles meant for the Special Battalion and then sold them. He had hoped that somehow Delaney might discover some evidence in the War Department, but his hopes had been dashed.

"I can help you," Delaney said, "by being a lawyer."

"You mean you'll threaten Holborrow?"

Delaney sighed. "You are so blunt, Nate, so hopelessly blunt. How can I threaten him? I know nothing. I can, however, drop broad hints. I can insinuate. I can pretend to know what I do not know. I can suggest a formal investigation might be undertaken, and it is possible, just possible, that he'll come to an arrangement rather than call my bluff. How many men in the battalion?"

"A hundred and eighty nine."

"Ah, that's something. He's drawing rations and pay for two hundred and sixty." Delaney smiled, seeing an advantage. "I can tell you one other thing. Holborrow was never wounded by a Yankee bullet. That bad leg came from a fall off his horse and the damage isn't half so bad as he pretends. He doesn't want to go to war, you see? So he's playing up the wound. What he wants is a nice, safe, profitable war in plump Richmond, and I guess he'll do quite a lot to make sure he gets it. But what do you want, Nate?"

"You know what I want."

"Two hundred rifles?" Delaney shook his head. "The rifles will have been sold long ago. I doubt Holborrow can lay his hands on fifty, but I'll do my best. But do you really want to be sent to Lee's army?" That was Starbuck's main request; that Holborrow would affirm that the Special Battalion was ready for combat and so release it to the war. "Why?" Delaney asked in genuine puzzlement. "Why don't you just take the God-given rest, Nate? Haven't you fought enough?"

Starbuck was not really sure of the answer. One part of him, a great shadowed horrid part of him, feared combat like a small child feared the night-ghouls, but still he felt compelled to take his battalion to war. He doubted if he could live with the knowledge that he was skulking while other men fought, but it was more than that. All he now possessed in the world was his reputation as a soldier. He had no family, no wealth, and no position other than his Confederate commission and if he betrayed that commission by skulking then he was abandoning his pride. He did not want to go to battle, he only knew he had to go to battle. "I'm a soldier," he answered inadequately.

"I shall never understand you," Delaney said happily, "but maybe the next few weeks will give me an answer. I'm joining Lee myself."

"You?" Starbuck asked, astonished. He stopped on the sidewalk and looked at his friend. "You're going to the army?"

"My country calls!" Delaney said grandiloquently.

"To do what?"

Delaney shrugged and walked on. "My idea, really. No one ordered me to go, Nate, but it seemed like a good idea when it occurred to me. Lee's invading the North, did you know? Well, he is and there are bound to be tricky points of law involved. If a man steals from enemy property, is it theft? It might seem a trivial thing to you, even irrelevant, but when this war does end there's bound to be all sorts of legal settlements to be made between the two jurisdictions and it seems only prudent to try and anticipate the issues."

"You'll hate campaigning," Starbuck said.

"I'm sure I shall," Delaney said fervently. In truth the lawyer had absolutely no wish to join Lee's army, but the orders had come from an angry man in Washington, and Delaney, who was convinced the North would win the war and had no desire to be attached to the losing side, had weighed his future and decided that the discomforts of a brief campaign should prove a good investment. He still resented Thorne's peremptory demand that he should spy on Lee's headquarters, for Delaney had reckoned he could do all his spying from Richmond's comfortable parlors rather than from some muddy and dangerous bivouac in the countryside, and he doubted that he would be made privy to any useful information. It was all, he reckoned, a waste of time, but he dared not refuse Thorne's demand, not if he wanted the rewards that would be in Washington when the war ended, and so he had invented a reason for attaching himself to Lee's army and now, with a mixture of horror and apprehension, he planned to travel north. "Tomorrow morning!" he announced. "George has packed us some wine and tobacco, so we won't be comfortless." George was his house slave.

"You'll be a damned fool to carry expensive wine to war," Starbuck said. "It'll be stolen."

"What a suspicious mind you do have," Delaney said. He was hiding his fears, and so was pleased to have this evening's distraction at

Richmond's dueling ground. Duels were supposedly illegal, but still the Richmond Anti-Dueling Society had its headquarters not two doors down from Belvedere Delaney's expensive brothel and the society kept itself busy raising funds and prosecuting men known to have fought affairs of honor. But not all the pious efforts of a hundred such societies had succeeded in eliminating dueling from the Confederate states. Richmond's dueling ground lay just beyond the city's limits, beneath the Chimborazo Hill on which was built the sprawling military hospital. Starbuck led his companions up Elm Street, crossed a plank bridge that spanned the dirt and garbage through which the Bloody Run trickled down to the James, and so reached the patch of desolate land squeezed between the shoulder of the hill and the rusting rails of the York River Railroad. Scrubby, soot-darkened trees fringed the dueling ground, which was overshadowed by the tall, gaunt, and windowless facade of a sawmill.

Colonel Holborrow's carriage was standing at the end of a track that led from the sawmill, while Holborrow and Dennison were pacing up and down the worn length of turf where the fights took place.

"Potter!" Holborrow limped forward as Starbuck walked into the slanting late sunlight. "You're under arrest! You hear me, boy? You ain't fighting no duel! You're going back to Camp Lee, where I'm going to break you down to private unless you can explain yourself. Just where the hell have you been all day? Are you drunk, boy? Let me smell your breath!"

"I ain't Potter, Holborrow," Starbuck said. "That's Potter." He pointed to the half-clothed lieutenant, who was weakly leaning against the balustrade of the wooden bridge that crossed the Bloody Run. "Sorry son of a drunken bitch, ain't he? And that's his wife with him. You want to go talk to them while I teach Dennison some manners?"

The effect of Starbuck's words was everything he could have wished. Holborrow's confused face turned between Potter and Starbuck, but no words came, only a spluttering indignation. Starbuck patted the colonel's shoulder and walked toward Dennison. "Ready, Captain?" he called.

"Who are you?" Holborrow shouted after him.

Starbuck looked into Dennison's eyes while he answered. "Major Nathaniel Starbuck, Colonel, once of the Faulconer Legion, now commander of the Second Special Battalion. And, according to Captain Dennison, a goddamned Yankee who ain't worth fighting for. Isn't that what you said, Captain?"

Dennison blanched, but did not answer. Starbuck shrugged, unbuckled the sword belt, and took off his jacket. He drew the saber, tossed its scabbard onto the coat then gave the blade two hissing cuts through the evening air. "I kind of reckoned you'd have the Colonel arrest me, Captain," he said to Dennison, "on account of your being a coward. I knew you wouldn't want to fight me, but you ain't got any choice now." He gave another practice cut, then smiled into Dennison's scarred face. "There was a fencing society at Yale," he said in a conversational tone, "where we goddamned Yankees learned to fight." Starbuck had never joined the society, but he did not need to make that plain to his opponent. "It was larded with European rubbish, of course. *Derobement* of the *prise de fer.*" He gave the naked blade an impressive twisting cut. "Bind from *quarte* to *seconde.*" He gave the sword another meaningless flourish before bringing it up into the salute. "Ready, Dennison?" he asked. "I got business to do tonight, so let's get it over with."

"That's Potter?" Colonel Holborrow had hurried back to Starbuck's side, even forgetting to limp in his haste. "Are you telling me that's Potter?"

"Don't shout so!" Starbuck said chidingly. "Lieutenant Potter is badly hung over, Holborrow. I found the sorry son of a bitch down in the Hells."

"Hell," Holborrow said, still thoroughly confused. "Then what in hell's name were you doing at Camp Lee?"

Starbuck smiled. "Looking you over, Holborrow, so I could report back to the War Department. See that short, plump fellow there? That's Major Belvedere Delaney from the Legal Department. He's my second tonight, but he also wants a word with you." Starbuck looked back to Dennison. "I decided against bringing a surgeon, Captain. I know it's against the rules printed in Wilson's *Code of Honor*, but I never did think that a duel was proper unless it ends in death, don't you agree?"

"He's from the Legal Department?" Holborrow rapped Starbuck's arm with his cane and gestured toward Delaney.

"He heads the department," Starbuck said, then turned back to the aghast Dennison. "Ready, Captain?"

Holborrow again demanded Starbuck's attention with a tap of his cane. "Are you really Starbuck?" he asked.

"Yes."

"Then you're a slippery son of a bitch," Holborrow said, but not without some admiration.

"It takes one to recognize another," Starbuck said.

"Inside the carriage, Colonel?" Delaney had joined them and gestured at the vehicle. "I find our sort of business is best done in privacy. Let's leave Starbuck to his slaughter, shall we? He enjoys slaughter," Delaney smiled at Dennison, "but I find the sight of blood upsetting before supper."

Holborrow clambered inside the coach, Delaney followed, and the carriage door slammed shut. The Negro driver watched impassively from the high box as Starbuck gave his saber another practice cut. "You ready, Captain?" he asked Dennison.

"You're Starbuck?" Dennison asked in a faint voice.

Starbuck frowned, looked left and right as though for inspiration, then gazed back into Dennison's face. "Sir," he said, "I'm a major and you're a captain, so that makes you a shad-bellied piece of ordure, otherwise known as a captain. Isn't that right?"

"Sir," Dennison said miserably.

"Yes," Starbuck answered the original question, "I'm Starbuck."

"I ain't got a quarrel with you," Dennison said, then, after a pause, "sir."

"But you do, Dennison, you do. Would it matter whose wife you insulted? As it happens, that lady is not my wife," he gestured toward Sally, who watched from the ground's far end, "but she is a dear friend."

"I didn't mean to give offense, sir," Dennison said, desperate to escape the wicked curved blade in Starbuck's hand.

"The offense you gave me, Dennison," Starbuck said, hardening his voice, "was by thinking you could bully a man of lower rank. Do that again in my battalion, Captain, and I'll whip your backside bloody and break you down to private. You understand me?"

Dennison stared into Starbuck's eyes for a second, then nodded. "Yes, sir," he said.

"Now let's discuss your disease, Captain," Starbuck said.

Dennison glanced up into Starbuck's eyes again, but could find nothing to say.

"It sure ain't ringworm," Starbuck said, "and it ain't psoriasis, and I've never seen a case of eczema that bad. Just what is your proper doctor giving you?"

"Turpentine," Dennison said softly.

Starbuck laid the flat of his saber blade against one of the open, gleaming sores on Dennison's cheek. The Captain flinched from the pain, but then submitted meekly to the weapon's touch. "It ain't turpentine, is it?" Starbuck asked. Dennison said nothing. Starbuck twitched the blade, making Dennison flinch. "It's croton oil, Captain, that's what it is, and no doctor gave it to you. You're rubbing it on yourself, ain't you? Every morning and every night you slap the stuff on. Must hurt like hell, but it makes damn sure no one can transfer you to a fighting battalion, ain't that it? Keeps you away from the nasty Yankee bullets, don't it?"

Dennison could not even meet Starbuck's eyes, let alone speak as Starbuck drew the blade slowly back along the sore. Starbuck remembered croton oil, the foul purgative that Lieutenant Gillespie had forced down Starbuck's throat in an effort to force an admission that he was a Northern spy. Where the oil had spilled onto Starbuck's cheeks it had formed smallpox-like pustules, and it was plain that Dennison was using the purgative as a means of fabricating an illness that would keep him safely in Richmond. "What will it be next, Captain?" Starbuck asked. "Swallowing gunpowder to make yourself vomit? I know all the tricks, you bastard, every last one of them. So what you're going to do now is throw away your croton oil, you hear me?"

"Yes, sir."

"Throw it away, wash your face in good clean water, and I guarantee you'll be as handsome as ever by the time you face the Yankees in battle."

Dennison forced himself to look up at Starbuck and the look was of utter hatred. He was a proud man and he had been utterly humbled, but he had no belly to try and retrieve his pride by fighting his new commanding officer. Starbuck picked up his scabbard and coat. "We've started badly, you and I," he told Dennison, "but no one but you and me knows what passed between us here, and I won't be telling. So you can go back to Camp Lee, Captain, repair your face, and make damn sure that your company is ready to fight. Because that's what I intend to do with the battalion, fight." He had meant his words to be conciliatory, but he saw no grateful response in Dennison's dark eyes, only bitterness. Starbuck was tempted to let Dennison go and let the bastard rot in his own self-inflicted misery, but he needed every officer he could get and besides, why should Dennison evade his duty? Dennison must fight like every other man defending his country.

The carriage door opened suddenly and Delaney jumped awkwardly down to the turf. Colonel Holborrow followed, but more slowly because he was exaggerating his limp. Delaney took Starbuck's arm and steered him out of earshot of Dennison or the colonel. "The Colonel and I have come to an understanding," Delaney said. "He believes it his patriotic duty to spare the Confederacy an expensive inquiry into his handling of the Special Battalion, even though, of course, he avers that nothing would be discovered by such an inquiry, and he also feels that under your leadership the battalion could well acquit itself nobly in battle."

Starbuck felt a pang of terror at the news. He had got what he wanted. "We're going north then?"

"Isn't that what you wanted?" Delaney asked. He had caught a whiff of Starbuck's fear.

"Yes," Starbuck said, "it is."

"Because you're going in two days," Delaney said. "I don't think Holborrow wants you in his sight a moment longer than possible."

"Jesus!" Starbuck swore. Two days! "What about my rifles?"

"Thirty."

"Thirty!" Starbuck protested.

"Nate! Nate!" Delaney held up a cautionary hand. "I told you I had no ammunition to force that issue. The rest of the rifles are sold, I know that and you know that, but Holborrow's never going to admit it. But he says he can find thirty good rifles, so be grateful. You'll just have to steal the others off the enemy. Aren't you supposed to be good at that?"

Starbuck swore again, but his anger ebbed as he considered the deal Delaney had struck. He had got what he wanted, a battlefield command, and somehow in the next few days he had to make the Special Battalion into a unit that could stand against the Yankees. He would make it so damned special that other Confederate battalions would wish that they too were punishment units. "Thanks, Delaney," he said grudgingly.

"I am overwhelmed by your gratitude." The lawyer smiled. "And now, I suppose, you want to spend an evening of dissipation at my expense?"

"No," Starbuck said, because if the Yellowlegs really were going north then he had work to do. He had men to train and boots to find and a battalion to shake into efficiency and only two days to work his miracle. Two days before they went to where the Yankees waited. Before the Yellowlegs went back to war.

ADAM FAULCONER HAD RARELY FELT SO USELESS, or so unwanted, for he realized after just a half day at McClellan's headquarters that he had nothing whatever to do. For a time those headquarters had stayed obstinately in Washington, where the Young Napoleon had insisted there were necessary arrangements that could not be made from the saddle nor by telegraph from the field, and so the blue-coated army moved slowly westward while their commander slept in the bed of his comfortable house on Fifteenth Street. A nervous silence descended on Washington when the troops departed; a silence enervated by rumors of rebel activity. Gray horsemen were reported in Pennsylvania, a barn had been burned in Ohio, the state militia was assembling to protect Philadelphia, but in all the rumor there was not one hard fact. No one actually reported seeing Lee or the redoubtable Jackson, though Northern newspapers were more than ready to print elaborate fancies in the factless vacuum. The rebels were said to be 150,000 strong, they were planning to take Baltimore, they had designs on Washington, they were marching against New York, and even Chicago was threatened. The newspapers were eagerly read by the blue army that was bivouacked not far from Washington, in the green Maryland fields, where they waited for McClellan. Meanwhile the Young Napoleon rode about the Federal capital leaving visiting cards in a score of fashionable houses, each scrap of pasteboard carefully inked with the initials PPC, which had the recipients puzzled until the French ambassador explained that the letters stood for *Pour Prendre Congé* and were the polite manner of indicating that a soldier was leaving home to go on campaign.

"*Pour Prendre Congé!*" Colonel Lyman Thorne snarled at Adam. "Who the devil does he think he's impressing?"

Adam had no answer. It worried him that he was always so tongue-tied in Thorne's presence. He would have liked to have impressed the colonel, but instead he found himself trapped into either monosyllabic answers or else saying nothing at all. This time he said nothing, but just kicked his heels gently back to coax an ounce more speed from his horse, then he leaned into the mare's neck as she rose to a snake fence.

Thorne's horse thumped down a second after Adam's. The two men were riding westward through a countryside apparently bereft of inhabitants; a countryside of neat farms and tidy orchards and well-drained fields. "Where is everybody?" Adam asked after they had cantered past another immaculate white-painted farm with a swept yard, a woodlot where the cut logs were aligned between the elm trees as neatly as soldiers in one of the Young Napoleon's beloved reviews, and a newly painted springhouse, but without any sign of a human presence.

"Indoors," Thorne answered. "Didn't you see the upstairs drapes twitch? These people aren't fools. Where would you be if two armies were close by? You put your valuables in the cellar, bury the cash in the kitchen garden, load the shotgun, dirty your daughters' faces so they don't look attractive, harness the wagon, then wait to see who comes."

"No rebels coming this way," Adam said, trying hard to make conversation with the forbidding Thorne, but even that cheerful observation met with a scornful reply.

"Damn the rebels, where are our cavalry patrols? Damn it, Faulconer, but Lee's been two days in the North and we don't know the first damn thing about what he's doing. And where are our scouts? This countryside should be thick with damn scouts. They should be tripping over each other, but McClellan won't release them. He doesn't want their precious horses to get hurt." Thorne's derision was sour and angry. "Little George will inch his way forward like a virgin edging into a barrack room," he said, "and Lee will be running wild. Did I show you Pinkerton's latest work of fiction?"

"No, sir."

The two horsemen had stopped their mounts on the crest of a long green watershed that offered a distant view westward. Thorne took out a massive pair of binoculars, wiped the lenses with the skirt of his coat, then peered at the distant view for a long time. He saw nothing to alarm him and so lowered the glasses. "Pinkerton claims that Lee has one hundred and fifty thousand men in Maryland and he reckons another sixty thousand are poised just south of the Potomac ready to mount an attack on Washington when McClellan goes to deal with Lee." Thorne spat. "Lee's no fool. He won't throw away his army in an attack on Washington's forts! He doesn't have enough men. If Lee even has sixty thousand men fit to fight I'd be surprised, but it's no good pointing out facts to frightened George, it just makes him more stubborn. Little George will believe what he wants to believe, and he wants to believe he's outnumbered because that way there's no disgrace when he doesn't fight. Hell, they should give me the army for a week. There'd be no rebellion at the end of that week, I can promise you."

The colonel fell silent as he unfolded a map. Adam desperately wanted to know why the army did not give Thorne a fighting command, but he did not like to ask the question, but then the colonel answered it anyway. "I'm not one of the elect, Faulconer. I wasn't in Mexico, I wasn't at West Point, I didn't spend my peacetime nights flattering other uniformed fools with damnfool stories about slaughtering Comanches. I was brought into the peacetime army to build barracks, so I'm not supposed to understand soldiering. I'm not part of the mystical brotherhood. Have you ever seen Little George talk about soldiering? He weeps! Goes misty at the eyes!" Thorne hooted his derision. "Damn the weeping until you've given someone something to weep about. You can't win a war without taking casualties, lots of casualties, blood from one end of the country to the other. After that you can weep. But don't give me all this podsnap about sacred bonds, brotherhood, honor, and duty. We have a duty to win, that's all."

"Yes, sir," Adam said dully. He was not sure he liked what the colonel was saying, for Adam had an idea that war was somehow mystical. He knew all war was a bad thing, of course, a terrible thing even, but when it was touched by honor and patriotism it was subtly transformed into nobility and Adam did not want to think of it as mere uniformed butchery.

He took the glasses that the colonel offered and dutifully trained them westward. He was wondering why the older man had so suddenly appeared at the army's headquarters to suggest this long ride into Maryland, but Adam, lonely himself, had no idea of the colonel's loneliness, nor of the colonel's fears. Thorne, watching his army led by fools, feared that it would be thrown away before it could win the war and he feared that nothing he could do would prevent that tragedy, but still he must do what he could. "One man," he said suddenly.

"Sir?" Adam lowered the glasses.

"One man can make a difference, Faulconer."

"Yes, sir," Adam said, cringing at the inadequacy of his answer and wanting to ask Thorne more about the strange spy who had given Thorne Adam's name. How was Adam supposed to contact the man? Or the man Adam? Adam had already asked Thorne these questions and received an honest answer; that Thorne did not know, but Adam would have liked to probe the matter further in search of some clue that would tell him how he might prove useful in this campaign.

Thorne took back the field glasses. "I reckon that's Damascus," he said, pointing to a small group of houses clustered atop a low ridge some four or five miles away, "and if the rebels were advancing on Washington, which they're not, they'd be there." Thorne folded the stiff map and shoved it into a pocket. "Let's take a late lunch in Damascus, Faulconer. Maybe we'll be struck by enlightenment on the road."

The horses trotted down the long green slope to where a herd of cows was standing belly deep in a gentle creek. Ahead of Adam now was a long stretch of valuable bottomland, well watered, lush, studded with stands of trees and cut by a tangle of small streams. Doubtless the land had once been all swamp, but generations of hard work had drained the wetland, tamed it, and made it useful, and Adam, looking at the results of that honest labor, was almost overcome by love for his country. That love was real for Adam, real enough to have driven him from his native Virginia to fight for the greater entity of the United States. Other countries might boast grander ceremonies than America, they might boast mighty castles, and possess splendid cathedrals and vast-halled palaces, but nowhere, Adam fervently believed, displayed the virtue of modest, hard, honest labor like America. This was a plain man's country and Adam wanted it to be nothing more, for nothing, he believed, was worth more than simple, painstaking achievement.

"Daydreaming, Faulconer?" Thorne growled, and Adam jerked his head up to see that three horsemen had appeared from a stand of timber a mile ahead. Three horsemen in gray. "Our friends have their cavalry scouts afield, I see," the Colonel said dryly, curbing his horse, "so it seems we won't be eating in Damascus after all." He took out his field glasses and inspected the rebel trio. "Down at heels, that's for sure, but I'll warrant their carbines are well looked after." He edged the glasses up to stare at the ridge on which Damascus stood. He was wondering if he was wrong and that Lee was advancing on Washington, in which case he expected to see some evidence of gun batteries on the high ground, but he saw nothing. "It's just a patrol," he said dismissively, "nothing more. Lee's not headed this way." He turned his horse. "No point in being captured, Faulconer, let's retire."

But Adam had kicked his horse forward. The Colonel turned back. "Faulconer!" he snapped, but Adam ignored Thorne. Instead he kicked his heels again and the mare tossed her head and lifted her hooves as she began to canter.

The three rebels unslung their carbines, but did not take aim on the lone horseman who rode toward them. The Northerner did not have a saber drawn, nor was he holding any weapon, he was simply riding in a straight line toward his enemies. For a few seconds Thorne wondered if Faulconer was defecting back to the south, then the young man swerved his horse, leapt a brook, and cantered at an angle to the rebel scouts, who suddenly understood his purpose. They whooped like hunters seeing the fox in open ground and kicked back their heels. It was a race, pure and simple. Adam was challenging them, and the three rebels accepted the challenge by racing to catch him. It was a country game as old as time, only this day the prize was survival and the penalty imprisonment. Adam held his horse back, watching over his shoulder as the three pursuing horses lurched into the full gallop. He teased them by continuing to curb his good mare, and only when the closest man was within thirty or forty paces did he let go the curb rein and so give the mare her head.

She flew. She was no ordinary horse, but one of the prize beasts from Washington Faulconer's stud at Faulconer Court House in Faulconer County, Virginia. This was a mare with Arab blood, but crossed with a hardy American strain and Adam trusted his father's horse-breeding far more than he trusted his political judgment. He whooped himself, echoing the wild cries his pursuers made. This, at last, was war! A challenge, a race, a contest, something to stir the blood and add piquancy to days of boredom. The mare leapt a stream, gathered herself, took three or four paces, jumped a fence, then settled into a thumping gallop across a stretch of land newly plowed for winter wheat. The furrows made the going hard, but the mare seemed not to notice.

Thorne, watching the race as he rode eastward in parallel to the young men, saw at last some quality in Adam above the stolid, worried demeanor that the young Virginian usually displayed. But what Thorne saw he was not sure he liked. Adam, he thought, would seek sensation to test himself, not to amuse himself, not to taste wickedness, but simply to put himself through the crucible of his own expectations. Adam, he thought, might very well kill himself to prove that he was a good man.

But not now. Now he was humiliating a trio of Jeb Stuart's vaunted horsemen. The chase across the plowed field had widened the gap between Adam and his pursuers, so once again he slowed down and the three rebels, seeing the deliberate curbing, became even more determined to catch their mocking enemy. They could see his horse was tired and whitened by sweat and they believed that another half mile would surely bring it to a panting stop and so they raked back with sharp spurs and whooped their hunting call.

Adam slowed even more. Then, picking his path, he suddenly kicked his heels and put the mare toward a wider stream that meandered through steeply cut banks. Rushes fringed the stream, disguising where the banks ended and the stream began, but Adam, who had ridden since the day he could first straddle a pony, showed no hesitation. He did not ride hard at the wide stream, but instead let the mare look at it, pick her own pace, and then he touched her flanks to let her know what was expected of her. To Thorne, watching from afar, it seemed as if the mare was going far too slowly to clear the water, but suddenly she gathered herself and soared effortlessly across the wide run. Adam let her run out her jump on the far bank, then he turned her round and stopped to watch his pursuers.

Two of the rebels swerved aside rather than attempt the water jump. The third man, braver than his companions, kicked back his heels and attempted the jump at a gallop. His horse took off from the same spot where Adam's mare had started her jump, but the rebel's beast crashed down short to plunge into a stiff stand of reeds. The horse's front legs folded and its shoulder thumped with bone-cracking force into the hidden bank. The rider was thrown clear, sprawling in the stream and cursing as his injured horse struggled to its feet. The beast stumbled again, then screamed from the pain of its broken shoulder.

Adam touched the brim of his hat in ironic salute, then turned away. Neither of the two surviving horsemen bothered with their carbines, though the third man, splashing in the welter of mud and water being churned by his wounded horse, drew his revolver and prayed that the half dunking he had received had not soaked the powder loaded into the cylinder's chambers. He cocked the weapon, then cursed his loss. Southern cavalrymen provided their own horses, and a good horse was worth gold. His own horse was useless now, a thing in pain, a broken-shouldered gelding of no use to anyone. He grabbed the bridle and hauled the horse's head toward him. He looked into the beast's terrified eye for a heartbeat, then aimed and fired. The sound of the single shot faded across the warm countryside as the horse, a bullet in its brain, thrashed briefly, then died. "Son of a bitch," the rebel said, watching Adam ride calmly away, "son of a god damned bitch."

The train crept forward, jerking its couplings in a metallic rattle that concertinaed down the long line of cars, then it stopped again.

It was nighttime. The engine panted for a few moments, then went silent. A trail of moon-silvered woodsmoke trickled from its huge-bellied funnel to drift across dark fields and black woods. Far off in the night a yellow light showed where some soul was still awake, but other-wise the land was swallowed by blackness shot through with moon-cast shadows. Starbuck rubbed the pane of glass by his elbow and peered out, but he could see nothing beyond a window glazed gold by the flickering light of the car's lamps and so he stood and edged his way through the sleeping bodies to the platform at the car's rear, from where he could keep a wary eye on the dozen boxcars that formed the train's tail and which held the men of his Special Battalion. If any of his men wanted to desert, then this stuttering nighttime journey gave them a prize oppor-tunity, but the land either side of the stalled train seemed empty. He looked back up the car to see that Captain Dennison was awake and playing solitaire. His face was still not cured, but the sores had dried up and in a week or two there would be no trace of the croton oil's ravages.

It was three days since Starbuck had faced Dennison at the dueling ground, three days in which the Special Battalion had scrambled to pre-pare itself for this journey north, a journey that had already taken them as far as Catlett's Station, where they had disembarked from the first train and then marched five miles across country to Gainesville where they had waited until this train of the Manassas Gap Railroad had appeared. The cross-country march had saved the battalion from the chaos at Manassas where Confederate engineers where still trying to patch together the junction recaptured from the Yankees the previous month. "Consider yourself lucky," Holborrow had told Starbuck, "that they're sending you by train." The truth, Starbuck knew, was that the authorities did not believe the battalion would survive the long march north. They reckoned the men would either straggle disastrously or else desert in droves, and so the battalion was being carried in comparative luxury to where they must fight. North to Manassas, west now across the Blue Ridge Mountains, and in the morning they would face a two-day march north along the Valley Turnpike to Winchester, which had become Lee's depot for the campaign across the Potomac.

Dennison scooped the cards up, yawned, then shuffled them with practiced fingers. Starbuck, unseen, watched him. Dennison, he had discovered, had been raised by an uncle who had punished the boy because his parents had died impoverished. The result was a vast pride in Dennison, but that knowledge had not increased Starbuck's sympathy for the captain. Dennison was an enemy pure and simple. He had been humbled by Starbuck and he would choose to take his revenge when he could. Probably, Starbuck reflected, in battle, and the thought of facing Yankee shells and bullets immediately made Starbuck shudder. The cowardice was debilitating him, sapping his confidence.

The locomotive suddenly roared. The firebox was momentarily opened so that the furnace glare blazed across the fields, then the light snapped off as the train crashed and juddered forward. Matthew Potter swayed down the crowded car and pushed open the door. "I don't think," he said, "that we've traveled faster than ten miles an hour since we left Richmond. Not once."

"It's the rails," Starbuck said. "Old, misaligned, half-loose iron rails." He spat into the darkness. "And you can bet the Yankees ain't coming toward us on broken-down rails."

Potter laughed, then offered Starbuck a lit cigar. "Do I hear an echo of Northern superiority?"

"They can build railroads up there, that's for sure. We just have to pray they don't start making soldiers half as good as ours." Starbuck drew on the cigar. "I thought you were sleeping."

"Can't," Potter said. "It must be the effect of sobriety." He half smiled. He had not taken a drop of drink in three days. "Can't say as how I feel any better," he said, "but I guess I've felt worse."

"Your wife's all right?" Starbuck asked.

"She seemed so, thanks to you," Potter said. Starbuck had inveigled Delaney into paying the Potters' arrears of rent, then he had arranged for Martha Potter to stay with Julia Gordon's parents in Richmond. Julia herself now lived at the Chimborazo Hospital where she was a nurse and Starbuck had only seen her for a few moments, but those moments had been enough to confuse him. Julia's grave intelligence made him feel shallow, gauche, and tongue-tied, and he wondered why he could summon the courage to cross a rain-soaked cornfield into the maws of Yankee guns, but could not raise the nerve to tell Julia he was besotted by her. "You're looking miserable, Major," Potter said.

"Martha will be happy enough with the Gordons," Starbuck said, ignoring the Lieutenant's comment. "The mother can be overpowering, but the Reverend Gordon is a decent man."

"But if she stays too long in that house," Potter said grimly, "I'll find myself married to a born-again Christian."

"Is that so bad?"

"Hell, it ain't exactly the quality that attracted me to Martha," Potter said with his lopsided grin. He leaned on the platform's balustrade and stared at the passing countryside. Small red sparks whirled in the locomotive's smoke trail, some sinking to the ground to lie like fallen fireflies that vanished behind as the train labored up the eastern flank of the Blue Ridge. "Poor Martha," Potter said softly.

"Why?" Starbuck asked. "She's got what she wanted, ain't she? Got a husband, got away from home."

"She got me, Major, she got me. Life's short straw." Potter shrugged. Much of the lieutenant's charm, Starbuck had discovered, lay in just such frank admissions of unworthiness. His good looks and bad ways attracted women's compassion like moths to a candle flame, and Starbuck had watched, amazed, as both Sally and Julia had made a fuss over him. But it was not just women who tried to protect Potter, even men seemed taken by him. The Special Battalion was united in little except resentment, but they had combined in an extraordinary surge of protective affection for Matthew Potter. They were amused by his fallibility, envious, even, of a man who could spend three days drunk, and they had made the Georgian the battalion's unofficial mascot. Starbuck had thought the Lieutenant would prove a liability, but so far he was the best thing that had happened to the despised Yellowlegs, because Potter entertained by simply existing.

But they would need more than one charming rogue to unite them. Starbuck had done his best in the two days before this journey began. He had persuaded Colonel Holborrow to produce boots, ammunition, canteens, and even the battalion's arrears of pay. He had marched the men up and down the Brook Turnpike and had rewarded them with cider from Broome's Tavern after one particularly grueling march, though he doubted that either the reward or the experience would matter much when they joined Jackson's hard-marching troops. He had made them load their antiquated muskets with buck and ball, an antiquated charge of shot that fired a musket ball with a scatter of buckshot, then he had purloined two dozen of Camp Lee's shabbiest tents to use as a target. The first volley had riddled the tents' ridges with holes but left the lower canvas almost unmarked, and Starbuck had made the men inspect the tents. "The Yankees don't stand high as a ridge," he had told them. "You're shooting high. Aim at their balls, even their knees, but aim low." They had fired a second volley and this one had ripped the worn canvas at the right height. He could spare no more ammunition for such target practice, but just hoped the Yellowlegs remembered the lesson when the men in blue were advancing.

He had talked to the men, not telling them that they were being given a second chance, but saying instead that they were needed up north. "What happened to you at Malvern Hill," he said, "could have happened to anyone. Hell, it almost happened to me at the first battle." At Malvern Hill, he had learned, part of the battalion broke and ran after a Yankee shell had struck plumb on their Colonel's horse while he was leading them forward. The horse had been torn into bloody shreds that had blown back into the faces of the center companies, and that shock introduction to war had been enough to scare a handful of men into full retreat. The others, thinking they were being ambushed, followed. They were not the first battalion to inexplicably break into flight, but it was their misfortune to do it a long way from where the real fighting was going on and to do it in full view of a score of other battalions. The shame clung to them still and Starbuck knew that only battle could wash it away. "The time will come," he told the battalion, "when men will be proud to say they were a Yellowleg."

Starbuck had talked to the officers and then to the sergeants. The officers had been sullen and the sergeants uncooperative. "The men ain't ready for battle," Sergeant Case insisted.

"No one's ready," Starbuck had answered, "but we've still got to fight. If we wait till we're ready, Sergeant Case, the Yankees will have conquered us."

"Ain't conquered us yet," Case answered, "and from what I hear, sir," he managed to invest the honorific with a dripping scorn, "we're the ones doing the conquering. Just ain't proper to take these poor boys off to a war they ain't ready to fight."

"I thought you were supposed to have got them ready," Starbuck said, unwisely letting himself be drawn into the argument.

"We're doing our job, sir," Case said, carefully enrolling the other sergeants onto his side of the argument, "but as any regular soldier will tell you, sir, a good sergeant's work can be undone in a minute by a glory-boy." He offered Starbuck a feral grin. "Glory-boy, sir. Young officer wanting to be famous, sir, and expecting the lads to die for his fame. Bloody shame, sir."

"We go tomorrow," Starbuck had said, ignoring Case. "The men will cook three days of rations and draw ammunition tonight." He had walked away, ignoring Case's snort of derision. Starbuck knew he had handled the confrontation badly. Another enemy, he thought wearily, another damned enemy.

"So what's happening?" Potter now asked as the train swayed up the incline.

"Wish I knew."

"But we're going to fight?"

"I reckon."

"But we don't know where."

Starbuck shook his head. "Get to Winchester and fetch new orders. That's what I'm told."

Potter drew on his cigar. "You reckon the men are ready to fight?" he asked.

"Do you?" Starbuck turned the question back.

"No."

"Nor me," Starbuck admitted. "But if we'd waited all winter they wouldn't be any more ready. It ain't their training that's wrong, it's their morale."

"Shoot Sergeant Case, that'll cheer them up," Potter suggested.

"Give them a battle," Starbuck said. "Give them a victory." Though how he was to do that with his present officers and sergeants, he did not know. Even to get the men as far as a battlefield, Starbuck thought, would be some kind of miracle. "You were at Shiloh, right?" he asked Potter.

"I was," Potter said, "but I have to confess it was mostly a blur. I wasn't exactly drunk, but sober don't describe it either. But I do remember an exhilaration, which is odd, don't you think? But George Washington said the same, do you remember? When he wrote how he was elated by the sound of bullets? Is it, you think, because we seek sensation? Like being a gambler?"

"I reckon I've wagered enough," Starbuck said grimly.

"Ah," Potter said, understanding. "I only had the one battle."

"Manassas twice," Starbuck said bleakly, "God knows how many times in the defense of Richmond, Leesburg, the fight at Cedar Mountain. Some brawl in the rain a few days back." He shrugged. "Enough."

"But more to come," Potter said.

"Yes." Starbuck spat a shred of tobacco under the train wheels. "And still there are some sons of bitches who think I can't be trusted because I'm a Yankee."

"So why are you fighting for the South?" Potter asked.

"That, Potter," Starbuck said, "is a question I don't need to answer."

The two men fell silent as the train wheels screeched on a curve. The stink of a hot axle-box's grease soured the woodsmoke aroma of the locomotive. They had climbed high enough now for the eastern land to lie revealed beneath the moon. A scatter of tiny lights showed faraway villages or farms, while the livid glow of small grass fires betrayed the double-curving path the train had followed up the gentle slope. "You ever done any skirmishing?" Starbuck asked suddenly.

"No."

"Reckon you could handle it?" Starbuck asked.

Potter, faced with a serious question, seemed nonplussed. "Why me?" he finally asked.

"Because the captain in charge of skirmishers has to be an independent son of a bitch who ain't afraid to take risks, that's why."

"A captain?" Potter asked.

"You heard me."

Potter drew on his cigar. "Sure," he said, "I guess."

"You get your own company," Starbuck said. "Forty men. You get the thirty rifles, too." He had been thinking about this all day and finally decided to take the plunge. None of the four existing captains struck him as men willing to take on responsibility, but Potter had an impudent nature that might fit him for the skirmish line. "You know what skirmishers do?"

"Crudely," Potter said.

"You go out ahead of the battalion. Spread out, use cover, and shoot the damn Yankee skirmishers. You fight those sons of bitches hard to push them back so you can start killing their main battle line before the rest of us arrive. Win the skirmisher's battle, Potter, and you're halfway to winning the real thing." He paused to suck smoke into his lungs. "We won't announce it till we've done a day's real marching. Let's see which men can take the pace and which can't. There's no point in putting weaklings into the skirmish line."

"I assume," Potter said, "that you were a skirmisher?"

"For a time, yes."

"Then I shall be honored."

"Damn the honor," Starbuck said. "Just stay sober and shoot straight."

"Yes, sir." Potter grinned. "Martha will be pleased to be a captain's wife."

"So don't disappoint her."

"I fear my darling Martha is doomed to disappointment. She believes it is possible, even essential, for all of us to be Sunday school good. Honesty is the best policy, she tells me, a stitch in time saves nine, neither a borrower nor a lender be, be honest as the day is long, do unto others, and all that noble stuff, but I'm not sure any of that's possible if you have a thirst and a little imagination." He tossed the stub of his cigar off the platform. "Do you ever wish the war would last forever?"

"No."

"I do. Someone to feed me, to clothe me, to pick me up every time my wings fold. You know what I'm frightened of, Starbuck? I'm frightened of peace, when there'll be no army to be my refuge. There'll just be people expecting me to make a living. Now that's hard, that's hard, that's real cruel, that is. What the hell will I do?"

"Work," Starbuck said.

Potter laughed. "And what will you do, Major Starbuck?" he asked knowingly.

Hell if I know, Starbuck thought, hell if I know. "Work," he said grimly.

"Stern Captain Starbuck," Potter said, but Starbuck had gone back into the car. Potter shook his head and watched the passing night and thought of all the trains clanking and banging and thrusting through this night carrying their loads of blue-coated troops to meet this train that rattled and screeched and shuddered its lonely way north. All mad, he thought, all mad. As flies to wanton boys. He could have wept.

If there was one thing that terrified Belvedere Delaney it was the fear of being discovered and captured, for he knew only too well what his fate would be. The cell in a Richmond prison, the merciless questions, the trial before scornful men, and the vengeful crowd staring white-faced at the high scaffold where he would stand with a rope about his neck. He had heard that men pissed themselves when they were hung, and that if the executioner bungled the job, and the executioner usually did bungle it, then death was agonizingly slow. The onlookers would jeer while he pissed himself and as the rope bit into his neck. The very thought made his bowels feel liquid.

He was no hero. He had never thought of himself as a hero, but merely as a quick-witted, amoral, genial sort of fellow. It amused him to make money, just as it amused him to be generous. Every man thought Delaney a friend, and Delaney took care to keep it that way. He disliked rancor, reserving his enmities for his private thoughts, and if he did wish to hurt someone he would do it so secretly that the victim would never suspect that Delaney had engineered the misfortune. It was thus that Delaney had betrayed Starbuck during the North's spring campaign to capture Richmond, and Starbuck had come as close as a whisker to a Northern scaffold, and Delaney would have genuinely regretted that fate, but he had never once regretted his part in so nearly causing it. Delaney had been pleased when Starbuck returned, delighted even, for he liked Starbuck, but he would still betray him tomorrow if he thought there was profit in the treachery. Delaney did not feel badly about such a contradiction; he did not even perceive it as a contradiction, merely as fate. Some Englishman had just written a book that was upsetting all the preachers because it implied that man, like all other species, had not originated in a divine moment of creation, but was muckily descended from God knows what primitive things with tails and claws and bloody teeth. Delaney could not recall the author's name, but one phrase from his book had lodged in Delaney's mind: the survival of the fittest. Well, Delaney would survive.

And survival was his own responsibility, which was why Belvedere Delaney took such exquisite care not to betray his own treachery. Colonel Thorne knew he was a Northern spy, and maybe Thorne had confided in one or two others, though Delaney had asked him not to, but other than Thorne the only human being who knew Delaney's true loyalty was his manservant, George. Delaney was punctilious in describing George as a manservant, he never called him a slave, though he was one, and he treated George with a grave courtesy. "We make each other comfortable," Delaney liked to say, and George, hearing the description, would concur with a smile. When visitors came to Delaney's exquisite apartment on Richmond's Grace Street the servant would behave like any other, though when Delaney and George were alone it seemed they were more like companions than master and slave, and some shrewd folk had scented that closeness and were amused by it. It was simply another part of Delaney's eccentricities and they supposed that master and slave would grow old together and that, if Delaney died first, George would inherit much of his master's wealth along with his own freedom. George had even taken Delaney as his surname.

On the occasions when Delaney had cause to send news to Thorne it had always been George who took the risks. It was George who carried the messages to the man in Richmond who passed them on northward, but George could not carry the messages now. George was as uncomfortable as his master at being among the rebel army, and George had no skills that could take him through a soldier's picket line. George could dress a salad, roast a duck, or whip up an exquisite custard. He could reduce a sauce to perfection, had a nose for fine wine, and could play with equal facility upon a flute or violin. He could take a coat made at Richmond's finest tailors and, with a few hours' work, so remake it that a man would swear it came from Paris or London. George had a connoisseur's eye for fine porcelain and many a time he had returned to Delaney's apartment with news of a fine piece of Meissen or Limoges being sold by a family impoverished by the war and which would fill a gap in his master's collection, but George Delaney was no man for hiding in thickets like a sharpshooter or riding across country like one of Jeb Stuart's cavaliers.

And those, Delaney knew, were the skills he would need if he was ever to send any useful intelligence to Thorne. Weeks before, when Thorne had despaired of the North's ability to spy on its foe and had demanded that Delaney somehow inveigle himself into Lee's headquarters, Delaney had foreseen the problem. George lacked the skills to carry the messages, while Delaney lacked both the skills and the nerve, and so Delaney had suggested that Adam Faulconer should be the courier, yet even Delaney had not yet devised any means of actually contacting Adam. It was all so very frustrating.

As Delaney had journeyed north he had not let the problem worry him. He very much doubted whether he would discover any intelligence worth passing on to Thorne; indeed the whole expedition, to both Delaney and to George, was a desperate inconvenience, but Delaney knew he needed to show willingness if he was ever to garner the rewards of his secret allegiance, and so the lawyer had resigned himself to a few weeks of discomfort after which he could return home, soak in a hot bath, sip cognac, and smoke one of his carefully hoarded French cigarettes before sending a message to Thorne in the old safe manner. That message would regret his silence of the past few weeks and explain that he had discovered nothing worth passing along.

Only now he had discovered something. Indeed, within minutes of arriving at Lee's headquarters, Delaney knew he held the fate of North and South in his hand. Damn it, but Thorne had been right all along. There was a place in Lee's headquarters for a spy, and Delaney was that spy, and Delaney now knew everything that Robert Lee planned and Delaney might as well have been on the far side of the moon for all the ability either he or George possessed to send that information to the Northern army.

Delaney had caught up with Lee's men at Frederick, a fine town that lay among wide Maryland fields. Nine streets ran east and west, six north and south, a concentration sufficient to persuade the inhabitants that their town should properly be called Frederick City, a name that was proudly painted above the depot of the spur line that ran north from the Baltimore and Ohio Railroad. The spur had carried the region's fat harvest of wheat and oats east to Baltimore and south to Washington, leaving only the corn waiting for harvest, though now much of that crop had been stripped by hungry rebels. "I'd rather find shoes than corn," Colonel Chilton said querulously. Chilton was a Virginian and, like any senior officer who had been stationed in Richmond, was well known to Delaney. Chilton, a fussy man in his middle forties, was now Lee's chief of staff, a position he had gained through his punctilious diligence rather than from any flair for soldiering. "So Richmond sends us a lawyer instead of shoes," he greeted Delaney's arrival.

"Alas," Delaney said, spreading his hands. "I would it were otherwise. How are you, sir?"

"Well enough, I suppose, considering the heat," Chilton said grudgingly, "and you, Delaney? Never expected to see a fellow like you in the field."

Delaney took off his hat, ducked into Chilton's tent, and accepted the offer of a chair. The shade of the canvas offered small respite from the heat wave that had made his journey a hell of dust and sweat. "I'm well," he answered and then, asked to explain his presence, launched himself into his well-rehearsed rigmarole about the War Department

being concerned about the legal repercussions of actions that, if undertaken on Confederate soil, might be considered felonious, but that, done
to the enemy, fell into an unknown category. "It is *terra incognita*, as we
lawyers would say," Delaney finished lamely. He fanned his face with
his hat brim. "You wouldn't, I suppose, have any lemonade?"

"Water in the jug," Chilton gestured at a battered enamel pot,
"sweet enough to drink without boiling. Not like Mexico!" Chilton liked
to remind people that he had served in that victorious war. "And I can
assure you, Delaney, that this headquarters knows quite well how to
treat enemy civilians. We're not barbarians, despite what those damned
newspapers in the North say of us. Carter!" he shouted toward an adja-
cent tent. "Bring me Order One-ninety-one."

A sweating clerk with ink-stained hands came to the tent with the
required order, which Chilton scanned quickly, then thrust into
Delaney's hands. "There, read it for yourself," the Chief of Staff said. "I'll
be back in a few moments."

Delaney, left alone in the tent, almost did not bother to read
beyond the first paragraph of the order, which was headed "Special
Orders, No. 191. Hdqrs. Army of Northern Virginia. September 9, 1862."
In pencil, next to the heading, a clerk had written "Gen. D. H. Hill." The
first paragraph, which Delaney idly scanned, was a prohibition against
soldiers going into the town of Frederick without written permission
from their divisional commander. A provost guard was stationed in the
town to enforce the order, which was designed to allay the inhabitants'
fears about being overrun and looted by a rapacious horde of half-
starving, ill-dressed soldiers. The paragraph entirely met the manufactured concerns that justified Delaney's presence in the army. "And quite
right, too," Delaney said to no one in particular, though in truth he
would not have cared if the soldiery had dismantled Frederick City shingle by shingle.

He poured himself a mug of warm water, drank, grimaced at the
taste, then, for lack of anything else to read, went back to the order. The
second paragraph arranged that local farm vehicles be commandeered
to transport the army's sick to Winchester. "Poor bastards," Delaney
said, trying to imagine the rigors of a fever-racked journey in a dung-

stinking farm wagon. He fanned himself with the order, wondering where in hell Chilton had vanished. He leaned forward to look out of the tent and saw George standing stiffly beside the horses, but no sign of Chilton.

He leaned back and read paragraph three. "The army will resume its march tomorrow," the paragraph began, and suddenly Delaney went chill as his eyes scanned the rest of the closely written page. The order might have begun with commonplace arrangements for policing the army and providing transport for its wounded, but it ended with a complete description of everything Robert Lee planned to do in the next few days. Everything. Every destination of every division in all the army.

"Sweet Jesus," Delaney said, and was overcome by a rush of terror as he thought what would follow his capture. One part of him wanted to thrust the order away and pretend he had never seen it, while another yearned after the glory that would surely be his if he could just smuggle this paper across the lines.

General Jackson will recross the river and, by Friday morning, take possession of the Baltimore and Ohio Railroad. He would occupy Martinsburg and cut off the road by which the Federal garrison at Harper's Ferry might retreat.

General Longstreet was ordered to advance to Boonsborough, wherever in hell that might be. General McLaws would follow Longstreet, but then branch off to help capture Harper's Ferry. General Walker was to cooperate with Jackson and McLaws by cutting off another road to Harper's Ferry, and once that Northern garrison was taken, the three generals were to join the rest of the army at Boonsborough or Hagerstown. Hagerstown? Delaney's geography was shaky, but he was fairly certain Hagerstown was a Maryland town close to the Pennsylvania border while Harper's Ferry was in Virginia! Which surely meant one part of Lee's army was going north, the other south, and so leaving the two parts vulnerable to separate attacks.

Delaney's hands felt almost nerveless. The paper fluttered. He closed his eyes. Maybe, he told himself, he did not understand these things. He was no soldier. Perhaps it made sense to split an army? But it wasn't his responsibility to decide if it made sense, but merely to send this news to the Northern army. Copy it, you fool, he told himself, but just as he opened his eyes to search Chilton's table for a pen or pencil, he heard footsteps outside the tent.

"Delaney!" a cheerful voice called.

Delaney ducked out of the tent to see that Chilton had returned with General Lee himself. For a moment the usually suave Delaney was lost in confusion. The order was still in his hand, and that flustered him, then he remembered he had been given it by Chilton and so no guilt could be attached to its possession. "Good to see you, General," Delaney finally managed to greet Lee.

"You'll forgive me if I don't shake hands?" Lee said, holding up his splinted and bandaged hands as explanation. "I had an altercation with Traveller. Well on the mend, now. And the other good news is that McClellan is back in command of the Federals."

"I heard as much," Delaney acknowledged.

"Which means our foes will dawdle," Lee said with satisfaction. "McClellan is a man of undoubted virtues, but decision-making is not one of them. Chilton tells me you're here to make sure we behave ourselves?"

Delaney smiled. "I'm truly here, General, because I wanted to see some action." He told the lie smoothly. "Otherwise," he continued, brushing his gray coat, "it would seem to me that this uniform is not properly earned."

Lee returned the smile. "Witness your action, Delaney, by all means, but don't get too close to McClellan's men, for I should be sorry to lose you. You'll dine tonight?" He turned as the clerk who had brought the copy of Order 191 to Chilton's tent reappeared with a sheaf of envelopes that he hesitantly held toward Colonel Chilton. "That's the order?" Lee asked Chilton.

"Seven copies," the clerk confirmed, "and Colonel Chilton's original is in that gentleman's possession," he indicated Delaney, who guiltily flourished the original copy.

"Eight copies in all?" Lee frowned and took the envelopes from the clerk and, as swiftly as his awkward bandages allowed, leafed through them to read the addressees' names. "Do we need one for Daniel Hill?"

Lee asked, flourishing the empty envelope addressed to General D. H. Hill that was evidently waiting for the original copy of the order in Delaney's hand. "Jackson will surely copy Hill the relevant parts?" Lee said.

"Best to be sure, General," Chilton said soothingly, retrieving the envelopes from the general and the single copy from Delaney. He folded the order and slipped it inside the envelope.

"You know best," Lee said. "So, Delaney, what news from Richmond?"

Delaney retailed some government gossip while Chilton placed the last copy of Order 191 in General Hill's envelope, which he laid with the others at the edge of a table just inside his tent. Lee, in an affable mood, was telling Delaney his hopes for the next few days. "I'd have liked to march north into Pennsylvania, but for some reason the Federals have left their garrison in Harper's Ferry. That's a nuisance. It means we have to snap them up before we march north, but the delay can't be long and I doubt McClellan will summon the nerve to interfere. And once we've cleared Harper's Ferry we'll be free to make a nuisance of ourselves. We'll cut some Pennsylvania rail roads, Delaney, while McClellan makes up his mind what to do about us. In the end he'll have to fight and when he does I pray we can so mangle him that Lincoln will sue for peace. There's no other point in coming north, except to make peace." The general made this last pronouncement gravely for, like many other Southerners, he worried about the propriety of invading the United States. The legitimacy of the Confederacy's war depended on being the aggrieved party. They proclaimed that they merely defended their land against an external aggressor, and many men questioned their right to carry that defense outside their border.

Lee stayed a moment or two longer with Delaney, then turned away. "Colonel Chilton? A word?"

Chilton had been summoning the dispatch riders, but now followed Lee across to the general's tent. Delaney was again left alone and the bowel-loosening terror almost swamped him as he looked at the pile of orders awaiting dispatch. General Hill's envelope was uppermost on the pile. Dear God, Delaney thought, but dare he do it? And if he did, how would he ever send the stolen order across the lines? His hand was shaking, then an idea struck him and he ducked into Chilton's tent and sorted through the piles of paper on the trestle desk. He found a copy of Lee's proclamation to the people of Maryland and that, he reckoned, would have to serve his purpose. He folded the proclamation twice, hesitated, looked into the innocent sunlight, then snatched up the envelope with Hill's name. It was still unsealed. He took out the order, inserted the proclamation, then pushed the stolen paper deep into a pocket of his jacket. His heart was thumping terribly as he placed the still unsealed envelope back on the pile and then stepped out into the sunlight.

"You look feverish, Delaney," Chilton said, returning to his tent.

"It will pass, I'm sure." Delaney sounded weak. He was amazed he could even stand upright. He thought of the gallows' raw pine beams oozing turpentine and dangling with a noose of rough-haired hemp. "The heat of the journey," he explained, "brought on a stomach fever, nothing else."

"Tell your man to add your baggage to ours. I'll give you a tent, then get some rest. I'll send you some vitriol for your stomach if it's still troubling you. You're dining tonight with us?" Chilton spoke about these domestic arrangements as he gummed a wafer over the unsealed envelope's flap. He had not looked inside the envelope and so had not detected Delaney's substitution. "Signatures, gentlemen," he reminded the junior officers who would now carry the orders to their destinations. "Make sure they're all signed for. On your way, now!"

The staff officers rode away. Delaney wondered if Hill would think it odd to receive Lee's proclamation, for surely he would already have received his own copy of the document that tried to justify the South's invasion of the North. "Our army has come among you," the proclamation said, "and is prepared to assist you with the power of its arms in regaining the rights of which you have been despoiled." But Delaney, if he was not caught, and if he could just devise a way of reaching Thorne or Adam Faulconer, would despoil the South of its victory. There would be no peace, no truce, no Southern triumph; just Northern victory, complete, crushing, and implacable.

If only Delaney knew how to achieve it.

S TARBUCK NEVER DID LEARN THE COLONEL'S NAME. HE
was a tall, wispy-haired man in his late fifties who was plainly overwhelmed by the responsibilities that had been thrust on him. "The
town," he told Starbuck, "isn't fit to be a depot. Isn't fit, you hear me?
The Yankees have been here more than once and what they didn't steal
our own skulkers took. You need boots?"

"No."

"You can't have any. General Lee demands boots. What boots?" He
gestured about his cluttered office that had once been a dry goods store
as if to demonstrate the obvious absence of any footwear. "You don't
need any?" The colonel suddenly understood Starbuck's reply.

"No, sir."

"Do you have any to spare?" the colonel asked eagerly.

"Not a pair, sir. But I do need axes, tents, wagons. Especially a
wagon." The battalion's only transport was a handcart that had proved
a brute on the short marches the Yellowlegs had so far completed. The
cart carried the precious rifles and as much spare ammunition as could

be piled on top, but Starbuck doubted whether the rickety vehicle would last another ten miles.

"No good asking me for wagons," the colonel said. "You can try commandeering from the local farms, but I doubt you'll have any luck. Too many troops have been through this place. They've stripped it bare." The colonel was in charge of the town of Winchester, which lay at the northern end of the Shenandoah Valley and was now the supply base for Lee's army across the Potomac. Starbuck's battalion had abandoned its train at Strasburg and marched north through a glorious summer dawn. Now, as the sun's heat grew stifling, the exhausted men waited in Winchester's main street as Starbuck reported for his orders. "I don't have any orders," the colonel said as he finished searching among his disordered papers. "None for you, anyway. Who do you say you are?"

"Starbuck, sir, Special Battalion."

"Special?" The colonel, who had introduced himself to Starbuck, but so quickly that Starbuck had never caught his name, sounded surprised. "Special," he said again in a puzzled tone, then he remembered. "You're the Yellowlegs!" He shuddered slightly, as though Starbuck might be contagious. "Then I do have orders for you, indeed I do. But aren't you called Maitland?"

"Starbuck, sir."

"Orders are addressed to Maitland," the colonel said, feverishly searching again among the papers on the shop's counter. All the doors and windows were propped open, but the ventilation scarcely alleviated the day's oppressive heat. The colonel was sweating as he searched. "Is Maitland coming?" he asked.

"I replaced Maitland," Starbuck said patiently.

"Someone has to get the short straw, I suppose," the colonel said. "Can't say I envy you. It's bad enough taking willing men to war, let alone a bunch of skulkers. How many did you lose between here and Strasburg?"

"Not one."

"No?" The colonel drew the word out to show his incredulity.

"I marched at the back," Starbuck said, and touched the Adams revolver at his side.

"Quite right, quite right," the colonel said and went back to his search.

Starbuck had shaded the truth. Some men had dropped out, and those men he had collected and forced back onto the road, though by the time they had finished the short march the stragglers were near beat and had feet with blisters so bad that blood was seeping out of the ill-sewn shoes they had been issued at Camp Lee. Most of the shoes, Starbuck guessed, would not last a week, which meant they would need to take some off the Yankees. Other men had fallen out of the column with diarrhea, yet despite their sickness and frail feet, all the men were now present in Winchester, but still the march had been a bad augury. The battalion was simply unfit.

"You know what's happening here?" the colonel asked.

"No, sir."

"We're about to throttle the Yankees out of Harper's Ferry. After that, God only knows. You need ammunition?"

"Yes, sir."

"We do have that, but no wagons." The colonel scribbled on a chit of paper that he gave to Starbuck. "Authorization to draw cartridges. You'll find them stored in a barn at the top end of Main Street, but if you ain't got a wagon, Major, you'll be hard put to carry a proper supply, and I can't find you a wagon." He gave Starbuck another piece of paper. "That's a War Department form entitling a civilian to be paid for any wagon you commandeer, but I doubt you'll find one. Too many other regiments have plowed this town. Ah, and you should go to the Taylor Hotel, Major."

"Taylor Hotel?"

"Down the street, just a few steps. Place with a big porch and not much paint. Not much left to eat there either, but it's still the most comfortable place in town. Your fellow's waiting there."

Starbuck, completely confused, shook his head. "My fellow?"

"Officer! Didn't you know? Fellow called Captain Tumlin. A good one, too! First-class fellow. Got captured at New Orleans and has been in Yankee jails ever since, but he managed to escape and reach our lines. Capital fellow! Richmond assigned him to your battalion for the duration of the campaign, so I kept him here. Seemed pointless to send him all the way to Richmond while you were coming here. He's even got some men for you! Skulkers and coffee-chasers, of course, every last one of them, but you must be used to that kind of scum. I shall be sorry to lose Billy Tumlin. He's an amusing fellow, capital company. Here we are." He found Starbuck's orders and tossed them up onto the counter. "I hope to God you're not staying in the town," he added anxiously. "I'm hard put to feed the men I've got without feeding more."

Starbuck slit open the orders and scanned them. He smiled, cracking the sweaty dust that was caked onto his face. "Good," he said, then, in response to the colonel's raised eyebrow, explained his pleasure. "We're assigned to Swynyard's Brigade."

The name meant nothing to the colonel. "You're leaving today, I trust?" the colonel inquired anxiously.

"We're either to wait here or at Charlestown, whichever's convenient, for more orders."

"You'll want to be in Charlestown then," the colonel said emphatically. "That's a very pleasant town. A long day's march from here, but you'll have to make it sooner or later."

"We will?"

"You will if you're going north. Charlestown is just this side of Harper's Ferry. Get there early, Major, and you'll have first pick of the bivouacs before the rest of the army arrives. And first pick of the girls. If there are any girls left, of course, which there might not be. Place has been picked over by both sides, but it's still very fair, very fair."

"Any Yankees there?"

The colonel pursed his lips and shrugged. "Maybe a few. Doubtless the Harper's Ferry garrison scavenge for corn thereabouts."

In other words, Starbuck thought, the very pleasant Charlestown was Yankee-haunted, stripped clean of supplies, and half deserted. "We'll march this morning," Starbuck said, much to the colonel's relief. "You can give us someone to show us the way out of town?"

"No need, my dear fellow. Straight up the road. Straight up. Can't miss your way."

Starbuck pocketed the orders and went out to the sidewalk and called Potter to him. "You're a rogue, Potter."

"Yes, sir."

"So be a rogue now and find a wagon. Any wagon. You're allowed to commandeer civilian vehicles, but you must sign for it so the owner can get reimbursement from Richmond, understand?"

"Yes, sir."

"Then you collect ammunition and follow us north. Take a dozen of your men to load and haul." He gave Potter the two pieces of paper. "Lucifer!"

"Major?" The boy ran up to Starbuck.

"Captain Potter is on a looting expedition, and you're good at that so you can help him. I want a wagon, anything on wheels that we can fill with cartridges. If the townspeople see soldiers combing the streets they'll hide anything valuable, but they won't notice you, so go and spy on them."

"Yes, Major." Lucifer grinned and ran off.

"Dennison!" Starbuck shouted. Dennison was the senior captain and thus, whether Starbuck liked it or not, the second in command of the battalion. "Get 'em up, get 'em moving," Starbuck said. "Straight up the road. Just keep going and I'll catch up with you." There was no point in waiting. The men might be tired, but the more they marched the fitter they would be, and the longer they rested in Winchester the more reluctant they would ever be to leave the town's dubious comforts.

"You staying to enjoy the town, Major?" Dennison asked cattily.

"I'm staying to collect some more men. I'll be ten minutes behind you. Now move."

The men climbed reluctantly to their feet. It was promising to be another day of terrible heat, no day for a march, but Starbuck had no intention of traveling all day. He planned to take a few miles off the journey, then find a field in which the battalion could have an afternoon of rest, then finish the journey in the next day's cool dawn.

He walked down the sidewalk and found the Taylor Hotel, which proved to be three impressive stories of pillared balconies dominating the street. Captain Tumlin's room was on the third floor and, because the captain was nowhere to be found in the public rooms, Starbuck climbed the wooden stairs and knocked on the room's door.

"Go away," a voice said. Starbuck turned the handle and found the door locked. "And don't come back!" the voice added.

"Tumlin!"

"Go away!" the man called. "I'm at my prayers."

A woman giggled. "Tumlin!" Starbuck shouted again.

"I'll meet you downstairs. Give me a half hour!" Tumlin answered.

The door's lock splintered at a simple push and Starbuck stepped inside to see a plump, sweating man rolling out of a disordered bed to reach for his holstered revolver. The man checked as he saw Starbuck's uniform. "Who the hell are you?" Tumlin asked.

"Your new commanding officer, Billy," Starbuck said, then tipped his hat to the girl who was clawing the grubby sheet to cover her breasts. She was a pretty black girl with a fine head of curls and sad, dark eyes. "Morning, ma'am," Starbuck said, "sure is a hot one."

"You're who?" Billy Blythe asked as he settled back under the sheet.

"Your new commanding officer, Billy," Starbuck said again. He walked to the louvered doors that opened onto the hotel's top balcony and pushed them open. From the balcony he could see the battalion forming its ranks, ready to march away, but the job was being done with pathetic slowness. Dozens of men were resting in the shade of verandahs and the sergeants were doing nothing to stir them. "Sergeant Case!" Starbuck shouted. "Show me how a proper soldier gets a battalion moving. Snap to it! The name's Starbuck," he called over his shoulder to Tumlin, "Major Nathaniel Starbuck."

"Jesus," Billy Blythe said. "You the son of the Reverend Starbuck?"

"Sure am. That worry you?"

"Hell, no," Billy Blythe said. "Just seems strange, you being a Yankee and all."

"No stranger than a man being in bed on a fine morning when there are Yankees to be killed," Starbuck said cheerfully. The street beneath him was at last showing some signs of vigor, so he turned back into the room. "Now get the hell up, Billy. I hear you've got some men for me. Where are they?"

Billy Blythe flapped a hand. "In camp, Major."

"Then get your boots on, Billy, and let's go fetch them. You know where I might find a wagon in this town?"

"Lucky if you can find a wheelbarrow," Tumlin said. "Hell, there ain't nothing here but bad soldiers and good women." He slapped the black girl's rump.

Starbuck saw some cigars on the washstand and helped himself to one. "You don't mind?"

"Hell, no, help yourself," Billy Blythe said. "There's a flint and steel on the mantel." He waited until Starbuck's back was turned, then swung himself out from under the yellowing bedsheet.

Starbuck turned. "Billy," he said reprovingly. "You go to bed dressed?" The pinkly naked Tumlin had a pouch belted round his stomach. "That's no way to treat a lady," Starbuck added.

"Just keeping it safe, Major," Tumlin said, scrambling into a pair of long underpants. He blushed, felt in the pouch, and took out two silver coins. "You'll forgive me, Major?" he asked and tossed the coins onto the bed. "Sorry about the interruption, honey."

The girl snatched the money as Starbuck lowered himself into a cane chair and put his dusty boots up on the washstand. "You were in a Yankee jail, I hear?" he asked Tumlin.

"Most of this year," Blythe said.

"They fed you well," Starbuck said as Tumlin buttoned a shirt round his plump belly, which was distended by the money pouch.

"I was four times this size when I got took," Blythe said.

"Where were you held?" Starbuck asked.

"Union, Massachusetts."

"Union?" Starbuck asked. "Where the hell's Union?"

"Out west," Blythe said. He had met Starbuck's father and knew the family came from Boston, so placing his mythical town of Union in the west of the state seemed a safe bet.

"In the Berkshires?" Starbuck asked.

"I guess," Blythe said, sitting on the bed to tug on his boots. "What are they? Hills? Not that we saw any hills, Major. Just big walls."

"So how many men have you got for me, Billy?"

"A dozen."

"Stragglers?"

"Lost sheep, Major," Blythe said, offering Starbuck a lazy grin, "just little lost sheep looking for a shepherd. Hell, I'm looking for a comb."

"Here." Starbuck saw the comb on the washstand and tossed it across the room. "So you escaped?"

Blythe winced as the comb caught in a tangle of his long hair. "Walked south, Major."

"Then you'll have good hard feet, Billy, all ready for some marching."

"And where the hell are we marching, Major?" Blythe asked.

"My guess," Starbuck said, "is Harper's Ferry. And once we've bagged the Yankees there, over the river and keep going north till the Yankees beg us to stop."

Blythe pulled on his gray coat. "Hell, Major," he grumbled, "you have one hell of a way of making yourself known to your officers."

"Coat's too small for you, Billy," Starbuck said with a grin. "When were you made a captain?"

Blythe paused to think as he buckled on his revolver. "Last year, Major. November, I guess, why?"

"Because that makes you senior to my other captains, which means you're my second in command. If I'm killed, Billy, my heroes are all yours. You ready?"

Blythe collected his few belongings and stuffed them in a bag. "Ready enough," he said.

Starbuck stood, walked to the door, and tipped his hat again to the girl. "Sorry to have disturbed you, ma'am. Come on, Billy. Let's go."

They caught up with the battalion three miles north of town. Starbuck marched the tired men another two miles, then swerved aside into a stretch of pastureland that edged a wood and a stream and had plainly been used many times before as a bivouac. The grass was stained where tents had stood too long, scorch marks showed where campfires had burned, while the margins of the woodland were nothing but ragged stumps where troops had cut their firewood. The railroad that led north from Winchester was a half mile away, its steel rails torn up and carried away by one side or the other while the turnpike that ran parallel to the ruined rail line had been deeply rutted by the marching and counter-marching of the armies that had fought for possession of the Shenan-doah Valley ever since the war's beginning. The pasture was a much-abused place, but it was still pleasant enough and just far enough from Winchester to deter any man who might have been tempted back to the town's taverns.

Captain Potter had no need of the taverns. He had brought the ammunition to the encampment, but after that he had somehow found himself a jug of whiskey and by late afternoon he was wildly drunk. Star-buck was drawing up lists of the new companies, which now numbered five. He had begun to choose men for Potter's skirmishing company and was writing their names when he became aware of a surge of raucous laughter. At first he thought it a good omen, maybe an upwelling of spirit among the resting men, but then Captain Dennison stooped under the crude cotton awning that served Starbuck as a tent. Dennison was picking his teeth with a wood splinter. "Nice desk, Major," he said.

"It serves," Starbuck said. He was using a tree stump as a crude writing desk.

"You might want to redo those lists," Dennison said with amuse-ment, " 'cos I reckon you just lost yourself a captain."

"Meaning what?"

"Potter boy's drunk. Drunk as a skunk. Hell, drunk as ten skunks." Dennison spat a shred of food. "Looks like he can't be trusted after all."

Starbuck swore, picked up his jacket and belt, and ducked outside.

Potter was playing the fool. A group of men who still had some energy after the day's marching had started a game of baseball and Pot-ter had insisted on being allowed to take part. Now, swaying slightly, he faced the pitcher and kept demanding that the ball be thrown at perfect hitting height. "Groin height!" he shouted, and the fielders egged him on by pretending not to know what he meant. Potter unbuttoned his pants to expose himself. "That's the groin! There! See?"

The pitcher, hardly able to throw for laughing, tossed an underhand lob that went wide. Potter swung madly, staggered, and recovered. "Try it closer, closer." He paused, stooped to pick up his stone jug, and took a swig. He saw Starbuck as he lowered the jug. "Captain Ahab, sir!"

"Are you drunk?" Starbuck said when he was close to Potter.

Potter grinned, shrugged and thought about the question, but could not come up with anything witty. "I guess," he said.

"Button yourself, Captain."

Potter shook his head, not in refusal, but in perplexity. "Just a bit of horseplay, Captain Ahab."

"Button yourself," Starbuck said quietly.

"You're going all stern on me, ain't you? Just like my father—" Potter stopped abruptly as Starbuck hit him in the belly. The younger man folded over, retching just as he had when Starbuck had first found him in the Hells.

"Stand up straight," Starbuck said, kicking over the stone bottle, "and button yourself."

"Let him play!" a voice shouted sullenly. It was Sergeant Case. "Nothing wrong with a game," the sergeant insisted. "Let him play." A few men muttered their support. Starbuck, they reckoned, was spoiling their day's one small moment of enjoyment.

"Good Sergeant Case," Potter said, cuffing spittle away from his chin. "My supplier of whiskey." He stooped to the fallen bottle, but Starbuck kicked it away before crossing to face Case.

"You gave Potter the whiskey?"

Case hesitated, then nodded. "Ain't against the law, Major."

"It's against my law," Starbuck said, "and you knew it."

Case rocked back and forward on his heels. He had drunk some of the whiskey himself, and maybe that gave him the courage to convert his hostility toward Starbuck into open defiance. He spat close to Starbuck's boots. "Your law?" he jeered. "What law is that, Major?"

"The rules of this battalion, Case."

"This battalion, Major," Case exploded in fury, "is the sorriest damn collection of bloody bastards ever put under a flag. This ain't a battalion, Major, it's a rabble of skulkers who weren't wanted in any proper regiment. This ain't a battalion, Major! This ain't nothing! We ain't got nothing. No wagons, no axes, no tents, no doctor, no nothing! We weren't sent here to fight, Major, but to get ourselves killed."

There were louder murmurs of agreement. Men who had been resting had come to see the confrontation, so that nearly all of the battalion was now grouped around the makeshift playing diamond.

"A month ago," Starbuck raised his voice, "I was in a battalion that got raided by Yankees. They killed half our officers, burned our wagons, destroyed all our spare ammunition, but we still fought a week later and won. This battalion can do the same."

"The hell it can," Case said. His fellow sergeants had come to his support, a phalanx of tough, grim-faced men who stared with blank hatred at Starbuck. "The hell it can," Case said again. "It might be good for guarding prisoners, or fetching and carrying supplies, but it ain't any good for fighting."

Starbuck turned slowly, looking at the worried faces of the men. "I think they can fight, Sergeant." He turned all the way round to face Case again. "But can you?"

"I've been there," Case said curtly, "and I know what it takes for men to fight. Not this!" He waved a scornful hand at the battalion. "No proper officer would take this rabble to war."

Starbuck stepped closer to Case. "Do I take that to mean that you won't lead them into battle, Sergeant?"

Case sensed he might have gone too far, but he was unwilling to back down in the face of his supporters. "Lead them into battle?" He scoffed Starbuck by crudely imitating his Boston accent. "Sounds like a fine Yankee phrase to me, Major."

"I asked you a question, Case."

"I ain't afraid to fight!" Case blustered and, by refusing to answer the question, implicitly backed away from the confrontation.

Starbuck could have let Case off the hook, but chose not to. "I asked you a question," he said again.

"Hell," Case said, cornered, "these men ain't fit to fight!"

"They're fit enough," Starbuck said, "it's you that ain't fit." He could have left it there, but sheer devilment made him rack the tension higher. "Take your stripes off," he said.

Case, faced with losing his rank, accepted the showdown. "You take 'em, Major," he said, "if you can." His fellow sergeants greeted the defiance with hand-clapping.

Starbuck turned away and walked to the vacated pitcher's spot. From the very first he had worried about imposing his authority on this despised battalion, and he had never done it. He had assumed that if he led they would follow, not because he inspired them, but because men usually do what is expected of them. In time, he had hoped, battle would wipe out the regiment's past history and unite it in purpose, but instead the crisis had come now, which meant that the solution could not wait for battle, but would have to be imposed now. He would exhaust the formal route first, but he knew it was doomed even as he turned back to the group of sergeants who slowly ended their clapping as he stared at them. "Sergeant Webber? Cowper?" he said. "Arrest Case."

The two sergeants spat, but neither made any other movement.

"Captain Dennison?" Starbuck turned.

"Ain't my business," Dennison said. "Finish what you started, Starbuck, ain't that what you once told me?"

Starbuck nodded. "When I've finished here," he raised his voice, "every company will elect new sergeants. Case!" he snapped. "Bring me your coat."

Case, driven to mutiny, brazened out the moment. "Come and get it, Major."

There was a moment's silence as the men watched Starbuck; then he took off his coat and revolver. He was apprehensive, though he took care not to show it. Case was a tall man, probably stronger than Starbuck, and probably no stranger to casual violence—any man who had survived fourteen years in a European army had to be tough— while Starbuck had been reared in the gentler world of respectable Boston, which eschewed violence as a means of resolving argument. Respectable Boston believed in reason leavened by Godliness, while

Starbuck's career now depended on beating down a bullying thug who had probably not lost a fight in a dozen years, but he was also a thug who was more than slightly drunk and that, Starbuck reckoned, should help him. "The trouble with you, Case," he said as he walked slowly toward the taller man, "is that you've spent too long wearing a red coat. You ain't a fusilier now, you're a rebel, and if you don't like the way we do things then you ought to get the hell out of here and go back to Queen Victoria's petticoats. You probably ain't man enough to fight Yankees." He was hoping to provoke Case into a rushed attack, but the big man had the sense to hold his ground and let Starbuck come to him. Starbuck broke into a jog, then aimed a massive kick at Case's groin, but a heartbeat later he jarred his left foot forward to stop his forward momentum.

Case half turned away from the kick and flicked out a hard punch with his left hand, only Starbuck did not run into the punch, but instead rammed his right boot forward into Case's knee. It was a brutally hard kick and Starbuck recoiled from it, safe out of Case's reach. Starbuck had hoped to do more damage, but the big man's quick left hand had stalled him.

Case stumbled as pain buckled his leg. The pain made him grimace, but he forced himself upright. "Yankee," he spat at Starbuck.

Starbuck knew this had to be quick. If the fight dragged on then his authority would be abraded with every blow exchanged. Victory had to be swift and total, and that meant taking some punishment. Case's tactics were obvious. He intended to stand like a rock and let Starbuck come to him, and every time Starbuck was in range he would inflict pain until Starbuck could take no more. So take the pain, Starbuck told himself, and put the son of a bitch down.

He walked forward with his eyes on Case's hard eyes. He saw the right hand coming and half raised his left hand to block the blow, but his head still rang as the fist crashed home on the side of his skull. Starbuck kept going forward, forcing himself into the stink of Case's unwashed wool uniform and the stench of tobacco and whiskey on the big man's breath, and the big man smelled victory as he reached to grab Starbuck's hair and pulled his head down onto his left fist.

Then Case gagged, choked, and his eyes widened as he tried to breathe.

Starbuck had hit the sergeant in the Adam's apple. He had rammed his right hand up and forward, knuckles outward, and as much by luck as judgment had slammed the blow under the sergeant's jutting beard to land dead on the inviting target of Case's unnaturally long neck. It was a wicked blow, taught him long before by Captain Truslow, who knew every nasty trick in the devil's book.

Case was staggering now, his hands at his throat where a terrible pain was threatening to cut off his airway. Starbuck, his own head ringing from the sergeant's blow, stepped back to watch the big man totter, then stepped forward again and gave Case's left knee another hard kick. The big man buckled. Starbuck waited again. He waited until Case was half down, then he brought his knee up into the man's face. Blood splashed out of the broken nose as Starbuck grabbed Case's hair and rammed his head back onto the knee. He let go of the greasy hair and this time Case dropped to all fours and Starbuck kicked him in the belly, then put his foot on Case's back and pushed him down into the grass. The breath rasped and rattled in Case's throat. He twitched as he tried to subdue the gagging pain, but nothing could stop the pitiful whimpering that sounded between each desperate attempt to breathe. Starbuck spat on him, then looked up at the other sergeants. "All of you," he said, "take your stripes off. Now!"

None dared oppose him, not with Case retching into the grass. His face had gone red, the breath was hoarse in his constricted throat, and his eyes were wide with terror. Starbuck turned away. "Captain Dennison!"

"Sir?" Dennison was white-faced, appalled.

"Get a knife, Captain," Starbuck said calmly, "and cut Case's stripes off."

Dennison obeyed while Starbuck retrieved his coat and revolver. "Anyone else here think they know better than me how to run this battalion?" he shouted at the men.

Someone began clapping. It was Caton Rothwell, and his applause spread among the many men who had hated their sergeants. Starbuck waved the clapping to silence, then looked at Captain Potter. "You come to me when you're sober, Potter," he said, then walked away. He felt that he must be shaking, but when he looked at his bruised right hand it seemed quite still. He ducked into his makeshift tent, then suddenly the tension flowed out of him and he shuddered like a man with fever.

Lucifer, without being asked, brought him a mug of coffee. "There's some of Captain Potter's whiskey in it," he told Starbuck. "I rescued it from the bottle." He stared at Starbuck's left ear that was throbbing painfully. "He hit you hard."

"I hit him harder."

"Man won't like you for it."

"He didn't like me anyway."

Lucifer watched Starbuck warily. "He'll be wanting you."

"Meaning?"

Lucifer shrugged and touched his Colt revolver that Starbuck had restored. "Meaning," the boy said, "you should take care of him properly."

"Let the Yankees do it," Starbuck said dismissively.

"Hell, they can't do nothing proper! You want me to do it?"

"I want you to get me supper," Starbuck said. His ear was hurting and he had work to do, even more work now that his new company lists had to be rewritten to accommodate the names of the newly chosen sergeants. Some of the old sergeants were reelected, and Starbuck suspected threats might have been used to ensure those choices, but Case's name was not on the list. The last company to report was E, the half-formed company of skirmishers, and Caton Rothwell brought that list written in clumsy letters on the back of a tobacco wrapper. Rothwell's own name was at the top of the page. Starbuck was seated outside his tent, close enough to a fire for the flames to illuminate the page that he first read and then handed to Billy Tumlin, who had come to share a late-night mug of coffee. "Good," Starbuck said to Rothwell when he saw Rothwell's name on the list. "Don't make the mistake I did."

"Which was what?" Rothwell asked.

"Being too easy on the men."

Rothwell looked surprised. "Hell, I don't reckon you're easy," he said. "Case don't, either."

"How is he?" Starbuck asked.

"He can walk in the morning."

"Make sure the son of a bitch does."

"Where are we going tomorrow?" Rothwell asked.

"North past Charlestown," Starbuck said.

"Past Charlestown?" Billy Blythe asked, accenting *past*. "I kind of hoped we'd find billets there."

"We're joining Old Jack's men to attack Harper's Ferry," Starbuck said, "and they won't be lollygagging in Charlestown, so nor will we. You want some coffee?" he asked Rothwell.

Rothwell hesitated, then nodded. "Kind of you, Major."

Starbuck shouted for Lucifer, then gestured Rothwell to sit. "When I first met you, Sergeant," he said, using Rothwell's new rank for the first time, "you told me that your wife was in trouble, which was why you walked away from your old regiment. What was the trouble?"

It was a blunt question and Rothwell met it with a hostile stare. "Ain't none of your business, Captain," he finally said.

"It is my business if it happens again," Starbuck answered just as curtly. His curiosity was not prompted by prurience, but rather because he suspected that Rothwell could be a leader in the battalion and he needed reassurance about the man's dependability. "And it is if I need new officers, and Yankee bullets have a way of creating vacancies."

Rothwell considered Starbuck's words, then shrugged. "Won't happen again," he said grimly, and seemed content to leave it at that, but a moment later he spat into the fire. "Not unless the Yankees rape her again," he added bitterly.

Tumlin, sitting next to Starbuck, hissed in evident disapproval.

Starbuck, embarrassed by the answer, did not know what to say and so said nothing.

"A Southron did it," Rothwell said, "but he was riding with the Northern cavalry." Now that he was launched on the story his reluctance to tell it had disappeared. He probed inside his top pocket to bring out a square of oilcloth that was tied with string. He carefully unknotted the string, then just as carefully unfolded the waterproof cloth to reveal another scrap of paper. He handled the paper as though it were a relic, which to him it was. "Bunch of Yankee cavalry raiders came to the farm, Major," he told Starbuck, "and left her this. The Southron took my Becky to the barn that day, but he was stopped. He burned the barn though, and the next week he came back and burned the house and took my Becky out to the orchard. Beat her bloody." There were glints in the corners of Rothwell's eyes. He sniffed and held the paper out to Starbuck. "This man," he said bleakly.

The paper was an official U.S. government form, printed in Washington, that promised payment for supplies taken by U.S. forces from Southern householders. The payment, which would be made at the war's end, was dependent on the family being able to prove that none of its members had carried arms against the U.S. government. The paper, in brief, was a license for Northerners to steal whatever they liked, and this paper carried a penciled signature that Starbuck read aloud. "William Blythe," he read, "Captain, U.S. Army."

Tumlin did not move, did not speak, did not even seem to breathe. Starbuck carefully folded the form and handed it back to Rothwell. "I know about Blythe," he said.

"You do, Major?" Rothwell asked with surprise.

"I was with the Faulconer Legion when cavalry attacked us. Blythe trapped some of our officers in a tavern and shot them down like dogs. Women too. You say he's a Southerner?"

"Speaks like one."

Tumlin let out a long sigh. "Reckon there are bad apples in every basket," he said, and his voice was so shaken that Starbuck looked at him with surprise. Somehow Tumlin had not struck Starbuck as a man easily moved by tales of hardship and Starbuck reckoned it was to Tumlin's credit that he had taken Rothwell's story so hard. Tumlin sighed. "Reckon I wouldn't want to be Mister Blythe if you got your hands on him, Sergeant," he said.

"I reckon not," Rothwell said. He blinked. "Farm belonged to my father," he went on, "but he weren't there when this happened. He's going to rebuild, he says, but how, I don't know." He stared into the fire that whirled a stream of sparks into the air. "Nothing left there now," Rothwell said, "just ashes. And my Becky's real hurt. And the children are scared it'll happen again." He carefully retied the string, then put the package back in his pocket. "Kind of hard," he said to himself.

"And you were arrested," Starbuck asked, "for trying to be with her?"

Rothwell nodded. "My Major wouldn't give me furlough. Said no one gets furlough before the Yankees are beat, but hell, we'd just whipped the bastards at Manassas so I reckoned I'd take my own furlough. Ain't sorry I did, either." He swallowed the lukewarm coffee, then glanced at Starbuck. "You arresting Case?" he asked.

"He's already in a punishment battalion," Starbuck said, "what else can they do to him?"

"They can shoot the son of a bitch," Rothwell said.

"We'll let the Yankees do it," Starbuck said, "and save the government the price of a bullet."

Rothwell was unhappy. "I reckon he ain't a safe man to keep around, Major."

Starbuck agreed, but was unsure what else he could do. If he was to have Case arrested then he would need to send the man under escort to Winchester and he could not spare an officer to lead such a party, nor the time to write up the paperwork for a court-martial. He could hardly have Case shot on his own authority, for he had invited the fight, and so the best course seemed to let things lie, but to tread warily.

"I'll keep an eye on him," Tumlin promised.

Rothwell stood. "Grateful for the coffee, Major."

Starbuck watched him walk away, then shook his head. "Poor man."

"Poor woman," Blythe said, then let out a long sigh. "I suspect that Mister Blythe will be long gone," he added.

"Maybe," Starbuck said. "But I was fond of one of the girls who died in that tavern and when this war is over, Billy, I might just go looking for Mister Blythe. Give me something to do in the piping time of peace. But for now, what the hell do I do with Potter?"

"Nothing," Blythe said.

"Nothing? Hell, I make him up to captain and he rewards me by getting blind drunk."

Blythe stretched out a cramped leg. Then he leaned forward and snatched a burning stick from the fire and used it to light a pair of cigars. He handed one to Starbuck. "I guess I'm going to have to tell you the truth, Major."

"What truth?"

Blythe waved his cigar toward the flickering camp fires. "These men here, they ain't an ordinary battalion any more than you're an ordinary major. They don't know much about you, but what they do know, they like. I don't say they like you, because they don't even know you, but they sure as hell are intrigued by you. You're a Yankee for a start, and you ain't inclined to follow the rules. You make your own rules and you fight your own fights. They like that. They don't want you to be ordinary."

"What the hell has this got to do with Potter?" Starbuck interrupted.

"Because men going into battle," Blythe went on as though Starbuck had never spoken, "don't want their leaders to be ordinary. Men have to believe in something, Major, and when God chooses to stay in heaven they're forced to believe in their officers instead. In you," he prodded the cigar toward Starbuck, "and if you show you're just an ordinary officer then, hell, they'll lose their faith."

"Tumlin," Starbuck said, "you're babbling."

"No, sir, I am not. I'm telling you that an ordinary officer would fall back on army regulations. An ordinary officer would humiliate Potter and that, sir, would be a mistake. Hell, give Potter a scare, put the fear of God in the bastard, but don't bust him back to lieutenant. The men like him."

"Let him off?" Starbuck asked dubiously. "That's weakness."

"Hell, Major, no one thinks you're weak after what you did to Case. Besides, Potter did you real proud with the wagon."

"He did that, right enough." Or rather Lucifer had done the battalion proud for, on his exploration of Winchester's side streets, the boy had glimpsed a magnificent hearse parked inside a shed. The shed had been locked tight by the time Potter's detail arrived and the owner swore there was nothing inside but baled hay, but Potter had forced the lock and revealed the black-painted vehicle with its etched glass windows, velvet curtains, and high black plumes in their silver holders. He had filled the hearse with ammunition, then, lacking horses, his men had dragged the quaint vehicle northward. "He sure did us proud," Starbuck admitted again, then pulled on his cigar. In truth he did not want to punish Potter, but he feared to send the battalion a signal of lenience. "I'll give him hell," he said after a while, "but if the bastard does it again I'll break him down to cookboy. You want to go find the son of a bitch and send him to me?"

"I'll do that," Tumlin said and shambled into the night.

Starbuck prepared himself for Potter's tongue-lashing. In truth, he thought, it had not been a bad day. Not a good day, but not bad either. The battalion had lost no one to straggling, he had faced down his enemies, but he had not made those enemies into friends. Perhaps that would never happen, but if it did, he thought, it would be in the fierce crucible of battle. And the sooner, the better, Starbuck thought, then he remembered the cornfield at Chantilly and recalled his gut-loosening fear. Oh God, he thought, let me not be a coward.

Late that night Starbuck toured the picket line that was not set against the incursion of enemies, but against the possibility of his own men deserting, then, wrapped in his dirty blanket, he slept.

Lucifer sat nearby. The boy was tired, but he was determined not to sleep. Instead he sat just outside the glow of the dying fire and he watched the makeshift tent where Starbuck slept and he watched the fire-dotted field where the battalion rested, and every now and then he would caress the long barrel of the Colt revolver that lay across his knees. Lucifer liked Starbuck, and if Starbuck would take no precautions, then Lucifer would guard him against the demons. For that, Lucifer knew, was what they were; white demons, bad as they came, just waiting to take revenge.

I T WAS PROBABLY THE WORST DAY OF DELANEY'S LIFE. AT
any moment he expected to hear that one of the precious copies of
Special Order 191 had gone missing and then he would have to face the
rigors of a full-scale inquiry, but to his astonishment no one seemed to
notice that a copy had been purloined. The army rested in blissful, blind
ignorance. Much of it left Frederick City on the morning after Delaney
stole the order. They marched in the early dawn to encircle the trapped
federal garrison at Harper's Ferry, while the rest of Lee's men prepared
for their own departure the next day. Cavalry patrols went eastward and
reported that the Northern army was only a day's march from Frederick
City, but was showing no eagerness to advance. George McClellan was
behaving true to his old form, creeping timidly forward and fearing
every imaginary threat while posing none himself. "Though he's not a
man I'd care to attack, not if he knew I was coming," Lee said generously at lunch. The general's broken hands had been rebandaged with
lighter splints and he was constantly flexing his fingers with a look of
astonished gratitude that their use was partly restored. "McClellan

would make a very good defensive general," he said, clumsily spooning beans to his mouth.

"There's a distinction?" Delaney asked.

"Oh, indeed." Lee cuffed spilled beans off his beard. "An attacker has to take more risks. Imagine playing chess, Delaney, where you don't have to make a single move until your opponent has developed his attack. You should win every time."

"Should?"

"A good attacker disguises his blows."

"As you are now, General?"

Lee smiled. "Poor McClellan will be getting reports from here, there, and everywhere. He won't know where we are or what we're doing. He'll know we're besieging Harper's Ferry, of course, because he'll hear the guns, but I doubt if McClellan will raise a finger to help those poor men. Ah, Chilton! You look harassed."

Delaney felt a surge of fear, but Colonel Chilton's harassment arose from a lack of varnish rather than the loss of Special Order 191.

"Varnish?" Lee asked, finally abandoning his attempt to manipulate fork and spoon with hampered fingers. "Are we trying to smarten this army? A hopeless task, I should have thought."

"News from the North, sir. Parrott guns." Chilton collapsed into a camp chair and fanned his face with his hat brim.

"You've lost me, Chilton," Lee said. "Varnish? Parrott guns?"

"The tubes of the twenty pounders are liable to explode, sir. One of our fellows in the North knows an inspector in the factory and he claims they reckon it's because of friction inside the shell caused by the sudden acceleration upon firing. That friction ignites the shell and causes it to explode inside the tube. The factory's solution is to empty the shells of their explosive and varnish the interior walls before refilling them. Worth a try, I'd say, only we can't find any varnish."

"Grease?" Delaney suggested, "or wax?"

"We could try that," Chilton said grudgingly. "But wouldn't wax melt?"

"Try grease," Lee said, "but eat first. The beans are excellent." The general wiped sweat off his forehead. The heat was again stupefying.

Delaney might have suggested a solution for exploding Parrott guns, but he had still not devised a method of passing the stolen order back to McClellan's army. During the night, as he had tossed sleeplessly on the hard ground, he had imagined riding desperately eastward until he met a Yankee cavalry patrol, but he knew his horsemanship was not up to such cross-country work. Besides, any rebel cavalry seeing him would be bound to be curious and that curiosity could well lead to the gallows' steps. Now, desperate to rid himself of the incriminating document, he had hit upon one last pathetic idea. "I thought, if you wouldn't mind," he said to Lee, "that I might look at the town before we leave?"

"By all means," Lee said. "Chilton will write you a pass."

"No danger of the Yankees arriving today?" Delaney asked anxiously.

"My dear Delaney!" Lee laughed. "None whatsoever, not with McClellan in command. We'll leave tomorrow, but I doubt he'll be here for at least another three days."

"There's nothing to see in the town," Chilton observed sourly, resenting that he was required to write Delaney a pass.

"One of my mother's cousins was a minister there for a time," Delaney said, inventing a reason for his curiosity, "and I have a notion he might be buried there."

"Your mother's cousins?" Lee said, frowning as he tried to remember Delaney's family tree. "So he was a Mattingley?"

"Charles Mattingley," Delaney said, and there was indeed a Reverend Charles Mattingley who had been a cousin of Delaney's mother, though so far as Delaney knew the Reverend Charles was still alive and ministering to heathen tribes in Africa. "Thomas's second son," he added.

"I never knew that branch of the family," Lee said. "They moved to Maryland, aren't I right?"

"Creagerstown, General. Thomas was a physician there for many years."

"And his son's dead, eh? Poor fellow, he can't have been very old. But it's odd, Delaney, to think of you being related to a minister?"

"Charles was an Episcopalian, General," Delaney said reprovingly. "It hardly counts."

Lee, an Episcopalian himself, laughed, then fumbled open the lid of his pocket watch. "I must be at work," he announced. "Enjoy your afternoon, Delaney."

"Thank you, sir."

An hour later, equipped with the pass that would take him past the provosts guarding the stores in Frederick, Delaney walked into town. In his pocket was the copy of Special Order 191 and he felt sure that the provosts would stop him, search him, and then march him at gunpoint on the journey that would end at a Richmond gallows, but the men guarding the town merely touched their hats as he showed them Chilton's pass.

The town had a deserted air. The presence of the rebel army had stopped all traffic on the rail spur and had inhibited the country folk from coming to do their marketing in Frederick City. The shops, protected by the cordon of provosts, were open, but few people were in the streets. One or two houses flew the rebel flag, but the gesture seemed desultory, a mere formality, and Delaney guessed that when McClellan's army reached the town it would suddenly be gaudy with stars and stripes. The people of Maryland did not seem overgrateful for being liberated by the Southerners. Some were enthusiastic, but only a handful of young men had volunteered to join Lee's army.

Delaney strolled past a carpenter's shop sandwiched between two churches. A bearded man was turning chair legs in the shop and he looked up as the rebel officer passed, but did not return Delaney's greeting. A cripple, probably a man wounded in one of the war's early battles, sat on a porch taking in the sun. He ignored Delaney, which suggested he had fought for the North. A black woman, probably a slave, came toward Delaney with a bundle of laundry on her head, but turned aside into an alley rather than confront him. A solemn little girl watched him from behind a window, but ducked out of sight when he smiled at her. A pair of cows were being driven down the street, probably to give milk that would be sold to the rebel army, and Delaney called a cheerful greeting to the girl who herded them, but she just nodded curtly and hurried on, probably fearful that he would try to take the cows from her. The stifling heat seemed to condense the town's aroma of sweet hay and animal ordure into a rank stink that offended Delaney's nostrils. He stepped around some fresh cow dung and it occurred to him, with the astonishment that comes from a moment of self-revelation, that the reason he was betraying his country was simply to escape from the constriction of small church-haunted towns like Frederick City with their suspicious populations and their glorification of simple virtues and honest toil. Richmond was a rung above such places, but Richmond stank of tobacco, Washington was a rung higher still, but Washington stank of ambition, while New York and Boston were higher yet, but the one stank of vulgar money and the other reeked of Protestant virtue and Delaney wanted none of them. His reward for treachery, he decided, would be an ambassadorship: a permanent and salaried post in Rome or Paris or Athens, all of them cities that stank of jaded tastes and languid nights. He touched the pocket in which he had the special order concealed. It was his passport to paradise.

He found the post office on Main Street. The idea of employing the U.S. mail to deliver the stolen order amused Delaney. There was something obvious, yet also quixotic, in the idea that appealed to his sense of mischief. He doubted whether Thorne would approve, for the vital news in the order was already a day old and it would probably be two or three days staler by the time it reached the U.S. army, but Delaney had no other idea how to send his message.

The postmaster had a cubbyhole office at the back of the building that had the usual wooden counter, a wall of pigeonholes for letters awaiting collection, and two long tables where the mail was sorted. "Not again," the postmaster groaned when he saw Delaney.

"Again?" Delaney asked, puzzled.

"We had a Captain Gage in here this morning," the postmaster protested, "and another fellow yesterday. What was his name, Lucy?" he shouted to one of the women seated at a sorting table.

"Pearce!" She called back.

"A Major Pearce," the postmaster said accusingly to Delaney. The postmaster was a big-bellied, truculent man with a red beard. He was also a Northern sympathizer, or at least he had defiantly kept a stars and stripes hanging on his cubbyhole wall. "But they're all there," he added, gesturing at a pile of mail in a basket on his desk, "so help yourself. But nothing's come in since Captain Gage checked."

Delaney took the mail from the basket and suddenly understood what the postmaster was saying. All of the letters were addressed to places in the North, and all were from Confederate soldiers. Someone, he assumed the provosts, was making certain that no one was trying to send information to the Yankees and so they had opened and read the letters before initialing the envelopes to show that the contents had been checked. "I wasn't here to read the mail," Delaney said, but opened one of the letters anyway. It was from a Sergeant Malone and addressed to his sister in New Jersey. Betty had given birth to another son, but the child had died at a month old. Mother was as well as could be expected. Cousin John had been wounded at Manassas, but not seriously. " 'These are sad times,' " Delaney read aloud, " 'but we remember you in our prayers.' " He shrugged, slipped the letter back in its envelope, then dropped the pile back into the basket. "Would you," he asked the post-master, "have an envelope you could donate to the army?"

The postmaster hesitated, then decided there was little point in being obstructive. He opened a drawer and handed Delaney an enve-lope. Delaney, making no attempt to hide what he did, took the copy of Special Order 191 from his pocket and slipped it inside the envelope, then folded the flap inside. "May I?" he asked and reached over the desk for the postmaster's pen. He dipped it in the inkwell, drained the excess ink from the nib, then wrote Captain Adam Faulconer, U.S. Army, Gen. McClellan's Hdqtrs., in block letters. "It's nothing that needs bother Captain Gage or Major Pearce," he said to the postmaster, then bor-rowed a pencil and, very carefully, copied Gage's initials. "There," he said, the job done. "I suppose you'll charge me for a stamp now?"

The postmaster looked at the addressee's name, then at the forged initials, and finally up into Delaney's face. He said nothing.

"He's an old friend," Delaney explained airily, "and this might be my last chance to write to him." There was a risk that the postmaster was not a Northern supporter at all, but that was a risk Delaney had to run, just as he had to risk that the provosts did not check the basket of mail a third time.

"You're all leaving then?" the postmaster asked.

"By tomorrow," Delaney said, "the army will be gone."

"Where?"

"Over the hills and far away," Delaney said lightly. Sweat trickled down his cheeks. "But I imagine," he went on, "that the Federals will be here soon?"

"Like as not," the postmaster said with a shrug. He weighed the letter in his hand, then ostentatiously put it in the drawer rather than with the other mail from the Confederate army. "It'll be delivered," he promised, "but I don't know when."

"I'm obliged to you," Delaney said.

Once outside the post office Delaney had to lean against the wall. He was shaking like a man with the fever. Dear God, he thought, but he had no stomach for this kind of thing. He felt a sudden need to vomit, but managed to hold it back. Sweat poured off him. He had been a fool! He had been unable to resist flamboyance. He had deliberately tried to impress a man he thought was a Northern sympathizer, but he knew the risk had been stupid and the thought of the hangman's noose made him gag again.

"Are you unwell, Major?"

Delaney looked up and saw an elderly minister in Geneva bands watching him with a sympathetic, but wary, look. Doubtless he feared Delaney was drunk. "It's the heat," Delaney said, "nothing but the heat."

"It is warm," the minister agreed, sounding relieved that it was not liquor that had caused Delaney's distress. "Do you need help? A cup of water, maybe?"

"No, thank you. I shall manage just fine." Delaney suddenly looked up as a rumble of thunder sounded in the distance. There were no threatening clouds in sight, but the sound of the far-off storm was unmistakable. "Maybe the rain will break the heat," he said to the minister.

"Rain?" The minister frowned. "That isn't thunder," he said, realizing what Delaney had meant. "Those are guns, Major, those are guns." He stared west down main street to where the green fields and heavy trees and lines of rebel tents showed. "Harper's Ferry," the minister said, "it must be Harper's Ferry. God help all those poor men."

"Amen," Delaney said, "amen." For the fighting had begun.

The guns slammed back on their trails, spewing smoke sixty feet ahead of their muzzles and scattering flaming scraps of wadding onto the grass where small fires flickered from the previous shots. The sound of the guns was huge, so huge that it was more than just a sound, but a physical sensation as though the very earth was being buffeted in space. The shells screamed across the valley to leave little smoke trails from their burning fuses, then exploded in gouts of dirty gray-white smoke above the farther ridge. The smoke trails twisted in the wind, became feathery and tenuous, then another battery fired and the grass in front of the muzzles flicked flat again as another set of smoke trails whipped across the sky. Cannon barrels hissed as the wet swabs were thrust down the muzzles. On the far ridge a Yankee battery returned the fire, but the Northern guns were outnumbered and the rebel guns were well laid and their fuses well timed, and so the Northern gunners died man by man as the shell fragments hissed among them.

The Northern guns pulled back across the ridge, leaving its defense to infantry alone. The Southern cannon changed their aim, scattering shells among the trees, bushes, and rocks of the ridge. Some cannon were firing percussion-fused shells that plunged into the ground to gout wagonloads of dirt and leaves, others used case shot that banged apart in the air to spit musket bullets down on the Yankee defenders.

"Skirmishers?" Lieutenant Colonel Griffin Swynyard galloped his horse toward Starbuck. "Skirmishers?" he called again.

"They're out there, Colonel," Starbuck said. The Yellowlegs were on the far right-hand flank of Swynyard's Brigade, and immediately to the left of the Legion, and Starbuck had taken good care that his skirmishing company had gone forward before Maitland threw the Legion's skirmishers down onto the valley floor. Starbuck had picked his skirmishers carefully, drawing them from the men who had held up best on the marches north from the railhead. Most of his men had taken those marches hard, limping slower and slower on bloody, blistered feet as the battalion crawled painfully to reach this valley north of Charlestown just as the first of Jackson's infantry swung in from their long march that had taken them west from Frederick City to loop clean about Harper's Ferry to this ground that lay south of the besieged Federal garrison.

That garrison was attempting to defend the high ground about the river town, but so far their defense was halfhearted. The Yankee cannon had given up the fight quickly; now it was the infantry's turn to be tested. Starbuck's detached company of skirmishers was already in action, the smoke of their rifles blowing in small gray puffs across the valley floor. The answering puffs were well up the farther slope, and Starbuck was mentally urging Potter to press harder, though in fairness his skirmishers were doing well. They were far ahead of the Legion's skirmishers. The sound of that skirmishers' battle came as a series of intermittent cracks that were only audible in the intervals between the cannon fire. Swynyard was using field glasses to watch the rebel shells fall on the far ridge. All Starbuck could see there was an erratic and broken cordon of blue-coated infantry beneath their bright flags. The line was not continuous. It was interrupted by the gaps between regiments or where bushes or rocky outcrops interfered with the line's alignment, and sometimes the defending line vanished altogether where the Yankees sheltered in dips of the ground or behind boulders. "I don't see any rifle pits, Nate," Swynyard said.

"For small mercies, God, thank you," Starbuck answered.

Swynyard grimaced, but did not protest Starbuck's blasphemy. Instead he pointed to the left-hand end of the Yankee line. "Reckon you could take that ground?" he asked. "Say everything from the end of the crest to where the guns were?"

"I guess," Starbuck answered. In truth he had no idea how the Yellowlegs would behave in battle. Nor did he know how he would behave in this first battle since the terror had overwhelmed him in the rain-swept fight near the mansion of Chantilly. He could feel that terror hovering near again. It gave him a curiously disembodied sensation, as though his spirit were merely watching his body and marveling that it could react so calmly to Swynyard's orders.

"Wait for the line to advance," Swynyard said, then he turned his horse and rode toward Lieutenant-Colonel Maitland, who was mounted behind the Legion's center company.

Starbuck walked to the center of his own line where Captain Billy Tumlin stood with the color party. The color was a four-foot-square flag issued from the state armory and it looked a sorry thing compared with the thirty-six-square feet of colored silk that flew above the Legion. Starbuck told Tumlin what the orders were, then walked out ahead of the battalion.

Starbuck's job was to reassure his men. They had been dubbed failures by the army, then issued with antique guns, and now he had to persuade them to be winners. "They ain't got cannon!" he shouted, "just muskets." Almost certainly the Yankees were all armed with rifles, but this was no time for literal truths. "They're frightened as hell," he went on. "They'll probably break just as soon as you get within shouting distance, but if you hesitate, they'll rally. Not one of you will be killed crossing the valley. Remember that! They don't have cannon! We're going to walk across and when I give the order you charge the bastards! Hold your fire until then. No point in wasting a musket shot at long range. Hold your fire, wait for the order to charge, then scream at them! The faster they run, the more equipment they'll leave behind, and the more you kill, the more boots we get. Now fix bayonets!"

He turned to stare across the ground over which they would advance. The land dropped steeply away to the left where a small stream tumbled toward the Potomac. Harper's Ferry lay where that river was joined by the smaller Shenandoah, and the confluence was surrounded by three high spurs of land that overlooked the small town. Jackson's troops now commanded the approaches to all three spurs, and all three were under pressure. Push the Yankees off the high ground and the garrison in the town, which had been swollen by other Northern troops driven to shelter by Jackson's advance, would be dominated by rebel artillery. Local people had slipped through the Northern lines to tell the rebels that close to twenty thousand Yankees were trapped there, and even allowing for exaggeration, that meant that the town must be crammed with food, weapons, and supplies; all the things the Special Battalion lacked.

Starbuck turned back to look at the battalion that now stood with fixed bayonets. It was a tiny battalion, but no smaller than many others that had been shrunken by war. The Legion was larger, but still Starbuck reckoned that the Legion was down to half the number of men who had marched to Manassas for the war's first battle. Captain Truslow strolled out from the Legion with a rifle on his shoulder, which, like Starbuck's, carried no badges of rank. "Your boys, eh?" Truslow said, nodding at the battalion.

"My boys," Starbuck agreed.

"Any good?"

"About to find out."

"Maitland's no damned use," Truslow said, spitting a stream of tobacco juice, "and he don't like me neither."

"Can't think why."

Truslow grinned. "He reckons I ain't born to it. How was Richmond?"

"Hot," Starbuck said, knowing that was not the answer Truslow wanted. "And I did see Sally," he added.

"Reckoned you might. How is she?" The question was gruff.

"Living in luxury. Making money, learning to speak French, winding the world round her little finger."

Truslow grimaced. "Never did understand her. Always reckoned I should have had a son, not a daughter."

"She ain't that much different from you," Starbuck said, "just one hell of a lot prettier. She sends her love."

Truslow grunted, then glanced at Starbuck's left ear. "Someone thump you?"

"Tall man, third from the right, rear rank," Starbuck said, jerking his head toward Captain Dennison's Company A, which lay at the right of his line. "He reckoned he ought to run the battalion instead of me."

Truslow grinned. "You put him down?"

"I thought of what you would do to him, then did it."

"The hell you did. He's still alive, ain't he?"

Starbuck laughed. "And probably praying for a chance to put a bullet in my back."

"Captain Truslow!" Colonel Maitland, mounted on his horse and with a drawn sword resting on his shoulder, trotted out from the Legion's ranks. "To your company, if you please."

Truslow spat. "Never reckoned I'd say it to you," he said to Starbuck, "but you'd sure be welcome if you come back."

"I'm working on it," Starbuck said.

Truslow shambled back toward the Legion, ignoring Maitland, who trotted past him to raise a hand in greeting to Starbuck. "So you got them here?" Maitland said, gesturing at the Special Battalion.

"You ever thought I wouldn't?"

Maitland ignored the question. Instead he turned and watched the skirmishers at work. "No problems here?" he asked.

The question had been asked lightly, but Starbuck sensed the nervousness behind the elegant Colonel's words. This was Maitland's first proper battle, though it hardly counted as a battle to Starbuck. The enemy guns were gone, the waiting Yankee infantry was probably taut as a cocked revolver's leaf spring, and all this action promised to be was a simple advance with a few casualties as the price of the ground gained. What lay beyond the crest was another matter, but there should be no problems here. "Should be easy," Starbuck said. A bullet whistled overhead and Maitland gave an involuntary wince that he hoped Starbuck had not noticed. "You know what he was aiming at, Colonel?" Starbuck asked.

"Us, I assume."

"You," Starbuck said. "Man on a horse with a sword. There's a bastard up on that ridge with a long-barreled sharpshooting rifle. Right now he's pushing the loader back onto the muzzle and reckoning he'll do better next time."

Maitland gave a wan smile, but did not move. Instead he glanced at Billy Tumlin, then back to Starbuck. "I'm glad you got Tumlin."

"You know him?"

"My lads rescued him. I'd have liked to keep him for the Legion, but Swynyard insisted we do things by the book."

"I like him well enough," Starbuck said, "and my need of good officers is greater than yours, Colonel."

"You really think so?" Maitland asked pointedly.

"That sharpshooter, Colonel," Starbuck said, "is tapping the bullet through the loader now. Got a breech charged with real good powder, a nice measured amount, and he's reckoning on giving you four feet of correction for the wind and to fire a wee bit lower than last time. So tell me, do you want to be buried here or is there a Maitland family plot?"

"I think Hollywood Cemetery would be more appropriate," Maitland said lightly, though he looked uncomfortable. "Discretion, you're advising, is the better part of valor?" he asked.

"Seems to work that way."

"Then I'll bid you good day, Starbuck," the Colonel touched his hat, "don't want to expose you to sharpshooters!" He turned his horse away.

Starbuck unhitched his own rifle, from which he had finally blown out the damp powder by dint of working a wire through the nipple and trickling a tiny amount of dry powder into the clotted charge that had finally, reluctantly, exploded when he fired the gun. He loaded it, then pushed a percussion cap onto the cone, hoping it was not one of the bad caps that had suddenly started emerging from the Richmond factories. Rumor said that the Negro workers were deliberately sabotaging the army, and certainly there had been a spate of bad caps filled with anything except fulminate of mercury. He lowered the hammer onto the cap, slung the rifle again, and walked back toward the battalion.

Lieutenant Coffman, who had been appointed as an aide to Swynyard, ran down the back of the brigade's line. His pouches and scabbard flapped as he ran, while he held his hat on with one hand and carried a rifle in the other. "We're to advance!" he shouted at Colonel Maitland, then ran on toward Starbuck.

Starbuck waved to show that he had heard. "Battalion! Forward! Get them moving!" he shouted. With the Legion he would probably have gone ahead of the companies, but today he planned to follow his men into the fight, not out of fear, but simply to make certain they did advance. "Forward!" he shouted again, and he heard Dennison, Peel, and Cartwright echo the call. Billy Tumlin, revolver drawn, walked behind the right-hand companies. Tumlin had no company of his own, but Starbuck had given him supervision of those two right-hand companies, as well as asking him to look after the adjutant's responsibilities, for which Potter was signally inept. "Drive 'em on, Billy!" Starbuck shouted, then moved to his own place behind Lippincott's and Peel's companies. "Forward now! Smartly!"

The four-line companies walked forward willingly enough. The rebel artillery fired over their heads, the shells sounding like great barrels rolling across the sky. Some of the men were made nervous by that sound and by the percussive blasts of the guns themselves, but Starbuck shouted at them to hurry as they instinctively crouched beneath the huge noise. "They're on your side!" he shouted, "now keep going! Sergeants! Look to the line! Look to the line!" Some men were hurrying, either out of eagerness or else a desire to get the advance over, and their haste was making the battalion ragged.

The Legion had not started forward yet, or rather some companies had advanced when Starbuck's men began walking, but Maitland had called them back into alignment and now he fussily dressed the ranks while on either side of his regiment the other battalions of Swynyard's Brigade advanced down the gentle slope. The battle flags lifted in the small breeze. The day was ragged with explosions, punctured by the hammer of cannons, splintered by rifles, and filled now by the sound of hundreds of feet swishing through the grass. A skirmisher limped back toward the Special Battalion, another lay dead with a bullet in his brain and with his arms outflung like a man crucified. Someone, probably one of the skirmishers armed with an old Richmond Musket, had already taken the man's rifle.

The Legion started forward at last. Starbuck's right-hand company, under Dennison, was lagging, maybe in the hope that the Legion would catch up and support them. "Keep 'em up, Billy!" Starbuck shouted, "chivvy them!"

Billy Blythe lumbered over to Dennison's company and waved his arms impressively. This morning's action was not to Blythe's liking. He was happy enough to shelter in the Special Battalion until the tide of war took him close enough to the Yankee lines, but he had no wish to fight, and no wish whatsoever to fight as an infantryman, but he knew he would have to keep up the pretense for a good while yet. There was no point in jumping over to these Yankees in Harper's Ferry for they were surrounded and doomed. He must wait till the battalion was across the river and so nearer to McClellan's main force. Until then he had decided he would do as much as was needed and no more. "Keep them moving, Tom!" he called to Dennison, but did not push the men himself.

Dennison called for the company to speed up, but without any conviction in his voice, and though the company did pick up its heels, some of the men, led by Case, deliberately dawdled. Starbuck himself ran over. "Move!" he shouted. "Move! Faster!"

Case slowed even more.

Starbuck dragged out the revolver and put a bullet into the turf behind Case's heels. "Move!" he shouted, "move!" He fired a second bullet, this one well wide of anyone. He had not looked at Case, nor at any other man as he fired, for he had not wanted another confrontation, just to keep the company moving, and the two revolver shots had the happy effect of moving the laggards on like startled rabbits. "Keep them going, Billy!" Starbuck snarled. "Captain Dennison! Move them!"

Billy Blythe was too shocked to respond. He stumbled on, chivvying Dennison's company with his arms, suddenly more frightened of Starbuck than of the Yankees waiting on the ridge. The sheer force of Starbuck's anger had startled him, but he recognized it as genuine power. Starbuck was one of those men who could shift whole battalions by his personality and it was Starbuck's anger and resolve that was keeping the Yellowlegs moving across the valley under the rippling thunder of rebel shells that arched above their heads. Starbuck, Billy Blythe reflected, was the kind of man who got other men killed. Or got killed himself. "What's your name, Case?" Blythe fell into step beside Case who, to show his independence, had again started to lag a few paces behind the rest of A Company.

"Sounds like you already know it, Captain," Case said in a voice that was still hoarse from the terrible blow Starbuck had landed on his throat.

"I meant your Christian name, Sergeant," Blythe said, deliberately restoring Case's lost rank.

Case hesitated, then decided that Captain Tumlin's friendly tone deserved an answer. "Robert," he admitted.

"Hell, I got a brother called Bobby," Blythe lied. "Real nice fellow. Maybe a bit too fond of his liquor, but Lord, can our Bobby tell tales." He saw the sidelong look of resentful hatred that Case gave Starbuck. "You shoot him now, Sergeant," Blythe said quietly, "and there'll be a hundred witnesses and before you can spit on his grave you'll be standing under the guns of a firing squad. Just ain't the sensible thing to do, Bobby. Besides, you think he ain't got his eye on you? Just keep moving, Sergeant, keep it brisk. Look like we're trying to win the war, will you? That way he forgets you." Case said nothing, but he did hurry his pace fractionally. A rebel shell that had been fired too low screeched just overhead, making some of the men duck. The shell exploded among the battalion's skirmish line, making Captain Potter scurry long-legged for a patch of bushes. The battalion laughed. "Starbuck's pet clown," Billy Blythe said softly.

Case gave Blythe a long, hard look as it dawned on him that the battalion's second in command might really be an ally. "If Starbuck dies," Case broke his silence, "you get command, Captain."

"I sure do thank you for pointing that out to me, Bobby," Blythe said, "and if that ever did happen, why, I'd be looking for experienced men to be my officers. No glory boys, ain't that the phrase? Just good experienced men. Proper soldiers. Know what I mean? Jesus!" This final imprecation was startled from Blythe by the sudden thunder of Yankee cannons. Enemy shells screamed into the valley to explode among the advancing infantry in eruptions of dirt, smoke, flame, and flesh.

The Yankees had kept some concealed artillery on the crest and now the gunners had hauled aside the screen of branches that had masked the cannon and opened fire on the advancing infantry. Their opening salvo was of shells, but they reloaded with canister so that every shot was now like a giant blast of buckshot fanning out from the muzzle. The canister broke apart at the cannon's mouth to spread its charge of musket balls and Blythe, appalled, saw the grass ahead of the brigade flick as though a huge, invisible broom was whipping toward the attackers. There was a pattering noise like hard rain, then a sudden scream of wind as the cloud of musket balls slashed through the ranks. Men fell, spun, retched, or staggered. One man near Blythe had a rib sticking through the weave of his butternut coat. The man stared at the splintered white bone with a look of utter incomprehension, then bubbling pale blood welled at the rent in his coat and slopped down his belly. More blood flooded his gullet, he fell to his knees, tried to speak, then collapsed onto his face.

Blythe and Case found shelter behind a boulder, where they shared a cigar as the canister rattled and sighed and slapped the air around them. Dennison's company had scattered in confusion. A few kept going forward, others lay flat, but most ran panicking toward their left where the battalion's remaining companies offered an illusion of shelter. Case hunched down beside Blythe. "This is nothing to Sevastopol," he said. "The damned Ivans shelled us day and night, day and night. Never let up for a minute."

"Experienced men, that's who I'll be looking for," Blythe said, handing the cigar back to his companion.

Case grimaced. "So what do we do about Starbuck?" he asked.

"Just wait on the good Lord, Bobby, wait on the Lord and He will provide. Don't the good book say that?"

"Is that what you're doing?"

"I'm biding my time, Bobby, but that time will come. I don't see no point in being too eager in battle. Hell, we need heroes, but some of us have to live to go home at war's end. Otherwise the Yankees will be plowing our wives and we'll be rotting in our graves."

Case peered about the boulder, looking at Starbuck's distant figure. "Can't do much without a rifle."

"Rifles will be found. Hell, I don't want to command no battalion without rifles." Blythe laughed. He was lining up his allies and doing what he loved to do. He was surviving and thriving, and he reckoned he was good at that because he took a long view of life, and dying in battle was no part of that view. He would survive.

The crash of the enemy guns stunned Starbuck into silence. He had promised his men there would be no cannon and that they could walk through the valley without fear of slaughter, but now the enemy gunners were swabbing, reloading, and ramming another volley of canister.

The fear roared in Starbuck, weakening his legs and threatening to make him whimper like a whipped child. He kept going forward, not out of bravery, but because he seemed incapable of changing his direction or pace. He wanted to shout at Potter to take his skirmishers up the slope toward the gunners, but no sound would come, and so he stumbled blindly on with his mind groping for a prayer that he could not articulate. The terror was unmanning him, and that thought jarred him and he wondered if he could ever face a terror like it again. His foot slipped in a crusted patch of cow dung and vomit rimmed his throat. He fought it down, gasping for air, and he was sure that the men of the Special Battalion, whom he was leading into a murderous cannon fire just as he had led the Legion into a Yankee artillery trap at Chantilly, were despising him. He looked to his right and was astonished to see a vast gap in the brigade's line. The Legion was missing, though beyond the gap he could see the kinked line of attacking men sweeping across the smoke-smeared pasture beneath the red and blue flags. Dennison's company had vanished and half of Cartwright's was gone, but the rest of the battalion was still going forward, though no longer in neat ranks. The men had spread into the gap left by Dennison's company and some part of Starbuck's scrambled thoughts recognized that the scattering would protect them from the canister.

Another storm of missiles flicked at the ground and snatched men back like puppets caught on whiplashed strings. The Yankee gunners were doing well, aiming their canister just short of the advancing rebels so that the massed musket balls bounced up into their faces. The taste of vomit was sour in Starbuck's throat, but somehow he was managing to say the Twenty-Third Psalm to himself, and the realization that he was falling back on the faith of his father both surprised him and gave him a steadying moment. He saw that the battalion had crossed the floor of the valley and was beginning to climb its farther slope. The Northern infantry had almost disappeared, not by retreating, but by taking cover among the rocks and bushes on the crest. Below them the Yankee skirmishers were hurrying back up the slope between the smoke bursts of the rebel shells, then suddenly the crest itself was crowned by smoke as the defending infantry opened fire. The sound rippled across the valley, a splintering crackle that came an instant after the smoke appeared. The bullets whistled overhead, though a few thumped into bodies with a dull sound like a butcher's cleaver falling. Blood misted as men fell backward. "Keep moving!" someone shouted behind Starbuck. "Keep moving! Go on! Go on!" Starbuck was in the broken ranks now, pushing on ahead, his body behaving like a leader even if his mind was still reeling between terror and the need to keep his left-hand companies moving up the slope.

Confederate artillery at last targeted the Yankee guns and shell-bursts cracked in the hot air above the sweating gunners. "Come on!" Starbuck screamed, amazed he could speak at all, "come on!" Every nerve in his body was screaming for him to turn and run, to find a hole and shelter for the rest of his life while the world went mad about him, but the shreds of pride and stubbornness kept him going and even made him go faster. He turned to shout encouragement to his stark-faced, clumsy men encumbered by bedrolls and packs and pouches and scabbards so that they lumbered forward with open mouths. "Come on!" he called, anger in his voice, though the anger was only at himself. The battalion was still two hundred yards from the crest, too far to order the charge, but he sensed that if he did not keep the battalion moving now, then it would go to ground and refuse to advance ever again. The Yellowlegs had already achieved far more than they had in their first battle, but to wipe the stain off their reputation they needed to keep going to victory. Rebel shells were screaming close overhead, their explosions punching the eardrums and throwing up fountains of dirt and smoke along the crest. The Yankee rifle fire had become ragged as men fired whenever they were loaded and Starbuck, seeing how sporadic were the bursts of muzzle smoke, realized that there was little more than a heavy skirmish line left on the crest. The Yankees were not going to fight for this ridgeline, but just inflict some casualties before slipping away and that thought gave him encouragement. Maybe he would not die in this cow-dunged pasture, but maybe he would give the despised battalion the victory it so badly needed, and he shouted again for his men to keep going forward, only this time the shout turned into a rebel yell and suddenly the remaining attackers were shrilling the sound with him as they broke into a clumsy run.

The canister fire had stopped. Starbuck was aware of only the sounds he was making himself. The thump of boots, the harsh scrape of breath, the desperate yelping of the war cry, the clank of his tin mug against the cartridge box, the slapping of the revolver holster against the back of his thigh. Something was burning on the crest, pumping a thick smoke into the air. Another rebel shell burst, its blast bending a bush sideways and shredding leaves among the smoke. Potter's men were in the ranks now and Potter himself was running close to Starbuck and screaming like a wild man. Starbuck blundered through a scorched, smoking patch where a shell had exploded. A Yankee skirmisher lay beyond, his head back, his hands curled, and his guts spilt into the churned dirt. Men were at last visible on the crest. They stood, aimed, fired, then dropped to reload. A bullet whistled its eerie minie sound near Starbuck, and he began to scream like Potter, a feral, terrible noise that came from the battle-mix of terror and glee. All he wanted to do now was punish the bastards who had so nearly unmanned him. He wanted to kill and kill.

"Come on!" he shouted, drawing out the last word as at last the attackers reached the gentle crest. Colonel Swynyard had been wrong and there were rifle pits along the ridge, but the Yankees were already abandoning them and going back to their next defense line, which lay on a farther ridge. The Yankee cannon were being dragged by horses back to that ridge where more guns waited and more infantry, but Starbuck had no orders to attack that far ridge. His job had been to push the Northern forces off this ridge and it was done, and he was running into clear air, blessed air, air untouched by bullets or shells, though he knew it would only be seconds before the far guns opened fire.

"Kill them!" he shouted, then leapt into a vacated rifle pit and leveled his rifle across the pile of soil at its rear. He aimed at a retreating Yankee and pulled the trigger. The hammer dropped onto a useless percussion cap and he swore, broke a fingernail levering the cap away, put another in its place, and tried again. The rifle hammered into his shoulder and its cloud of smoke hid his target. Potter was beside him, laughing. The rest of the battalion, those who had stayed the course, were in the other abandoned rifle pits and firing at the Yankee infantry as they hurried away.

The far Yankee cannon opened fire. The shells flashed overhead and thumped behind as Swynyard's Brigade went to ground on the captured ridge. Starbuck reloaded the rifle then turned to see where his men were. He could see the color sticking up from a rifle pit, he could see a scatter of wounded men crawling slowly on the slope beyond, and he could see the Legion still climbing the hill. He turned to look north and was amazed to see the land drop away to where, between the shoulders of two humped hills, he could glimpse a silver river sliding eastward. Beyond the river, in Maryland, there was smoke on the hills where other Confederate troops were tightening Jackson's grim ring about Harper's Ferry.

"Sweet Jesus, but I enjoyed that," Potter said.

Starbuck meant to tell him that he should have taken his skirmishers up against the gunners, but instead he vomited. He emptied his belly into the floor of the rifle pit. "Jesus," he said when he had finished heaving. "Jesus."

"Here," Potter handed him a canteen, "it's only water."

Starbuck rinsed out his mouth, spat, then drank. "I'm sorry," he said to Potter.

"Something you ate," Potter suggested tactfully.

"Fear," Starbuck said harshly.

A shell banged into the turf a few yards ahead of their pit. It did not explode, but instead tumbled end over end to embed itself in the spoil thrown up by the Yankee diggers. "I think we might seek other quarters," Potter said, eyeing the shell. The air above the metal shimmered from the heat of the missile's passage.

"Go on," Starbuck said. "I'll join you." Once alone he squatted in the pit, pants about his ankles, and voided his body. He was sweating and shaking. The ground thumped softly from the fall of the shells. The sky above the pit was laced with smoke, but suddenly the fear drained away and Starbuck stood and clumsily pulled up his pants, belted them, then buttoned his fraying jacket and rebuckled his revolver belt and straightened his bedroll. He climbed out of the pit and, with shouldered rifle, walked among the other pits to congratulate his men. He told them they had done well, told them he was proud of them, and then he walked back down the slope to watch his stragglers climb sheepishly toward the crest. Captain Dennison was pretending to be busy as he chivvied the laggards, but he took care to avoid Starbuck, though Captain Tumlin walked eagerly across the slope with his hand outstretched.

"Hell, Starbuck, if you ain't the bravest man I ever saw then my name's not Tumlin," Blythe said.

Starbuck ignored both the outstretched hand and the compliment. "What happened to your companies?" he asked coldly.

Tumlin seemed unconcerned by Starbuck's brusqueness. "I managed to keep most of Cartwright's boys moving, but A Company?" He spat. "They're mules, Starbuck, mules. I got up here once, went back for the bastards and still they weren't moving. Did my best. Hell, Starbuck, I know you're disappointed, but I did my God honest best."

"I'm sure." Starbuck was convinced of Tumlin's sincerity. "Sorry, Billy."

"You look kind of washed up, Starbuck."

"Something I ate, Billy, nothing worse." Starbuck found a broken cigar in his pouch and lit the largest remnant. "You want to make me a list of the casualties, Billy?" he asked, then walked back to the crest as the Yankee cannon fire increased in intensity, but the shells were no longer aimed at the captured ridge, but toward a second rebel attack that was coming from their left flank. Swynyard's men had cleared the ridge to prevent its defending Yankees from flanking that second attack, which was the real assault intended to take the high ground that formed the southern skyline of Harper's Ferry. The sound of the battle thumped and snapped, filling the air with gray-white smoke.

Starbuck pulled the bayonet off his rifle as he watched the Legion climb the last few yards. Maitland had deliberately held them back from the canister fire, and the men knew it, and while they were doubtless grateful to have been spared the last stuttering fire of the Yankee's melting resistance, they also looked ashamed. The despised Yellowlegs had outperformed them, and Starbuck's men called jeering greetings to the arriving Legion. Starbuck did not try to stop them, though he knew that Dennison's company did not deserve the reward of a little pride. "Captain Dennison!" Starbuck shouted.

Dennison slouched along the crest where his men were spreading into empty rifle pits. Dennison expected a reprimand, but instead Starbuck pointed across the crest to the rifle pit he had vacated. "Your men can form the picket line," he said. "Skirmish order a hundred paces down the hill. You can stay up here." He pointed toward the rifle pit that he and Potter had vacated. "Make that rifle pit your headquarters."

"Yes, sir."

"Don't worry about the shell. It's dead. Go on, hurry. Jump in before some bastard sharpshooter starts practicing on you."

"Yes, sir," Dennison said, then shouted at his men to follow him to the forward slope of the hill. Starbuck watched as Dennison jumped into the pit, then he turned away.

"What are you laughing at, Nate?" Colonel Swynyard, his horse abandoned for the battle's duration, came striding along the hill.

"Just a petty revenge, sir." He was ashamed of it now, but he could not undo the juvenile prank. "Nothing to worry you," he added.

"Your lads did well," Swynyard said, "real well, and I guess they'll prove just as sound when we have to fight a proper battle. Well done, Nate, well done." He paused. "You know why the Legion was slow?"

"No, sir."

"Then I'd better find out," he said grimly and paced toward Maitland.

And Starbuck tipped back his hat and wiped the sweat off his face. His battalion had fought its first proper fight. The Yellowlegs had not run away and life seemed suddenly sweet.

ADAM FAULCONER HAD ONCE OPPOSED THE WAR. Before it began, when debate had raged like prairie fire across America, he had been passionate in his quest for peace, but that passion had been overwhelmed by the bitterness of his country's division. Adam had then returned home to fight for his native state, but he could find no allegiance there. His love stayed with a *United* States and so, risking breaking his family's heart, he had crossed the lines and replaced his gray coat with a blue.

He had not regained his passion in the North. Instead he had found a dull anger that served as a replacement for what he now perceived had been youthful fervor touched with youthful ignorance. One man, Lyman Thorne had told Adam, can make a difference, and Adam wanted to be that man. He wanted the war to end, but he wanted it to end with complete Northern victory. The man who had once opposed war now embraced it like a lover, for war would be God's punishment on the South. And the Southerners, Adam believed, had to be punished, not because they were at the heart of American slavery, but because they had broken the Union and so defiled what Adam knew to be God's country. The South was the enemy of God, and Adam His self-appointed champion.

But a champion who felt useless. True, Colonel Thorne had given him a task and it was a task that could make the difference Adam craved, but Thorne had been unable to give Adam any guidance as to how that task might be completed. He was living by hope, not by plans, and felt nothing but frustration.

The frustration was made worse by General McClellan's sluggishness. News arrived on Thursday afternoon that the rebel army had finally abandoned Frederick City to march westward, but McClellan merely filed the report and instead spoke about the need to preserve Washington. The withdrawal from Frederick could be a ruse, he claimed, a device to suck the 100,000 men of the federal army away from Washington while a second army of rebels poured across the lower Potomac to engulf the capital. Or else, McClellan feared, the rebel withdrawal might be merely a bait to draw the Northern army out of its camps and onto a battlefield of Lee's choosing, and Lee, McClellan now believed, possessed 200,000 fighting men; 200,000 wolf-colored demons who attacked with fearful shrill cries and a desperate ferocity. McClellan would not risk that ferocity, nor uncover Washington. He would be steady.

And so, while the rebels vanished beyond the barrier of mountains that lay west of Frederick City, McClellan's army inched its way forward. There was no pursuit of the rebels and even the news that the fifteen thousand men at Harper's Ferry were under siege did not provoke the Young Napoleon into haste. Harper's Ferry must look after itself while McClellan, fearing every rumor, tried to protect his army against all eventualities. The army, he decreed, would advance on a broad front, but there was to be no unseemly haste. Caution ruled.

Adam had no say in the matter. Adam was an unwanted major attached to McClellan's headquarters and Adam's opinion was of no interest to anyone, least of all to Allen Pinkerton, who commanded McClellan's Secret Service Bureau. Adam attempted to influence Pinkerton, and through Pinkerton, McClellan, by arguing with Pinkerton's chief of staff, who was a friend of Adam's and the older brother of Adam's erstwhile friend, Nate Starbuck. James Starbuck was utterly unlike Nate. He was a Boston lawyer, honest, careful, and conscientious, and his cautious nature only reinforced Pinkerton's inflated estimates of the rebel's numbers. Adam, arguing with James at supper on the Thursday evening when they had first heard about the rebels leaving Frederick City, protested that Lee could not possibly muster 200,000 men, not even 100,000. "Maybe sixty or seventy thousand," Adam said, "but probably no more than fifty."

James laughed at the figure. "We are meticulous, Adam, meticulous. Give us credit for that. We have hundreds of reports! I know, I collate them. I compare them."

"Reports from who?" Adam demanded.

"You know I can't say," James said reprovingly. He paused to extract a scrap of chicken bone from between his teeth then laid the bone chip carefully on the edge of his plate. "But the contrabands tell the same tale, the exact same tale. I interviewed two more today." The contrabands were escaped slaves who were brought to Pinkerton's tents and quizzed about the rebel forces. They all told the same story; thousands upon thousands of rebels, endless marching columns and vast guns crushing the dusty roads beneath their iron-rimmed wheels. "Even if we allow for some small exaggeration," James said with a flourish of his fork, "we must still credit Lee with a hundred and seventy thousand. And that's far more men than we have!"

Adam sighed. He had ridden with the rebel army as late as the spring campaign and knew there could never be 170,000 men in gray coats. "How many were bivouacked at Frederick City?" he asked.

James looked owlishly solemn. "At least a hundred thousand. We have direct reports from the town."

Adam suspected the townspeople's reports were about as much use as the rumors printed in the newspapers. "What does our cavalry say?" he asked.

James frowned and probed his cheek with a forefinger before extracting another sliver of bone. "Very skeletal, this chicken," he said disapprovingly.

"Maybe it's rabbit," Adam said. "So what did the cavalry say?"

James peered at his food in the candlelight. "Don't think it's rabbit. Rabbits don't possess wishbones, do they? I'm sure they don't. And I don't think our cavalry were ordered as far as Frederick City today. In fact, I'm sure they weren't. Maybe the problem is that our cooks can't joint chickens properly. I found one kitchen fellow attacking a carcass with a cleaver! Can you credit that? With a cleaver! No attempt to joint the bird, just hacking it apart. Never seen such behavior. Wasn't even plucked properly either. I told him, do as your mother does, I said, run the skin over a candle flame and that will get rid of the feather-gristle, but I don't think he listened."

"So why don't you and I go to Frederick City," Adam ignored the culinary problems, "tomorrow morning. At dawn."

James blinked at Adam. "For what purpose?"

"Because if a hundred thousand men were encamped at Frederick," Adam said, "they'll have left traces. Fire-marks. Say ten men to a campfire? So if we count the scorched patches in the fields we'll have a shrewd idea of Lee's numbers."

James laughed gently. "My dear Adam, do you have any idea how long it would take two men to count ten thousand burned patches of grass?" He shook his head. "I appreciate your interest, I surely do, but I don't think we need, if you'll forgive my bluntness, amateur help in the Secret Service. Mind you, if you can help us with some signaling problems, we would be grateful. You're something of an expert on telegraphy, aren't you? Our fellows seem unable to grasp the equipment. They probably send their messages with cleavers!" He snorted with amusement at the thought.

But Adam had no time for heavy-fisted telegraphers, but only to indulge his dull anger at the slowness of the North's army and the plodding obtuseness of its Secret Service. He decided he would ride to Frederick City himself in the dawn, not to count fire patches, but to talk to the people in the town who might give him some indication of Lee's numbers. Civilians, Adam knew, usually overestimated numbers of troops, but maybe there was someone in the town who could give him some facts that the U.S. Cavalry had not found time to seek out themselves.

He saddled his horse before the dawn and was well through the picket line by the time the sun blazed up behind to cast the horse and rider's shadow long across the verge of the white dusty road. He breakfasted as he rode, eating bread and honey and drinking cold tea as his path wended north eastward in parallel with the unfinished railbed of the Metropolitan Rail Road. He felt redundant and useless. In truth he had small purpose for visiting Frederick, for he knew that whatever he discovered, if he found anything at all, would be discounted by Pinkerton's staff, who were busy constructing their own elaborate picture of the rebel army, but Adam was filling in time because any activity was better than another indolent day in McClellan's camp.

The countryside was curiously silent. It was the absence of cocks crowing that was strange, but that, Adam knew, was because rebel foragers must have combed these gentle farms for their supplies. It would be a hungry winter in Maryland.

He watered his horse at Middlebrook, then rode on past the bottomland where he had outgalloped the rebel patrol. His spirits, which had been depressed by the futility of his assignment, began to rise with the sun as he rode through the good country. Haystacks stood neatly in well-tended fields and woodlots were stacked high, though doubtless the advancing army would soon make short work of all that hard labor. It was an image of peace and it warmed Adam's soul that now soared into a sunlit daydream of the war's ending. He doubted he could go back to Virginia, and doubted that he even wanted to return. Instead, he thought, he would go to New England and study for the ministry. He had a vision of a shingled town built about a steepling white church amidst the heavy woods; a place of honesty and hard work, a place where a man could study and preach and minister and write. He saw a study heavy with books, and maybe with his father's ivory-hilted saber, which Adam had captured and now wore at his side, hanging above the fireplace. The saber had been a gift to Adam's great-grandfather from Lafayette, and its blade was handsomely inscribed. "To my friend Cornelius Faulconer," the inscription read in French, "who joined me in the fight for liberty, Lafayette," and Adam imagined his own great-grandchildren treasuring the weapon as a memento of two wars in which virtue had triumphed over evil. He envisioned a kitchen with a heavy black range, steaming pots, drying herbs, and heaped bowls of fruit picked from his own yard. He thought of Julia Gordon in Richmond, and wondered if at the war's ending she would acknowledge the South's sins and come north to share his imagined haven in the deep, pious silence of the New England woods.

These thoughts carried him through Clarkstown, Hyattstown, and Urbana, until at last he crossed the Baltimore and Ohio. The rebels had prized up the rails and uprooted the ties to leave a scar across the good land, but Adam knew the North's engineers would soon repair the track and have the cars running east and west again. Ahead of Adam now was Frederick City, but all around him was nothing but deserted fields dotted with the pale marks where tents had stood and the dark smears where fires had burned. The rebels had vanished.

It was late morning when he entered the town. "Hey! Soldier!" a woman called, spotting Adam's blue coat, "where are the rest of you?"

"They're coming, ma'am," Adam answered, courteously touching the brim of his hat.

"Lee's boys are gone, all gone," the woman said, then plunged her washing down the scrub board. "Thought you'd be here sooner."

The townsfolk greeted Adam happily. There were more Northern sympathizers than rebel adherents in the town, and the appearance of a single Yankee soldier was sufficient to prompt a display of Stars and Stripes. The flags were hung from upper story windows or hoisted on makeshift poles. Men came to shake Adam's hand and some pressed gifts on him; cigars or flasks of whiskey. Adam tried to refuse the gifts, but was embarrassed by his own apparent ingratitude and so he pretended to drink from one flask, then thrust a handful of the cigars into a coat pocket. He dismounted at Main Street. A dozen people were all talking at once to him, telling him how the rebels had gone, telling him how large their army had been, but admitting that the Southern forces had not laid the town to waste. They had expected to be pillaged, but the rebels had behaved themselves, even if they had insisted on paying for their supplies with Confederate money that was next to worthless. The townsfolk wanted to know when McClellan's army would arrive and when the rebel invasion would be whipped back out of the rest of Maryland. Adam, as he tried to cope with this blizzard of talk, noticed how some people crossed the street to avoid him and others even spat as he passed. The loyalties of Frederick, despite the display of Northern flags, was plainly confused.

Adam wanted to find the mayor or a selectman, but instead he was pressed to go into a nearby tavern and celebrate his one-man liberation of the town. Adam shook his head. He was close to the post office and he decided that the postmaster, being a federal official, might be a source of some authoritative information, and so he tied his horse's reins to a hitching post, took Thorne's gold from the saddlebag to protect it from thieves and, shaking off the importunate crowd, edged into the office. "Sweet Lord above," a woman greeted his appearance, "so you got here."

"Only me, I'm afraid," Adam said, and asked if the postmaster was available.

"Jack!" the woman called, then gestured at the empty tables. "No business this last week," she explained. "Guess we'll be catching up soon enough."

"I guess," Adam said, then greeted the postmaster, a big, red-bearded man who emerged from a small office at the back of the building. Some townsfolk had crowded into the post office behind Adam and, to lose their ebullient company, Adam followed the postmaster to the tiny office.

The man proved less than helpful. "I can tell you there was a mighty number of the rogues," he told Adam, "but how many?" He shrugged. "Thousands. Thousands and thousands. What did you say your name was?"

"Major Adam Faulconer."

The postmaster stared at Adam with a look close to suspicion. "You're a major? Not a captain?"

It seemed an odd question, but Adam confirmed his rank. "I was promoted a week ago," he explained. He had hung Thorne's bag of gold coins from his belt and the dull chink of the coins embarrassed him.

The postmaster seemed not to notice the sound of the money. "What's your posting, Major?" he asked.

"I'm at General McClellan's headquarters."

"Then I guess you knew to come here, Major," the postmaster said mysteriously, and unlocked a desk drawer out of which he took a stiff brown envelope that, to Adam's astonishment, had his name written on it. The handwriting was in capital letters and was unfamiliar to Adam, but he felt a tremor of excitement as he pulled the envelope open and unfolded the single sheet of paper.

The excitement turned to astonishment, almost to disbelief, as he read the Special Order. At first, scanning the opening two paragraphs, he wondered why anyone should have bothered to send him what seemed nothing more than a set of routine housekeeping instructions, but then he came to the third paragraph and, barely able to contain his excitement, he saw that he had been given all of the rebels' dispositions. He had in his hand the whole strategy of the rebel army, the positions of every last division in Lee's forces. The paper was gold, pure unalloyed gold, for Robert Lee had scattered his army. Part was at Harper's Ferry, parts were moving north toward Pennsylvania, and others were presumably guarding the road between. Adam read the order twice and suddenly knew he was not serving his country in vain. Even McClellan, given this paper, would surely realize the opportunity. The Young Napoleon could fight each part of Lee's army separately, defeating them one after the other until the rebellion, at least in Virginia and its neighboring states, would be utterly destroyed. "Who gave this to you?" Adam asked the postmaster.

"Didn't give his name."

"But he was a rebel officer?"

"He was." The postmaster paused. "I reckoned it was important, because the fellow kind of acted strange. So I kept it separate from the other letters."

Suppose it was a trap? Adam stared at the signature, R. H. Chilton. He knew Chilton, though not well. Was this a lure? But that was not his decision to make. "What did the man look like?" he asked the postmaster.

The man shrugged. "Small," he said, "plumpish. A bit, how would you say? Delicate? Like he wasn't supposed to be a soldier."

"Did he have a beard?"

"None."

Delaney? Adam thought. Belvedere Delaney? Not that the identity of Thorne's spy mattered now, all that mattered was that this precious piece of paper should get back safe to McClellan. "Thank you," Adam said fervently, then he picked up the discarded envelope, but in his haste he tore it as he tried to put the order back inside.

"Use this." The postmaster gave him a larger envelope, which Adam used to hide the order. He went to put the envelope in his pocket, but found it filled with cigars.

"Have these, please," Adam said, spilling the cigars on the desk.

"Not all of them!" the postmaster protested Adam's generosity.

"I've more than enough," Adam said. He did not smoke, but Lyman Thorne enjoyed his cigars, so Adam put the last three into the envelope before shaking the postmaster's hand. "Thank you again," he said fervently.

He hurried back to the street where he thrust the curious onlookers aside and pulled himself into the saddle. He transferred the gold back to its saddlebag and pushed his horse through the crowd until at last he broke free of them and could spur down the street toward the rail depot. A butcher in a bloodied apron came out of a shed as Adam trotted past. "You want to be careful, soldier!" the butcher shouted. "There were some bushwhackers west of the town not long ago."

Adam reined in. "Rebels?" he asked.

"Weren't wearing blue," the butcher said.

"I thought the rebels were gone?"

"These are bastards from over the river. Come to pick up some plunder, like as not. But they were well to the west when I saw them, but they'll be circling round to the south to look at the rail depot. You go out that road," the man pointed due east, "and you'll be well clear of them. After ten or twelve miles you'll come to Ridgeville and you can turn south there."

"Thank you," Adam said, then he turned the horse, kicked his heels back, and urged the horse into a trot. He had a long journey ahead and he had to save his mare's strength and so he curbed his instinct to spur her into a canter. He touched his pocket, scarce daring to believe what was hidden there. Delaney? Was Delaney the traitor? And Adam was shocked at himself for having used the word "traitor," even in his thoughts, for whoever had sent the order was no traitor to the United States. But was it Delaney? Somehow Adam could not imagine the foppish, clever lawyer as a spy, but he could think of no one else who fit both the postmaster's description of the rebel officer and Colonel Thorne's portrait of his reluctant agent. Delaney, the sly Richmond lawyer with the glib tongue, skin-deep smile, and watchful eyes.

Adam's astonishment took him past a schoolhouse, then by an empty livery stable and a Negro chapel. He splashed through a ford and spurred up the far bank onto a long stretch of road that left the town behind to run between fields blotched with the scars left by rebel camps. He passed a small orchard that had been stripped bare by soldiers and it was just past that orchard, where the road bent leftward and began to run gently down toward the Linganore Run, that he saw the rebel horsemen.

He reined in. The five men were a quarter mile away, motionless, and watching him almost as if they had been expecting him. Two of the horsemen were on the road, one was well to the north, while the others were in the pasture south of the road. For a few seconds the six men all watched each other without moving, then Adam wrenched his mare's head around and spurred her back toward the town.

He had thought of trying to outrun the handful of rebels, but his horse had covered too many miles on a hot day to be capable of a lung-stretching gallop across miles of country. A McClellan-like caution was the best plan and so he kicked his heels to urge the mare back past the plundered orchard.

Adam felt a tremor run through the mare, then she stumbled, and he had to lean to his right to help her keep her balance. For a second he thought she must have put a foot into a hole, but then the sound of the shot arrived. He kicked his heels back again and the mare tried to respond, but a bullet had hamstrung one of her back legs and there was

no more she could do for him. She tried one last gallant pace, then buckled and whinnied aloud with the pain. Her blood splashed bright on the
dusty road.

Adam kicked his feet free of the stirrups. The dying echo of the single carbine shot crackled about the hot countryside, fading into the heat
haze that cloaked the day. He glanced behind and saw the five rebels
spurring toward him. He pulled the gold free, then scrambled away
from the thrashing horse. He ran into the trees and drew his revolver.
Sweat stung his eyes. The horse was crying pitifully, her hooves banging
on the road as she fought against the pain in her leg.

Adam steadied himself against the trunk of an apple tree and leveled
the revolver. The enemy was still two hundred yards away, a hopelessly
long shot for a revolver, but he might be as lucky as they had been with
their one fateful shot and so he emptied the cylinder chamber by chamber, aiming at the two closest men who were advancing on the road
itself. His view of the enemy was blocked by the smoke of his shots and
he had no idea where his bullets were going. He fired his last round,
then ran back into the orchard where he crouched, panting, as he
reloaded the gun. He was hurrying, and so he fumbled with the cartridges before forcing himself to be methodical. Fear battered him, but
he kept it at bay by reminding himself of the stolen order in his pocket.
He had to survive.

He pushed percussion caps onto the revolver's cones, then peered
eastward. The two horsemen on the road had paused, reluctant to ride
closer to his fire, but the other three men had vanished and Adam suddenly realized they must be riding north and south to outflank him. He
would be trapped in the orchard and hunted down like a cornered fox.

He ran to the orchard's western edge. The town did not look so far
away and there were stands of trees, a straggling hedge, and the remnants of a haystack to give him cover. He looked left and right and could
see no enemy and so, committing his safety to God, he ran into the sunlight.

He aimed for the haystack that had been pulled apart by rebels seeking bedding, but there was enough hay left to offer hiding while he gathered his breath for the next stretch back to Frederick. Would any

townsfolk hear the gunfire and come to his aid? He ran hard, expecting to hear the whistle of a bullet at any second, then threw himself into the warm, scented hay where he dragged great breaths of humid air into his lungs.

Two rebel horsemen appeared to the south a second or two after Adam had taken cover. The two rebels paused, staring at the orchard, and Adam was tempted to keep running, but knew they would spot him as soon as he left the broken stack. He twisted in his nest of hay to look north, but he could see no enemy there, but then a rumble of hooves made him look south again to see a whole troop of enemy horsemen spurring toward the orchard. The sound of the shots had not brought the townsfolk, but a whole pack of rebel soldiers instead.

They were not Jeb Stuart's cavalry. These men, as the butcher had said, were bushwhackers. They were from the northern counties of Virginia, farmers by day and fighters by night, only on this day they had given up farming to come north and see what pickings could be gleaned from the abandoned rebel camps and to ambush any Northern cavalry patrols probing west toward Lee's army. Their uniforms were the same coats they wore when they wrestled with a plow or gelded a calf, their weapons were hunting rifles and ox-killing pistols, while their hatred of Yankees had been intensified by the frequent federal invasions of their farmland. They had been robbed, they had been insulted, they had been impoverished, and now, with the fervor of starving dogs seeking carrion, they sought revenge.

Adam checked the percussion caps on his revolver, then looked up to see the newly arrived troop trotting toward the orchard. Dust from the hay clung to the grease on Adam's gun while the smell of the dry grass reminded him of childhood games with his sister Anna, then, with a shameful pang, an unwanted memory came to his mind of the time when he had glimpsed his father clamber off a haystack, carrying his clothes on his arm, then turn to give a hand to Bessie. She had been a house slave then. A year later his father had freed all his slaves, making them servants instead, but for years Adam had been frightened of Bessie because of what he had seen. He had been confused at the time, but later he was tormented by the memories of her lissome, gleaming black body and the bright sound of her laughter as she had jumped down beside his father and pulled her pale blue dress over her head. Adam hated slavery.

But the men who hunted him now, he knew, were no slaveowners. They had barely enough money to own a horse, let alone a Negro, and they did not fight to preserve slavery, but to defend their land, and in that defense they were grim and unforgiving. He wriggled deeper into the hay, pulling great clumps of it over his body, but keeping a loophole free through which he could watch his pursuers.

The rebels had surrounded the orchard and now the majority of them dismounted, hitched their horses to tree trunks, and walked into the apple grove with rifles leveled. Adam's horse was still whinnying with pain, but a sudden shot brought silence. None of the mounted rebels who had stayed outside the orchard was looking toward the haystack and that lack of vigilance persuaded Adam to twist round and look for an escape route. There was a patch of dead ground a hundred paces away, and beyond it, in a field of long grass, a surviving rail fence offered a hint of cover that might let him work his way back to the town, where he would be much safer than in this warm but treacherous refuge. When the rebels discovered that he had escaped from the orchard they were bound to search the haystack and Adam did not want to be found hiding like a child and so he crawled to the haystack's edge, looked back once to check that he was unobserved, then burst out of the hay and ran in a low crouch toward the dead ground.

His saber scabbard tangled in his legs, making him sprawl noisily onto the grass. He unbuckled the saber's belt, let it fall away, then ran on. He heard the shout almost at once and ran as fast as he could. He should have twisted and turned like a beast trying to escape pursuing dogs, but he ran straight toward the dead ground and so gave the rebel who had first spotted him an easy target.

The rebel fired and the bullet slammed into Adam's right buttock. The sledgehammer force of the shot twisted Adam round and threw him forward so that he slid on his back into the shallow valley where he was momentarily hidden. There was blood on the grass, pain in his hip, and tears in his eyes. He gritted his teeth and forced himself upright.

The pain was terrible, like a poisoned mist that clouded his thoughts, but he retained enough sense to know that he must save the stolen order. He limped north, intent on reaching the rail fence even though he knew it offered him no salvation now, but he was convinced that if he could just reach the fence he would somehow survive. He forced himself on, though every time he put his weight on his right leg he gave an involuntary cry of agony. Behind him he could hear the whooping calls and galloping hooves of the rebels.

He was trapped. He dropped the bag of gold from his belt, hoping that the loss of its weight would give him speed, but the pain was getting worse and, in a moment of clarity, he knew there was no chance of escape now. The hooves were getting louder. He had seconds, just seconds, to decide what to do, but all that was left was sheer despair and so he staggered up the hollow's far lip, where he plucked the envelope with its cigars and the special order from his pocket, then skimmed it into the long grass. A bullet stung the air near him as he twisted back toward the lower ground. The envelope had fallen in the meadow's long grass and Adam could only pray that the rebels had not seen him discard it and would not find it. McClellan's army must come to these fields in time and maybe the order would be discovered. Or maybe not, but Adam had done what he could and now, he knew, he must suffer capture.

He struggled another dozen paces eastward, then collapsed. His right pant leg was soaked in blood. He lifted the revolver, waiting for his enemies to appear, and he felt a terrible regret for all he had missed in his life. He had never taken a girl into a haystack. He had been dutiful, so very dutiful, and now he could have wept for all his uncommitted sins, and that thought made him close his eyes and utter a prayer for forgiveness.

His eyes were still closed as the rebels gathered about him. They were wiry, hard-faced men who smelled of tobacco, manure, horses, and leather. They slid out of their saddles and one man plucked the revolver from Adam's nerveless fingers. The gun had been his father's and was an English-made Adams, a beautifully engineered weapon with ivory grips, and the rebel who had taken it gave a yelp of triumph as he recognized the gun's quality.

"Got ourselves a Yankee major," a second man said, peering at Adam's badges. "A real major."

Someone kicked Adam's right leg to see if he was conscious. Adam cried aloud in pain and opened his eyes to see a ring of bearded, sun-tanned faces. One of the men stooped and began searching Adam's pockets, pulling his coat roughly and jarring pain through Adam's side with each tug. "A doctor, please," Adam managed to say.

"Sorry son of a bitch, ain't he?" a man said, then laughed.

Another man had found the gold and that caused new whoops of excitement, and then a third man brought the wondrous saber from the field where Adam had discarded the blade. The leader of the rebels, a thin, clean-shaven man, took the saber and slid it from the scabbard. He read the inscription and, though he knew no French, he could recognize the names. "Faulconer," he said aloud, then, with wonder in his voice, "Lafayette! Son of a bitch." The man wore a black hilted saber at his side, a weapon as crude as a butcher's blade, and now he replaced it with Adam's belt and scabbard before looking again at the inscription on the French made blade. "Faulconer. That's a Virginia name."

"His name's Faulconer," the man who had searched Adam said. He had found the letter from the Inspector General's Department in Washington that appointed Adam to McClellan's army. The letter stated he was inspecting signal arrangements and it was the piece of paper designed by Colonel Thorne to explain Adam's presence in the Federal Headquarters. Now it only served to make things worse.

"What the hell's a signal inspector doing in Frederick?" the rebel leader asked.

"And carrying gold," another man added.

The leader squatted at Adam's feet and pushed the saber's tip into the underside of Adam's chin. "Are you a Virginian, Major?"

Adam stared up at the blue sky.

"I asked you a question, boy," the leader said, giving the saber a prod.

"An American," Adam said. He was feeling faint. He could sense the blood flowing out of his wound, seeping into the ground and making him delirious, but the pain was magically subsiding. He was warm, almost comfortable. "I'm an American," he managed to say.

"Hell, we're all Americans," the rebels' leader said. "But are you a Virginian?"

Adam said nothing. He was thinking of Bessie, who had looked so black and slim and beautiful as she had pulled the blue dress over her smiling face. He thought of Julia Gordon in Richmond. He thought of the dream in New England; the preacher's house, the books, the kitchen, the sound of children laughing in a tree-shaded yard.

"Son of a bitch is crying," one of the rebels crowed.

"So would you if your ass had been shot off," another man said, provoking a gust of laughter.

"Hell of a shot, Sam," a third man said admiringly, "must have been forty rods if it was an inch."

"Fifty at least," Sam said.

The saber pricked at Adam's chin. "What were you doing here, Major?"

"No damn good," one of the rebels answered for Adam, then laughed.

"Son of a bitch," the rebel leader said, then stood and sheathed the lovely saber. He pulled out his revolver and aimed it at Adam's head. "I don't have all day, Major, and nor do you, and I ain't got the patience to wait on you seeing sense. So talk now, you son of a bitch. Just what were you doing here?"

Adam closed his eyes. In heaven, he was telling himself, there would be no tears and no pain and no regrets. No tangle of crossed allegiances. No war. No slavery. There would just be joy and peace and endless calm happiness. He smiled. Such happiness in heaven, he thought, such warm, dreamy happiness.

"He ain't going to talk," a man said.

"He's Faulconer's son," a new voice intervened. "You remember? The son of a bitch deserted in the spring."

"Faulconers never were any damned good," a voice growled, "nigger-loving rich bastards."

The rebel leader fired. The sound of the shot crackled along the hollow and faded as the bullet thumped with a terrible force into the dirt beside Adam's head. "What's your name?" the leader demanded.

Adam opened his eyes. "Faulconer," he said proudly, "and I'm a Virginian."

"So what were you doing here, you bastard?" the rebel asked.

"Dreaming of heaven," Adam said and would say no more.

"You're a traitor, you son of a bitch," the leader said when he realized Adam was determined to stay silent. He fired a second bullet, and this one slammed into Adam's head, making it jerk up once as the bullet drove a fist-sized chunk out of the back of his skull. The head flopped back, blood on the fair hair and with its eyes open, then was still.

The rebel holstered the revolver. "Leave the son of a bitch where he is."

A fly crawled onto one of Adam's eyeballs, then flew down to the wound in his open mouth. The rebels walked away. They had made a good haul: gold, a fine saddle and bridle, a saber and a revolver. They did not find the envelope.

When the Virginian horsemen had gone back south a group of men came from the town to investigate what the shooting had been about. They discovered Adam's body. One of them sent for two slaves and a handcart on which the corpse was wheeled into the town, where there was a discussion about what to do with it. Some wanted to wait until McClellan's army reached Frederick City and then hand the body over, but the Episcopalian minister insisted that no one knew whether the Northern army would even come to the town and that by the time anyone did arrive the corpse would surely be stinking and so a hole was dug in the graveyard where Adam, uncoffined, but in the uniform of the country he had loved, was buried with prayers. The postmaster remembered the dead officer's name, though not how to spell it, and "Adam Falconer" was burned into the wooden cross that marked the heap of soil.

While out in the pasture, close to the hollow and near to some scars of old rebel campfires, the envelope lay unnoticed in the grass.

Billy Blythe stood next to Captain Thomas Dennison and watched Starbuck. Neither man said a word, neither had to. They were both experiencing the same mix of envy and dislike, though in Dennison the dislike was nearer to hatred.

Starbuck was oblivious of their scrutiny. He was stripped to the waist, sheened with sweat, and hauling on a ten-pounder Parrott gun that needed to be taken to the final crest overlooking Harper's Ferry. The route up the hill was too steep for horses or oxen, and so the gun had to be manhandled to the summit and the Yellowlegs had drawn the duty. A dozen other guns were being similarly dragged uphill and so far the Special Battalion had made the best time, but even with fifty men hauling on ropes and another half-dozen heaving at the gun's wheels, their efforts were now blocked by a deep cleft in the rocks, and by a screen of tough undergrowth. "Son of a bitch," Sergeant Rothwell cursed the heavy weapon, then chocked its wheels with rocks so that the gun would not roll back down the last few precious yards gained. There were only fifty paces to go, but those yards could prove to be the most difficult of the climb, and could also cost them the first place in the unofficial race to reach the crest.

Starbuck smeared sweat out of his eyes then pulled free his bayonet and tried to saw through the base of one of the tangling shrubs. "Cut them down," he explained to the men around him, "and fill the gap." He gestured at the fissure in the rock just beyond the clump of bushes, but when he stooped back to the bush he found that the bayonet would not do the job. The tough, fibrous trunk took a clean initial cut, then just stubbornly resisted the steel.

"We need saws and axes," Rothwell said.

Lieutenant Potter, who had been offering encouragement rather than muscle, jerked his head northward. "There are some Georgian boys with saws over there," he said.

Starbuck straightened up, winced at a sudden pain in his back, and wiped the bayonet clean against his pants. He sheathed the weapon. "Lucifer!" The boy clambered up the slope. "Mister Potter knows where there are some saws that need stealing," Starbuck said.

"So much for the Sixth Commandment," Potter said, raising a laugh among the exhausted men.

"Go," Starbuck said, "both of you."

Potter and Lucifer hurried away on their larcenous expedition while Starbuck went back down the slope to help the men hauling the gun's limber. Halfway down he met Captain Peel, who was climbing up with two dozen full canteens of water for the gun's hauliers. "Reckoned you'd be thirsty," Peel panted.

"Well done. Thank you," Starbuck said, pleasantly surprised. Peel, of the four original captains, was proving by far the most useful. He had transferred his allegiance from Dennison to Starbuck and if he was a weak ally, he was still a welcome one. Cartwright and Lippincott did their duties, but without enthusiasm, while Dennison was downright sullen. Billy Tumlin alone seemed able to talk sense into Dennison and for that Starbuck was grateful.

Billy Blythe was talking to Dennison now. The two men had found a private hollow just below the crest and settled there to smoke cigars. "I lost my ma and pa, just like you," Billy Blythe told Dennison. In truth his father had not been lost so much as never found after impregnating Blythe's mother, who was still very much alive but very far from her son's thoughts. "Hard being an orphan," Blythe said.

Dennison, grateful for the sympathy, but still sullen, shrugged.

"Reckon it was harder for you, Tom, than for me," Blythe said generously.

Dennison gave a slight nod, then sucked on the cigar. From far away came the muted thud of big guns bruising the air. He guessed it was a federal battery shelling the rebels on the hills north of the trapped garrison. "I survived," he said grimly.

"Oh, sure, we survive," Blythe agreed energetically, "but it's more than that, Tom. What people like Starbuck never see is that we orphans are harder than most. Tougher. Got to be. I mean you and I didn't have proper homes, did we? Not like Starbuck. Or maybe he does see. Maybe he does understand that we're tougher, which is why he's jealous."

"Jealous?" Dennison asked. He had never thought Starbuck jealous of him. Scornful, maybe, but never jealous.

"Stands out a mile," Blythe said seriously. "That's why he holds you down, Tom." Blythe paused to pluck a shred of tobacco from his mouth. "Hell, he knows you ought to have been the battalion commander. The thing about these men," here Blythe jerked his cigar toward the men crowded about the stalled cannon, "is that they need discipline. Real hard discipline. Starbuck plays up to them, wants them to like him. He's easy on them. Hell, you or I would have whipped the rank off Potter the moment he got drunk, but not Starbuck. He went easy on him. Soft. But being soft with this sort of battalion won't work, not in battle. You know that and I know that."

Dennison nodded agreement. "Starbuck let Rothwell off the horse. The day he arrived at Camp Lee. Soft, you're right," he said.

"Rothwell!" Blythe said. "Now there's a dangerous man." He fell silent, apparently thinking. "Don't help, not being soft on men like Rothwell," he went on. "Not that I'm the right fellow to bring discipline. I know that. I'm too easygoing. I can see what's wrong, but I ain't got the nature to do anything about it, but then I ain't aiming to stay on here anyway."

"You're not?" Dennison inquired a little too eagerly.

"Hell, no. I'm fixing to go back to Louisiana. That's my patch, Tom, not Virginia. I didn't ask to be put here, I wanted to go home where I belong, and just as soon as this campaign's done I aim to be going south. Five weeks? Six, maybe? Then Billy Tumlin goes home. I'd rather be fighting Yankees in Louisiana than up here, and besides, a Virginia regiment ought to be led by a Virginian, don't you reckon?"

"Yes," Dennison, a Virginian, said fervently.

"And Starbuck, he ain't no Virginian," Blythe went on. "Hell, he ain't even a Southron. What's the point of fighting a war to be rid of the Northerners if you get a Northerner giving you orders?" Blythe shook his head. "Don't make no sense, leastwise none I can see."

"I thought you liked Starbuck," Dennison said resentfully.

"Hell, Tom, there ain't no profit in being an open enemy, not of no man! Besides, it ain't in my nature to act disgruntled, but that don't stop me seeing what's plain as a boil on a whore's backside. If I was Swynyard, and thank the Holy Lord I ain't, I'd take Starbuck away from this battalion and put you in charge." In truth Blythe despised Dennison for a boastful coward, and found it hard even to sit close to the man whose face was a cluster of scabrous patches left over from his sores, but cowardice, as Blythe well knew, was no barrier to a man's ambitions and he saw a desperate ambition in Dennison. "You should be in command," he went on, "with Bobby Case as your second. Then you should all go back to Camp Lee and put in some proper training. That's how to make this battalion into a fine fighting regiment, not Starbuck's way." Blythe shook his head as though in despair.

"Case is a good man," Dennison said. In truth he was terrified of Case and had been somewhat astonished when Tumlin called him Bobby, but Dennison did understand that Case was now a natural ally in the private war against Starbuck.

"You won't find a better man than Case," Blythe agreed vigorously, "salt of the earth. And he respects you, Tom. Told me so." Blythe sniffed as though he had been profoundly moved by Case's confidence. "And I'll tell you something else," Blythe went on. "We shouldn't be here." He waved his cigar in a gesture intended to embrace the whole siege of Harper's Ferry. "The battalion ain't ready to fight. It ain't equipped proper and it ain't trained proper." He spoke emphatically, and Dennison nodded eager agreement. "What this battalion needs," Blythe said, "is a good few months training. The responsible thing to do, Tom, is to survive this campaign. Do no more than you have to, then take the battalion in hand for a winter's training. I won't be here to help you, because I'll have gone south, but you and Bobby Case can get the job done. But to do it, Tom, you have to survive, and Starbuck's mighty careless with men's lives in battle. You saw that yesterday. Maitland and you had the sense to hold back, you had the sense to spare your men, but not Starbuck. He was waltzing up that hill like a preacher smelling a free ride in a brothel! He gets men killed, Starbuck does, and that ain't the way to win wars. You know that and I know that."

"So what are you suggesting?" Dennison asked, scratching at one of the flaky scabs on his face.

Good God, Blythe thought, what was he supposed to do? Paint a target on Starbuck's back and put a gun in Dennison's hands? "Hell, I ain't suggesting nothing," he said, "except that maybe you and Bobby Case should be running this battalion. Once I've gone south, Tom, it won't make no difference to me, but it hurts, it hurts real bad, to see talent being held back. It ain't in my nature to say nothing when I see that, and you and Bobby are being held back."

A burst of cheering made both men turn to see that Captain Potter and Lucifer had returned with a pair of bucksaws that were swiftly put to work. A squad of outraged Georgians were following the thieves, intent on retrieving the saws, and Starbuck's men were working fast to rip down the bushes before the confrontation.

"That goddamn slave of Starbuck's," Dennison said softly, "he watches all the time. Stays awake at night, watching."

"Hell, down south we know how to treat uppity niggers," Blythe said scornfully, "specially niggers with guns. He wouldn't last a day down south."

A burst of laughter sounded. Potter, with a face of utter innocence, was claiming that he thought the bucksaws had been discarded. He launched into an elaborate story of just chancing upon the two saws, and while he talked the Yellowlegs ripped the blades to and fro and hurled the sawn bushes up into the small ravine.

The Georgian captain demanded the saws' immediate return. Starbuck, sweat and dirt on his chest, introduced himself. He agreed that theft was a serious matter. "You can identify the saws?" he asked the Georgian.

"Hell, we saw the nigger snatch them!"

"Lucifer!" Starbuck called. "Did you take this gentleman's saws?"

Lucifer shook his head. "Captain Potter said they were lost, sir. Said I should take care of them." Another two bushes were cut through and the men scrambled up to the next tangle of brush and began work again.

"The saws were lying on our coats!" the Georgian protested.

"I think the proper procedure would be a full inquiry," Starbuck said. "If you'd like to make a report to your brigade commander," he told the Georgian, "I'll warn mine that the paperwork is coming. Captain Potter? You can write a detailed report on the circumstances under which you encountered the saws?"

"How many copies, sir?" Potter asked.

"Three at least," Starbuck said.

The Georgian shook his head. "Hell, mister," he said to Starbuck, "my boys can just take the saws now. Kind of spare you the ink. Come on, boys." He led his dozen men toward the saws, but a score of Starbuck's men offered to defend them and the Georgians checked at the odds.

Potter patted the stalled gun. "Shall we load with canister, sir?" he asked Starbuck.

Starbuck grinned, then turned to see that the last of the bushes were being cut down. He waited till the saws had done their work, then collected them. "Thank you for the loan," he told the Georgian Captain, holding out the saws. "Appreciate it."

The Georgian laughed, took the saws, and walked away while Starbuck's men stooped to the gun traces and began hauling. The heavy gun creaked and rocked as it gathered way, then it bounced up over the sawn stumps and crashed over the makeshift bridge that filled the ravine. Starbuck ran alongside the gun, cheering the men on. The gunners ran with him, eager to site the weapon and so begin the bombardment that would doom the trapped garrison of Harper's Ferry. A cheer announced the gun's emplacement, the first gun to be sited above the doomed town. The limber still had to arrive, but Starbuck's men had won the race. And in two days, Starbuck reckoned, they ought to be inside the town and with any luck there would be a rich haul of axes, spades, boots, saws, ammunition, rifles; all the things his Special Battalion needed. And after that they would go north and then, Starbuck knew, he would have to face the Yankees in battle. And maybe, he dared to hope, this would be the last battle, for that was the hope of this rebel campaign. Go north, show the Yankees that the South could not be beaten, and then make peace. That was the dream, the reason to cross the Potomac; the hope that the slaughter would end.

THE NORTHERN ARMY GROPED CAUTIOUSLY INTO THE deserted Maryland farmlands, where General McClellan left nothing to chance. He watched his flanks, secured his communications, and advanced his forward units at the pathetic pace of ten miles a day. Pinkerton, head of the army's Secret Service, assured McClellan that he faced at least 200,000 well-armed rebels, and McClellan imagined that horrid horde waiting to ambush him like Apaches falling on an army supply train. The White House urged McClellan on while the War Department sent him contrary dispatches declaring that the further he went from the capital the more likely it was that the rebels would swarm over the river to assault the city. McClellan just inched forward, always ready to spring back if danger threatened.

Colonel Thorne had abandoned his Washington office. He could not stand the oppressive heat in the capital, where the only news from the army was grudging while every rumor of Lee's apparent ambitions was only too readily reported by the press. Philadelphia was expecting a siege; the city fathers of Baltimore had forbidden the sale of alcohol to protect the nerves of their fearful citizens; while the British Ambassador, a genial aristocrat, was reported to be packing his bags in preparation for a declaration of war against the United States. "All nonsense, Thorne," Lord Lyons told the colonel at a White House reception. "No point in going to war with you," he added lightly, "at least not until Bobby Lee's won the thing for us. We might come in then, of course, to pick up the pieces and get some revenge for Yorktown."

"It might come to that, Ambassador," Thorne had answered gloomily.

Lyons, hearing the colonel's despair, patted his arm. "It won't, Thorne, and you know it won't. Not while you've got that man." He nodded across the crowded room at the president of whom Lyons was famously fond. "I admit that some in Britain are not unhappy to see you embarrassed, Thorne," the ambassador went on, "but I don't think we wish to risk embarrassment ourselves. Believe me, I'm packing no portmanteaus. Pay a call on us, see for yourself."

But Thorne had no patience for Washington's diplomatic niceties, not while the fate of the Republic was being decided in Maryland and so, with the president's permission, he packed his saddlebags and rode west to join McClellan's headquarters where, seeking Adam, he found that his protégé had disappeared. Allen Pinkerton's Chief of Staff, James Starbuck, whom Thorne had encountered earlier in the war, declared that Adam had ridden toward Frederick City two days before. "If he did," McClellan, who was visiting Pinkerton's quarters, had overheard the comment, "then he deserved what he got."

"Which is what, pray?" Thorne asked.

"Capture, I suppose. The man had no business there. I thought he was here to advise our signal people?"

"He was," Thorne lied, and knowing that McClellan knew he lied.

"Then he should have been working with the telegraphers, not exercising his horse. Unless, of course, he was here for another purpose?"

Thorne stared into the general's young, fresh face, which was set in the perpetual scowl of a man always trying to look older and more severe than his inmost fears made him feel. "What purpose might that have been, General?" Thorne asked spitefully.

"You'd know, Thorne, you'd know," McClellan snapped. He knew full well that Thorne had the president's confidence, and he feared, justifiably enough, that the white-haired colonel was feeding Lincoln with a constant stream of unofficial news. No wonder the fool in the White House had no idea how to win the war! If the ape would just let McClellan be slow and systematic then the Union would be saved, but no, he was forever prodding and urging McClellan to go faster. And what did Lincoln know of war? My God, the man was a railroad lawyer, not a soldier. McClellan let these resentments brood in his mind as he listened to the distant grumbling of the heavy guns at Harper's Ferry.

A stirring of the thick, warm air caused that grumbling sound to swell into a sudden staccato. Thorne wondered why McClellan did not launch an army corps toward the beleaguered garrison to rescue the thousands of Northern soldiers and their tons of precious supplies from the rebels, but such an ambitious lunge was beyond the Young Napoleon's thinking. "You wouldn't mind, I suppose," Thorne asked, "if I rode toward Frederick City?"

"Your choice, Colonel, your choice, but I can't spare men to protect you. Besides, I confidently expect to camp there tonight, but if you care to ride ahead, it's your risk. Now, if you'll excuse me, I have a war to prosecute."

Thorne did ride ahead of the advancing army, but in the event he arrived much later than McClellan's vanguard. The colonel's horse threw a shoe and by the time he had discovered a blacksmith and had the shoe nailed back onto the hoof, the Federal army was already moving into the scarred fields that had held the rebel army just a few days before. Axes sounded in the woods as men cut firewood, and everywhere drab tents unfolded in long lines. Latrines were dug, horses led to water, and pickets set to watch the empty fields.

Thorne rode into the town that was filled with curious Northern soldiers who were disappointed not to hear tales of rebel rapine and pillage. Stars and Stripes flew from windows, rooftops, and balconies, but Thorne cynically suspected that just as many rebel flags had greeted the arrival of Lee's army. Barrels of water and lemonade were placed on the sidewalk to slake the soldiers' thirst, while women handed round trays of cookies. One enterprising shopkeeper was doing a brisk trade in Confederate flags; crude things that Thorne guessed had been run up on a sewing machine, but the soldiers were eager enough to buy the souvenirs that would be dirtied, shot at, then sent home as battle trophies. Even the despised Confederate paper money, which had no real value outside the South, was being bought as keepsakes. Four young women in widely hooped skirts and fringed shawls, carrying paper parasols, walked brazenly down the center of Main Street. They were no local girls, that much was obvious, for their pinchbeck sophistication was far too flashy for Frederick City's tastes. Thorne guessed they were four of the hundreds of Washington whores who had followed the army west and were said to have their own transport, tents, and cookhouses.

A tall, white-haired preacher frowned at the sight of the girls, and Thorne, deciding that the preacher looked like a man of sense, approached, introduced himself and, without any real hope of learning anything useful, asked about Adam.

It took the preacher only a few moments and a half dozen questions to identify the missing officer. He hauled off his wide-brimmed hat and gave Thorne the terrible news. "Buried in my own churchyard, Colonel." The minister led Thorne to the graveyard, and to the mound of freshly turned earth with its makeshift wooden cross on which Adam's name had been misspelled. Someone, Thorne was glad to see, had put flowers on the grave. "You poor bastard," Thorne said too softly for the preacher to hear, "you poor innocent bastard."

So that, he thought despairingly, was that, and he rode dejectedly back to the growing Federal encampment. The desperate throw had failed. Thorne had always known it was a reckless and ramshackle chance, but he had deceived himself into believing that somehow it might work. Yet how was Adam ever to have reached Delaney? It had been a waste of a good man and, when Thorne reached the camp and found where his servant had erected his tent, he forced himself to endure the penance of writing to Adam's father. He did not know if Adam's mother still lived, and so he addressed the letter to General Washington Faulconer and assured him that his son had died a hero. "It will doubtless grieve you that he perished while fighting for his country rather than for his native state, but Almighty God saw fit to repose that patriotism in his heart and God's ways are ever inscrutable." The stilted words were hopelessly inadequate, but what words could ever suffice to tell a father of his son's death? Thorne told the General where Adam's body lay, then finished the letter with his sincere regrets. A drop of sweat smeared his signature, but he blotted it dry, sealed the letter, then pushed it to one side. Damn, he thought. The one chance to goad McClellan into a semblance of energetic soldiering had passed. Thorne had played and lost.

Except he had not lost. Two Indiana soldiers, a sergeant and a corporal, had finished pitching their tents and had wandered north out of their camp lines, across a dip in the pastureland, to a cleaner stretch of grass that was unsoiled by rebel litter. They planned to make a fire and boil some coffee away from the predatory gaze of their comrades and so they walked toward a rail fence that had miraculously remained unbroken during the rebels' stay. Rails made good firewood, and the coffee would help pass the long hot afternoon, but just before they reached the fence Corporal Barton Mitchell saw an envelope lying in the grass. It had a curiously bulky look and so he picked it up and shook out the contents. "Bless me, Johnny," he said as the three cigars appeared. He sniffed one. "Damn good too. You want one?"

Sergeant Bloss took the offered cigar, and with it the sheet of paper that had served to wrap the precious find. As he nipped the cigar's end with his teeth he glanced at the paper and, after a few seconds, frowned. There were names here he recognized—Jackson, Longstreet, and Stuart—while at its foot the paper was signed by command of General R. E. Lee.

The coffee was forgotten. Instead the two men took the paper to their company commander, who passed it up the chain of command until at last a prewar colleague of Colonel Chilton's recognized the handwriting. It seemed the order was genuine and it was hurried to General McClellan's tent.

Thorne heard the excitement and, pulling on his blue coat, ducked out of his tent and strode across to where a throng of people was gathered about the General's headquarters. Many in the crowd were civilians come to gape at the federal general who, convinced that the order was the real copper-bottomed thing, was exultant. McClellan saw Thorne and brandished the paper triumphantly. "Here's a paper with which I can whip Bobby Lee, Thorne! And if I can't I'll go home tomorrow!"

Thorne, astonished at this sudden enthusiasm on McClellan's part, could only gape.

"Tomorrow we'll pitch into his center!" McClellan boasted, "and in two days we'll have him trapped!"

Thorne managed to secure the order. His astonishment grew as he read it, for here were written all Lee's dispositions and those dispositions revealed the enemy commander to be a consummate gambler. Lee must have known that McClellan's army was marching westward, but such was his contempt for his enemy that he had divided his army into five parts, then scattered them across western Maryland and northern Virginia. Most of the Confederate forces were besieging Harper's Ferry, others had gone north to prepare for the invasion of Pennsylvania, while smaller forces barred the hills that faced McClellan's troops. It was true that the order was now four days old, but the constant mutter of the distant guns confirmed that the rebels were still swarming about Harper's Ferry and that sound suggested that the dispositions detailed in the order were still in place, which meant that if McClellan really did march quickly then there was a genuine chance that the Northern army could be placed between the scattered units of Lee's army. Then they would be destroyed, one by one, slaughter by slaughter, surrender by surrender, page after page of history being made.

"Rebellion's end, Thorne," McClellan said as he retrieved the paper.

"Indeed, sir," Thorne said, and felt a pang of distaste for the short general whose hair was so carefully waved and whose mustaches so gleamingly brushed. A gelded cockerel, he thought, and was ashamed that he should so resent this gift of utter victory being given to such a creature.

"You don't doubt the order's genuine?" McClellan inquired, unable to hide his nagging anxiety that the order might be a ruse, though the circumstances of its finding suggested gross carelessness rather than sly design. "Pittman vouches for the handwriting," the general went on. "It's Chilton's penmanship, right enough, or so Pittman says."

"I trust Colonel Pittman's memory on the point, sir," Thorne admitted.

"Then we've won!" McClellan crowed. The ape in the White House might take the credit for preserving the Union, but George Brinton McClellan was content that the voters at the next presidential election would know who was truly to thank. McClellan in '64! And '68, by God, and maybe forever once the voters realized that only one man in the country had the nerve, prudence, and wisdom to steer America! McClellan luxuriated in that vision for a moment, then clapped his hands. "Marching orders!" he announced, then shooed his visitors away so that he could work in peace.

Thorne found Colonel Pittman, and from Colonel Pittman he traced the order's discovery back to Sergeant Bloss and Corporal Mitchell. From them he learned where the envelope had been found, and after that he rode into Frederick City and found a man who had helped retrieve Adam's body. To Thorne's delight he discovered that the body had been found only yards from where the envelope had lain, and that circumstance convinced Thorne that the copy of Special Order 191 was genuine, and not a subtle trap laid by an outnumbered enemy. "So it wasn't in vain," he told Adam in his grave. "You did well, Faulconer, you did well." He solemnly saluted the grave, then said a prayer of thanks. God, it seemed, had not abandoned His country. And well done, Delaney, Thorne added silently. The Richmond lawyer had earned a reward.

For already the first Federal troops were preparing to march with new haste and sudden purpose; preparing to march west to where Lee's betrayed army was spread so carelessly across the summer-heated land. The Young Napoleon had been offered victory and now, with uncharacteristic verve, he sprang to take it.

At dawn Harper's Ferry was shrouded in a mist that flowed like twin white rivers from the Shenandoah and the Potomac valleys to meld softly above the town. The mist flowed in utter silence, but it was an ominous silence, for by now the rebel troops commanded all the high ground about the river town and their great guns had been dragged forward to the crests so that their cold, dew-beaded barrels were pointing down to what lay hidden by the soft white vapor. The gunners had loaded and rammed their pieces, and their most distant cannon was scarcely a mile from the mist-concealed federal defenses, a mere six and a half seconds of flight for the nineteen-pound shells that were nestled inside the barrels against the two-pound charges of coarse powder that would explode when Jackson gave the signal. There were guns to the north of the town, guns to the south, and guns to the west. A ring of guns, all silent now, all waiting for that shroud of mist to lift from the doomed town.

General Thomas Jackson paced the rocky crest of the Bolivar Heights west of the town from where he scowled at the valley mist as though it were a devilish device planted to thwart his victory. His cadet cap was pulled low over his brooding eyes, but those eyes missed nothing as he walked up and down, up and down, sometimes dragging a cheap watch from his pocket and peering at its slow-moving hands. The gunners tried not to catch his gaze. Instead they busied themselves with unnecessary tasks like greasing already lubricated elevating screws or straightening the friction primers that came bent from the factory so that they would not accidentally ignite and cause an explosion. Shirt-sleeved infantry carried ammunition up the hill trails and stacked their loads beside the waiting guns.

Most of the rebel infantry would be spectators of this battle and the hills were crowded with lines of gray and butternut uniforms waiting for Old Jack's firework display. Starbuck's battalion was close to a mixed battery of ten- and twenty-pounder Parrott guns, their trails all burned with the initials USA, evidence that Jackson had equipped his batteries with cannon taken from the Yankees. Captain Billy Blythe carried a cup of coffee as he joined Starbuck. "That's Old Jack?" he asked, nodding at the shabby, bearded figure who stumped in his huge square-toed boots up and down beside the guns.

"That's Jackson," Starbuck confirmed.

"Queer-looking fellow," Blythe said.

"Frightening as hell," Starbuck said.

"Specially to Yankees, eh?" Blythe said, then sipped at the coffee that was bitterly sour. He could not wait to get back to the North where the coffee was rich and fragrant, and not this adulterated dirt that the rebels drank. "You met him?"

"I met him." Starbuck was never particularly communicative in the morning and spoke curtly.

Blythe did not mind. "You reckon he'd say howdy?" he asked Starbuck.

"No."

"Hell, Starbuck, I'd like to shake the man's hand."

"Shake mine instead," Starbuck said, but instead of offering it he stole Tumlin's coffee and sipped it. "And if you swear in front of him, Tumlin, you'll wish you'd never met him."

"Keep the coffee, Starbuck," Blythe said magnanimously, "ain't nothing but goober pea shit anyhow. Morning, General!" he called aloud as Jackson's pacing brought the general close to Starbuck's men. "Fine one for a victory, sir!"

Jackson looked astonished at being addressed and stared at Blythe as though surprised to see a soldier on the hill, but he said nothing. Blythe, unfazed by this cold response, strode forward as if the general was his oldest friend. "Prayers are being answered, sir," Blythe said vigorously, "and the enemy will be crushed in the very nest where John Brown defied our legitimate aspirations."

"Amen," Jackson said, "amen. And you are, sir?"

"Tumlin, General," Blythe said, "Captain Billy Tumlin, and proud to meet you, sir. I prayed for you these many months and am grateful that the Lord has seen fit to hear me."

"'Vengeance is mine, saith the Lord,'" Jackson said, turning to look at the mist through which the topmost part of the town and the pinnacle of a church in the lower quarter was now showing. The vapor was thinning, promising to lay bare the Yankee defenses. "You're saved in the Lord, Captain?" Jackson asked Blythe.

"Praise His name, yes," Blythe lied glibly.

"I didn't hear," Jackson snapped and cupped a hand to his ear. Years of artillery work had deadened the General's hearing.

"Praise His name, yes!" Blythe shouted.

"We are a Godly nation, Captain, and a righteous army," Jackson growled. "We cannot be defeated. Fight with that assurance in your heart."

"I shall, sir, and amen," Blythe responded, then held out his hand, which the general, with some surprise at the gesture, finally clasped. "God bless you, sir," Blythe said as he shook Jackson's hand, then he turned and walked back to Starbuck. "See?" Blythe chuckled. "Easy as feeding crumbs to a bird."

"So what did you say to him?"

"I told him I was one of God's anointed, told him I prayed for him daily, and offered him God's blessing."

"You ain't a saved Christian, Billy Tumlin," Starbuck said sourly. "You're nothing but a miserable sinner."

"We have all sinned, Starbuck," Blythe said earnestly, "and fallen short of the glory of God."

"Don't preach to me, for Christ's sake, I've had my bellyful of preaching."

Blythe laughed. He was pleased with himself for having shaken the great Jackson's hand, and the tale would be a good boast in the comfortable days after he had crossed the lines. He was pleased, too, for having fooled Jackson into thinking he was with a fellow Christian. Be all things to all men, that was Billy Blythe's belief, but make sure you profit from the deceptions. "So what happens now?" he asked Starbuck.

"What do you think? We shoot the hell out of those poor sons of bitches, they surrender, then we go and shoot the hell out of the rest of the sorry bastards." Starbuck checked suddenly, arrested by the distant sound of gunfire. It was very distant, much too muted and far away to be the guns on Harper's Ferry's farther side. The same distant grumbling had trembled across the sky the previous evening, just before the sun had set in a blaze of western scarlet, and Starbuck had climbed to the ridge top to see a small billow of whiteness on the far northeastern sky-line. That far whiteness, which had been touched pink by the dying day, could have been an errant wisp of cloud, except that the noise had betrayed what it truly was—gunfire. A skirmish or battle was being waged deep inside Maryland. Starbuck shuddered and was glad he was here and not there.

The last mist shredded from the valleys to reveal the small town of Harper's Ferry huddled at the point between the merging rivers. The fame of the place had somehow persuaded Starbuck that it would prove a large town, almost the size of Richmond maybe, but in truth it was a tiny place. It must have once been a pleasant, tree-shaded village built on a spur of hill that dropped to the banks of the Potomac and Shenandoah rivers, though now many of the buildings were charred ruins out of which brick chimney stacks reared gaunt. An undamaged church flew a flag that, when Starbuck borrowed a gunner's binoculars, he saw to be the British flag. "I thought those bastards were on our side," he told the gunner officer.

"Who cares? Kill 'em anyway." The gunner laughed, reveling in the wealth of targets that the lifting mist had revealed. There were federal earthworks on the edge of the town and naked batteries waiting to be shelled. The two rivers were edged by a sprawl of industrial buildings that had once been the federal arsenal and a rifle factory but which were now nothing but scorched roofless walls, while the massive bridge that had once carried the Ohio and Baltimore's rails over the Potomac had been reduced to a series of stone piers like the stepping stones of a giant. The only passage across the wide Potomac now was a pontoon bridge erected by Northern engineers, but as Starbuck watched a great fountain of water exploded out of the river beside the bridge, making the pontoons tug on their chains. A few seconds later there came the sound of the rebel gun that had fired the shell from the distant hills.

Jackson looked startled, for he had not yet ordered his signalers to wigwag the order to begin the bombardment, but someone in the rebel lines on the north side of the Potomac had tired of waiting and suddenly all the guns on all the hills about the town crashed back on their trails and pumped smoke and shells toward the trapped garrison. The watching infantry cheered as the wispy smoke trails of the shells' burning fuses arced down to the battered town where the Yankees waited.

And where they now died. The rebel gunners worked like fiends to sponge out, reload, and ram their guns, and shell after shell screamed down the slopes to explode in gusting swathes of smoke, flame, and dirt. The Yankee earthworks outside the town seemed to disappear in blasts of smoke, and when the smoke drifted clear the watching rebels could see their enemies running back toward the town's war-scarred buildings. A few Yankee guns tried to answer the destructive barrage, but the Northern batteries were swiftly battered into silence by the rebel artillery. To the watchers on the hills it seemed as though the river town was being turned into a pit of hell. Flames leaped up from burning limbers, smoke drifted thick, and huge trees shivered like saplings as the shells blasted the leaves away. Sweat poured down the gunners' faces and bare chests. Each recoil slammed the guns violently back so that their trails gouged deep troughs in the dirt. The wet sponges that extinguished any trace of red-hot explosive remaining in a barrel after each shot hissed and steamed as they were rammed down to the breach, then, the second that the sponge was withdrawn to be thrust into a bucket of dirty water, the loader would shove the next round into the muzzle to be rammed hard down while the rest of the team maneuvered the gun back to its proper aim. "Ready!" the gunner would shout and the team would duck aside with hands over their ears as the command to fire was shouted. The gunner yanked the lanyard that scraped the friction primer over its incendiary tube and a heartbeat later the gun would crash back behind its billow of smoke and another shell, its fuse smoking, screamed toward the town.

"I was there once," Billy Blythe said to Starbuck.

"You were?"

"Saw Mister Brown hung," Blythe said contentedly. "Smug son of a bitch."

"What were you doing there?"

"Buying horses," Blythe said. "That was my trade, see? And once in a while we came north to find a nag or two. Stayed at Wager's Hotel."

He stared at the town and shook his head. "Burned to a cinder, by the look of things. A pity. I was hoping to renew my acquaintance with a girl there. Sweet as honey, she was, only a lot cheaper," he laughed. "Hell, she and I were watching out of a bedroom window when they hung that smug son of a bitch. Hung him higher than an angel. Kicked like a mule, he did, and all the time I was making that sweet little honey moan for pleasure."

Starbuck felt a flicker of distaste for his second in command. "I met John Brown," he said.

"You did?"

"He came to Boston wanting funds," Starbuck explained, "but he didn't get none from us." At the time he had been puzzled that his father had refused to help the famous abolitionist, but now, looking back, he wondered if the Reverend Elial Starbuck had been jealous of the stern, ravaged-faced Brown. The two men had been very alike. Had his father feared such a formidable rival in the abolition movement? But Brown was dead now, and in the wake of his hopeless rebellion there was a plague of death across America. "He told me I'd be a warrior against the slavocracy," Starbuck recalled the meeting in his father's parlor, "guess he got that wrong."

"You're fighting to keep the slaves, is that it?" Blythe asked.

"Hell, no. I'm fighting because I've nothing better to do."

"Slaves won't be freed anyway," Blythe said confidently.

"They won't?"

"Not this side of heaven, and if God's got any sense, not there neither. Hell, who's going to pay the lazy sons of bitches wages?"

"Maybe they're only lazy because they don't get wages," Starbuck said.

"Sound like your pa, Major."

Starbuck bit back an angry retort. He was surprised at his sudden suspicions of Billy Tumlin and wondered if he was being unfair to the man, but he sensed that Tumlin's glibness concealed a sly dishonesty. Billy Tumlin lied too easily, and Starbuck had seen proof of that when Tumlin talked with Jackson, and now he wondered how many other lies Tumlin had told. There was something that did not ring true about

Tumlin, and Starbuck found himself wondering why a man who had ostensibly escaped from a Yankee prison was so well fed and so handsomely equipped with a money belt. "I'm going to get myself a map in Harper's Ferry," he said just after the nearest gun had thumped back on its trail.

"A map?" Blythe asked.

"I want to see where Union is in Massachusetts, Tumlin. You kind of piqued my interest. I thought I knew half the back towns in Massachusetts on account of going with my father when he preached up-country, but I sure as hell don't remember a Union. Where was it near?"

"Hell, it weren't near nowhere!" Blythe was suddenly defensive. "It was a prison, remember. Maybe the Yankees made the name up?"

"I guess that must be it," Starbuck said, content that he had unsettled his second in command, but as Tumlin moved away to find more congenial company Starbuck found himself wondering how many enemies he could afford to make in the Special Battalion. Case would kill him as soon as give him the time of day, and Starbuck suspected Dennison would do the same if he could ever summon up the courage. He could not depend on Cartwright or Lippincott, who did their duty, but with a singular lack of enthusiasm. Potter was a friend, and Caton Rothwell too, but Starbuck's enemies far outnumbered his friends. He had experienced the same divide of loyalties in the Legion and Starbuck, reflecting on the schisms, feared it was because of his personality. He envied men like Colonel Elijah Hudson, the North Carolinian whose battalion had fought alongside the Legion at Manassas and whose men seemed united in affection for him. Or Pecker Bird, still recovering from his wound, who had inspired nothing but loyalty during his time as the Legion's commander. Then Starbuck noticed Old Mad Jack pacing up and down beside the busy guns. The general, as he so often did, was holding his left hand in the air as though he was testifying to God's goodness, though in truth he only held the hand in the odd position because otherwise, he believed, the blood would puddle around an ancient wound. Starbuck watched the general and thought that there was a man who made enemies as well as friends.

Jackson chose that moment to glance up and catch Starbuck's eye.

For a moment the two stared at each other with the uncomfortable sensation of recognition, but with nothing to say either, then Jackson made a growling sound as he lowered his left hand. "Have you found your Savior yet, Mister Starbuck?" he called, evidently recalling his last conversation with Starbuck.

"No, General."

Jackson veered toward Starbuck, trailing a gaggle of staff officers behind him. "But you are searching?" he inquired earnestly.

"I'm thinking about something else right now, General," Starbuck said. "I was kind of wondering why a soldier makes enemies of his own side just by doing his duty."

Jackson blinked at Starbuck, then frowned at the dirt beside his ungainly boots. He was plainly considering the question, and giving it hard thought, for he remained staring at the ground for what seemed like a full minute. One of his aides called to him, but the general flapped an irritated hand to show that he did not want to be disturbed, and when the aide called again he simply ignored the importunate man. Finally his fierce eyes looked up at Starbuck. "Most men are weak, Major, and the reaction of the weak to the strong is usually envy. Your job is to make them strong, but you cannot do that alone. Do you have a chaplain in your battalion?"

Starbuck wondered if the general assumed he was still in command of the Legion. "No, sir."

"Sir!" the aide called from beside the guns.

Again Jackson ignored the man. "Sheep need shepherds, Major," he told Starbuck, "and greater strength comes from a man's faith than from his sinews. I am, God knows, the weakest of mortals!" This was proclaimed in the energetic voice of a man sure of his own soul. "But God has given me duties and granted me the strength to perform them."

"Sir! Please!" The aide stepped closer to Jackson.

Jackson, in a surprising gesture, touched Starbuck's arm. "Remember, Major," he said, " 'They that wait upon the Lord shall renew their strength; they shall mount up with wings as eagles; they shall run, and not be weary; and they shall walk, and not faint.' Isaiah."

"Chapter forty," Starbuck said, "verse thirty-one."

Jackson smiled. "I shall pray for you, Major," the General said, then turned to his aide and his smile vanished. "What is it?"

The aide was carrying a pair of field glasses that he offered to the general. "The enemy, sir," he said, pointing down toward the beleaguered town, "is surrendering."

"Cease fire! Cease fire!" It was the nearest battery commander who, lacking any orders, had decided to end the bombardment on his own authority.

Jackson seized the field glasses, but even without their aid it was possible to see two Yankees walking with a white flag between the patches of smoke that drifted from the exploded shells. The Yankees were holding a grubby white flag hoisted on a pole. "It was a pitiful defense," Jackson growled angrily. "They should be ashamed of themselves." He hurried away, shouting for his horse to be fetched.

"Cease fire!" another gun commander shouted. The rebel guns on the farther hills had still not seen the white flag and they went on firing until the signalers managed to wigwag their flags with the message about the enemy surrender, and so a silence gradually fell across the smoke-veiled, explosive-torn valley, though it was not a total silence, for out of the distant, heat-hazed north, from across the river and the faraway hills, came the sound of other guns. Someone was fighting hard, but who, or where or why, no one in Harper's Ferry knew.

Belvedere Delaney was seeing his first battle and finding it far more terrifying than anything he could have imagined or feared. He had ridden to the range of hills that barred the Yankees' approach from the east and had arrived in time to witness McClellan's attack on the southernmost of the two passes that had been guarded by pitifully small numbers of rebel troops. Prudence would have dictated that the passes be more heavily manned, but Lee had gambled on McClellan's usual supine performance and so had stripped the defenders bare to add to the men assaulting Harper's Ferry.

But McClellan was no longer supine. McClellan knew his opponent's mind and now he lunged to break the rebel army.

To Delaney, watching from a high vantage point north of the pass, it seemed as though waves of blue-clad troops were washing up the wide valley like ocean waves running toward a beach. The foam of the breaking surf was the rill of smoke caused by exploding Yankee shells that crashed and flamed along the rebel defenses, while behind the smoke the long lines of blue infantry came remorselessly forward. Delaney was too far away to smell the blood or see the heavy coils of men's guts spewed across the summer grass, but the noise alone carried a violence that was almost unbearable. The crash of the guns was percussive, deafening, disorientating, and, worst of all, unending. How any man could live under that barrage was beyond Delaney's comprehension, yet live they did, and the occasional splintering crack of rifle volleys told him that some rebel units still fought back against the onrush of Yankees.

The Yankee tide did not come forward smoothly, indeed, to Delaney, it often seemed inexplicably slow. He would watch a line of infantry advance under its flags and then, for no apparent reason, the line would stop and the men settle down. Another line would jerk forward while busy horsemen galloped in what seemed aimless errands between the advancing lines. Only the big guns never stopped, filling the shallow pass with smoke and noise and terror.

Behind the pass, stretching out toward the gentler farmland of eastern Maryland, a mass of Federal troops was gathering. McClellan's army was crowding behind the attack ready to stream through the pass and ram their guns and rifles between Lee's scattered troops. To the west, behind the rebel lines, there was no such show of strength, only country roads carrying wagons of wounded back toward the unseen Potomac.

"I guess our message got through," Delaney said to George.

George, a handsome, light-skinned Negro, nodded. "Something stirred them," he agreed in an amused tone.

Delaney, recalling his terror at being found out, felt an immense relief. He unstoppered a silver flask and drank from it, then handed the flask to George. "A toast to Northern victory, George."

"To victory," George said, and tipped the flask to his lips. He savored the wine, then smiled. "You brought some of the '49 hock."

"Only one bottle."

"A pity it isn't chilled," George said reprovingly.

"When Richmond falls," Delaney said, "we shall bathe in chilled hock."

"You might, not me."

Delaney laughed. Rome, he was thinking, Rome was the place to go, or if Rome was pitching it too high, then perhaps Athens or Naples. He would be an ambassador for freedom in a place of sun-touched beauty and decadent luxury. He would uniform George in a curled wig and a gilt-encrusted coat, and dine to the sound of a string quartet playing beneath heavy-scented flowers. By day he would lecture the natives on the arts of government and by night be lectured by them on the arts of decadence.

Beneath him, struggling to make that dream come true, the blue lines suddenly surged forward. The rebels were breaking. Men who had fought and beaten Yankees on fields across Virginia were now tasting defeat. Their defenses were shredding and breaking. Small groups of men ran westward, some shrugging off equipment so they could run faster, while others were left dead or wounded on the shell-torn turf as the victorious Yankees swept across the captured positions. The surviving rebel guns were being limbered up and whipped away, their encampments were abandoned, and everywhere the Stars and Stripes came forward. "Time to go, George," Delaney said, watching the rout.

"But to where? Richmond?"

"Back to Lee, I think. I should like to be a witness of the bitter end," Delaney said. He thought there might well be a book in it. A tragedy, probably, for though Lee was his country's enemy, he was a good man, but Delaney doubted whether goodness was the quality that won wars; only might, hard resolve, and low treachery could do that.

Delaney turned his horse and cantered west. He had betrayed the Confederacy to McClellan and now prayed he would be a witness to its destruction.

The federal general who formally surrendered the Harper's Ferry garrison was splendidly uniformed in gold-braided blue with a shining scabbard hanging from his belt, while Jackson, accepting the great prize, was in a filthy homespun coat, shabby boots, and with his battered cadet cap crammed over uncut, dirty hair. Jackson, even in victory, looked grim, though he did allow himself a smile when Starbuck's hearse came into view. The vehicle was being pulled by the skirmishers of Potter's company, while Potter himself was riding on the box from where he cracked an imaginary whip. The Yankee General, still at Jackson's side, wondered for the hundredth time why McClellan had not come to the garrison's rescue and then, at the sight of the hearse, was overcome with mortification as he realized the utter shame of being defeated by such ragamuffin troops. None of the victorious rebels was better dressed than their general, and most were worse; indeed some of Jackson's men limped into the town on bare feet while the beaten Yankees were outfitted with the best products of the industrial North.

Colonel Swynyard came hurrying down the column in search of Starbuck. "You can jettison your death-cart, Nate!" the colonel called. "The town's crammed with wagons. New wagons, fine wagons. I've left young Coffman guarding a pair for you. Told him to shoot any rogue who dared lay a finger on them. And I daresay we can give most of your fellows rifles now, there must be thousands here! And food. It's like Manassas Junction all over again."

For once again Jackson had captured a major Federal supply base, and once again his hungry, footsore, ill-dressed troops were given run of the North's largesse. Whoops of joy greeted each opened crate. Tinned meat was prized open with bayonets and real coffee set to boil on fires made from splintered crates that had carried brand-new rifles. Jackson's commissary officers did their best to see that the most needy units received the pick of the plunder, but the chaos was too great and the first arrivals grabbed most of the choice pickings. Starbuck's men were early enough to find some rifles, boots, food, and ammunition, but not enough for every man, yet Starbuck was able to give two of his four musket-carrying companies brand-new Springfield rifles still coated in their factory grease. The rifle locks were inscribed 1862 and were handsomely engraved with an American eagle and U.S. SPRINGFIELD. The hearse and one of the two wagons were loaded up with cartridges for the new rifles.

Swynyard frowned at the hearse. "Are you sure you want to keep it?" he asked Starbuck.

"The men like it. It makes them feel special."

"I suppose it would," Swynyard said, then raised his head to listen to the far off sound of gunfire. "We're marching in the morning," he said grimly. "No rest for the wicked."

"What's happening?"

"Yankees are attacking," Swynyard said vaguely, then shrugged as if to say that he knew no more. "Lee wants us all together again. It'll be hard marching, Nate. Tell your fellows they have to suffer the blisters and keep going. Just keep going." The colonel had a map that he unfolded to show Starbuck the route they would take. "We go up the southern bank of the Potomac," he said, tracing the westward road with a nail-bitten finger, "to a ford here, near Shepherdstown, then we march east as far as here." He tapped the map.

Starbuck peered at the rendezvous, which was a town situated at a road junction just a few miles inside Maryland. "Sharpsburg," he said. The map showed a small town positioned on a wide strip of land formed by the Potomac River and one of its tributaries, Antietam Creek. "Sharpsburg," Starbuck said again. "Never heard of it."

"You're sleeping there tomorrow night," Swynyard said, "God willing."

"My men's feet willing, more likely," Starbuck said. He lit one of the captured cigars that Lucifer had discovered along with a haul of new underwear, shirts, sugar, and coffee. "Did we get any horses for the wagons?" he asked.

"A few, none of them good." The colonel folded his map. "Early start, Nate. Get some sleep."

Getting sleep was easier said than done, for the men did not want to sleep. They had won a victory and the ease of that victory was cause for celebration and the Yankee supplies had yielded enough liquor to make that celebration rousing. Others, like Starbuck, wanted to look at the sights. They marveled at the captured cannons that were lined wheel to wheel in the armory yard and that would now take their place in the Confederate battle line, then they explored the engine house where

John Brown had been surrounded with his hostages. The little fire-fighter's building had a handsome cupola, reminding Starbuck of the widow's walks on the houses beside the sea in Massachusetts, though this cupola, like the engine house's brickwork, was pitted by the scars made by the bullets of the U.S. Marines who, under Colonel Robert Lee's command, had forced John Brown's surrender. Some rebels were all in favor of pulling the engine house down in case it became a Yankee shrine, but no one had the energy for the demolition and so the building remained intact. Starbuck climbed to the church flying the British flag to discover it was a Catholic building that had sheltered its parishioners beneath a neutral flag. A nearby church had been shelled to destruction, but the Catholic congregation had escaped the bombardment.

The Yankee prisoners marched disconsolately out of the town, going to the heights where they would bivouac before being sent south to the prison camps. Harper's Ferry was left to its new owners who, as night fell, lit cooking fires that flickered low as men rolled themselves in blankets and slept on ground still littered with fragments of shell casing. Starbuck had made his quarters in an abandoned railroad box wagon, but he could not sleep and so he pulled on his boots and, careful not to wake Lucifer who, after nights of watching Starbuck, had at last fallen fast asleep, slipped out of the wagon and walked between his sleeping men toward the bank of the Shenandoah.

He was bone tired, but he could not sleep, for the same fears that had prompted his morning conversation with Jackson were nagging at him. He felt presentiments of failure and suspected they sprang from within himself. He had failed to unite the Special Battalion, just as he had failed with the Legion. No battalion, he told himself, could fight well if it was riven with jealousies and hatred, but discerning the problem did not help him find a solution. It was true that he had made some allies in the battalion, but they numbered fewer than half of the total, and many of the rest were bitter enemies. He thought about Elijah Hudson and Pecker Bird and Robert Lee and decided that their popularity sprang from character, and if character was lacking, he chided himself, leadership was a hopeless ambition. Griffin Swynyard had changed his character through the grace of God and that had made all the difference;

a once-hated major had become an admired colonel. Starbuck picked up a piece of rubble and tossed it into the river that here flowed fast and white over rocky outcrops to its junction with the Potomac.

So was God the answer? Was there nothing he could do for himself? Starbuck, gloomier than ever, suspected that the ambition in his own soul was the flaw that revealed itself to his men. That and the cowardice that he saw in himself. Or perhaps Maitland was right, and some men were born to lead. Starbuck swore softly. He had a vision of a perfect battalion, one that operated as smoothly as the newly greased mechanism of the captured Springfield rifles. A machine that worked.

Jackson had said that only God could give a man strength, and only strength could make a battalion work together. A battalion was composed of men with different fears and suspicions and ambitions, and the trick of it was to swamp those desires with a greater desire: the desire to work together toward victory. In a day or two, Starbuck feared, the Yellowlegs would face a real Yankee army, the same army that had made the northern horizon vague with smoke these last two days, and how would they fight then? Of the officers Potter alone was loyal, and Potter, God knew, was a weak reed. Starbuck closed his eyes. A part of him yearned for the grace of God to drench him with strength, but whenever he was tempted to yield to his Maker's will another temptation intervened, and this was a more beguiling temptation. It consisted of memories of firelit bodies, not dead and twisted and lice-ridden and scarred and filthy, but bodies on sheets. Sally pushing her hair back from her face. The girl who had died under Blythe's bullets at the tavern. He remembered her crouching by the fire, her red hair falling down her naked back, laughing as she toasted a scrap of bread on which she had melted a scrap of cheese taken from a mousetrap. Heaven, Starbuck liked to think, lay in those moments and he was unwilling to call them hell. His father had always said that being a Christian was not easy, but it had taken these last two years to show Starbuck how desperately hard it really was. He did not want to abandon sin, yet he feared that he would fail as a soldier if he did not. He wondered if he should pray.

Maybe a prayer by this hurrying river would hurtle its way through the smoky air to the ear of God, who alone could give a man the strength to overcome temptation.

A stone slid on stone to Starbuck's right. He opened his eyes and saw a shadow flicker among the rubble and stunted trees on the river-bank. "Who's there?" he called.

No one answered. He decided it must have been a rat, or else one of the rake-thin cats that lived wild in the ruined armory. The lights of the town showed through trees, but they revealed nothing on this broken riverbank where weeds grew thick among fallen stones. He turned back to the water. Maybe, he thought, he should pray. Maybe he should claw and crawl his way back to God, but where would that journey end? On the Yankee side? On his knees to his father?

A click sounded and he knew it was a gun being cocked. For a second he froze, hardly daring to believe what he suspected, then he threw himself backward just as a gun flamed and banged to his right. The shot screamed over his head and a billow of smoke gusted across the water. He scrambled into a half-choked culvert that was brimming with scummy water and he dragged the Adams revolver from his holster. He heard footsteps, but could see no one. A sentry was shouting, demand-ing to know who had fired and why, then Starbuck saw a shape silhou-etted against the tree-shrouded lights of the town and he leveled the revolver. Then a second man sprang up and he changed his aim, but both were running away, bent double, unrecognizable, scuttling toward the rusted tracks of the Baltimore and Ohio rails. He fired once, but over their heads for if he had aimed and missed then the bullet could have struck home among the encamped soldiers. More men were running toward the river, shouting warnings and questions.

Starbuck dragged himself out of the filthy water. A sentry saw him and dropped to one knee with his rifle leveled. "Who are you?" he shouted.

"Major Starbuck. Swynyard's brigade." Starbuck holstered the re-volver and brushed stinking water off his pants. "Put the gun down, lad."

An officer arrived demanding to know who had fired and why. Starbuck gestured at the river. "Thought I saw a man swimming. I reckoned it was an escaping Yankee."

The officer stared at the moon-glossed river that foamed over the rocks. "I can't see anyone."

"So I was dreaming," Starbuck said. "Now I'm going to bed."

He walked away. He heard the word "drunk" being used, but he did not care. He knew what he had seen, but he had not known whom he had seen. Two men, his men, he guessed, and somewhere in the battalion they were still loose and waiting for their chance.

Them and a hundred thousand Yankees. Across the river. Marching toward a town no one had ever heard of. Called Sharpsburg.

~ PART TWO ~

PART TWO

T HE CREEK WELLED FROM A MOSSY SPRING IN A LOW
pass of the South Mountains, then flowed west and south through
a rocky landscape of thin soil and old trees. Little disturbed the stream's
flow in its first few miles, for there were no settlements in that part of
Pennsylvania, but just east of Waynesborough the creek flowed into
farmland and became muddied with the feet of cattle. There were still
no bridges, for the stream was shallow enough to be forded even during
the winter spate, and so it flowed on across the border into Maryland
where, deepened and broadened by other streams, it reached its first
bridge at Hagerstown. Fish lay in the bridge's shadow, and in summer
children played in the waist-deep water.

Past Hagerstown the creek ran southward, flowing deeper and
stronger as more tributaries joined, but still it was little more than a
stream. In places it ran shallow over rocks, foaming and swirling
through the flickering shadows of the woods before it swung in great
serpent loops between lush green fields. Deer drank from the creek,

men fished from it, and cattle stood in its summer pools to cool themselves.

The Beaver Creek joined the stream five miles south of Hagerstown and now the creek was almost a river. It could still be forded by horsemen, but the local folk had built handsome stone bridges to keep their feet dry. The creek flowed on, still looping, but hurrying now to its confluence with the Potomac River, where the creek was swallowed into the massive flow of water running to the eastern sea.

Some four miles north of where the creek joined the Potomac River there was a spot where a shelving bank of shingle edged the water beneath a stand of great elms. It was a pretty place, cool in summer and a favorite spot for children who liked to run into the river down the shingle bank or else swing on a rope hung from an elm bough above the water, but on a couple of Sunday mornings every summer there was no playing at the place, for on those days a procession would walk up the Smoketown Road, skirt the East Woods, then follow a track across the Miller farmland that led to the creek's steep, wooded slope. There might be fifty people in the procession, rarely more, and they walked in a solemn silence that would only be broken when someone started a hymn. Then they would all join in, their voices strong as they wended between cornfields and woods toward the water. The men would be in their suits, all of them ill-cut from a dark, thick cloth, but the discomfort of the formal clothes was a tribute to the day. The women were shawled and bonneted while the children were held firmly by the hand so that no unseemly behavior would mar the occasion. At the head of the procession strode a preacher in a wide-brimmed black hat.

Once at the river the preacher would wade into the creek and pray to the God of Abraham and of Isaac and of Jacob that He would bless this day, and bless these good people, then one by one those souls who had come to be baptized in the presence of their neighbors would walk into the water and the preacher would fold their hands on their breast, place another hand at their back, and then, with a joyous shout of blessing because a soul was being received into the heavenly host, he would thrust them backward into the creek so that the water flowed over their heads. He would hold them there for a second, then haul them upright as the congregation on the bank called loud praises for God's mercy to miserable sinners. Almost always the newly baptized men and women wept for happiness as they waded out of the creek to join the dark-suited congregation singing for them.

They sang in German. Many of the local settlers had come from Germany and they worshipped in a small, whitewashed church that had no spire, no porch, no pulpit, no decoration of any kind, though in tribute to the hard winters there was a black-bellied iron stove standing between the well-made pews. From the outside the church looked more like a humble house than a shrine, though inside it was surprisingly spacious and would be filled with light on sunny days. The Germans were Baptists, though their English-speaking neighbors good-naturedly described them as Dunkers, because of their custom of baptism by full immersion. On the Sabbath the Germans might worship in one place and the English-speakers in another, but during the week the Poffenbergers and Millers, Kennedys and Hoffmans, Middlekaufs and Pipers were good enough neighbors and hard-working farmers, and all agreed that they shared good land. Limestone might break the rich fields here and there, but a blessed living could be made from these farms so long as a family worked diligently, trusted in God, and had patience. That was why they had come to America, to thrive and live in peace beside a Maryland creek that flowed from a low pass in the South Mountains down to the wide Potomac River.

The creek was called the Antietam and the Dunker church lay just north of a village called Sharpsburg, and hardly a soul in America outside of Washington County, Maryland, had ever heard of either.

But then the armies came.

The rebels came first. Dirty, tired, ragged men with bleeding feet, boils on their skin, and lice in their beards. They marched south down the Hagerstown Pike raising a cloud of dust behind their gunwheels and shabby boots. Some had no boots at all, but walked barefoot. More rebels limped in from the east, crossing the creek on the handsome stone bridges. These rebels from the east wore bandages and had red-rimmed eyes and faces stained with black powder. They had fought to delay the Yankees at the passes in the hills and they had lost, and now they came to join Robert Lee's army at Sharpsburg.

It was a tiny army. Seventeen thousand men spread into the pastures and woodlots north of the village and the farmers could only watch as their precious rail fences were dismantled to make firewood or shelters. The army's guns, with their blackened muzzles and dirt-stained wheels, were lined on the high ground above the creek. The guns faced east.

The Yankees came next; sixty thousand blue-coated troops who crossed the Red Hill on the creek's eastern bank and then stopped. Just stopped.

The rebel guns had opened fire, bouncing their solid shot off the farmland and up over the first Northern troops to show on the river's far bank. General McClellan, told that the enemy had formed a fighting line on the creek's far bank, ordered the halt. He knew that thought must be taken, plans made, and fears understood, and so the Northern troops scattered into encampments and the rebel guns, seeing that their enemy was making no attempt to cross the creek, ceased their firing.

The gunsmoke drifted over the creek's valley and was touched pink by the setting sun. General Robert Lee watched the stalled enemy across the river, then turned to walk back toward the Hagerstown Pike where an ambulance waited to carry him to the army's headquarters just west of Sharpsburg. The general's hands were still bandaged and that made riding difficult, and so he walked while one of his aides led Traveller by the reins. Lee seemed curiously diminished out of the saddle. On horseback he looked like a tall man, but on foot he was revealed as only of average height. The ambulance was waiting beside the whitewashed Dunker church, which looked bright against the dark woods behind. The church's pews were being chopped for firewood by a battalion of Georgians who were billeted about the small house of worship.

The General had hardly spoken as he walked back from the gunline, but now he saw Major Delaney sitting slumped beside the pike that ran in front of the church. Lee smiled. "So you're alive, Major?"

"Happily, sir." Delaney struggled to his feet.

"And you have seen what you came to see, yes?"

"Fighting," Delaney said grimly.

"Rather more than I hoped you'd see," Lee said ruefully. "It seems McClellan has greater energy than I credited him with." Lee gestured to the ambulance. "Hardly a conquering general's carriage, Major, but you're welcome to share it back to headquarters. I assume you'll pitch camp with us again?"

"If I may, General."

"Unless you'd rather go home?" Lee suggested charitably. He might need every man he could muster to fight McClellan, but he could hardly imagine this pale, tired lawyer being of any great help.

"Are we to fight?" Delaney asked, climbing into the ambulance and leaving George to lead his two horses behind the slow-moving vehicle.

"Oh, I think so," Lee answered mildly. "I rather think we must." He leaned back against the ambulance's side and looked momentarily weary, then he frowned at his bandaged hands as though frustrated by the limitations they forced on him. "At least," he said ruefully, "it stops me biting my nails." The ambulance swayed and rocked on the dry road. It was a Yankee vehicle, captured at Manassas, and highly sprung to relieve the pain of its wounded occupants, but even the best springs could not smooth out the ruts of the Hagerstown Pike as it dropped into Sharpsburg. "You know what Frederick the Great once said?" Lee asked suddenly, his thoughts reverting to the trial that lay ahead. "That the unforgivable crime in war is not making the wrong decision, but making no decision. And I think we have to fight here."

"Why?" Delaney asked, then hastily added, "I'm curious, sir," in case the General thought he was challenging his decision.

Lee shrugged. "We invaded the North, Delaney. Are we to slink away with nothing accomplished?"

"We captured Harper's Ferry, sir," Delaney pointed out.

"So we did, so we did, but we set out to do a great deal more. We came north, Delaney, to inflict hurt on the enemy and that we still have to do. I had planned to inflict that pain well north of here, but I confess General McClellan has surprised me, so now I must hurt him here rather than on the Susquehanna. But here or there, what matters is to hurt him so badly that the North cannot invade us again, and Europe will see that we can defend ourselves and are thus worthy of their support. Hurt them once, Delaney, and there's a chance we'll not have to inflict pain again, but if we just slip away then McClellan will follow and we shall have to fight him on our own soil. And poor Virginia has suffered enough, God knows." The general spoke softly, rehearsing his arguments out loud, and always conscious that Belvedere Delaney carried weight in Richmond's political circles. If things went badly in the next few hours then it would be as well to have a man like Delaney retailing the general's motives to the Confederacy's leaders.

"McClellan outnumbers us," Delaney said, unable to hide his nervousness.

"He does indeed, but he always has," Lee answered dryly, "though this time, I confess, his preponderance is significant. We guess he has eighty thousand men. We have less than twenty." He paused, smiling at the outrageous imbalance. "But Jackson's men are marching toward us. We might line up thirty thousand against him."

"Thirty?" Delaney was appalled at the odds.

Lee chuckled. "Poor Delaney. You really would be happier in Richmond, I think? It would do you no dishonor to leave us. Your work here is surely done?"

Better than you know, Delaney thought, but answered instead with a quotation from Shakespeare. " 'The fewer men, the greater share of honor.' "

Lee smiled, recognizing Shakespeare's line from *Henry V.* "A few men beat a great army in that battle," he said, "and I do know one thing about these men." He gestured with a bandaged hand at his ragged troops in their bivouacs. "They are the best fighting men, Delaney, that this poor world has ever seen. They make me feel humble. Wars might be won by strategy, but battles are won by morale, and if you and I, my friend, should live to be a hundred we shall never see troops as good as these. McClellan is nervous of them, very nervous, and tomorrow he has to attack them and he will do it gingerly. And if he is as cautious as I expect, then we shall have a chance to tear his army into pieces."

Delaney shuddered at the thought of battle. "He hasn't been cautious these last few days, sir," he said warningly.

Lee nodded. "He got wind of our dispositions. We don't know how, but some sympathizers at Frederick sent us a message telling us that McClellan was boasting that he had us in the bag. Well, so he did, but it's one thing to have a bag and it's quite another to stuff the wildcat inside the bag. Believe me, Delaney, his caution will return. It already has returned! If I was across that river I wouldn't be bivouacking now. I'd be pushing brigades over the valley, I'd be thrusting hard, I'd be fighting, but McClellan is waiting, and every hour that he waits brings Jackson's men closer to us."

But even when Jackson's men came, Delaney thought, Lee's army would be less than half the size of McClellan's. The rebellion was surely doomed and Delaney, rejoicing in that thought and in the part he had played in the destruction, still felt a regret for Lee. The General was a good man, a very good and honorable man, but Lee had no ambassadorships in his pocket and so Delaney prayed that on the morrow he would watch the Confederacy die in the ripe fields beside the Antietam.

Tuesday, September 17, dawned hot and sultry. The Confederate pickets, warned of an enemy attack, stared across the river through a heavy fog that slowly lightened as the sun rose above the Red Hill. The pickets feared the blast of cannons loaded with canister and the splashing of men carrying bayonets and loaded rifles through the river's fords, but no such attack came. McClellan, if he did but know it, had succeeded in the dearest wish of all fighting generals: He had trapped his enemy's army while it was split into two parts, and if McClellan had lunged across the stream he could have destroyed Lee's small army, then marched against Jackson's scattered men as they hurried north from Harper's Ferry.

But McClellan did not move. He waited.

The sun burned the last of the fog from the creek and nervous rebel pickets stared across the water at green leaves from which the smoke of campfires drifted gently. Confederate cavalry reconnoitered the Antietam's banks north and south of Lee's position, but no Northern troops were attempting the crossing, nor, astonishingly, were any Northern cavalry making similar patrols in the drowsy, heavy countryside. There were Yankee troops marching, but those men formed the tail of McClellan's huge army as it crossed the hills toward the Antietam's eastern bank. The sixty thousand Yankees became seventy-five thousand and still McClellan did not advance. He waited.

He waited just two and a half miles east of the Dunker church, on the Yankee bank of the Antietam, in the Pry family farmhouse. The farm had a substantial house, ample barns, and well-drained fields that sloped from the Red Hill down to the creek's banks. Most of the fields were stubble now, though some were tall with corn that was almost ready to be harvested. One meadow was stacked with hay, a second had a fine crop of clover, while the higher fields had just been plowed for the planting of winter wheat. Yankees were bivouacked in all the meadows and had torn down the haystacks to make their mattresses. Some played baseball, some wrote home, others lay reading in whatever shade they could discover on this hot, humid day. Once in a while a man would peer through the trees at the distant line of rebel guns crowning the western skyline, but until they received orders to attack they were content to rest. Little Mac would see them right. The newspapers might call McClellan the Young Napoleon, but to the Northern soldiers he was always Little Mac and the one thing they knew and loved in Little Mac was that he would never risk their lives unnecessarily. They trusted him, and so they were content to wait.

Colonel Thorne was not content. At dawn he was riding his horse down the Antietam toward the Potomac, and by the time the fog had lifted he had marked a half dozen crossing places on his map. He had attempted to cross one ford and been repelled by an alarmed shout from a gray-clad picket who had hastily cocked his rifle and fired a wild shot that whipped over Thorne's head. Further upstream he had watched a stone bridge and tried to count the number of rebels dug into their rifle pits on its far side. He saw them go down to the creek to fill their canteens, watched them wash, and listened to their laughter.

Now, as the morning dragged somnolently onward, he discovered General McClellan comfortably ensconced in the Pry house. Telegraphers were running wire up the hill to a signal station on the Red Hill's summit from where messages would be semaphored by relay stations until another telegraph station could send McClellan's news to Washington. One message already waited to be sent and Thorne, discovering the telegraphers setting up their equipment in the Pry's parlor, picked it up. "This morning a heavy fog has thus far prevented us doing more than ascertain that some of the enemy are still there," the message read. "Do not know in what force. Will attack as soon as situation of the enemy develops." Thorne snorted as he dropped the message. You don't wait for the enemy, he thought. My God, but Adam Faulconer had died to put the Northern army into this place and all McClellan needed to do was order his troops forward. Those troops were in high enough spirits. They had chased the rebels off the mountain passes and rumors were whipping through the Northern ranks that Lee was wounded, maybe dead, and so were Jackson and Longstreet. The troops were willing enough to fight, but McClellan was waiting for the situation of the enemy to develop, whatever that meant. Thorne strode out of the parlor to discover the General sitting in one of a number of well-upholstered armchairs that had been placed on the lawn to give a view of the ground across the river. A telescope stood on a tripod beside the General, while in front of the armchairs, on the lawn, which sloped steeply downhill, a barricade had been erected from fence rails and tree branches. The barricade suggested that McClellan believed he might have to make his last stand here on the farmhouse lawn, firing his revolver from the comfort of an armchair while his defeated troops streamed past on either side.

"I have been south," Thorne said abruptly. McClellan, chatting with Pinkerton, who occupied the armchair next to his, had pointedly ignored the colonel's arrival and so Thorne simply butted in.

"South where?" McClellan finally asked.

"South down the creek, sir. There are fords there, and none of them properly guarded by the rebels. One had a picket, but only a handful of men. The best crossing is at Snaveley's Ford." Thorne held out his notebook in which he had penciled a crude map. "Cross there, sir, and within a mile we'll have cut off Lee's retreat."

McClellan nodded, but otherwise seemed to take no notice of Thorne's words.

"For God's sake, sir," Thorne said, "attack now! Lee can't have twenty thousand men under arms."

"Nonsense." McClellan was goaded into the argument. "Believe that, Colonel, and you'll believe anything." He laughed and his aides sniggered dutifully.

"Sir." Thorne deliberately made his voice respectful. "We know when Harper's Ferry surrendered, sir, and we know that Jackson's troops cannot have reached Sharpsburg yet. No troops can cover that distance that fast, but if we wait till this evening, sir, they'll be here. Then Lee will have forty or fifty thousand men waiting for us."

"General Lee," McClellan said icily, "has eighty thousand men already. Eighty thousand!" His voice rose in indignation. "And if this benighted government saw fit to provide me with the men necessary to prosecute a successful war I would already have attacked, but I cannot attack until I know, with utter certainty, the enemy's dispositions!"

"The enemy's disposition, sir, is desperate!" Thorne insisted. "They're tired, they're hungry, they're outnumbered, and in three hours, sir, you can have a victory as complete as any in history."

McClellan shook his head in anger, then glanced at Allen Pinkerton, who slouched low in his flower-printed armchair. He wore an ill-fitting jacket and had a hard, round hat on his blunt head. "Colonel Thorne believes we outnumber the enemy, Major Pinkerton," McClellan gave the chief of his secret service his honorary rank, "is that your determination?"

"Wish it was, chief!" Pinkerton took a stubby pipe out of his mouth, then went on in his broad Scottish accent and with a tone of utter confidence. "There are many more of them than of us, that I'll wager. We had a laddie ride the creek bank yesterday, what was his name? Custer! That's the fellow. Hordes of them, he says, just hordes! A good lad, young Custer."

"You see, Thorne?" McClellan asked, vindicated.

Thorne pointed west and southward to where a smear of hazy whiteness was smudged across the midday sky. "Sir," he appealed. "You see that white cloud? It's dust, sir, dust, and it marks where Jackson's leading men are hurrying to reinforce Lee, but they're ten miles off yet, sir, and so I beg you, sir, I beg you, just go now! Attack!"

"War is always a simple matter to amateurs," McClellan said, his voice dripping with scorn. "Lee would not be standing against us with twenty thousand men, Colonel, though I've no doubt he'd like us to think he has so few. It's called setting a trap, Colonel Thorne, but I'm too old a dog to fall for that one." McClellan's staff officers laughed at this evident shaft of wit. The General smiled. "You heard Major Pinkerton's evaluation, Colonel," he said, "do you doubt him?"

Thorne's opinion of Pinkerton was unpronounceable, but he made one more effort to hammer sense into his opponents. "This man who rode the lines yesterday," he demanded of Pinkerton. "Did he cross the river?"

"Now how could he do that?" Pinkerton asked, tamping down the tobacco in his pipe. "There are eighty thousand rebels across that river, Colonel, and young Custer's too canny a lad to commit suicide." The Scotsman laughed.

"Eighty thousand," McClellan repeated the figure, then pointed to the cloud of dust, "and that dust tells us that more are coming." He stretched his legs to prop his boots on the strange, fortress-like barricade and, for a time, with his head sunk on his chest, he frowned toward the distant plateau that was edged by the rebel gunline. "By tomorrow, gentlemen," he announced after a long silence, "we shall doubtless face a hundred thousand enemies, but we shall do our duty. America expects no more of us."

It does expect more, Thorne thought savagely. America expects victory. It expects its sons to be spared slaughter in the coming years, it expects an undivided Union and to have Washington's gutters awash in beer while the victory parade marches past, but all McClellan prayed for was survival, and Thorne, appalled at the man's obduracy, could do nothing more. He had tried, and in the cause for which he pleaded

Adam Faulconer had died, but McClellan commanded the army and the battle would be fought in the Young Napoleon's own good time. And so the Yankees waited.

Nothing could have prevented straggling. For a time Starbuck had snarled at his limping, bleeding, struggling men, but one by one they dropped back in helpless weakness. The road's verges were littered with other stragglers who had dropped out of battalions further up the road, while here and there a brave soul hobbled on using his rifle as a crutch and with his feet leaving bloody footprints on the road's dust.

Starbuck's battalion at least had boots, but the boots were ill-made and were coming apart at the seams. Their real problem was plain weakness. They were unfit, and the handful of marches they had made in the last few weeks were no preparation for this hot, hard road where Jackson's staff officers goaded the troops on. Most of the other battalions were suffering from a lack of food. The army had outrun its supplies, and though the men had gorged on the Yankee delicacies captured at Harper's Ferry, that rich food had only made them ill. Now they were back on a diet of apples and corn snatched from the unharvested fields, and even the men who kept up the grueling pace were plagued by diarrhea. The column pounded on between lines of exhausted, sick men and the ever-present stench of feces.

Colonel Swynyard finally gave up trying to prevent straggling in his brigade. "It's no good, Nate," he said, "let them be." Swynyard was leading his horse. He could have ridden, as Lieutenant Colonel Maitland of the Legion rode, but he preferred to rest his horse's back and to set an example to his men.

Starbuck grudgingly let the sickest men fall out, but he would not allow any of the officers to leave the column. Billy Blythe was the worst affected. He was sweating in his tight coat and stumbling glassy-eyed, but whenever he veered toward the grass verge Starbuck would shove him onward. "You're an officer, Billy," he said, "so set an example." Blythe viciously spat out the efficacious word, but he was more frightened of Starbuck than of his weakness and so he limped on. "I thought you walked all the way south from Massachusetts," Starbuck added.

"I did."

"Hell, this is a stroll compared with that. Keep going."

Sergeant Case displayed no weakness. He marched steadily, untiringly, with Billy Blythe's bedroll over his own. When, each hour, the column halted for a ten minute rest, Sergeant Case would find water and bring it to Blythe. Starbuck watched the two and wondered if it had been they who had tried to kill him in the Harper's Ferry night, but now, under the unrelenting sun, that murder attempt seemed like a bad dream. He wondered if he had been mistaken. Maybe the shot had merely been some man's attempt to clear his musket of fouled powder, or perhaps a drunk had loosed a bullet into the night. He had seen two men running away, but that proved nothing.

Potter's company led the battalion. They lost no one to straggling, nor should they, for they were the cream of the Special Battalion. Potter marched happily enough, singing with his men, telling stories and jokes, and sometimes helping to haul the hearse with its precious load of ammunition. More ammunition was carried on the wagon, but the draft horses taken at Harper's Ferry were proving fatally weak. The wagon fell farther and farther behind, causing chaos as gun teams and battalions tried to pass it on the road.

"I assume," Potter said to Starbuck, "that there is a purpose to this exertion?"

"If Old Jack marches like this," Starbuck said, "you can be sure he's going to battle."

"You like him, don't you?" Potter observed with amusement.

"Old Jack? Yes, I do." Starbuck was faintly surprised at the admission.

"You emulate him."

"Me?" Starbuck was surprised. "Never," he said dismissively.

"Not in the matter of God," Potter allowed, "nor, perhaps, in his eccentricities, but otherwise? Yes, you do. Single-minded Starbuck, not yielding an inch, tougher than boot leather. You despise weakness."

"This ain't a time to be weak."

"I can think of no better time," Potter said dryly. "The weak are liable to fall out and be spared the slaughter. It's you strong ones who'll march gallantly into the Yankee guns. Don't worry, Starbuck, I'll be with you, but I have to tell you there's a jug of whiskey in my pack in case things get too bad."

Starbuck smiled. "Only one?"

"Alas, only one, but it's marvelous what one bottle will achieve."

"Just keep some for me."

"A sip, maybe." Potter walked on, following the hearse with its dusty plumes. "I am astonished at my forbearance," he said after a while. "I have a whole jug and I haven't unstoppered it."

"So you are strong."

"Temporarily, maybe."

"Jackson says that strength comes from God," Starbuck said.

"He would, wouldn't he?" Potter said, casting a sidelong look at his Major. "Do I detect a soul in trouble?"

Starbuck glanced to his right to see a stretch of the Potomac showing between heavy trees. The march was taking them northward along the Potomac's southern bank, but soon, he knew, they must cross the river and thus pass into the North. "I was just thinking about God last night," he said evasively. He wondered if he should mention the murderous attempt on his life, but decided it would all sound too fanciful. "Hell," he said after a while, "when you're going into battle you're bound to think about God, aren't you?"

Potter smiled. "Has anyone determined whether Christians survive battle in greater numbers than unbelievers? I should like to know. Hell, if getting saved is my ticket to survival then you can lead me to the mercy seat right now."

"It ain't living or dying," Starbuck said, trying to ignore the burning pain in his leg muscles and the ache of the boils on his back and the harsh taste of the dust in his throat. "It's what happens after death."

"That's hardly a reason to be converted," Potter said. "I spent enough time in my father's church not to want to spend eternity with the same people." He shuddered. "Good people, yes, but oh so disapproving! I think I'll take my chances at the other destination." He laughed, then checked his amusement as a rumbling noise bruised the sky. "They've begun proceedings without us?" he suggested chidingly.

"That's not gunfire," Starbuck said, "just thunder. Summer thunder." There were clouds in the east and maybe by evening there would be a hard rain that might break the sweltering humidity that was making the march so hard.

A half hour later they turned and forded the Potomac River. A strong battery of Confederate artillery guarded the ford's Virginia bank, evidence that this was Lee's only way of escape if disaster struck the Confederate army. The water came up to their waists so that men had to hoist their cartridge pouches and cap boxes clear of the stream. Once on the far bank, in Yankee territory at last, they crossed the bridge over the Chesapeake and Ohio Canal and began walking toward a small village just four miles eastward. "Sharpsburg," Swynyard told Starbuck, "and this," he gestured at the road up which they trudged, "is our only line of retreat. If the Yankees whip us, Nate, we'll be running for our lives down this road and if they cut us off from the ford we'll be done for."

"They won't whip us," Starbuck said grimly. Rebel encampments stretched untidily on either side of the road; evidence that the column was at last nearing its destination. This was the army's rear area, the place where the transport wagons and artillery parks were sited, the place where the field hospitals readied their scalpels and probes and bandages. The village of Sharpsburg itself was a small grid of neat frame houses with whitewashed porches and carefully watered yards that had been stripped bare of vegetables and fruit. Some civilians put out barrels of water for the marching column, but claimed they had no food to give. "We're starving ourselves, boys," a pregnant woman explained.

"Get your victuals off the Yankees, lads," an old man, evidently a Southern supporter, shouted, "and God bless you!"

They turned left off the village's main street onto the Hagerstown Pike, which climbed steeply toward the higher ground. A staff officer galloped down the column, found Swynyard, and directed him northward along the pike that ran straight between fields rich with clover.

They passed the Dunker church, taking it for a roadside cottage, and there they turned right onto the Smoketown Road and walked the last half mile to reach a shady wood of tall elms and heavy oak. The wood stretched to the north, while south of the road was a plowed field newly sewn with winter wheat. A family's graveyard was set in the field's center, and it was there that Swynyard established his headquarters. His brigade, thinned by straggling and worn out by a summer's campaigning, collapsed in the plowed field and in two fields of stubble that lay to the east. The ground here fell gently away toward the creek and Starbuck, throwing down his bedroll in the shade of the trees just across the road from the plowed field, could see Yankee guns on distant pastures across the river.

But there was no time now to reconnoiter the ground. What was left of the battalion had to be shown where to bivouac, then a working party had to go to the springhouse of the nearby farm to find water. A few stragglers limped in and a handful of others arrived on wagons that had been sent back down the road to collect the weary. Starbuck ordered a sullen Captain Dennison down to the town to find any other stragglers and direct them up to the high ground.

Swynyard summoned his battalion commanders to the small graveyard. He showed them where the brigade's small reserve store of ammunition was being stored, then walked the officers eastward to the rebel gunline, which overlooked the deep, wooded valley of the creek. Lee had evidently decided against defending the creek's bank, but would instead let the Northern army cross the water and then climb the steep slope into the face of his guns, rifles, and muskets. "With God's help, gentlemen," Swynyard said, "we shoot them down here."

It was an open stretch of fields, a place where men would stand in the smoke and trade volleys with a horde of Yankees coming up from the woods. Maitland had his expensive field glasses trained across the valley to a plowed field where a battery of Northern guns was being sited. "Parrott guns, by the look of them," he said, "and aimed right at us."

"Near on two miles away," John Miles, the commander of the

small 13th Florida regiment opined. "Maybe the sons of bitches will lose us in the smoke."

"Hell, they'll fire at the smoke," Haxall, the Arkansas man, observed.

"Our guns will deal with them," Swynyard said, cutting the pessimism short.

Maitland had turned his attention to the group of farm buildings that stood below the graveyard on the rebel held slope. "Can we turn that farm into a fortress?" he asked Swynyard. "Our Hougoumont," he added.

"Our what?" Haxall asked.

"The château of Hougoumont," Maitland answered with his insufferable air of superiority. "A fortified farm that Wellington held all day against Napoleon's men. At Waterloo," he added condescendingly.

"He also fortified the farm at Mont St. Jean," Swynyard said, unexpectedly trumping Maitland's knowledge of military history, "and he lost it because the French surrounded it and the poor men inside ran out of ammunition. And tomorrow the Yankees will be all round that farm. It's too far forward."

"So we just ignore it?" Maitland asked, reluctant to give up the thought of a solid stone wall between himself and the Yankee rifles.

"Yankees won't ignore it," Starbuck put in. "They'll fill the place with sharpshooters."

"So we burn it," Swynyard decided. "Miles? Your men can fire the buildings tonight?"

"Reckon they'd enjoy that, Colonel."

"Then do it," Swynyard said, then briefly sketched the brigade's dispositions. The big Virginia regiment would hold the right of the brigade line, then would come the smaller units from Florida and Arkansas, with Maitland's men of the Faulconer Legion on the left. "You're in reserve, Nate," Swynyard told Starbuck. "Keep your men in the woods. That might give them some cover from the Yankee guns."

"I thought our guns were going to silence their guns?" Maitland observed cattily.

Swynyard ignored the comment. "It'll be a plug-ugly infantry fight, gentlemen," he said grimly. "We'll have plenty of artillery, though, and the enemy's coming uphill. The side that stands longest and shoots best will win, and that's going to be us." He dismissed the officers, but put an arm into Starbuck's arm and led him northward toward the woods. "The Legion's got good men," he told Starbuck, "but I don't trust Maitland. He's yellow. Thinks his white skin is too precious to be punctured by a bullet. That's why your men are right beside his. If Maitland starts to go back, Nate, step in."

"Step in?" Starbuck asked. "He outranks me."

"Just step in. Hold the Legion for me till I can get rid of Maitland. May not happen, Nate. Or maybe the good Lord will see fit to take me home tomorrow, in which case Maitland takes over the whole brigade, and God help these men if he does." Swynyard stopped and stared down the long slope. "Just have to shoot them down, Nate, just shoot them down." He said it sadly, imagining the blue masses that would swarm up the hill next morning.

But Swynyard was wrong. The Yankees might well be planning to cross the river and climb the hill, but first they intended a flank attack and late that afternoon, as Starbuck's men were mauling the trees and raiding the remnants of rail fences for their camp fires, a mass of Northern troops crossed the creek by a bridge that lay well north of the rebel positions. The Yankees climbed to the higher ground and kept marching westward until they reached the Hagerstown Pike and there they camped. Rebel pickets fired at the Yankees, and every now and then the sound of rifles crackled angry and loud as Northern skirmishers tried to drive the Confederates away, but neither side made any attempt to attack the other's main body. General Lee watched the Federal troops making their camp to his north and their presence told him what to expect in the morning. The Yankees would march south in what promised to be a massive attack straight down the Hagerstown Pike.

But that assault, Lee knew, would be only one attack. Others would come across the creek, and maybe other Yankees would try to curl around his southern flank. So be it. He did not have the men to guard every river crossing, only to hold the high ground around the village and the Dunker church. But at least his army was growing. Two-thirds of Jackson's men had come from Harper's Ferry and the remaining third, once they had finished sending the Federal prisoners south to the camps, would hurry toward him the next day. He would start the battle with less than thirty thousand men and he knew that more than twice that number were readying themselves to attack him, but if McClellan was not fought here then he would have to be fought in Virginia. It was better here, Lee decided, where the Yankees would have to climb the hills from the creek into the face of his guns.

But the Yankees encamped to the north would have no hills to climb, for they were already on the high ground. Those men would attack down the line of the pike where two long stands of timber, the West Woods and the East Woods, formed a natural funnel some six or seven hundred yards wide. The funnel was a swathe of farmland that led into the heart of Lee's position. Not that the Yankees could be seen yet from that heart, for, though they were camped in the woods that grew at the northern lip of the funnel, a thirty-acre cornfield stood between them and the rebel line. The corn stretched across the funnel and was near to harvest and so stood as tall as a paraded regiment. The stalks whispered together in the small evening breeze; a screen to hide two enemies from each other, and in the morning, Lee guessed, a place where the attacking Federals would meet his hard-bitten troops.

"So you're not my reserve after all, Nate," Swynyard said when news of the Yankee flanking march arrived. The Yellowlegs were camped at the base of the East Woods and that meant they guarded one lip of the funnel and so could expect to fight the Yankees in the dawn. "I can change you over," Swynyard volunteered.

"They'll fight," Starbuck said of his men. Besides, it was dusk, and to change the position now would mean confusion among men too tired to change bivouacs. "You ain't expecting an attack up the slope now?" he asked, indicating the farmland where the battalion commanders had met and where the farm buildings now blazed from the work of Miles's incendiarists.

"Maybe they'll come both ways," Swynyard said. "If McClellan's got any sense, that's what they'll do. And that'll mean hard work, Nate. But those boys," he waved a hand northward to indicate the Yankees who were camped higher on the turnpike, "are closest, so worry about them first." He dragged his hand with the missing fingers through his tangled beard. "Earn our pay tomorrow, that's for sure. Your boys are all right?"

"They'll fight," Starbuck said, ignoring his doubts about Tumlin and Dennison.

"Tell them I'm holding prayers in half an hour," Swynyard said. "I'll invite you, even though I know you won't come."

"I might," Starbuck said unexpectedly.

Swynyard was tempted to make a joke of Starbuck's answer, then he saw that maybe his prayers for Starbuck's soul were being answered and so he bit back his jest. "I'd like it if you did, Nate," he said instead.

But Starbuck did not come to the colonel's prayer meeting. Instead he walked to the very right-hand end of his short line where Captain Dennison's A Company was bivouacked. Starbuck was nervous that the gesture he was about to make would be construed as weakness, but the bad blood inside the Special Battalion needed to be lanced and so he looked for Private Case and, finding the big man, jerked his head toward the trees. "I want you," he said.

Case glanced at his companions, shrugged, then ostentatiously picked up his rifle and checked that it was primed. He followed Starbuck into the trees, taking care to keep a half dozen paces behind. Starbuck remembered the shot in the Harper's Ferry night, but that was not why he had summoned Case because Case would never admit to having been one of the two men. Instead, on the eve of battle, Starbuck wanted to make peace.

Starbuck stopped when they were out of earshot of the rest of the battalion. "So what," he asked, "would the Royal Fusiliers be doing different?" Case seemed bemused by the question and did not answer. Starbuck looked into the ugly face and was amazed again by the flat brutality of Case's eyes. "Even in the Royal Fusiliers," Starbuck said, "sergeants don't get away with defying their officers. What the hell did you expect me to do? Let you keep your stripes?" Again Case did not answer. He just turned his head and spat a thin stream of tobacco juice onto a hump of limestone.

"Tomorrow," Starbuck went on, but feeling as though he was wading through a lake of molasses, "we're going to fight, and if A Company fights as feebly as it did the other day, you're all going to die." That got Case's attention. The feral gaze shifted from some distant point among the trees to stare into Starbuck's eyes. "You know how to fight, Case, so make damn sure the rest of the company fights like you. Do that, and you get your stripes back. Understand?"

Case paused, then nodded. He shifted the tobacco from one cheek to another, spat again, but still did not speak. Starbuck was about to launch himself into an earnest peroration about men not being able to serve two masters, about the need for discipline, about the value of experienced men like Case to a battalion like the Yellowlegs, but he managed to check the words before he even began. He had said all he needed to say and Case had heard all he needed to hear and the rest was up to Case himself, but at least, Starbuck thought, he had given the tall man something to look forward to beyond mere revenge. "When tomorrow's over, Case," he said, "you can go to another regiment if that's what you want, and you can go as a sergeant, but tomorrow you fight with us. You understand me?"

Case paused. "You through?" he finally asked.

"I'm through."

Case turned and walked away. Starbuck watched him go, then walked east until he came to the edge of the wood and could stare across the valley. Distant fires flickered in far woods. Somewhere behind him, on the plateau, a gun fired. There was a pause, then a Yankee cannon answered. A battery of rebel artillery, poised on a hill to the turnpike's west, had seen the Northern gunners emplacing a battery and so had opened fire. The two sides dueled as the night fell, and fought on into the darkness so that their gunflashes lit the farmland in sudden bursts of unnatural light that spewed their powdery glare across green fields and cast black shadows among the heavy trees. To the east, on the slope that fell down to the creek, the burning farm buildings churned thick smoke and bright sparks into the night air. The cannon fire died slowly and finally ceased altogether, but then, in the echoing silence, it began to rain. Starbuck, rolled at last in his blanket beneath the trees, heard the drops pattering on the green leaves and tried to sleep, but sleep would not come. He had marched to Sharpsburg and he was more frightened than he had ever been in all his life. Because tomorrow he must fight.

I T'S REAL COFFEE," LUCIFER SAID, SHAKING STARBUCK AWAKE, "from Harper's Ferry."

Starbuck swore, tried not to believe what was happening, then swore again when he realized it was happening. It was not yet dawn. The mist in the trees was mixed with the acrid smoke of half-dead fires. The leaves dripped. The Yankees were coming today.

"You're shivering," Lucifer said. "You got a fever."

"I don't."

"Like a baby. Shivering." Lucifer prodded the nearest embers with a stick, trying to stir life into the fire's remnants. "Yankees didn't have fires," he said, then grinned. "They're hiding from us. Reckon they're more frightened of us than we are of them."

"They're on your side," Starbuck said gracelessly.

"I'm on my side," Lucifer insisted angrily, "and no one damn else is."

"Except me," Starbuck said, trying to mollify the boy. He sipped the coffee. "Did you stay awake all night?"

"I stayed awake," Lucifer said, "till I was sure they was asleep."

Starbuck did not ask who "they" were. "There's nothing to worry about," he said instead. He hoped that was true. He hoped he had defused Case's smoldering anger. He hoped he would survive this day.

"You don't worry 'cos I do," Lucifer said. "Did I hear Captain Tumlin tell you he saw John Brown hung in Harper's Ferry?"

Starbuck had to think to remember the conversation, then recalled Tumlin talking about watching with his whore from an upper window of Wager's Hotel. "Yes," he said bleakly, trying to imbue the syllable with disapproval for Lucifer having eavesdropped. "So?"

"So," Lucifer said, "Mister Brown wasn't ever hung in Harper's Ferry. He was hung in Charlestown. Everybody knows that."

"I didn't."

"Your Captain Tumlin," Lucifer said sourly, "don't know shit from a sugarcone."

Starbuck sat up and pushed the clammy folds of the blanket away. He was shivering, but he guessed it was just the damp. That and apprehension. He heard twigs snapping in the woods, but there was a strong picket line to the north so the sound had to be his own men stirring. He wondered how long it was till dawn. The mist was thick as gunsmoke. Everything was damp—the wood, the ground, his clothes. His rifle was beaded with dew. The day was chill now, but it promised to be burning hot, a day of rank humidity, a day when the spent powder would choke the rifle barrels like soot clogging a chimney.

"Shit from a sugarcone," Lucifer said again, trying to provoke a response.

Starbuck sighed. "We're a makeshift battalion, Lucifer. We get the dregs." He snapped one of his laces as he tied his boots. He swore, wondering if the small accident was a bad omen. He fiddled out the broken lace and, in the dark, rethreaded what was left and tied a knot. Then he stood up, every bone and muscle aching. Fires were coming to life in the fields and wood, the flames dulled and misted by the fog. Men coughed, spat, grumbled, and pissed. A horse whinnied, then there was a clatter as a man blundered into a stand of arms. "What's for breakfast?" he asked Lucifer.

"Hardtack and half an apple."

"Give me half of the half."

He strapped on his belt, then checked that the cartridge pouch was full, the cap box filled, and the revolver loaded. For hundreds of years, he thought, men had woken thus to a day of battle. They had tested their spear points, felt their sword edges, made certain musket flints were tight, then prayed to their gods that they would live. And hundreds of years from now, Starbuck supposed, soldiers would still wake in a gray dark and go through the same motions with whatever unimaginable means of death they carried. He hefted his rifle, checked the percussion cap, then slung it on his shoulder. "To work," he said to Lucifer. "Earn our pay."

"What pay?" Lucifer asked.

"I owe you," Starbuck said.

"So I ain't a slave?"

"You're free as a bird, Lucifer. You want to fly away, then you fly. But I'd miss you. But if you stay today," Starbuck added, knowing full well that Lucifer would stay, "then you keep out of harm's way. This ain't your fight."

"White men only, eh?"

"Fools only, Lucifer. Fools only," Starbuck said, then walked slowly through the dark wood, feeling his way where the feeble light of reviving fires did not show a path. He talked to waking men, stirred the laggards, and organized a work party to fill the battalion's canteens. Biting bullets off cartridges filled the mouth with salty gunpowder so that an hour into a fight men were parched and water was worth its weight in gold. He sent another party to bring up spare ammunition from the graveyard so that the battalion could have its own reserve supply at the wood's edge. It was there, where the wood bordered the road, that he stopped to listen to an unseen band of men who softly sang a hymn among the dark mist-shrouded trees. " 'Jesus, my strength, my hope,' " they sang, " 'On thee I cast my care; With humble confidence look up, And know thou hear'st my prayer.' " The familiar words were strangely comforting, but someone else had also been listening and started to sing another hymn in a voice much louder than those of the men who had gathered for their morning prayers.

" 'Hark how the watchmen cry!' " Captain Potter sang in a remarkably good clear tenor voice, " 'Attend the trumpet's sound. Stand to your arms, the foe is nigh, The powers of hell surround.' "

Starbuck discovered Potter among the trees. "Let them be," he chided Potter gently for disturbing the prayers.

"I just thought my choice more appropriate than theirs," Potter said. He was in a feverishly excited mood, so much so that for an instant Starbuck wondered if the stone bottle of whiskey had been emptied, but there was no smell of liquor on Potter's breath as, more quietly, he sang the hymn's last quatrain. " 'By all hell's host withstood, We all hell's host o'erthrow, And conquering them through Jesus' blood, We on to conquer go.' " He laughed. "Funny, isn't it? The Yankees are probably singing that as well. Both of us clamoring to Jesus. He must be confused."

"How are your pickets?" Starbuck asked.

"Awake. Watching for the host of hell. I came to fetch them a bucket of coffee. I guess proceedings won't begin till light?"

"I guess not."

"And then," Potter said with unholy relish, "we can expect something very nasty. Is it true they outnumber us?"

"So far as we know, yes." Starbuck felt a trembling that seemed to begin in his heart and flicker down his arms and legs. "Maybe by two to one," he added, trying to sound laconic as though he faced battle every day. And what day was it? A Wednesday. There was nothing special about Wednesdays at home. Not like Sundays that were given to God and solemnity, or Mondays that were his mother's wash-day and when the whole Boston house would be busy with servants and steam. Wednesdays were just Wednesdays, a half marker between Sundays. His father would be saying prayers with the servants. Did anyone in the house wonder where the second son was today?

There was a glimmer of lightening in the fog that lay to the east. " 'Per me si va ne la città dolente,' " Potter said suddenly and unexpectedly, " 'per me si va ne l'etterno dolore, Per me si va la perduta gente.' "

Starbuck gaped at him. "What the hell?" he asked.

" 'Through me you enter the city of sorrows,' " Potter translated dramatically, " 'through me you come into eternal pain, through me you join the lost people.' Dante," he added, "the words inscribed above the Gates of Hell."

"I thought it said 'Abandon all hope, all ye who enter here'?" Starbuck said.

"That, too," Potter said.

"When the hell did you learn Italian?"

"I didn't. I just read Dante. There was a time, Starbuck, when I fancied myself a poet, so I read all the poetry I could. Then I discovered a quicker way to Elysium."

"Why in God's name did you study medicine?"

"My father believed I should be useful," Potter said. "He believes in usefulness. Saint Paul was a tentmaker, so Matthew Potter must have a trade, and poetry, my father believed, was not a trade. Poetry, he declared, is not useful unless you're a psalmist, in which case you're dead. He thought I should be a doctor and write uplifting hymns in between killing my unsuspecting patients."

"You'd make a good doctor," Starbuck said.

Potter laughed. "Now you sound like my mother. I must find that coffee."

"Matthew," Starbuck stopped Potter as he walked away. "Look after yourself today."

Potter smiled. "I have a conviction that I shall live, Starbuck. I can't explain it, but somehow I feel charmed. But thank you. And may you survive too." He walked away.

Beyond the fog the sun was lightening the eastern sky, turning the dark to gray. There was no wind, not a breath, just a still, silent sky heavy with the sullen gray wolf-light, the light before dawn, before battle.

Starbuck flinched, then closed his eyes as he tried to compose a prayer to fit the day, but nothing came. He thought of his younger brothers and sisters safe in their Boston beds, then went to form his men into line.

Because it was a windless, lovely dawn beside the Antietam.

Gunners begin most battles. The infantry will win or lose the fight, but the gunners start the killing and even before the fog had lifted the Yankee gunners across the Antietam began their bombardment. They had positioned their guns the previous evening and now, with nothing to guide their aim but the tops of trees protruding through the fog, the gunners opened fire.

Shells screamed eerily through the vapor. The Federal guns that had been brought across the river joined the cacophony, banging their missiles over the cornfield into the whitened vacancy where the rebels waited. The rebel guns answered, aiming blind at first, but as the fog thinned they were able to fire at the diffused glare of muzzle flames that made livid patches in the mist whenever an enemy gun fired.

Shells plowed the fields newly sewn with winter wheat. Dirt vomited up from each impact and for once, Starbuck noted, it was brown dirt rather than the redder Virginian soil. The smoke of each explosion hung motionless in the windless air. A loose gun horse galloped across the field behind Starbuck's battalion. It had been struck by a shell fragment and blood was gleaming on its left hindquarter. The horse caught sight of the waiting infantry and stopped, eyes white, red flank shivering. A gunner finally caught the gelding's bridle and, patting the beast's neck, led it back toward the battery. Each time the rebel guns fired the fog shuddered.

Starbuck paced slowly behind his men. Some were lying down, some were crouching, and some kneeling. The Yankee guns to the north were firing shells that rumbled overhead. Some of the shells whistled. Once, looking up, Starbuck saw a tiny trail of fuse-smoke in the fog, a streak of white vapor thicker than the whiteness about it. The gray light had turned white. It was thinning out.

The gunners worked as though they believed they could win the battle by themselves. The shells plunged and cracked into the high rebel ground and the noise ricocheted about the plateau. One man in Starbuck's battalion was telling his beads. "Jesus, Mary, and Joseph," he prayed, "Jesus, Mary, and Joseph." He said the names again and again, and each time a shell exploded he would twitch. One shell struck high in a nearby tree and the crash of the explosion was followed by a slow, awful creaking as a branch slowly tore away. "Jesus, Mary, and Joseph," the man wailed desperately.

"Where are you from?" Starbuck asked the man.

The soldier looked up at Starbuck. His eyes were empty and scared.

"Where are you from, soldier?"

"Richmond, sir." He had an Irish accent. "Venable Street."

"And before that?"

"Derry."

"What was your trade, lad?"

"Saddler, sir."

"I'm glad you're a soldier now."

"You are?"

"I thought the Irish were the best fighters in the world?"

The man blinked at Starbuck, then smiled. "They are, sir. Had lots of practice."

"Then I'm glad you're here. What's your name?"

"Connolly, sir. John Connolly."

"Then pray hard, John Connolly, and shoot low."

"I will that, sir."

Starbuck's battalion, a tiny regiment, was at the southern edge of the pastureland, a hundred paces behind the cornfield. His two left-hand companies were in the open, facing the corn, while his right companies were huddled in the East Woods. Potter's skirmishers were higher up the wood, waiting for the Yankees. The rest of Swynyard's Brigade was bent back at right angles, lining the wood's edge and then strung across the plowed field toward the family graveyard.

Swynyard joined Starbuck. "A quarter to six," he announced, "or thereabouts. My watch stopped in the night." He glanced to the left. "They look good," he said of the neighboring brigade.

"Georgians," Starbuck said. He had introduced himself to the colonel of the battalion next to him and the man had been cordial, but Starbuck had seen the flicker of worry when the Georgian colonel had learned that the Yellowlegs were guarding his right flank.

Swynyard turned and stared southward across the pasture toward the Smoketown Road, which was just becoming visible in the thinning fog. "Lots of troops ready to back us up," he said.

"Lots?" Starbuck answered wryly, knowing that Swynyard was merely trying to reassure him.

"There are some, anyway," Swynyard admitted wryly. A new battery of rebel guns was being positioned in the pasture, its muzzles pointed ominously northward in a sign that Lee expected the first Yankee attack to come straight down the funnel between the woods. Straight across the cornfield. Straight at the waiting men who crouched beyond the corn. Some Georgian skirmishers were already up among the stalks that stood high as a standing man.

Swynyard dragged his maimed hand through his straggling beard, a gesture that betrayed his nervousness. He was worried about the eastern flank, the long slope that fell with ever-increasing steepness toward the creek. His fear was that the Yankees would embroil his brigade in a fight at the funnel's mouth, then attack up that slope to smash in behind his men. And once the Yankees were up on the high ground about the Smoketown Road there was nothing to stop them carving Lee's army into fragments, but so far there were no signs of Yankee activity on the creek itself. There were no reports of men trying to cross the river, no sounds of guns being dragged down to the fords and bridges, and no glimpses of blue-coated troops filing down the farm tracks toward the Antietam's eastern bank.

A new barrage of guns sounded. These were the rebel guns positioned on the hill to the west of the turnpike and they were firing slantwise across the funnel's northern mouth. "I suspect," Swynyard said, "that our erstwhile brethren are stirring."

"God help us," Starbuck blurted out.

Swynyard put a hand on Starbuck's shoulder. "He does, Nate, He does." The hand on Starbuck's shoulder suddenly convulsed as the sound of rifles crackled through the morning. The skirmishers were engaged. "Not long now," Swynyard said in the unconvincing tone of a dentist trying to soothe a nervous patient. "Not long." His hand convulsed again. "Last night," he said quietly, "I had to fight the temptation for a drink. It was as bad as those first few nights. I just wanted a mouthful of whiskey."

"But you didn't?"

"No. God saw to that." Swynyard took his hand away. "And this morning," he went on, "Maitland searched the Legion's packs. Confiscated their liquor."

"He did what?" Starbuck asked, laughing.

"Took every last drop he found. Says he won't have them fighting drunk."

"So long as they fight," Starbuck said, "what does it matter?" The neighboring battalion was fixing bayonets and some of Starbuck's men followed suit, but he shouted at them to put the blades away. "You'll need to kill a few with bullets first," he called to them. He could not see any enemy because the tall corn hid everything to the north. The field was a screen to hide a nightmare. He could hear gunfire in the woods and guessed that Potter had opened fire.

The neighboring battalion stood ready to give fire. "Get 'em up, Nate," Swynyard said.

"Stand!" Starbuck shouted and the two left-hand companies struggled to their feet. They were thin companies, still missing many of their stragglers, but the remaining men looked confident enough as they waited. The battalion's battle flag was at the center of the two companies, where it hung lifeless in the still air. "I wish I could see the bastards," Starbuck growled. His stomach was churning and the muscles of his right leg involuntarily twitching. He had been constipated for two days, but was suddenly scared that his bowels would void. He had been spared the worst of the cannon fire, for the East Woods served to hide his men from the Yankee guns across the creek and the guns to the north were firing overhead, but still the fear was sapping him. Somewhere ahead of him, somewhere beyond the mist-shrouded stalks of tall corn, there was a Yankee infantry attack coming and he could not see it, though now, dimly, he could hear the sound of boots and drums and men shouting. He looked for the enemy's flags, but could not see them and he guessed this opening attack had not yet reached the cornfield. The skirmishers' rifles cracked and every now and then a rifle bullet would flick a corncob aside and whistle just over the battalion's head. One such bullet came close to Swynyard, startling the Colonel.

"Ahab," Swynyard said.

"Sir?" Starbuck asked, thinking that Swynyard had joined in Potter's fancy about Captain Ahab, the *Pequod*, and Moby Dick.

"He was slain, remember, by a bow drawn at a venture. I always think it would be a pity to be killed by an unaimed bullet, but I suppose it's how most men die in battle."

"King Ahab," Starbuck said, realizing what Swynyard meant. "I don't suppose there's much difference between an aimed and an unaimed bullet." He was forcing himself to sound calm.

"So long as it's quick," Swynyard said, then gasped with surprise.

New Yankee guns had opened fire. The gunners had seen the rebel skirmishers in the corn and now, before their own infantry marched into the tall stalks, the gunners tried to weed the crop of enemy riflemen. The artillery was loaded with canister that scythed through the corn. Barrel after barrel fired, and patch by patch the corn was blasted aside. Each shot bent great swathes of corn that tossed as though they were caught in a hurricane. The bullets flicked up from the hard ground to twitch skirmishers aside and some kept going right through the crop to thud into the infantry waiting in the pasture. Two of Starbuck's men reeled backward, one with brains welling out from a shattered patch of skull. The other man screamed, clutching his belly. "There's a doctor in the graveyard," Swynyard said.

"Peel!" Starbuck shouted. "Get these men back!" He would use men from the two right-hand companies to take the casualties back to the graveyard. "Make certain your men come back here!" he called to Peel, then he cupped his hands and shouted at the two left-hand companies to kneel again. The corn was thrashing and whipping, and patches of it were being slung high into the mist that looked thicker to the north, but that thickness was just gunsmoke clogging the air. More canister slapped and slashed the corn, the bullets whistling as they ricocheted on overhead. The surviving rebel skirmishers were retreating. One man crawled on bloody hands through the stalks, another limped, a third collapsed at the field's edge. Still more canister poured into the bloody field, the worst of the fire going into the center, and so sparing Starbuck's companies the full force of the cannonade. Two rebel howitzers were lobbing shells over the corn, trying to find the enemy batteries, while the rebel cannon on the western hill scorched shells down into the pasture where the Yankees advanced. It was still an artillery fight, a complicated mesh of trajectories under which the infantry moved forward to death.

Then, as suddenly as it had begun, the Yankee canister ended.

The corn was still. The day almost seemed silent. Scores of guns were firing, and men were shouting, but it seemed silent. The corn stood thick in patches and lay crushed in swathes. Small flames flickered among the fallen stalks where the wadding from the skirmishers' rifles had started fires. And, at last, there were flags visible above the standing corn. Tall flags hanging limp from staffs that bobbed up and down as the color bearers marched through the cornfield.

Some of Starbuck's men aimed their rifles. "Wait!" he called. "Wait!"

The Yankees were at last visible through the remnants of standing corn.

They were a dark line in the cornfield's mist. They were a horde of men advancing beneath their brilliant flags. They were death in blue. There were thousands of them, a mass of men, a drum-driven multitude with bayonets on their rifles.

"Two brigades, I'd guess," Swynyard said calmly.

"Wait!" Starbuck called to his men again. The Yankee attack was wide enough to overlap the cornfield, which meant that the eastern end of the blue line was now in the woods. "Tumlin!" he shouted.

"Starbuck?" Tumlin appeared at the wood's edge. The trees above him had been made ragged by Yankee shells that had stripped some branches of leaves and ripped other branches away.

"Take Dennison's company and support Potter!" Starbuck shouted. "The sons of bitches are coming through the trees!" Tumlin ducked out of sight without acknowledging the order and Starbuck knew he should go and make certain Dennison's company did move up through the wood, but the sight of the Yankees coming through the shattered cornfield was holding him rooted to the pastureland. The nervousness had ebbed, displaced by the need to hold his men taut.

"Coffman," Swynyard called the young lieutenant. "Tell Colonel Maitland to advance in support here. He knows what to do. Go on, lad." Coffman ran.

"I'll put Truslow's company into the woods," Swynyard said, sensing Starbuck's nervousness about the battalion's right flank. A crash of exploding shells drowned the Colonel's next words. Some rebel staff officers had ridden to the Smoketown Road, from where they were staring north through big field glasses, and the Yankee gunners across the Antietam were doing their best to kill the mounted men. The salvo of shells gouged the road and its verges with craters. Smoke screened the horsemen. Somewhere a bugle was playing, its notes brazen and rousting. The Yankee drummers were rattling away.

Rebel guns fired from the woods to the west of the cornfield. They used solid shot that plowed into the Yankee lines. A flag went down, and was immediately snatched up. Starbuck had found one of the limestone ribs that hunched its way through the soil and was standing on it for a better view. He could hear hard and solid rifle fire in the woods, but none of his men was running out of the trees so the fight there had to be under control. Truslow's company from the Legion came running up the edge of the wood and Swynyard went to divert them into the trees. If Truslow was there, Starbuck knew, then he could forget the wood.

"Wait!" Starbuck called to his men. The Yankees were at the center of the cornfield now and it was their turn to be hit by canister. The strike of the bundled shot cut down swathes of corn and drove up spurts of dust from the dry ground. Huge gaps were being torn from the Yankee ranks, but every time the dreadful scythe cut down a handful of men there were others who jumped over the fallen bodies to fill the hole. The Yankees had fixed bayonets. Their flags hung as limp as the rebel battle flags. One brave man waved his banner to and fro so that the Stars and Stripes made a fine show, but his gallantry was rewarded with a blast of canister that snatched him and the flag backward. The flag flew over the heads of the advancing men. Starbuck could hear the boots trampling the corn. He could hear the Northern sergeants shouting harshly at their men to stay in line, to close up, to keep marching. He could hear the drummer boys frantically trying to win the war with the speed of their sticks.

"Aim low!" he told his men. "Aim low. Don't waste your shots! But wait! Wait!" He wanted the first volley to be a killer.

The misted air was full of noise. Shells rumbled overhead, bullets whistled, the boots splintered the corn. Rifles cracked in the woods. The rebel line looked a perilously thin thing to withstand the Yankee hammer blow. "Wait!" Starbuck called, "wait!" Yankee skirmishers were deep in the corn, sniping at his men. A corporal came out of the line with a bloody shoulder, another man choked on his own blood.

The Yankees were two hundred paces away. They looked fresh, well-clothed, and confident. Starbuck could see their mouths open as they shouted their war cries, but he could hear nothing. He stared at them and he suddenly thought that this was how the makers of America had seen the Redcoats. The rebels then had been just as ragged, and the enemy just as well armed and smartly uniformed, and his fear was abruptly swamped by a fierce desire to shatter this overweening enemy. "Fire!" he shouted, "and kill the bastards!" He screamed the last three words and his two companies opened fire a second before the rest of the rebel line fired to blanket the pasture with rifle smoke. "Kill them!" Starbuck was shouting as he walked up and down behind the line. "Kill them!" He pushed through the files and fired his own rifle, then immediately dropped the butt to the ground to begin reloading. His pulse was racing, the fire was in his veins, the madness of battle was beginning its magic. Perfect hate casts away fear. He rammed the bullet down.

"Fire!" Captain Cartwright encouraged his men. It was a straight infantry fight now. The Yankee gunners were unsighted and so the blue-coated riflemen had to fight and kill and endure the bullets coming back. The rebel guns drenched the attackers in canister, blasting new gaps in the surviving corn. A spray of blood misted the air and somewhere a man screamed terribly until his screams were cut short by the meaty thump of a bullet burying itself in flesh. Starbuck smelled the horrid stink of burned powder, he heard the whistle of a minie bullet whip past his ear, then the rifle was back in his shoulder, and he aimed low into the corn and fired.

The gunsmoke was hanging in the still air like a layer of fog. Some men, in order to see beneath the smoke, lay down to aim. Starbuck ducked and could see Yankee legs among the corn. He fired, then backed out through the files to see how his men were faring.

The Yellowlegs were sticking to the fight. They were ramming their bullets, priming the guns, pulling their triggers, but some were falling. Some were dead. The noise was obliterating sense; it was a deafening sky of fire, a numbing rattle laced with screams. More men fell. Starbuck's line was thinning, but suddenly Davies's company from the Legion was pushing into their ranks to add their fire. Davies grinned at Starbuck. "Christ," he said in awe.

"Fire!" Starbuck shouted. Survival now depended simply on outfiring the enemy. "Captain Peel!" He ran toward the trees to summon the last of his shrinking battalion. "Peel! Bring your men!" Peel's company still had the old-fashioned Richmond muskets that were loaded with buck and ball and Starbuck reckoned the smoothbore volleys might work a wicked slaughter in this close-range battle. "Into line! Anywhere!" He pushed men helter-skelter into the ranks, no longer caring whether the companies kept their cohesion. "And fire! Fire! Just kill them!" He screamed the words as he emptied his revolver chamber by chamber into the shroud of smoke. "Kill them!"

Bullets whipped back from the Yankees. Stabs of flame showed where they fired, and Starbuck saw that the flame lances were getting closer as the attackers advanced, their progress fed by the rear ranks, who moved up to take the place of the dead. The rebels were backing away, not in panicked retreat, but step by step, keeping their line, firing and firing at the blue horde that slowly, inexorably, like men wading against an outflowing tide, was forcing its way to the cornfield's southern edge. It was there that they stopped, not because the rebel fire grew worse, but simply because the field's margin served as a natural boundary. Behind them was the illusory cover of what corn remained standing, while ahead of the cornfield were open pastures and rebel batteries, and the Yankee officers could not persuade their men to march into the smoky, death-swept vacancy. The rebel line had also checked, aligned now on its guns, and there the two sides stayed and traded shot for shot and death for death. The wounded hobbled back from their line, but the rebels could spare no men now to carry the injured back to the surgeons. The rebel wounded must bleed to death or else crawl on hands and knees beneath the bruising noise of the big guns.

The Georgians were bringing in reinforcements, and then Colonel Swynyard appeared behind Starbuck with the big 65th Virginia battalion. "Nate! Nate!" Swynyard was only yards away, but the noise of the battle was so great that he needed to shout. "They're firing on the graveyard!" He pointed to the East Woods, meaning that Yankees had somehow reached the trees' southern end and were threatening Swynyard's reserve of ammunition. "Find out what's happening for me!"

Swynyard feared his right flank was about to be turned, but for the moment he would hold on in the pasture where he was tumbling his battalions into the tiny space where the firefight was hottest and where he would fight his brigade as though it were one single battalion. Starbuck, running to his right, sensed that this dawn slaughter was horrendous. He could not ever remember a battle swelling into horror so fast, nor ever seeing so many wounded or dead, yet miraculously his despised battalion had stood the fire and was still standing it and still giving back as good as they got. "Well done!" he shouted at them, "well done!" No one heard him. They were deafened by the blistering noise.

He ran into the trees. A score of wounded rebels had taken shelter beneath the closest trees, and some men, even though unwounded, had joined them there, but Starbuck had no time to stir those laggards back to their duty. Instead he ran northward in the cover of the trunks to where he could hear his skirmishers fighting. They were very close by, evidence that the Yankees had indeed pushed them hard back. Truslow's men were among Potter's skirmishers, who in turn were mixed up with a company of Georgian skirmishers who had retreated to the trees rather than risk the canister that had been cutting the corn short, and now they all fought together. Starbuck saw Truslow reloading his rifle behind an elm tree that was scarred by bullet strikes. He dropped beside him. "What's happening?"

"Bastards ran us back," Truslow said grimly. "Reckon they've reached the road on that side of the wood." He jerked his beard eastward. He was suggesting that the rebels now only held the southwestern corner of the trees. "Sons of bitches have breech loaders," Truslow added, explaining why the Yankees had been so successful.

Breech-loading rifles were much quicker and easier to load, especially when a man was lying down or crouching behind cover, and so the Yankee skirmishers were pouring a much heavier fire than the rebels could maintain, but now the fight had stalled in the corner of the wood where thick brush, scattered stacks of cordwood, and the limestone outcrops gave the rebels enough shelter to frustrate the withering Yankee fire.

"Seen Potter?" Starbuck asked Truslow.

"Who's he?"

"Thin fellow, floppy hair."

"Over to the right." Truslow jerked his chin. "Be careful going through here. Sons of bitches are good shots." A bullet whipped a chunk of bark off the elm. "Like Gaines's Mill," Truslow said.

"That was a hellhole."

"So's this. Be careful."

Starbuck gathered himself for the dash across the wood. He could hear the heavy firing from the cornfield, but that fight seemed distant now. Instead he had entered a different version of hell, one where a man could not see his enemy, but only spot the gouts of rifle smoke that marked where the Yankee sharpshooters lurked. It was dark under the trees, a darkness caused by the remnants of fog and the thickness of powder smoke. Starbuck wondered what time it was. He reckoned the Yankees had attacked at six o'clock and somehow it felt like midday already, though he doubted if even a quarter of an hour had passed since he had first glimpsed that blue mass marching steadily toward the cornfield. "Give my love to Sally if anything happens," he said to Truslow, then he sprinted away from the elm, dodging and darting among the trees. His appearance provoked an instant fusillade from the Yankees. Bullets lashed about him, thumping into trees like ax blows, whistling in the air, flicking through leaves, then a shot seared across his back. He knew he had been hit, yet he was still running and he guessed the wound was nothing but a near miss that had laid open his skin. He saw Potter behind a stack of cordwood and dived to join him. A Yankee jeered his plunge for safety.

"I'm almost tempted to pray," Potter said.

"Your prayers are answered," Starbuck said, "I'm here. What's happening?"

"We're holding," Potter said laconically.

"Where's Dennison?"

"Dennison? Haven't seen him."

"I sent him to reinforce you. Tumlin?"

"No sign of him," Potter said. Every few seconds the stack of wood was thumped by a Yankee bullet, and every thump would hammer a log a half inch out of alignment. "They're Pennsylvanians," Potter said. "Call themselves the Bucktails."

"How the hell do you know that?" Starbuck asked. He had rammed his rifle into a space between the logs and, without bothering to aim, fired toward the hidden skirmishers.

"We got one of them. Stupid man got too far ahead and Case pulled him down."

"Case? So Dennison's company is here?"

"Private Case is," Potter said, jerking his head west to show where Case was crouching behind a fallen tree. A dead Yankee was beside him and Case had taken the man's breech-loading rifle and was using it to fire steadily into the brush where puffs of smoke betrayed Yankee positions. "The fellow had a deer's tail pinned to the back of his hat," Potter went on. "Full of fleas, it was. He's dead now. It's difficult to live with a slit throat, it seems."

"Where's Sergeant Rothwell?"

"Sent him back for ammunition."

"What's happening out there?" Starbuck jerked his head toward the east, where the Smoketown Road angled through the trees.

"God only knows," Potter said.

Starbuck peered eastward, but could see nothing beyond the trees. He knew some of the Pennsylvanians had got past this point and were now firing toward the graveyard from the southern edge of the wood. For a second he thought about trying to lead an attack that would cut those men off from their companions, then he abandoned that idea. The Yankees were too thick on the ground and too good to be taken that lightly. A Yankee counterattack would destroy his skirmishers and open the brigade's flank to the fire of the Pennsylvania breech-loaders.

"There's blood on your back," Potter said.

"Bullet scrape. Nothing serious."

"Looks impressive." Potter had made a loophole in the cordwood and fired through it. The shot was answered by a half dozen bullets that made the whole log pile quiver. "The bastards can fire three bullets to our one," Potter said. "They're using Sharps rifles."

"I heard. Can you hold?"

"So long as the Yankees don't reinforce."

"Then hold on." Starbuck patted Potter's back, then dashed to his left. His appearance provoked a flurry of shots, but Starbuck had already dropped behind the dead tree where Private Case had found refuge. Case glanced at Starbuck, then peered back toward the enemy. The dead Yankee's throat was cut almost to the spine so that his head lolled back in a mess of fly-encrusted blood.

"Where's Captain Dennison?" Starbuck asked.

Case did not answer. Instead he aimed, fired, then levered down the trigger guard to expose the breech of the Sharps rifle. A puff of smoke curled from the open breech as he pushed a stiff linen-wrapped cartridge into the barrel. He pulled up the trigger guard and Starbuck noted how a built-in shear sliced the back off the cartridge to expose the powder to the firing nipple. Case put a new percussion cap on the nipple and aimed again.

"Where's Dennison?" Starbuck asked.

"Ain't seen him," Case said brusquely.

"You came up here with him?" Starbuck asked.

"I came because there were Yankees to be killed," Case said, as loquacious suddenly as he had ever been with Starbuck. He fired again and his shot was rewarded with a yelp of pain that turned into a wail of agony that echoed through the wood. Case grinned. "I do so like killing Yankees." He turned his flat, hard eyes on Starbuck. "Just love killing Yankees."

Starbuck wondered if that was a threat, then decided it was simple bravado. Case was doing his duty, which suggested that the awkward conversation in the dusk had done its work. "Then just keep killing them," Starbuck said, then waited until a sudden rattle of shots suggested that the nearest Yankees might be reloading before he sprinted back through the trees. He ran for three or four seconds, then twisted sideways and dropped behind a tree just a heart's beat before a rattle of shots whipped the air where he had been running. He crawled a few yards and rolled into cover, waited a few seconds, then ran back to the wood's edge.

The firefight in the pasture still raged, though now both sides were lying down rather than standing up to the killing volleys. Swynyard was crouching, an anxious look on his face. "Pray it's good news," he greeted Starbuck.

Starbuck shook his head. "Bastards have taken most of the wood. We've only got this corner. But they ain't there in force. Just skirmishers." A shell dropped just behind the two men, struck a limestone outcrop and, instead of exploding, bounced up to tumble through the air. It made a weird screeching noise that faded quickly away. "What's happening here?" Starbuck asked.

"Stalemate," Swynyard said. "They ain't coming forward, we ain't going forward, so we're just killing each other. The last man alive wins."

"That bad, eh?" Starbuck asked, trying to sound lighthearted.

"But it's going to get worse," Swynyard promised, "it's going to get one whole lot worse."

When the sun rose above the Red Hill it offered a slanting light to give the watchers at the Pry Farm a marvelous view of the battle, or at least of the battle's smoke. To General McClellan, ensconced in his armchair, it seemed as though the woods on the creek's far side were alight, so much smoke was hanging in and above the trees. That smoke, of course, denoted that the enemy was dying, but the General was still in an irritable mood, for none of his aides had thought to cover the arm-chairs in the night and consequently the upholstery was damp from the dew that now had seeped through his pants. He decided to make no complaint, mainly because a small crowd of civilians had gathered beside the house to stare at him in admiration, but he petulantly refused the first cup of coffee because it was too weak. The second was better, and came in a fine bone china cup and saucer. "A table would be useful," the general observed.

A side table was fetched from the house and somehow balanced on the sloping lawn behind the barricade. The general sipped the coffee, placed it on the table, then put an eye to the telescope that was conve-niently mounted on its tripod beside him. "All goes well," he announced loudly enough for his civilian admirers to hear, "Hooker is driving them." A shadow fell over the telescope and he looked up to see that Colonel Thorne had come to stand behind his chair. "Still here, Thorne?" McClellan asked testily.

"Apparently, sir."

"Then doubtless you heard me. All goes well."

Thorne could not tell, for the attack of Hooker's corps was hidden by trees and smoke. The noise told him that a considerable battle was being fought, for both artillery and musketry sounded hard and fast across the creek's valley, but no one could tell from the noise what was happening on the ground. All Thorne knew for sure was that the First Corps, under General Hooker, with thirty-six guns and over eight thou-sand men, was attempting to drive down the Hagerstown Pike toward the heart of the rebel position. That much was fine, but what Thorne did not understand was why McClellan had not launched his other troops across the Antietam. The rebels would have their hands full con-taining Hooker, and now was the time to hit them in the flank. If McClellan threw everything he had against the rebels then the battle would surely be over by lunchtime. The Confederates would be broken and fleeing to the Potomac where, piling up against the single ford that was their retreat, they would be easy pickings for the Northern cavalry.

"What of the other attacks, sir?" Thorne asked, gazing at the battle through a pair of field glasses.

McClellan chose not to hear the question. "Fine china," he said, inspecting the coffee cup that was prettily painted with pansies and forget-me-nots. "They live well here," he spoke to an aide and sounded grudging, as though a rural farmer had no right to possess such good china.

"The purpose of good government, sir, is to provide its citizens with a prosperous existence," Thorne snarled, then turned his glasses northward to where another corps of the Northern army was waiting beside the Hagerstown Pike while Hooker's men attacked. Two whole corps had crossed the river the day before, but only one was driving south. "Is Mansfield to back up Hooker?" he asked.

"Mansfield will do his duty," McClellan snapped, "as will you, Colonel Thorne, if you have any duty other than to bother me with questions that are none of your concern."

Thorne backed away from the reproof. He had done what he could to spur McClellan, and to do more was to risk arrest for insubordination. He paused beside the ever-growing crowd of local people who had come to cheer the North to victory and to observe the great Northern hero, McClellan, and, so far as Thorne could judge, Hooker's attack did seem to be deserving applause, but he still feared for the day. It was not defeat that Thorne feared, for the North outnumbered the South far too heavily to risk defeat, but he did fear a stalemate that would allow Lee to survive and fight another day. McClellan should be swamping the rebels with attacks, drowning them in fire and crushing them with his vast army, but all the signs suggested that the Young Napoleon would be cautious. So cautious that he was here, in his armchair, rather than in his saddle and close to the fighting. Lee, Thorne knew, would be close to where the dying was happening. Thorne had known Lee before the war and he admired the man, and Lee, Thorne knew, would not be admiring the china before a gallery of awestruck spectators.

But Lee was the enemy this day, and an enemy who needed to be destroyed if the Union was to be preserved. Thorne took out his notebook. He knew that whatever happened today, McClellan would paint it a victory and McClellan's supporters in the Northern press and in the Congress would demand that their hero should keep command of the army, but only total victory would justify McClellan keeping command, and Thorne was already seeing that happy outcome slip from the Young Napoleon's nerveless grasp. If Lee did survive to fight another day then Thorne was determined that the North would have a new general, a new hero, to do what should be done this day. Thorne wrote his notes, McClellan worried about a surprise rebel attack that would wrong foot his army, and across the creek men died.

The Confederate reinforcements swelled the defenders' fire, while the Yankees at the edge of the cornfield died. Their fire slackened and the rebels, scenting an advantage, began to advance in small groups. The Yankees retreated, yielding the cornfield's edge, and that prompted a sudden shrill outbreak of the rebel yell and the Georgian Brigade was charging into the corn with fixed bayonets. The surviving Yankees broke and ran. Swynyard held his men back, shouting at them to align themselves on the wood instead. "Bayonets!" he shouted. "Forward!"

The Georgians stormed into the cornfield. A few wounded Yankees tried to hold them off with rifle fire, but those brave men were killed with bayonets, and still the Georgians advanced through corn that had been cut down by canister, trampled by boots, scorched by shell fire, and dampened by blood. Beyond the ragged corn the Georgians could see a pasture thick with the retreating enemy and they gave the rebel yell as they hurried forward to chase the Yankees even further.

Then the Yankee gunners saw the rebels in the corn and the canister started again; great gouts of death fanning over the broken field to spin men down and douse the corn in yet more blood. The Pennsylvanians in the trees took the Georgians in the flank with fast rifle fire and the rebel counterattack stalled. For a moment the men stood there, dying, achieving nothing, then they too pulled back from the wrecked corn.

Starbuck found the remains of his three companies close to the wood. Potter's company was still fighting among the trees, while Captain Dennison's men had vanished. Cartwright was shaking with excitement, while Captain Peel was white-faced. "Lippincott's dead," he told Starbuck.

"Lippincott? Christ, I never even knew his first name," Starbuck said.

"It was Daniel," Peel said earnestly.

"Where's Dennison?"

"Don't know, sir," Peel said.

"I don't even know your name," Starbuck said.

"Nathaniel, sir, like you." Peel seemed embarrassed by the admission, almost as if he thought he was being presumptuous.

"Then well done, Nate," Starbuck said, then he turned as Lieutenant Coffman arrived with an order from Colonel Swynyard. Starbuck's men, along with the big 65th Virginia, were to attack into the trees to rescue the brigade's skirmishers from the deadly Pennsylvanian Bucktails. It took a few minutes to align the three Yellowleg companies; then, without waiting for the larger Virginian regiment, Starbuck ordered them into the trees. "Charge!" he shouted. "Come on!" He was screaming the rebel yell, wanting to put the fear of God into the enemy, but when the Yellowlegs charged past the skirmish line they discovered the Yankees were gone. The Bucktails had fired so fast that they had exhausted their ammunition and were already slipping back out of the wood. They left their dead behind, each corpse with a buck's tail on its hat. Swynyard's attack, denied its prey, slowed and stopped.

"Back where you started from!" Colonel Swynyard called. "Back to your positions! Back! Captain Truslow! Here!"

He put Truslow in charge of the wood, giving him every skirmisher in the brigade as his force. The Pennsylvanians would probably return, resupplied with their unique cartridges. Truslow had found one of the Sharps rifles and was exploring its mechanism. "Clever," Truslow said sourly, reluctant to praise anything Northern.

"Accurate, too," Starbuck said, looking at his own dead skirmishers. Sergeant Rothwell was alive, and so was Potter, but too many good men had died. Case was alive, leading a small coterie of his cronies. Case, like a couple of his friends, had pinned a dead Pennsylvanian's buck's tail to his own hat to show he had killed one of the feared skirmishers and Starbuck liked the gesture. "Case!" he shouted.

Case turned his gaze on Starbuck, saying nothing.

"You're a sergeant."

A flicker of a smile showed on the grim face, then Case turned away. "He don't like you," Truslow said.

"He's the one I fought."

"The one you should have killed," Truslow said.

"He's a good soldier."

"Good soldiers make bad enemies," Truslow observed, then spat tobacco juice.

The brigade formed again where it had started the day, though now its ranks had been thinned by death. Men from Haxall's Arkansas regiment helped the wounded back to the graveyard, while others brought water from the springhouse of the burned farm. Starbuck sent a dozen men to loot the cartridge pouches of the dead and distribute the ammunition. Lucifer brought Starbuck a full canteen of water. "Mister Tumlin," Lucifer said gleefully, "is in the graveyard."

"Dead?" Starbuck asked savagely.

"Hiding behind the wall."

"Dennison?"

"Him too." Lucifer grinned.

"Sons of bitches," Starbuck said. He turned to run over to the graveyard, but just then a bugle sounded and the Yankee artillery began to fire again and Starbuck turned back.

The second Northern attack was coming.

In Harper's Ferry the noise of battle was like distant thunder, but a thunder that never ended. Vagaries of wind would sometimes dull the sound to a grumble, or else magnify it so that the ominous crack of individual guns could be heard.

The captured Federal garrison had been marched away to captivity and now the last rebel soldiers prepared to leave the small, ransacked town. The troops were General Hill's Light Division, three thousand of Jackson's best men, and they had seventeen miles to march to reach the source of the bruising noise that filled the sky.

It promised to be a hot day, a searing hot day, a day when marching would be hell, but nothing to the hell that waited for them at their journey's end. General Hill wore his red shirt, a sign he expected to fight.

The Light Division began its march, while ten miles north, but blocked from them by the wide Potomac River, their comrades pushed new powder into blackened rifle barrels and a new mass of Yankees, more numerous then the first, came down the turnpike.

And the battle was scarcely a half hour old.

BILLY BLYTHE RECKONED HE HAD MISCALCULATED. HE HAD only ever seen one battle and that had been fought close to the Bull Run, where the hills were smaller and steeper than this high plateau between the Antietam and the Potomac, and at Manassas there had been far more woods, which had provided easy places for a man to hide while the battle's tide washed extravagantly past. He had planned on doing just that this day—slipping away in the confusion and finding some deep place in the green trees where no one would find him until the killing was over.

Instead he discovered himself on a high, bare place cut by fences and lanes, and where the only woods were either firmly in rebel hands or else were the scenes of savage fighting. And that meant there was nowhere to hide and nowhere to run, and so Billy Blythe sheltered behind the graveyard's low stone wall and wondered just how he was ever going to abandon the rebel army and join the Northern troops. He made what preparation he could. For a time he had busied himself among the wounded, though it was no act of mercy that had motivated him, but rather the need to discover a well-bloodied gray coat that he could exchange for his tight jacket. Then, wearing the blood-damp coat so that he looked like one of the wounded himself, he settled down to wait.

"You hurt?" Dennison saw Tumlin lying against the wall.

"Nothing that'll kill me, Tom," Blythe answered.

Dennison reloaded the rifle he had borrowed from one of the wounded. Every few moments he would peer over the stone wall's coping and fire a shot at the Yankee skirmishers who edged the East Woods. He had fled from those woods earlier, driven out by the terrifying fire of the Pennsylvanian rifles and now, with half of his company, he sheltered behind the graveyard wall. The other half of his company was lost. Dennison knew he should not be here, that he should have stayed with Starbuck's battalion, but he had been drowned by terror in the opening minutes because he had never imagined that battle could be so overwhelmingly violent. At Gaines's Mill, where the Yellowlegs had earned their derisory nickname, Dennison had never come close to the real battle, but somehow he had imagined that combat would prove to be a more decorous business, something like the prints of the Revolutionary War that hung on his uncle's walls. In those prints the two opposing lines always stood upright with noble expressions of grim resolve, the dead had the good manners to lie facedown so that their wounds were hidden, while the wounded were relegated to the edges of the pictures where they expired palely and gracefully in the arms of their comrades. That had been Dennison's expectation, but in the first few shattering moments of this bloody day beside the Antietam he had discovered that the reality of battle was a gut-loosening slaughter in which a man's wits were banished by noise and where the wounded died with their bellies slit open, their brains splattered on turf, and their voices screaming helplessly as they thrashed in agony. And all the while the noise banged on and on, and the bullets hissed and whistled, and the terrible shells crashed incessantly.

A doctor, his hands, sleeves, and shirtfront drenched in blood, saw Billy Blythe's coat and stepped over the recumbent bodies toward him. "You need help, soldier?"

"I'll be back on my feet right soon, doctor," Blythe answered. "Bleeding's stopped and I'll be back in the line when I've got my breath. You look after the others, sir."

"You're a brave man," the doctor said, and moved on to find another casualty.

Blythe grinned, then lit a cigar. "Reckon you're doing the right thing, Tom," he said to Dennison.

"I am?" Dennison had knelt ready to fire another shot, but just then a bullet struck the wall's top and ricocheted on into one of the trees that shaded the graves, and Dennison slumped back down beside Blythe.

"Keeping your men in reserve," Blythe said. "That shows you've got your wits about you. I admire that."

Dennison shuddered as a shell exploded nearby to rattle the stone wall's far side with scraps of metal. "We can't stay here all day," he said, some small part of him recognizing that there was a duty to fulfill on the field.

Blythe twisted round and raised his head above the wall. "You could take your men back to the woods now," he said. A few moments before those woods had been edged with Yankees firing at the grave-yard, but those marksmen seemed to have disappeared and, for the moment at least, the nearer edge of the trees seemed deserted, but another Yankee attack was coming, which suggested that the southern edge of the trees would once again become a battleground. Which meant that Blythe would wait. If the rebels regained a firm hold of the trees then he might go back and find a place to hide, but till then he would let the stone wall shelter him.

Dennison snatched a look at the shattered branches and riven trunks of the East Woods, which looked as though a giant ax-man had gone berserk among its trees, then ducked back. "Maybe I'll keep my men in reserve," he said.

"Good decision, Tom," Blythe said. "But I doubt Starbuck would agree. Starbuck just wants your men dead. Hell, he don't care." Dennison looked scared at the mention of Starbuck and Blythe shook his head. "Reckon you'll have to deal with Mister Starbuck if the Yankees don't oblige you. And that means dealing with his lackeys too. Like Sergeant Rothwell. Perhaps Bobby Case can help you?"

"I ain't seen Case," Dennison said. "Maybe he's dead."

"You'd better pray not. You're going to need friends, Tom, otherwise Starbuck will have you on a court-martial. I know you're doing the right thing, and you know it too, but will Starbuck know? You'd better make sure, Tom. I'd hate to see a good man like you sacrificed by a Yankee bastard like Starbuck. I reckon you'd best find Bobby Case and talk to him. Do your duty by the battalion and your country."

Dennison looked shocked at the thought of being court-martialed for cowardice. "Deal with Starbuck?" he asked faintly.

"Unless you want a few bad years in prison. Of course, they could just shoot you, but most court-martials end in prison, don't they? You and some niggers chained together picking cotton or breaking up rocks?" Blythe was making it up as he went along, but he could see his words were getting through to Dennison's dulled senses. "My name ain't Billy Tumlin," Blythe went on, "if you don't have an urgent need to take care of Starbuck. Starbuck and Rothwell."

"Starbuck and Rothwell?" Dennison asked.

"And Potter, too," Blythe said. "And that damned nigger boy. Get your enemies out of the way, Tom, then you can soar! You can be a great soldier. My, I envy you. I won't be here to see it on account of being back home in Louisiana, but I'll watch your career. Upon my soul, I will."

"You reckon Case will help me?" Dennison asked nervously. He was afraid of Case. There was something very dangerous in Case's big, brooding presence and unreadable eyes. "You sure he'll help?"

"I know he will," Blythe said firmly. It had been Case who had helped Blythe during the night in Harper's Ferry, but that attack on Starbuck had been both opportunistic and clumsy. Things would be much easier now, for what was one pair of deaths among so much carnage? "I told Bobby you'd make him into an officer," Blythe said. "I reckon Bobby Case deserves to be an officer, don't you?"

"I reckon," Dennison agreed vigorously.

"So find him, Tom, and do your duty. Hell, you don't want to see Starbuck throw a whole battalion away, do you?"

Dennison settled back to think about matters while Blythe leaned contentedly against the wall and drew on his cigar. It was as easy, Blythe reckoned, as stealing from a country church poor-box. He would have his inconvenient enemies killed, then he would somehow cross the lines to his reward in the North. He touched his federal commission, which was still hidden in his pants pocket, then waited.

To Starbuck it was like a nightmare from which he had awoken, only to find the nightmare was real. The rebel line had hurled one attack back, but now another identical assault tramped stolidly down the funnel between the East and West Woods. It was like Ezekiel's valley of dead bones on which the sinews were stretched, the flesh placed, and the skin wrapped before the breath of God animated the dry bones into a great army. And now, in this waking nightmare, that army advanced on Starbuck and he wondered, in the name of God, just how many more warriors the Yankees could produce.

The new attack again filled the space between the West and East Woods. It came beneath flags, accompanied by drums, trampling over the blood and horror of what was left of the first attack. Yankee skirmishers ran forward, dropped to their knees in the remnants of the corn, and opened fire.

The rebel guns, charged with canister, roared at the advancing line. Starbuck saw one skirmisher lifted from the ground by the strike of the canister and flung backward like a rag doll hurled by a petulant child. The man sprawled back to earth, then, amazingly, picked himself up, found his rifle, and limped away. A rebel skirmisher shot him in the back and the man pitched forward onto his knees, hesitated, then fell flat.

"Wait!" Swynyard was loping along the back of his line. His men were lying down and, at a casual glance, they looked like a solid brigade, but Swynyard knew that too many of the prone men were already dead. They had been killed in the first attack, and too many of the living would soon share their fate. Swynyard looked behind but could see no more reinforcements. "We hold them here, boys," he called aloud.

"Hold them here. Wait till you see their belt buckles. Don't waste bullets. Hold hard, boys, hold hard."

More Yankees were pushing through the East Woods. The rebels had nothing there but Truslow's heavy skirmish line, and after trading a handful of shots, that line pulled back rather than be overrun. Starbuck saw Potter emerge from the trees and ran over to join him. "What's happening?"

"Thousands of the sons of bitches," Potter said breathlessly. His eyes were bright, his face drawn, and his breath hoarse.

"Brigade attack," Truslow, who had followed Potter from the trees, offered more usefully. He put his men at the end of Swynyard's line where they crouched, waiting for the storm to break.

The rebel gunners had seen the gray skirmishers come out of the East Woods and, reckoning that there were Yankees to be killed, switched some of their fire onto the trees. Shells hammered into the timber where great elms swayed as if caught in a hurricane. Branches splintered down with the iron shards of shell fragments, leaf scraps blew like rain. More shells poured into the woods while the other rebel guns cracked their loads of canister at the Yankees in the cornfield, who were at last in range of the waiting rifles.

"Fire!" Swynyard called.

The rifles began their work, but every downed Yankee was replaced by more men from the rear ranks. The edge of the wood was infested by Yankees, who hid behind trees and shot at the rebels in the open pasture. The Northern skirmishers targeted the rebel gunners, trying to suppress the deadly canister, and minute by minute their bullets did their work. The Northern line came forward in small groups, knelt, opened fire, then darted forward again. The sound of the Northern volleys was like shredding calico or like a canebrake burning. There was no beginning and no end to the rifles' noise, just a continuous splintering horror that filled the air with whistling lead. The rebels began to glance behind, wondering where salvation lay in this open-air hell. The smoke stretched in another thin cloud above the cornfield.

Starbuck crouched among the men of Cartwright's company and fought as a rifleman. There was nothing else to do. There were no useful commands to shout, no reserves to fetch, nothing to do but fight. The fear that had haunted him for a month was still there, but at bay now, lurking like a beast in the shadows. He was too busy to be aware of it. For him, as for the others who still survived in the rebel line, the battle had become a tiny patch of earth circumscribed by smoke, blood, and burning grass. He had no conception of time, nor of what happened elsewhere. He heard the shells boom overhead and the unending thunder of the guns all around, and he knew that the foul-smelling air all about him was thick with bullets, but all his concentration was now on loading and firing. He picked his targets, watching one group of Yankees trying to work their way down the edge of the East Woods. He would choose one man, watch him, wait till the man checked to load his rifle, then fire. He saw an officer, shot at him, then dropped the rifle butt onto the ground as he pulled a cartridge from the bottom of his pouch. An enemy bullet hit the rifle's stock, almost snatching it from his grasp and driving great splinters from its butt. He swore, rammed the bullet home, brought the broken stock up to his shoulder, primed the cone, and saw the officer was still alive, still shouting his troops forward, and so he fired again. His shoulder was tender from the rifle's recoil and his fingernail was bleeding from picking the hot shattered caps from the cone. The rifle's barrel was almost too hot to touch. The man next to him was dead, shot through one eye, and Starbuck rifled the man's pouch to find six cartridges.

Truslow was hit in the thigh. He cursed, clapped a hand on the bleeding wound, then scrabbled in his pouch for a tin of moss and spider's web that he had kept for this moment. He ripped his pant leg apart, gritted his teeth, then stuffed the mixture into the entry and exit wounds. He rammed the moss and web in, suffering the pain, then picked up his rifle and looked for the son of a bitch who had shot at him. Robert Decker was crawling among the dead, rescuing cartridges, which he tossed to the living. Potter was firing and loading, firing and loading, always keeping his front toward the enemy so that no bullet struck the precious bottle of whiskey in his pack.

The Yankee line seemed to thicken rather than thin. More blue-coated troops were coming down the funnel to stiffen the attack, and now a Northern gun team galloped right into the cornfield and slewed about in a shower of dirt and broken stalks to position their cannon on a slight rise of ground that lay at the field's northern margin. A gun horse went down to a blast of rebel case-shot. It screamed and flailed at the air with its hooves. It thrashed its neck, spraying blood while a gunner cut it out from the rest of the panicking team that he ran back out of rifle range. Another gunner shot the wounded horse, then his companions fired their first shot—a shell that landed plumb in the center of the rebel line. The Yankee gunners were screaming at their own infantry to clear a field of fire so they could load with canister. "We can't last," Truslow growled to Starbuck.

"Jesus," Starbuck said. If Truslow sensed defeat, then disaster must be close. He knew Truslow was right, but still he did not want to admit it. The Yankees had come within an ace of breaking the fragile line, and when that line was dead or captured they would charge across the plateau's top to pierce the very center of Lee's army. The rebels were still enduring the Northern fire, but Starbuck guessed that most, like him, were simply too scared to run away. A man trying to retreat across the plateau would make himself an easy target and it seemed safer to crouch low behind barriers of the dead and keep on fighting.

The Yankee gun in the cornfield coughed a barrel of canister that churned dead and living flesh before ricocheting on into the pasture behind. A rebel gun was handspiked round to fire at the Yankee cannon, but a group of blue skirmishers killed the rebel gun crew. A color bearer in the Yankee lines waved a flag and Starbuck saw the arms of his home state, Massachusetts. A foolhardy Northern officer galloped a horse behind his men, encouraging them. Such men made choice targets, but the rebels were too few and too desperate to do anything now but pour a blind fire straight into the gunsmoke in hope of keeping the over-whelming Yankee mass away. More Northern canister crashed from the gun in the cornfield and more rebels died. Truslow's leg was soaked in blood. "You should see a doctor," Starbuck said. He was shaking, not with fear, but with a desperate excitement. He had one cartridge left.

Truslow gave a short efficient opinion of all doctors, then fired before dropping down behind a corpse that offered some cover as he reloaded. The corpse twitched as a bullet struck home with the meaty sound of an ax blow. Starbuck had reloaded his revolver during the pause between attacks and now fired all its chambers at the nearest group of Yankees. Truslow was right, he thought. They should retreat, but a retreat would become a rout. Better, perhaps, to lie here and let the victorious Yankees roll right over the line. He rammed his last cartridge into his rifle and peered across a corpse to find a final useful target. "Sons of bitches," he said vengefully.

Then, suddenly, there was a screaming sound, an exultant sound, a high-pitched wailing terror of a sound, and he looked to his left and saw a new rebel unit streaming across the pasture. Some of the newcomers were in gray, some in butternut, but most wore the remnants of the gaudy *zouave* uniforms with which they had begun the war. It was the Louisiana Tigers, a fearful regiment of scoundrels from New Orleans, and it charged right past the rebel line, with bayonets fixed and with their battle flag streaming in the smoke. A sudden salvo of shells burst among the regiment, but the ranks closed up and screamed relentlessly on.

"Forward!" Truslow shouted. "Come on, you bastards!"

Astonishingly, the frail rebel line rose from among the dead. The Yankees, taken by surprise, seemed to pause in sheer disbelief. It was their turn to see the dead come to savage life. "Come on!" Truslow shouted. He was limping, but nothing would stop him.

"Bayonets!" Starbuck shouted.

It seemed a terrible madness had cloaked the rebel line. It was on the verge of rout, but, spurred by the Louisiana Tigers, it charged forward instead of running back. Men were screaming the rebel yell as they ran. The Yankees in the cornfield offered one scattered volley, then began to retreat. Some, unwilling to abandon their victory, shouted at their comrades to stay in the cornfield and those men formed small groups to resist the broken rebel charge.

The rebel yell was the song of those men's deaths. For a few brief seconds the two sides clashed in the corn. Bayonets parried bayonets, but the rebels outnumbered the Northerners who had stayed to fight. Starbuck, unaware that he was screaming like a maniac, banged a rifle and bayonet to one side, then lunged his own blade into a face. He kicked the man as he fell, reversed his rifle, and hammered the bullet-splintered stock down into the bloody face.

A volley sounded. The Yankees had reformed north of the cornfield and were pouring volley fire at the Louisianians. More fire came from the woods on either side of the cornfield. There were Yankees in both.

"Back! Back!" someone shouted, and the rebels ran back through the cornfield to their old position. Starbuck paused long enough to loot the cartridges from the man he had wounded, then ran after his men. Bullets whipsawed from either side. He was aware of bodies everywhere: sprawling, broken, explosive-torn, mangled, dismembered bodies—white bones and brain, blue intestines, sheets of blood. Some men lay on their own, but most were in groups where they had been cut down by canister and some, horrifically, moved slowly beneath their carapaces of fly-crawling blood. A man moaned, another called on God, a third coughed feebly. Starbuck crouched as he ran, then at last he was out of the cornfield and back in the rebel line. Potter had been wounded. A bayonet had slashed off half his left ear, which now dangled amid a blood-soaked hank of hair. "Just a scratch," he insisted, "just a scratch. The whiskey's safe."

The rebel line lay down again. Men shared canteens and doled out cartridges they found in dead men's pouches. The Yankees had regrouped, but they seemed unwilling to go back into the cornfield that had become a slaughteryard for both sides. Instead they crouched while the rebel canister whipped the air overhead and their own guns returned the fire. The lone gun on the slight knoll in the field had been abandoned, but there were other Yankee guns close behind it and those guns were firing away. Starbuck aimed at one of the gunners, then decided to save his ammunition.

He stood. The blood in the small of his back had crusted his shirt and now that crust pulled painfully away to wash a gush of warm liquid down his buttocks. His throat was parched, his eyes raw with smoke, and his bones aching with weariness. He found the Irishman who had been telling his beads before the battle and sent him back to the springhouse with a dozen canteens. "Go easy now," he told him. "Give the trees a wide berth." The Yankee sharpshooters were back at the edge of the East Woods, though the smoke that lingered in the windless air was spoiling their aim, and their fire, which would have been terrifying in another circumstance, seemed puny after the tempest of rifle fire that had preceded the Louisianian charge.

Colonel Maitland was lying facedown close to the Smoketown Road. Starbuck did not recognize the man until he crouched beside him and tugged at Maitland's pouch in hopes of finding some pistol cartridges. "I'm not dead," Maitland's muffled voice protested, "I'm praying."

Starbuck touched the canteen at Maitland's belt. "You got water?"

"It is not water, Starbuck," Maitland said reprovingly, "it is cordial. Help yourself."

It was neat rum. Starbuck coughed as the raw liquor hit his powder-abraded throat, then spat the rest onto the grass.

Maitland rolled over and retrieved the canteen. "Good things are wasted on you, Starbuck," he said reprovingly. The colonel, having confiscated the Legion's liquor, must have drunk most of it, for he was helplessly drunk. A bullet hit a nearby gun barrel with a great clang like a cracked bell struck. The gunners spiked their piece around and gave the Yankees in the East Woods a dose of canister. Maitland lay back on the grass and stared at the gunsmoke churning in the blue sky. "When you were a child," he said dreamily, "did you find summer endless?"

"And winter," Starbuck said, sitting beside the colonel.

"Of course. You're a Yankee. Sleighbells and snow. I once rode in a sleigh. I was only a child, but I remember the snow was like a cloud around us. But our winter is slush and impassable roads." Maitland fell silent for a moment. "I'm not sure I can stand," he finally said in a pathetic voice.

"No need at the moment."

"I have been sick," Maitland said solemnly.

"No one knows," Starbuck said, though in fact the front of the colonel's elegant uniform was thick with vomit. It had caked in the yellow braid and lodged behind the glittering buttons.

"The truth is," Maitland said very solemnly, "that I cannot abide the sight of blood."

"Kind of a drawback for a soldier," Starbuck said mildly.

Maitland closed his eyes for a moment. "So what's happening?"

"We drove the bastards off again."

"They'll come back," Maitland said darkly.

"They'll come back." Starbuck stood and took the canteen out of the colonel's nerveless fingers and emptied the rum onto the ground. "I'll get you some water, Colonel."

"I'm very much obliged to you," Maitland said, still staring at the sky.

Starbuck walked back to the ravaged battle line. Swynyard was staring across the cornfield with vacant eyes. His right cheek was twitching as it had done when he had been a drunkard. He looked up at Starbuck and it took him a moment to recognize the younger man. "Can't do that again," he said grimly. "One more attack and we're done, Nate."

"I know, sir."

Swynyard took out his revolver and tried to reload it, but his right hand was shaking too much. He gave the gun to Starbuck. "Would you mind, Nate?"

"Are you hit, sir?"

Swynyard shook his head. "Just dazed." He stood up slowly. "I stood too close to a shell burst, Nate, but God spared me. I wasn't touched, just dizzied." He shook his head as if to clear his thoughts. "I've sent for cartridges," he said carefully, "and water's coming. There are no more men. Haxall's hurt bad. Got a lump of iron in his belly. He won't last. I'm sorry about Haxall. I like him."

"Me, too."

"I haven't seen Maitland," Swynyard said. "Thank you, Nate," this was for loading the revolver that the colonel now returned to its holster.

"Maitland's still here," Starbuck said.

"So he didn't run away? Good for him." The colonel glanced up and down his line. On paper he commanded a brigade, but the men left in the firing line would hardly have constituted a regiment in the prewar army and the brigade's various battalions had become inextricably mixed as Swynyard had fed men into the battle, so that now men simply clung to their friends or nearest neighbors while officers and sergeants looked after whoever was within sight. "The textbook," Swynyard said, "would probably suggest we disentangle ourselves and get back into our proper battalions, but I think we'll forget the textbook. They'll fight just as well as they are." He meant, Starbuck suspected, that they would die just as well, and indeed, at that moment, it seemed impossible that they should do anything but die. The Yankees were quiet, but that lull would not last, for Starbuck could see more blue coats showing beyond the jagged wreckage of the cornfield. The enemy had attacked twice, and twice they had been thrown back, but now the Yankees gathered their forces for the next advance.

Starbuck sent Lucifer to Maitland with a canteen of water. The boy came back grinning. "One happy man, the Colonel," he said.

"He's not the first to get drunk on a battlefield," Starbuck said.

"Mister Tumlin," Lucifer happily reported more news, "is wearing a new coat. All bloody."

Starbuck no longer cared about Tumlin, nor Dennison. He would deal with them after the battle, if there was anything left to deal with. Now, back among the dead who sheltered the living in the shell-blackened pasture, he waited for the Yankees.

Whose drums began to sound again. Whose guns opened fire again.

For the third attack was coming.

Two miles to the south, where the Antietam Creek turned sharply westward as it ran down to the Potomac, a whole corps of the United States army waited in hiding on the creek's eastern bank. Twenty-nine battalions of hardened troops, backed by guns, were ready to cross the river and slash north toward the road that ran west from Sharpsburg. Once that road was captured then all Lee's troops north of the town would be cut off from their retreat, and this corps was the lower jaws of that terrible trap.

Some of the troops were sleeping. Others cooked breakfast. The rebels knew they were there, for the rebel artillery across the creek kept up a harassing fire, but the Northern troops were concealed by woods and reverse slopes and the rebel shells whirred overhead to explode harmlessly in woods or pastures.

No orders came to cross the creek, and for that the commanders of the battalions closest to the water were grateful. The stone bridge that crossed the creek was narrow, and the far bank was precipitous and crowded with rebel infantry who had dug rifle pits into the slope so that any attack down the road and onto the bridge would be a bloody affair.

Still farther south a group of officers worked their way through thick brush and timber to where they could see a ford. The ford offered a way of outflanking the rebels defending the stone bridge, but when the officers came in sight of the creek their hopes fell. The far bank was just as steep as the slope that lay beyond the bridge, and the ford, far from being unguarded, had a picket line of gray infantry dug into its sharp slope.

"Whose idea was this?" one man, a general, asked.

"Some damned engineer colonel," an aide answered. "Thorne, he's called."

"The bastard can cross first," the general said as he peered through field glasses at the far bank. The sound of the battle in the north filled the sky, but above its din he could just hear the sound of voices coming from over the water. The rebels here seemed lighthearted, as if they knew that on this terrible day of slaughter they had drawn a long straw.

A trampling of feet in the woods made the general draw back from the trees' edge. Two of his aides were approaching with a farmer dressed in a thick wool coat and a shovel hat. Cow dung was plastered on the man's pants.

"Mister Kroeger," one of the aides introduced the farmer, who still retained enough Old World servility to pull off his hat when he was named to the general. "Mister Kroeger," the aide explained, "says this isn't Snaveley's Ford."

"Not Snaveley's," Kroeger agreed in a German accent. "Snaveley's down there." He pointed downstream.

The General cursed. He had fetched seven battalions and half a dozen guns to the wrong place.

"How far?" he asked.

"Long ways," Kroeger said. "I use it for the cows, yes? Too steep here for cattle." He motioned with his hand to demonstrate how steep the far bank was.

The general swore again. If he had been given cavalry, he told himself, he would have scouted these lower banks of the creek, but McClellan had insisted on the army's cavalry staying close to the Pry farm. God alone knew what good they were doing there, unless McClellan fancied that they would protect him during a fighting retreat.

"Is there a road to Snaveley's Ford?" he asked.

"Just pastures," Kroeger answered.

The general cursed a third time, prompting the farmer to frown in disapproval. The general slapped at a horsefly. "Send a reconnaissance party downstream, John," he told an aide. "Perhaps Mister Kroeger will guide them?"

"You want the troops in march order, sir?" the aide asked.

"No, no. Let them have their coffee." The general frowned in thought. If this dung-encrusted farmer was right and the ford was a good long way downstream, then maybe it was too far away to let his men outflank the defenders at the bridge. "I need to talk to Burnside," he said. "There's no great hurry," he added. It was, after all, still early. Most of America would not have had their breakfasts yet, certainly not the respectable part, and McClellan had sent no orders for the lower jaw of the trap to swing shut. Indeed, McClellan had sent no orders at all, which suggested there was plenty of time for coffee.

The officers walked away from the creek, leaving the woods there in peace. North of Sharpsburg the armies fought, but in the south they brewed their coffee, read the latest letters from home, slept, and waited.

The third Union attack was not centered on the cornfield, but rather drove down the turnpike toward the West Woods. Starbuck could see its progress by the thick cloud of smoke churned up by the rebel shells that tore into the leading blue ranks, then by the ripping sound of rifle fire exploding from the northern edge of the West Woods. The sound of the battle rose to a frenzy that matched the two previous fights at the cornfield's edge, but for the moment this was someone else's fight and Starbuck rested. His eyes were smarting and his throat, despite the mouthfuls of water he had gulped down, was still dry, but his pouch was half full of cartridges again; some were gleaned from the dead and the others from the brigade's last reserves that had been fetched up from the graveyard. The Yankee gunners had manned the cannon in the cornfield again, but its canister was being soaked up by the makeshift barricades of the dead, who protected the living riflemen in the gray line. The worst threat to his men came from the big federal guns on the Antietam's far banks, but those gunners were concentrating the worst of their fire on the rebel batteries that lay close to the Dunker church.

Potter scuttled across to Starbuck and offered him a canteen. "Your man Truslow's back in the woods."

"He ain't my man. His own, maybe. Yankees are gone?"

"They're still there," Potter said, jerking his head toward the northern part of the East Woods, "but not those bastards with the Sharps rifles. They've gone." Potter lay down, sharing the corpse that protected Starbuck from the canister. Potter's ear was crudely bandaged, but blood had seeped through the knotted length of rag to crust on his coat and shirt collars. "You want my men back in the woods?" he asked.

Starbuck glanced toward the woods and was rewarded by a flash of bright blue feathers. "Bluebird," he said, pointing.

"That ain't a bluebird. That's a bunting. Bluebirds have got reddish chests," Potter said. "So do we stay here?"

"Stay here," Starbuck said.

"I hear Colonel Maitland is stewed?"

"He ain't too sprightly," Starbuck admitted.

"This is my first stone-cold sober battle," Potter said proudly.

"You've still got the whiskey?"

"Safe in its stone bottle, wrapped in two shirts, a piece of canvas, and an unbound copy of Macaulay's *Essays*. It isn't a complete volume. I found it dangling in a Harper's Ferry privy and the first thirty pages had already been consumed for hygienic purposes."

"Wouldn't you rather have found his poetry?" Starbuck asked.

"In a privy? No, I think not. Besides, I already have swathes of Macaulay in my head, or what remains of my head," Potter said, touching the bloody bandage over his left ear: "'To every man upon this earth Death cometh soon or late, And how can man die better Than facing fearful odds.'" Potter shook his head at the appropriateness of the words. "Too good for a privy, Starbuck. My father hung the works of Roman Catholic theologians in our outhouse. It was, he said, the only thing they were fit for, but the insult misfired. I damn nearly converted to popery after reading Newman's lectures. Father thought I was constipated till he found out what I was doing, and after that we used newspapers like every other Christian, but father always made sure that any verses of scripture were cut out before the sheets were threaded on the string."

Starbuck laughed, then a warning cry from the mix of Georgians and Louisianians who lay to his left made him peer over the corpse, on which the flies were already crawling and laying their eggs. The Yankees were in the cornfield again. He could not see them yet, but he could see a trio of banners showing over the shattered field and it would only be a few seconds before the Northern skirmishers came into sight. He pulled back his rifle's hammer and waited. The flags, two Stars and Stripes and a regimental color, were well to his left, suggesting that these attackers were staying close to the turnpike rather than spreading across the whole cornfield. Still no skirmishers appeared. He could hear a band playing somewhere in the Yankee lines, its melody diluted to a delicate threnody by the insistent percussion of shells, canister, and rifle fire. Where the hell were the Yankee skirmishers? The heads of the leading rank of attackers were in view now and Starbuck suddenly realized that there were no skirmishers coming, just a column of formed troops advancing carelessly in the open. Maybe they believed the real battle was being fought in the West Woods where the cacophony of shell fire and rifles was loudest, but they were about to discover that the battered line of rebels in the pasture was not all dead men.

"Stand up!" a voice shouted from among the Georgian survivors.

"Stand!" Starbuck took up the cry and heard Swynyard echo it.

"Fire!" Starbuck shouted, and on either side of him the ragged remnants of the rebel line stood like scarecrows from among the bloodied dead and poured a volley into the compact Yankee formation. The attacker's front file collapsed, then a roundshot ripped through the remaining ranks like a ball thumping into skittles.

Starbuck rammed a bullet home, propped the ramrod against his body, fired, and loaded again. The Yankees were spreading out, running crablike across the cornfield to match the rebel line with a line of their own. More blue uniforms were streaming up behind. God, he thought, but was there no end to the bastards? The rebel line coalesced into groups as men instinctively sought the company of others, but then, when the Yankee fire became torrid, they lay down again to fight from behind the corpses. Men lying down fired more slowly than men standing, and the slackening of rebel fire persuaded the Northern officers to shout their men forward, but the advance was checked when the rebel guns opened fire with case shot—metal balls that exploded in the air to rain down a shower of musket balls—and that deadly shower persuaded the Yankees to lie down. Truslow's company was firing at the Yankees' open flank, evidence that no Northerners had attacked down the East Woods, but then Starbuck saw Bob Decker running zigzag in the pasture, crouching low and evidently looking for someone. "Bob!" Starbuck shouted to attract his attention.

Decker ran to Starbuck and dropped beside him. "I'm looking for Swynyard, sir."

"God knows." Starbuck raised himself to peer over the corpse that sheltered him and saw a Yankee flag carrier kneeling in the corn. He fired and dropped back.

"Truslow says there are Yankees beyond the wood, sir." Decker pointed east.

Starbuck swore. Till now that open flank had been blessedly free of Yankees, but if an attack did come from the open country to the east then there was no way that the survivors in the pasture could cope with it. The Yankees would sweep into the East Woods, then out into the pasture, and the Yankees pinned down in the cornfield would join the attack. "You find Swynyard," he ordered Decker, "and tell him I've gone to take a look."

He ran eastward. Bullets whipped past him, but the lingering smoke spoiled the Yankees' aim. Starbuck saw Potter and shouted at him to bring his company, then he was in the trees. He jumped a newly fallen branch, twisted past two rebel corpses, then ran on until he reached the Smoketown Road. He paused there, wondering if the Yankees still held the trees beyond, but he could see no movement and so he crossed the dirt track and ran on through the trees. A wounded Yankee called out for water, but Starbuck ignored the man. He headed toward the wood's edge through trunks gouged and splintered and drilled by bullets.

He dropped in the shadows at the tree line. To the east, where the land dropped away to the creek, he could see nothing, but to the north, where the Smoketown Road emerged from the trees to vanish beneath a crest neatly plowed into furrows, were Yankees. Another damned horde of Yankees. They were two wide fields away and for the moment they were not moving. Starbuck could see officers riding up and down the ranks, he could see the banners hanging in the still air, and he knew that the Yankees were being readied to attack. And all that stood between them and Lee's center were two shrunken companies of skirmishers.

"The good Lord is surely testing us today," Swynyard said, catching sight of Starbuck. The colonel knelt beside him and stared at the waiting Yankees. Potter was behind him with a dozen men; all that remained of his company.

Starbuck felt a vast relief that Swynyard had arrived. "What do we do, sir?"

"Pray?" Swynyard shrugged. "If we bring our men here then we open up the cornfield, if we leave them there, we open up this door."

"So we pray," Starbuck said grimly.

"And send for help." Swynyard backed away. "Leave someone here to watch them, Nate, and let me know when they advance." He ran off through the woods.

Starbuck left Sergeant Rothwell to watch the Yankees, while he led Potter and his men back across the Smoketown Road to the inner edge of the East Woods, where Truslow was harassing the Yankee flank in the cornfield. "What are those sons of bitches doing?" Truslow asked, meaning the Yankees formed on the Smoketown Road.

"Dressing ranks. Getting a speech."

"Let's hope it's a long one." Truslow had torn away the pants leg from his wounded thigh and bound the injury with a bandage torn from a dead man's shirt. He spat tobacco juice, lifted his rifle, and fired. He was aiming at the cannon that still stood on the knoll in the cornfield, keeping its gunners in shelter so they could not rake the rebel line with canister. He reloaded, took aim, then turned to his right before pulling the trigger. There were shouts among the trees and Truslow was suddenly shouting at his men to fall back. The Yankees were coming through the woods again.

Starbuck saw a banner among the shredded leaves. He fired at the color bearer, then fell back with Truslow's company. "Rothwell!" he shouted through the trees, knowing he would not be heard, but knowing he had to warn the Sergeant. "Rothwell!" He did not want the Sergeant marooned in the trees and he wondered if he should run to fetch the man.

But then all hell broke loose on the cornfield's far side.

General McClellan dabbed at his lips with a napkin, then brushed crumbs of toast from his lap. He was aware of the gaze of the civilian spectators and he kept a stern look on his face so that none of those onlookers would be aware of the worries that racked him.

He was risking a trap. He knew it instinctively, even if he did not know just what form the trap would take. Lee outnumbered him, he was sure, and Lee was fighting a defensive battle and that could only mean that the enemy was disguising his intentions. Somewhere in the landscape a mass of rebels was waiting to attack, and McClellan was determined not to be caught by that surprise assault. He would hold men in reserve to counter it. He would frustrate Lee. He would preserve the army.

"Sir?" An aide stooped beside McClellan's chair. "Dan'l Webster, sir, he's unhappy."

"Unhappy?" McClellan asked. Daniel Webster was his horse.

"The civilians, sir, they're plucking his tail hairs. As souvenirs, sir. We could ask them to move, sir? Up the hill, maybe?"

"There must be a stable?"

"He's in the stable, sir."

"Then shut it!" McClellan did not want to lose his audience. He rather enjoyed their admiration. Indeed, stretching his legs once in a while, he liked to chat with them and assure them that all was well. There was no need to worry mere civilians with his concerns, or tell them that he had telegraphed Washington with an urgent request that every Northern soldier available should be hurried west toward the army. Those soldiers could not of course reach the battlefield in time to join the fight, but they might provide a rear guard behind which his army could retire if Lee's masterstroke brought chaos. The hotheads in his army, fools like Colonel Thorne, might wonder why he did not unleash the men poised to cross the river and attack the rebels' flank, but those fools did not understand the army's danger.

More men marched down to the creek where the columns waited for the order to cross. One unit sang "John Brown's Body" as they marched close to the Pry farm and McClellan scowled. He hated that song and had tried to forbid it being sung. So far as McClellan was concerned there had been nothing to admire in John Brown's foolish adventure. The man had tried to start a slave rebellion, for God's sake, and his hanging, McClellan believed, had been richly rewarded. He tried to ignore the music as he stooped to his telescope to watch the troops on the creek's far side, who were forming up for a new attack on the smoke-wreathed woods. "That's Mansfield's corps?" he asked an aide.

"Yes, sir."

"Tell them to go!"

He would let Mansfield attack and see what happened. At best they would push Lee's men back and at worst they would provoke the dreaded riposte. McClellan almost prayed for that riposte to happen, for then, at least, the fears would take solid shape and he would know just what he had to deal with. But for now he would go on attacking in the north and stay alert for the horror he knew must come.

Three miles away, in a grove of trees near Sharpsburg, Robert Lee stared at a map. He was not studying the map, indeed he was hardly aware that he was looking at it. Belvedere Delaney was among the aides who hovered nearby. The general liked Delaney and had invited him to keep him company. It was good to have someone slightly irreverent, someone who offered amusement rather than advice.

A crescendo of firing sounded from the higher ground north of the town. In a moment, Lee knew, the gunsmoke would billow above the skyline to mark where the fighting had erupted so suddenly. "That's it," he said mildly.

"It?" Delaney asked.

Lee smiled. "Hood's men, Delaney, almost our last reserves. Not, to be honest, that they were reserves." Lee had ruthlessly stripped troops from the southern part of his battle line to preserve the army's northern perimeter so that now, beyond a fragile skin of troops that edged the creek, he had nothing to fight an outflanking attack from the south.

"So what do we do?" Delaney asked.

"Put our trust in McClellan, of course," Lee said with a smile, "and pray that Ambrose Hill reaches us in time."

The Light Division was marching as it had never marched before. It was still south of the Potomac and a long way from the ford at Shepherdstown, but the ever-present sound of the big guns was the summons that kept them moving. Staff officers rode up and down the long column urging the men on. Marching troops were usually given ten minutes rest an hour, but not today. Today there could be no rest, just marching. The dust kicked up from the dry road choked men's throats, some limped on bare bleeding feet, but no one straggled. If a man dropped out he dropped like the dead, dropped out of sheer exhaustion, but most kept grimly going. They had no breath to sing, not even to speak, just to march and march and march. To where the guns were sounding and the piles of dead grew high.

GENERAL JOHN HOOD'S DIVISION BURST OUT OF THE West Woods to hit the flank of the attacking Yankees like a tidal wave. Most of Hood's men were Texans, but he had battalions from Alabama, Georgia, Mississippi, and North Carolina in his ranks, and all were veterans. They stopped the Yankee advance dead on the turnpike, then spread their battle line across the pasture, where they faced north toward the cornfield. One volley was enough to decimate the Yankees advancing through the corn, then the Texans were screaming the rebel yell and plunging forward with bayonets. Some small groups of Yankees resisted and were cut down, but most just fled. The North's attack was spent, the rebel counter-attack was surging, and the survivors of the old defense line, the battered, bleeding men from Georgia, Louisiana, and Virginia, went forward with Hood's men.

The Yankee artillery by the North Woods took up the battle. They could not use canister, for the ground in front of them was littered with wounded northerners, and so they cut their shell fuses as short as they dared and opened fire. The shells crashed into the cornfield, flinging men aside and adding a new skein of smoke to the cirrus-like canopy that hung above the trampled crop. The noise reached a new and dreadful intensity. The Northern gunners worked frantically, double-shotting some guns to belch out pairs of shells that exploded a heartbeat after firing. The guns by the turnpike were unhampered by wounded men and they turned their canister on the Texans advancing on the road. One barrel load of bullets ripped up forty feet of snake fence and drove its splintered remnants into a company of rebels. Yankee infantry appeared from the North Woods to add their volley fire, and all the while the rebel cannon lobbed their long-fused shells over the flags of Hood's Division to harry the Northern gunners.

The Yankee gunners at the northern edge of the cornfield died hard. They tried to keep the fight going, but they were in easy range of the Texan skirmishers and one by one the guns were abandoned. Still the Confederates drove forward, skirting the piles of dead and dying in the cornfield, struggling through the rage of bullet and shell as though they could sweep the Yankees clear up to Hagerstown and beyond. Some officers tried to check their men, knowing they were advancing too far, but no voice could be heard in the tempest of iron and lead. The battle had become a gutter fight, rage against rage, men dying in a cornfield that had become death's kingdom.

A regiment from Mississippi pursued the broken Yankees toward the northern edge of the broken corn, sure they were chasing shattered troops to utter defeat, but the Yankees had Pennsylvanian infantry waiting at the rail fence. The blue-coated riflemen were lying down, resting their barrels on the fence's lowest rail. A standing man could see nothing but smoke, but at ground level the waiting infantry could see the legs of the attackers.

They waited. Waited till the rebels were just thirty paces off, then loosed a volley that ripped into Hood's men and silenced the screaming rebel yells in one curt blow. For an instant, an odd, mind-numbing instant, there was a silence on the battlefield as though the wings of death's angel were sweeping overhead, but then the silence passed as the Pennsylvanians stood up to reload and their ramrods clattered in hot barrels and the Northern guns jarred back on their trails to add more carnage to the slaughter in the corn. The front rank of the Confederates was a horror of writhing bodies, blood, and moans. A man snatched up the fallen banner of Mississippi and was shot down. A second man gripped the flag by its fringe and dragged it back through the corn as the Pennsylvanians fired a second volley that thumped into flesh with brutal force. The flag fell again, riddled with bullets. A third man seized the banner and raised it high, then walked backward from the blazing rifle fire until he was driven down with bullets in his belly, groin, and chest. A fourth man speared the flag on his bayonet and pulled it back to where the survivors of his battalion were forming a crude line to return the Pennsylvanian fire. The space between the two lines seemed to be a shifting mass of dirt, a heaving, crawling pile of giant maggots that blindly struggled to find safety. It was the wounded pushing the dead away and trying to rejoin their comrades.

The right flank of Hood's attack swept into the East Woods. There, protected by the battered trees from the effects of the Northern guns, the Texans drove into the Yankees, who were advancing southward. Men fought within spitting distance. For a time the two sides traded shots, neither willing to retreat and neither able to advance, but slowly the rebel fire gained the advantage as more men came from the pasture. The Yankees retreated and the retreat became hurried as the rebels pushed forward with bayonets.

Starbuck and his men were weary, bruised, wounded, and parched, but they fought among the trees with the desperation of soldiers who believed that one last effort would rid them of their enemies. Again and again the Yankees had come forward, and again and again they had been pushed back, and this time it seemed as if they could be pushed clear back out of the woods altogether. One group of Northerners turned a pile of cordwood into a miniature redoubt. Their rifle barrels spat long flames over the logpile, the tongues of fire oddly bright in the shadow of the trees. Starbuck used his revolver, firing at murderously close range into the Yankees, who suddenly abandoned the logs as a rush of screaming Texans swept up from their right. A small black dog stayed with its dead master, running back and forth and barking piteously as the rebels ran past. Starbuck unslung his rifle, paused to reload it, then ran on toward the fighting. He came to the road that ran through the woods and crouched at its edge, watching as Yankees dashed across to escape the charge. He fired, saw a man sprawl in the grass that grew down the road's center, then he sprinted over the dirt road himself. The fight seemed to be dying as the Yankees legged it out of the trees and so he squatted by a limestone knoll and began the laborious business of reloading the revolver.

Lucifer ran over the road, leading the black dog on a makeshift leash of two rifle slings. "You shouldn't be here," Starbuck said, making space for the boy behind the knoll.

"I always wanted a dog," Lucifer said proudly. "Got to find him a name."

"There are still Yankees in the wood," Starbuck said, pushing down the lever that rammed the revolver's chambers.

"I shot one," Lucifer said.

"You damn fool," Starbuck said fondly. "They're fighting for your freedom." He levered down the last chamber, then upturned the gun to push on the percussion caps.

"I'd have shot more," Lucifer said, "only the gun don't work." He offered Starbuck his revolver. The trigger hung limp.

"It needs a new stop spring," Starbuck said, handing the gun back, "but you shouldn't be fighting. Hell, these bastards are trying to liberate you and you're killing the poor sons of bitches." Lucifer did not answer. Instead he frowned at his gun and twitched the trigger in hope that it would engage on some part of the mechanism. The small dog whimpered and he soothed it. It was a puppy, scarce weaned, with coarse black hair, a snub nose, and a stump of a tail. "The bastards will kill you," Starbuck warned him. "You and your dog."

"So I die," Lucifer said defiantly. "And in heaven we get to be the masters and you all are our slaves."

Starbuck grinned. "I don't reckon on seeing heaven."

"But maybe your hell is our heaven," Lucifer said with relish. "Imp," he added.

"Imp?" Starbuck asked, "imp of Satan?"

"The dog! I'm going to call him Imp," Lucifer said delightedly as he ruffled Imp's ears. "Got to get you some meat, Imp." The stumpy tail suddenly wagged as the dog licked Lucifer's face. "I always wanted a dog," Lucifer said again.

"Then keep him safe," Starbuck said, "and keep yourself safe."

"I ain't going to be killed," Lucifer said confidently.

"Every corpse here thought that," Starbuck said grimly.

Lucifer shook his head. "I ain't," he insisted. "I ate a Yankee grave."

"You did what?"

"I found a dead Yankee's grave," Lucifer admitted, "and I waited till midnight, then I ate a scrap of dirt from the grave. No Yankee can kill me now. My mother taught me that."

Starbuck heard something pathetic in the last few words. "Where is your mother, Lucifer?"

The boy shrugged. "She's alive," he said reluctantly.

"Where?"

The boy jerked his head, then shrugged. "She's alive." He waggled the useless trigger. "But they sold me out. Reckoned I was worth something, see?" He touched his skin. "I ain't real black. If I'd been real black they'd never have sold me, but they reckoned I could be a house slave." He shrugged. "I ran away."

"So where is your mother?" Starbuck insisted.

"Hell, she's probably sold by now. The master never kept the niggers he'd slept with, not usually. I don't know where she is." He said the last words angrily, as if to demonstrate that he did not want to talk about the subject any more.

"And your mother taught you magic?" Starbuck asked.

"It ain't magic," Lucifer insisted, still angry. "It's a way of staying alive. And it ain't for you."

"Because I'm white?"

"Alice Whittaker," Lucifer said suddenly, not looking at Starbuck. "That's her name. Ain't he a fine puppy?"

"He's fine," Starbuck said. He wondered if he should ask more, but suspected that Lucifer had already revealed more than he wanted to. He leaned over and fondled Imp's ears and received a lick as a reward. "He's fine," he said again, "and so are you." He holstered his reloaded revolver and stood up. There was still sporadic firing higher up the wood, but he wanted to see what had happened to the formed troops who had been waiting on the Smoketown Road and so, warning Lucifer to stay where he was, he crept cautiously through the trees. He expected to find Yankee stragglers, but this part of the wood was almost empty. Two rebels limped past on their way to the doctors and a dead Pennsylvanian Bucktail lay against a tree with a look of surprise on his face, but otherwise the trees were deserted.

Sergeant Rothwell was lying down at the edge of the wood where Starbuck had left him. There was blood on his back and Starbuck's first thought was that the man was dead, then he saw an arm move. He ran to the sergeant's side and carefully rolled him over. Rothwell moaned. His teeth were chattering, his face was yellow, and his eyes closed. There was blood on his chest. "Rothwell!" Starbuck said.

"In the back," Rothwell managed to say, then he stiffened and his body shook in a terrifying spasm. Another moan escaped his throat. "In the back," he said again, "but I never turned my back. Honest to God, I didn't turn." He was desperate to deny that his wound denoted cowardice. "Oh, Jesus, sweet Jesus," he said. He was crying from the pain. "Sweet Jesus."

"You're going to be all right," Starbuck said.

Rothwell caught hold of Starbuck's hand and gripped it hard. His breath was coming in short, shallow gasps. His teeth chattered again. "They shot me," he said.

"I'll get you back to the doctor." Starbuck looked around for help. A dozen rebels were running north through the trees, but the deafening sound of the battle in the cornfield drowned out Starbuck's shout. The men ran on.

"In the back," Rothwell said, then suddenly he screamed as the pain whipped through his body. The scream faded to a pathetic moan. He gulped in air and the breath scraped in his throat. "Becky," he said, and the tears rolled down the dirt and sweat on his face, "poor Becky."

"Becky will be fine," Starbuck said helplessly, "so will you." He used his free hand to wipe the tears away. Rothwell's body heaved in a spasm and the tears came more freely. "It hurts," he said, "it hurts." He was a strong man, but now wept like a child and each breath came harder and harder. "Oh, Becky," he finally managed to say in a voice so feeble that Starbuck scarcely heard it. Rothwell was still alive, for his fingers were pressing on Starbuck's hand. "Pray," he said, then whimpered again.

Starbuck said the Lord's prayer, but before he had reached the words "Thy kingdom come" the sergeant died. His belly heaved up in a massive spasm and his mouth suddenly brimmed with blood that spilled down both cheeks. He shook his head, then slumped back still.

Starbuck prized the dead fingers away from his hand. He was shaking himself, terrified by the horror of Rothwell's death, and when he looked up to stare across the fields where the Yankees had been formed he could not see because of the tears in his eyes. He cuffed the tears away and saw that the Yankees were still waiting at the far side of the two wide fields. Other Northerners were retreating toward those troops, pursued by rebel bullets. For the moment the Yankees had been hurled clean out of the East Woods, but not, it seemed, out of the cornfield, for Starbuck could still hear the full fury of rifle and cannon fire still thundering and cracking on the far side of the woods.

He stood and slung his rifle. It was time to sort out the chaos, to find the survivors of his battalion and report to Swynyard. He walked through the trees and back across the Smoketown Road. A Yankee reeled in front of him—dazed, whimpering, and wearing a mask of blood through which his frightened eyes showed white. Two prisoners were being prodded toward the rear by a small man with a bristly beard and a smoothbore musket. Two squirrels, killed by shellfire, hung from the rebel's belt. "Dinner!" he called cheerfully to Starbuck, then pushed the two frightened Yankees onward. The wounded and dead lay in clumps where the fighting had been fiercest and everywhere a sheen of gunsmoke hung between the trees like a hint of autumn mist. So many scraps of leaf had been blown from the trees by shells and bullets that the ground between the trunks was green as parkland. Starbuck, suddenly overcome with weariness and with despair for Rothwell's miserable death, leaned against a bullet-scarred trunk. Sweat trickled down his face.

He was feeling in his pouch, hoping to find a cigar among the handful of remaining cartridges, when a familiar figure showed among the distant trees. There were a score of rebels in sight, most of them searching the dead for plunder and ammunition, but there was something peculiarly furtive about the plumpish figure who advanced through the trees with an elaborate caution, then suddenly saw something and darted to one side and knelt on the ground.

Tumlin. God damn Billy Tumlin. Starbuck pushed away from the tree and stalked the big man. Tumlin glanced to left and right once in a while, but saw nothing to disturb him. He was stripping the blue coat from a Yankee corpse and was so intent on dragging the sleeves off the dead man's awkward arms that he did not know Starbuck was near him until the warm rifle barrel touched the back of his neck. Then he jumped in alarm.

"You got a thing about coats, Billy?" Starbuck asked.

"Coats?" Blythe managed to say as he stumbled backward against an elm trunk.

"You're wearing a new one today. Ain't as small as your last one." Starbuck slung the rifle, then touched the blood patch on Tumlin's chest. "Got hit, Billy?"

"Nothing serious," Blythe said. He wiped sweat off his face and offered Starbuck a grin.

Starbuck did not return the smile. "So where have you been, Billy?"

Tumlin shrugged. "Saw a doctor," he said.

"He patched you up?"

"Kind of," Blythe said.

Starbuck frowned at the mess of blood on the gray coat. "Looks bad, Billy. Looks real bad. Man could die from that kind of chest shot."

Blythe gave what he hoped was a brave smile. "I'll survive."

"You sure?" Starbuck asked, then he punched the blood patch, punched it forcefully enough to push the heavy man back against the tree. Blythe winced at the blow, but he did not react like a man who had been hit on a fresh wound. "I hear you've been skulking in the graveyard, Billy," Starbuck said.

"No," Blythe said unconvincingly.

"You bastard," Starbuck said, suddenly overcome with a blinding anger, "you white-livered piece of shit." He punched Tumlin on the bloody patch again, and this time the man did not even flinch. "That ain't a wound, Billy. It ain't even your jacket." Blythe said nothing and Starbuck felt a pang of pure hatred for a man who did not do his duty. "Was John Brown wearing a coat when he was hung?" he asked.

Blythe licked his lips and glanced left and right, but there was no escape in sight. "John Brown?" he asked, confused.

"You saw him hang, didn't you?"

"Surely did," Blythe said.

"You and the whore, right? And she was leaning out the window and you were leaning on top of her, ain't that right?"

Blythe nodded nervously. "About the size of it," he said.

"So tell me about it, Billy," Starbuck said.

Blythe licked his dry lips again. He wondered if Starbuck had gone mad, but guessed he had to humor the fool whose face was so drawn and hard. "I told you," Blythe said, "we watched him swing on a gallows outside Wager's Hotel."

"In Harper's Ferry?" Starbuck asked.

Blythe nodded. "Saw it with my own eyes." He flinched as a shell crashed through the branches overhead and exploded farther down the wood. Leaf scraps sifted down.

Starbuck had not moved as the shell whipped overhead. "John Brown was hung in Charlestown," he said, "and that's a fair ways from Wager's Hotel, Billy." He took out his revolver. "So what other lies have you told, Billy?"

Blythe glanced at the revolver and said nothing.

Starbuck pulled back the revolver's hammer. "Take off the coat, Billy."

"I—"

"Take it off!" Starbuck shouted and rammed the revolver's muzzle up under Blythe's plump chin.

Blythe hurriedly unbuckled his belt, let it drop, then pulled off the borrowed coat. The only blood on his shirt was the small stain that had rubbed off from the inside of the jacket.

"Drop the coat, Billy," Starbuck said, grinding the foresight of the

Adams into the bulging flesh. "You don't deserve to wear that coat. You ain't a man, Billy Tumlin, you're a coward. Drop the coat." Blythe let the coat fall and Starbuck pulled the revolver back and lowered its hammer, making the gun safe. Blythe looked relieved, but then Starbuck whipped the pistol's heavy barrel across Blythe's face to open a cut on Blythe's right cheekbone. "Now you're really wounded, Billy," Starbuck said. "And get the hell out of my sight. Go on, go!"

Blythe stooped to retrieve his revolver, but Starbuck put his foot on the belt. "Without a weapon?" Blythe asked.

"Go!" Starbuck shouted again and watched the heavy man blunder away.

Starbuck picked up the revolver and walked in the other direction. "Lucifer!" He saw the boy leading his new dog. "Here! New gun for you." He tossed Tumlin's belt to the boy. "Now get out of here before a Yankee shoots you." He saw Truslow shouting at men to stop looting the dead and get themselves up to the wood's edge, then he heard something far worse. Drums and cheers. He turned and ran back to where Rothwell's body lay. Then swore.

Because the Yankees were coming again.

Billy Blythe was weeping as he worked his way back north through the woods. He was not weeping because of the cut on his face, but for shame at being humiliated by Starbuck. He imagined an exquisite revenge, but first he had to survive the horror of this battle and get back where he belonged—in the North.

He found the body he had been stripping of its jacket and, after checking that Starbuck was not in sight, he dragged the coat free. He looked for his revolver, but it was gone. He cursed, then pulled on the bloody gray coat, which still lay beside the elm tree. He bundled the blue jacket under his arm, then, touching his pants pocket to make sure his precious United States commission was still safe, went on northward. Men were running past him, going to the wood's eastern margin, where a new rattle of rifle fire was filling the trees with sound. They ignored Billy Blythe, taking him for another wounded man.

He went as far north as he dared and there discovered what he had been seeking. He found a log pile, and behind it were three Northern bodies, still warm, all of them bloody and all of them dead. Blythe crouched, peeled off the gray coat and pulled on the blue, then wriggled down beside the logs and heaved the three corpses on top of him. He knew the Yankees were attacking again, and this time, he reckoned, the rebels would not stand. Blythe believed the battle was turning, and it was time for him to turn with it. A shell whipcracked through the trees overhead, making him whimper, but then at last he was deep in the leaf mold beside the logs and protected by the warm bodies above. He lay still, feeling a dead man's blood trickle onto his back. He wished he could repay Starbuck for that blow across the face, but guessed Starbuck would not be alive to take the repayment. He hoped Starbuck's death was agonizing, and that thought consoled him as he waited under the corpses for rescue.

Billy Blythe had survived.

Belvedere Delaney was making himself useful. Lee had gone to the higher ground, but he had not invited Delaney to accompany him and so Delaney had searched for his servant, George, thinking it was time for the two of them to begin preparing for a tactful withdrawal. Delaney had discovered George carrying pails of water to the wounded men waiting for the surgeons in the garden of a house just north of the village.

These men were the fortunate wounded, the handful that had been brought down from the fighting to the comparative peace in the rebel rear. Most of these men were victims of Yankee shells, for the men with bullet wounds were too far forward to be fetched back by the handful of ambulance wagons and those men would suffer where they lay, but these men were receiving the best care the Confederate army possessed. The worst afflicted could not be cared for at all because the surgeons' efforts were being saved for the men who stood a chance of survival. Some ether was available and the lucky few were thus anesthetized before the saws and knives slashed at their broken legs, but most men were given a slug of brandy, a leather gag to bite on, then told to play the man, be quiet, and lie still. Orderlies held them firm on the table while a surgeon in a blood-soaked apron sliced into the mangled flesh.

Delaney's first instinct was to shy away from the horror, but an overwhelming pang of pity made him stay. He carried cups of water to wounded men, then held their heads up as they sipped. One man went into spasm and bit the cup's rim so hard that the china shattered. Delaney held another man's hand as he died. He wiped sweat from the forehead of an officer with bandaged eyes who would never see again. Six or seven women from the village were helping with the wounded and one of them was defiantly wearing a small Stars and Stripes pinned to her apron as she moved among the blood and vomit and stench of the garden. George crouched beside a South Carolina sergeant and tried to staunch the blood that kept hemorrhaging from a crudely bandaged slash at his waist. The man was dying and wanted reassurance that the battle was being won, and with it the war, and George kept saying over and over in a soothing voice that the rebels were charging forward, that the Yankees were falling back, and that victory was imminent. "Praise the Lord," the sergeant said, then died.

One man pleaded with Delaney to find his wife's daguerreotype at the bottom of his cartridge pouch. Delaney pulled out the rounds and there, under them all, was the precious scrap of copper sheet wrapped in a piece of chintz. The woman looked heavy-jawed and dull-eyed, but just glimpsing her face gave the dying man peace. "You'll write her, sir?" he asked Delaney.

"I will."

"Dorcas Bridges," the man said, "Dearborn Street in Mobile. Tell her I never did stop loving her. You going to write that down, sir?"

"You're going to be all right," Delaney tried to reassure the man.

"I'm going to be just fine, sir. Before this day's through, sir, I'll be with my Lord and Savior, but Dorcas now, she's got to manage without me. You will write to her, sir?"

"I'll write." Delaney had a stub of pencil and carefully wrote Dorcas's address on a scrap of newspaper.

Delaney collected a dozen other names and addresses and promised to write to them all. He would write, too, and he would say the same thing in each letter, that their husbands or sons had died bravely and without pain. The truth was that they had all died in horrid pain. The lucky lost consciousness, but the unlucky felt the agony of their wounds right till the last. At the rear of the house, where an herb garden grew, a pile of amputated arms and legs grew higher. A small child watched the pile with wide eyes, thumb in her mouth.

While on the high ground the guns went on and on.

Starbuck found the remnants of Potter's company still miraculously clinging together. They were close to Rothwell's body, lining the edge of the East Woods and firing toward the Yankees who marched south. A tatterdemalion mix of men were in the rebel line. There were Georgians, Texans, Virginians, Alabamians, and nearly all had lost touch with their officers, but were simply joining the nearest rebel line and fighting on. The noise in the wood was deafening. The Yankees had brought up new guns that were banging case shot into the trees, there were Northern skirmishers behind the limestone outcrops in the plowed fields, and all the while the fight in the cornfield was swelling into its old fury.

The Yankees were advancing in a column of companies, making themselves a tempting target for the rebel riflemen. "I wish we had cannon," Potter shouted to Starbuck, then pulled his trigger. Truslow fired steadily and grimly, each bullet thumping into the mass of blue uniforms that kept coming forward, though the closer the attack came to the trees, the more chaos was ripped into its leading ranks. Colonel Maitland had come into the woods, where he was swinging his sword and shouting drunkenly to kill the swine. Swynyard came running south through the wood and knelt beside Starbuck at the edge of the trees. He waited till Starbuck had fired. "They're in the woods again," Swynyard shouted, pointing north.

"How many?"

"Thousands!"

"Shit," Starbuck said, then poured powder into his barrel, spat in the bullet, picked up his ramrod, and shoved it down hard. His right arm was tired and his right shoulder one agonizing bruise from the gun's recoil. "Who's holding them?" he asked Swynyard.

"No one."

"Jesus," Starbuck swore again. He waited for the smoke to clear and suddenly, right in front of him, he saw a Yankee officer on horseback. The man was white-bearded, his uniform was heavy with braid, and he was shouting desperately at the milling Northerners who were recoiling from the fire from the woods. Starbuck wondered if the man was a general, then aimed at the inviting target. At least a dozen other rebels had seen the man and there was a small fusillade of shots, and when the rifles' smoke had thinned, there was only a riderless horse.

The firing in the cornfield reached a new intensity. Swynyard tapped Starbuck's shoulder. "See what's happening, Nate. I don't want to be trapped here."

Starbuck ran through the woods. Above him was the noise of bullets and case shot whipping through the leaves, provoking a constant shower of leaf scraps. The wood's center was empty, except for the dead and dying, but as he neared the western edge the rebels became thick again. They were firing at a single regiment of Yankees, which appeared to have made a lone charge through the broken corn. The Yankees seemed confused and abandoned, for no other battalions had supported their charge, and now, surrounded by rebels, they had huddled into a mass that was inviting a grim punishment from the rebels. One of the blue-coated men waved a New York flag to encourage his comrades, then a case shot cracked into smoke just above the flag that fell instantly. The Yankees began to retreat, and the rebels, heartened by the small victory, pushed forward into the corn again. It seemed to Starbuck that every rebel in Maryland was being thrust into the fight in one last desperate attempt to hold the position. Men were running from the West Woods to thicken the line that trampled forward into the corn. Captain Peel was there with more survivors from Starbuck's battalion and Starbuck ran to join them. The ground in the cornfield felt lumpy because of the fallen cobs and because so many blasts of canister and case shot had littered the earth. A skin of smoke hung at breast height above the corn, while everywhere there was puddled blood, broken men, flies, and shattered weapons.

The rebel line advanced clear through the cornfield, but was again stopped at its northern edge. The Northerners had their own battle line waiting and that line gave a terrible volley that cracked into the rebel counterattack. Cannons belched canister, battalions fired volleys, but the insanity of battle had gripped the Southerners and instead of retreating from the overwhelming fire, they stayed and fired back into the Yankees. Starbuck scrabbled among the last few cartridges in his pouch and listened to the terrible swish of canister raking through the fallen corn and to the thump of bullets striking home. Some men knelt to fight and others lay down to see beneath the thickening smoke band.

The fight seemed to last forever, though later, counting his cartridges, Starbuck knew it could only have been a couple of minutes. He was unaware of making any sound, but he was keening a high moaning noise that was the product of pure terror. On either side of him men fell, and at every second he expected to suffer the banging impact of a bullet, but he stayed where he was, loading and firing, and he tried to blot out the noise of the screams and the bullets and the guns by singing the high unchanging note. He was working slowly, his brain fuddled by the chaos, so that he had to think about each action. The spent powder had caked in the grooves of his rifle's barrel, making it hard to force each bullet down. He had propped his ramrod against his belly to make it easier to retrieve after each shot, but it kept falling into the corn and every time he stooped to pick it up he wanted to lay down and stay down. He wanted to be anywhere in all the world except here in death's kingdom. He loaded again and saw one of his men fold slowly over, gasping for breath. Another man dragged himself back through the corn, leaving a trail of blood from a shattered leg. A Yankee drum lay discarded in the corn, its skin punctured by bullets. Little flames flickered in the corn, where bullet wadding had started fires. A Georgian officer was on his knees, hands clasped at his groin as he heaved in small breaths and stared in desperate misery at the blood spilling down his thighs. The man looked up and caught Starbuck's eye. "Shoot me," he said, "for pity's sake, man, shoot me."

Then, from the northern part of the East Woods, a new volley crashed.

And the rebel line collapsed.

It had fought since dawn, but now, in the face of yet more Yankee attackers, the defense disintegrated. The collapse began with one battalion, then the panic spread to the neighboring units and suddenly a whole brigade was running. Starbuck was not aware of the panic at first. He had heard the massive volley off to his right and he was aware of screams and cheers from the edge of the woods, but he doggedly went on loading his rifle while the Georgian officer pleaded for death, but then a nearby man called out a warning and Starbuck saw Yankees running through the smoke. He snatched up his ramrod and ran with the other rebels. Some Yankees sprinted ahead, angling in front of Starbuck in their eagerness to cut off a retreating flag. He let the ramrod drop and dragged the revolver from behind his back and fired wildly into the blue coats. A rebel sergeant swung his rifle by the barrel to bring its heavy stock down on a Yankee head. Starbuck heard the impact of the rifle butt just as a bearded Yankee lunged at him with a bayonet. Starbuck stepped aside so that the blade went past him, he thrust the revolver into the man's belly, and pulled the trigger, but nothing happened. In despair, screaming, he swung his clumsy rifle so that the bullet-shattered stock slammed into the side of the Yankee's head. Starbuck could smell the man's uniform, the tobacco on his breath, then the man stumbled. Starbuck kicked him hard and ran on. He stumbled over cornstalks, canister balls, and bodies. There were cheers behind and panic in front. He expected a bullet at any second and dropped the broken rifle to gain a mite of speed.

The momentum of the Yankees' attack carried them down through the East Woods and caused more rebels to join the flight. The Northern guns on the Hagerstown Pike hurried the fugitives along with round after round of case shot. The rebels tumbled out of the yard of the burned farm, they abandoned the graveyard, they fled for the trees in the west and so abandoned the morning's hard-fought battlefield to the Yankees. Here and there groups of men retreated slowly, in ranks, firing as they went, but most of the gray-clad infantry simply ran and only slowed when they realized that there was no Yankee pursuit. The Northerners were as confused as the rebels and, though some men pushed doggedly on, more stopped in the cornfield to reload and fire at the rapidly vanishing enemy. Starbuck recognized some men from

Faulconer's Legion and joined them. He plucked up a Springfield rifle from a dead Texan and checked that it worked. A handful of the Yellowlegs were still with him, and then, on the Smoketown Road, he saw Lucifer and Imp walking west with Potter's company. He joined them, then crossed the dirt ruts of the Hagerstown Pike to reach the shadows of the trees beyond.

Colonel Swynyard was shouting his own name in an attempt to rally his brigade. Handfuls of men joined him, milling in confusion among the woods just north of the Dunker church. Behind them now was a stretch of pastureland that had been turned into hell's outpost—a swathe of killing ground littered with bodies and slick with blood, a smoke-hung graveyard of the unburied dead over which Yankee battalions advanced in uncoordinated pursuit of the rebel fugitives. Shell bursts punctured the pasture, scattering dead men and hurrying the last rebels toward the West Woods.

Some of the panicking rebels had not stopped in the West Woods, but had kept going into the farmlands beyond. Rebel cavalry were dispatched to round them up and send them back to the West Woods, where officers and sergeants bellowed out unit names. Here and there the vestiges of companies formed, and shattered battalions gathered under their torn and stained colors. Other officers did not worry about rejoining their battalions, but just tugged and pushed men into makeshift companies at the wood's edge and told them to open fire on the pursuing enemy. A wagon was whipped up the Hagerstown Pike and dropped off boxes of artillery ammunition for the gun teams that had hastily deployed in front of the woods. The wagon's team was hit by a Yankee shell and dying horses screamed as gallons of their blood washed down the road's deep ruts. The ground in front of the rebel batteries was at last free of fugitives and the gunners opened fire with canister that dropped more dead among the army of corpses that lay beneath the smoke.

For a moment it seemed as though the guns would hold the Northern advance, then lines of blue troops appeared in the smoke that hazed the land east of the batteries. Gunners desperately tried to handspike the guns about to face this new threat, but then a rippling volley whipped a storm of minie bullets that clanged off cannon barrels, drove splinters from gun wheels, and threw down the gunners. In the pause while the infantry reloaded, the surviving gun captains brought up their horse teams and dragged the guns back through the trees. A Yankee cheer sounded, then a battalion charged into the vacated ground where the grass had been flattened and scorched by the cannon blasts. No one opposed them and the troops, a big Pennsylvanian regiment, found their lodgment in the West Woods. They captured the Dunker church, which was filled with wounded men, and there they stopped, for the woods around them were alive with rebel survivors who began a galling fire. The Pennsylvanian commander sent messengers to the rear with pleas for support and ammunition. Some Northern guns came to help the Pennsylvanian, but the gunners unlimbered too close to the woods and rebel sharpshooters raked them with fire. The guns pulled back, one hauled by infantry because all its horses had been shot. The abandoned wagon had caught fire and its remaining load of shells banged off one by one to vomit a filthy smoke into the white-hot sky.

General Jackson raged up and down the wood shouting at men to form in company, to find their battalions, to turn and fight. He knew this was the moment for the Yankees to strike. If one Northern corps, even one brigade, should reinforce the Pennsylvanian lodgment about the Dunker church and carry the attack straight on through the woods, then the dizzied men in gray would break. The Yankees would win the day, the rebel army would be turned into a rabble fleeing for a narrow ford, and by winter the streets of Richmond would be filled with strutting Yankees. General Lee, recognizing the same danger, was assembling a line of guns on a ridge to the west of the woods so that if the triumphant Yankees did burst through the trees, they would be met by a killing barrage that might at least slow the pursuers and give his men time to make a fighting retreat toward the Potomac.

But the Yankees were as dazed as the rebels. The swiftness of the Northern advance had left their units scattered across the field. All of the ground that lay east of the Hagerstown Pike and north of the Dunker church was in Yankee hands, and some Northern units had crossed the Pike to find a dangerous shelter in the edge of the West Woods, but the reinforcements they needed were nowhere in sight. Rebel guns in the south of the battlefield were thrashing the beaten ground with shellfire and rebel infantry was firing from the woods, and so the pursuit stalled as the Yankees, like the rebels, tried to pull order out of chaos.

The rebel panic in the West Woods subsided. Men counted their cartridges and some glanced nervously behind in an effort to spot a route away from the carnage, but as the Northern firing died away the rebels began to reform. One by one the companies were remade, the gaps in the line were mended, and the cartridges replenished.

"I borrowed poor Haxall's watch." Colonel Swynyard joined Starbuck. "He won't need it in heaven, poor man, but I'll send it to his wife."

"He's dead?" Starbuck asked.

Swynyard nodded, then shook the watch and held it to his ear. "It seems to be working," he said dubiously, then looked at the watch's face. "Almost nine o'clock," Swynyard said, and Starbuck immediately frowned and wondered why it was not getting dark. "In the morning, Nate," Swynyard said gently, "in the morning."

The day was still young.

Yankees walked through the East Woods and out into the cornfield. One man vomited at the sight of the field. The stench of the place was worse than a slaughterhouse. Men lay shattered, their blood spilled wide, their bowels open in death. Sightless eyes gazed through smoke, mouths were open and filled with flies. Rebel and Yankee lay together. The wounded called for help, some wept, some called for a merciful shot to the head. A few, pitifully few, stretcher bearers had begun work. A chaplain, overcome by the horror, fell to his knees at the edge of the trees and let tears fall onto an open Bible. Other men moved among the horror in search of plunder; they carried pliers to take gold-capped teeth and knives to cut off wedding ring fingers or else to quiet their victims' protests. A battery of guns checked at the cornfield's edge, the team's drivers unwilling to run their heavy weapons over the field corpses, but an officer shouted at them to damn their squeamishness and so they cracked their whips and forced the guns across the bodies. Blood turned black. Steam came from the deeper blood pools. The sun was climbing, the very last mist had gone from the creek, and the day's sweltering heat was rising.

Mister Kroeger, the farmer who had undertaken to be the Yankees' guide to the Snaveley Ford, insisted on visiting his farm first. The cows needed milking, but as no orders had come from McClellan ordering an attack across the river, no one thought to hurry the farmer. The Yankee troops detailed to cross the bridge on the lower creek stared from their hiding places and wondered how in the name of a merciful God they were supposed to cross several hundred yards of open land, then cram themselves onto a bridge just twelve feet wide, all the while being raked by the rebels in the rifle pits who waited on the farther bank.

A new and heavier corps of Northern troops forded the river well to the north of the lower bridge. Their crossing was not opposed and the fresh troops began the long climb to the plateau where they would serve to reinforce the Yankees who had beaten the rebels out of the East Woods and the cornfield. Thirteen thousand men climbed the hill, their bands playing and colors flying as they drew nearer and nearer to the death-house stench that waited at the slope's summit. The long lines of advancing men paused and broke apart whenever they reached a rail fence, but once over the fence the long ranks reformed and pushed on. It would take the newcomers some fair time to reach the summit, and once there they would need to be shown where to attack, and all that while the rebels were desperately patching together the northern half of their army and so, for a while, the plateau was eerily silent. Once in a while a gun would fire or a rifle crack, but both sides were drawing breath.

One man, at least, had survived the battle and would fight in it no more. Billy Blythe waited until the sound of firing had died away and until the first excited rush of storming Yankee troops was long gone past his hiding place, and only then did he free himself from the deadweight of the men who concealed him. The woods were full of curious Yankees, but no one took any particular notice of Billy Blythe in his loose blue coat. He staggered to make himself look like one of the many wounded men waiting for help under the cover of the trees.

He found a dead rebel officer behind a rotting trunk and took the man's belt with its holstered Whitney revolver. Then, still staggering, he made his way east to the Smoketown Road, where a press of vehicles jammed the dirt track and its grass verges. Wagons were bringing new ammunition for the cannons and ambulances were lining up for the wounded. One of the ambulances was carrying the dying body of General Mansfield, who had been shot off his horse as he had tried to urge his men into the East Woods. "Can you walk back?" a sergeant shouted at Blythe.

Blythe mumbled incoherently and lurched more impressively.

"Come on, lad, up with you!" The sergeant boosted Blythe's heavy body onto the bed of an empty ammunition wagon that would trundle north to Smoketown before crossing the creek by the upper bridge.

Blythe lay in the wagon and stared at the sky. He smiled. Caton Rothwell, one of the two men who had sworn to kill him, was dead, shot in the back by Blythe himself, and Blythe had sown enough discord to be fairly sure that Starbuck would be removed before the day was through. He chuckled as he admired his own cleverness. Damn it, he thought, but there were few men to touch Billy Blythe for sheer cunning. He fingered his commission, then struggled to sit up. A Pennsylvanian Bucktail officer, wounded in the leg, sat beside him and offered him a cigar. "Hell," the Pennsylvanian said.

"Life is sure sweet," Blythe said.

The Pennsylvanian frowned at Blythe's accent. "Are you a reb?" he asked.

"A major in your army, Captain," Blythe promoted himself to celebrate his survival. "I was never a man to change allegiance to my country, certainly not on account of a pack of Sambos." He accepted the Pennsylvanian's cigar. "Hell," he went on, "I can understand fighting over land or women, but over darkies?" Blythe shook his head. "Just plain don't make sense."

The captain leaned back on the wagon's sideboard. "Jesus," he said faintly, still shaking after his time in the cornfield.

"Praise His name," Blythe said, "praise His holy name." For Billy Blythe was safe.

Captain Dennison was safe too. He was in the West Woods, where he had found Sergeant Case. The two men were some twenty yards behind the remnants of Starbuck's battalion, where they were concealed in the muddle of disorganized and leaderless men. "Captain Tumlin didn't make it," Dennison said nervously, "leastwise I ain't seen him. And Cartwright's dead. So's Dan Lippincott."

"So the battalion's yours," Case said, and then, after a pause, "or it will be when Starbuck's dead."

Dennison shuddered. He had been scared half to death by the retreat across the open country, a retreat marked by the whistle of minie bullets and the jeers of Yankees and the thump of exploding shells.

"Yours," Case said again, "and you promised to give me back my company. As a captain."

"I did," Dennison agreed.

Case pushed a rifle into Dennison's hands. "It fires true," he said, "and it's loaded."

Dennison stared at the gun as though he had never seen such a thing before. "Swynyard might not confirm me," he said after a while.

"Bloody hell, Captain, we all have to take our chances," Case said, then levered down the trigger guard of his captured Sharps rifle to make sure a round was in the breech. It was. That meant he had three rounds in all, and after they were fired the gun would be useless. Dennison looked up at Starbuck and tentatively raised the rifle to his shoulder, but Case pushed it down. "Not now, Captain," he said scornfully. "Wait till the Yankees come again. Wait till there's plenty of noise."

Dennison nodded. "You're firing too?" he asked, needing reassurance.

"Head shot," Case said. "You go for the body." He patted the middle of Dennison's back to show where the nervous Captain should aim. "One of us will get the bastard. Now wait." Case had not been fooled by Starbuck's offer of leniency. He guessed that the Yankee bastard was scared of him and had tried to buy Case off by returning his stripes, but Robert Case was not a man to let a grudge be settled cheaply. Starbuck had humiliated him, and Case wanted his revenge. He also wanted the commission. In a month, he reckoned, he could be commander of the

Yellowlegs and then, by God, he would whip the bastards into a disciplined unit. Maybe he could change their name, call them the Virginia Fusiliers, then have the bastards march into battle like they were on Aldershot's parade ground.

The two men crouched low, both waiting for the odd silence on the battlefield to end.

The first Yankee hammer blow had fallen, and under it the rebel line in the north of the battlefield had crumbled. The second blow now climbed steadily up from the middle part of the creek while the third, concealed in the hollows and trees beyond the Antietam, waited for the order that would launch them across the gently flowing stream to cut the rebels' retreat.

On the far side of the Potomac, the marching Light Division heard the sudden lull in the gunfire. Sweating men looked nervously at each other and wondered if the silence meant that the battle was already lost. "Keep going!" the staff officers shouted, "keep going!"

They had miles to march yet and a deep, wide river to cross, but they kept on toward the ominous silence and the pyre of smoke that dirtied a sky above a field of dead.

"Seventy-nine men, sir," Starbuck reported to Swynyard.

"The Legion's down to a hundred and four," Swynyard said bleakly. "Poor Haxall's men don't even make a company. The Sixty-fifth is a hundred and two." He folded the scrap of paper on which the totals had been penciled. "More men will come in," he said, "some are hiding, some are running." Swynyard's Brigade was shrunken small enough to be collected in a half-acre clearing of the West Woods. The Yankees holding the Dunker church were not more than two hundred paces away, but neither side had ammunition to spare and so each was treating the other gingerly. Now and then one of the rebel skirmishers who ringed the Pennsylvanians fired, but return fire was rare.

"God knows how many have died," Starbuck said bitterly.

"But your men stood and fought, Nate," Swynyard said, "which is more than the punishment battalion did at Manassas."

"Some stood and fought, sir," Starbuck said, thinking of Dennison. He had not seen the captain and did not care if he never saw him again.

With any luck, Starbuck thought, Dennison was dead or captured, and so, he hoped, was Tumlin.

"You did well," Swynyard insisted. He was watching an ammunition wagon stop on the track that led through the clearing. The wagon's rifle ammunition was for his brigade, a sign that their fighting was not done this day.

"I did nothing, sir," Starbuck answered, "except chase after my men." The battle had been chaos almost from the first. Men had become detached from their companies, they had fought with whoever they found themselves, and few officers had kept control of their companies. The rebel defense had been made by men just standing and fighting, sometimes without orders, but always with vast pride and a huge determination that had finally been eroded by one heavy attack after another.

"Charmed," Swynyard said sardonically.

"Sir?" Starbuck asked in puzzlement, then saw that Swynyard was staring at Lieutenant Colonel Maitland, who was strolling along the decimated ranks of the Legion. Maitland was grinning vacuously and spreading lavish compliments, but he was also having some trouble in keeping his footing. His men grinned, amused at the sight of their inebriated commander.

"He's drunk, isn't he?" Swynyard asked.

"He's soberer than he was," Starbuck said. "Much."

Swynyard grimaced. "I watched him in the cornfield. He was strolling through fire like it was the garden of Eden and I thought he must be the bravest man I'd ever seen, but I suppose it wasn't bravery at all. He must have drunk all that liquor he confiscated."

"I guess."

"He was telling me last night," Swynyard went on, "just how scared he was of not doing his duty. I liked him for that. Poor man. I didn't realize how scared he really was."

"If Old Jack sees how scared he is now," Starbuck said dryly, "he'll be lucky to keep his rank." He nodded to the left where Jackson was riding toward Swynyard's Brigade along the reformed line.

"Colonel Maitland!" Swynyard shouted in voice worthy of a sergeant. "To attention, if you please! Now!"

Maitland, astonished by the peremptory order, snapped to attention. He was facing his men so only they could see the surprised look on his face. Jackson and his aides rode their horses behind the drunken colonel and so noticed nothing. The general reined in close to Swynyard. "Well?" he asked curtly.

"They can fight, sir," Swynyard said, guessing what the curt question meant. He turned and pointed at the bullet-pocked wall of the Dunker church that was just visible through the leaves. "Yankees there, sir."

"Not for long," Jackson said. His left hand rose slowly into the air as he turned to gaze at Swynyard's ranks. "A brigade?" he asked, "or a battalion?"

"Brigade, sir."

Jackson nodded, then rode on down the line of exhausted men who he knew must soon fight again.

"Three cheers for Old Jack!" Maitland suddenly erupted and the Legion gave three rousing cheers that Jackson pointedly ignored as he spurred on toward the next brigade.

"What do you do with Maitland, sir?" Starbuck asked.

"Do?" Swynyard seemed surprised by the question. "Nothing, of course. He's doing his duty, Nate. He ain't running away. When this fight's done I'll have a word with him and suggest he might be better employed back in the War Department. But at least he'll be able to say he fought the good fight at Sharpsburg. His pride will be intact."

"And if he doesn't go?"

"Oh, he'll go," Swynyard said grimly, "believe me, Nate, he'll go. And once he's gone I'll put your boys into the Legion and give the whole lot to you."

"Thank you, sir."

Swynyard looked over Starbuck's shoulder and jerked his beard to suggest that there was someone needing Starbuck's attention. Starbuck turned and, to his astonishment, saw it was Captain Dennison who, very formally, was reporting for duty.

"Where the hell were you?" Starbuck snapped.

Dennison glanced at Swynyard, then shrugged. "Where I was told to be, sir. In the graveyard."

"Skulking?" Starbuck snarled.

"Sir!" Dennison protested. "Captain Tumlin ordered us there, sir. Said the Yankees had skirmishers attacking our wounded. So we went there, sir. Fought them, sir." He patted the black-muzzled rifle that now hung from his shoulder. "Killed a few, sir."

"Tumlin ordered you there?" Starbuck asked.

"Yes, sir."

"Son of a bitch," Starbuck said. "Where the hell is Tumlin?"

"Don't know, sir. Shall we fall in, sir?" Dennison asked innocently. A dozen men of A Company were with Dennison and none of them looked as tired, strained, or scared as the other survivors from the Yellowlegs.

"Fall in," Starbuck said. "And Captain?"

"Sir?"

"I gave Case his stripes back."

"He told me, sir."

Starbuck watched Dennison go to join the remnant of his company. Sergeant Case was there, the buck's tail still pinned to his gray hat, and, for a second, Starbuck wondered about that bullet in Caton Rothwell's back. Then he dismissed the suspicion. There had been enough stray Yankees in the woods to account for that miserable death. If it was anyone's fault, Starbuck thought, it was his for not leaving two men to watch from the wood's edge.

"What was all that about?" Swynyard asked when Dennison had fallen in.

"God knows, sir. Either he's lying, or Tumlin disobeyed me. But that bastard," Starbuck jerked his head toward Dennison, "ain't never been civil to me in the past, so the hell knows why he's starting now."

"Battle, Nate," Swynyard said. "It changes men."

A bugle sounded to the east. Starbuck turned and stared through the trees toward the horrid ground where so many had died. Till now he had been fighting an enemy who had come from the north, but the collapse of the rebel line in the cornfield meant that from now on they would be facing east. Another bugle called. "Bastards are coming again," Starbuck said.

"Then let us make ready," Swynyard said very formally.

Because the battle was still not lost, nor won, and the Yankees were coming again.

The first division of Union reinforcements came up from the creek in fine style, but when they reached the plateau there was no messenger to guide them to where they were needed. One Northern general was dead, another had gone back wounded, and so there was no one to tell the newly arrived troops where to attack. Their own general saw where the lingering gunsmoke hung thickest and pointed with his sword. "Keep going! That way! March!" A second Yankee division was climbing from the creek, but the general did not wait for it to join him. Instead he formed his men into three long lines of battle, one behind the other, and sent them through the East Woods. Once through the trees they reformed their lines and advanced across the cornfield where the wounded cried out to stop men treading on them.

The attacking division would have made a fine sight if it had been maneuvering on a parade ground, but on a battlefield the serried mass of men was an invitation to the tired rebel gunners waiting beyond the turnpike. The cannons opened fire. Case shot cracked gray above the attackers' heads while solid shot whipped through rank after rank of men, one shot sufficient to kill or wound a dozen men. The Yankees pushed on, closing their ranks after each bloody strike and leaving behind them a new trail of dead and injured men.

The Pennsylvanians around the Dunker church heard the guns and prayed that someone was coming to their support. Their attack had driven a deep wedge into the center of the rebel army, but their ammunition was now desperately low. Their colonel had sent for help, but none was coming. Skirmishers probed the woods around the church, looking for other Northern troops who might have found shelter in the trees, but there were no allies within reach and one by one the Pennsylvania skirmishers were killed or wounded by rebel sharpshooters. The Northern colonel looked behind him for help while his pickets reported the noise of troops gathering in the surrounding trees.

The troops were rebels. They were fresh and unblooded this day. In the dawn they had been guarding the bridges and fords across the lower part of the creek, but no Yankee attack had materialized and so, in desperation, Lee had stripped his southern defenses of every man that could be spared. Those men had marched through Sharpsburg and up the hill to where Jackson now hurled them at the Dunker church.

The rebel yell echoed in the woods. Volleys clattered against the church walls, thumped into trees, and ricocheted off stone. For a time the Pennsylvanians resisted the tightening ring, but they were isolated and outnumbered and finally they broke. They ran, abandoning their wounded, crossing the turnpike, and not stopping until they were out of range of the rebel rifles.

The rebels did not pursue. Jackson had freed himself of the Pennsylvanians and now he turned his men north to where the great parade ground attack had pushed across the cornfield and into the northern part of the West Woods. The attacking division had suffered horribly from the rebel guns, but enough men survived to reach the trees and sweep the rebel gunners out of their path. A handful of Confederate skirmishers fled, and suddenly the Stars and Stripes were being carried into the West Woods. "Keep going!" officers shouted, knowing their men would be tempted to stay in the shelter of the bullet-flecked trunks. "Keep going!" The three battle lines marched on westward as if they planned to push clean on down to the Potomac, but the guns Lee had placed behind the wood greeted their appearance at the tree line. Another cornfield lay beyond the wood and it was filled with rebel sharpshooters who, concealed by the standing corn, poured rifle fire into the blue ranks. The Yankees paused to reform lines that had been tangled by their advance through the trees.

The three impressive battle lines were jumbled together now, but still they faced westward, as though their general believed his object was to reach the distant Potomac. In truth the enemy lay to the south, where Jackson had collected every man he could find and was leading them through the trees against the unprotected Yankee flank. Guns hid the noise of the advancing troops. There were rebel guns firing from the western hill and Northern guns firing from higher up the Hagerstown Pike, but then, drowning even the thunder of the artillery, an almighty crash of rifle fire splintered across the sky with a sound like the very veils of heaven being ripped apart.

The second division of Yankee reinforcements had climbed from the creek. They were supposed to follow the first division, which was now isolated in the West Woods, but the second division had lagged behind and now, reaching the plateau, they could see no sign of the men they were supposed to reinforce. For a few moments they waited, their general officers seeking directions amid the chaos, but then, lacking any orders, they marched southeast toward the beckoning landmark of a white spire of a Sharpsburg church that could just be glimpsed above the trees. For a few moments the Yankees advanced across the open farmland unobserved and unhindered, but in their path was a farm lane and the lane was an attacker's nightmare. For years heavy farm wagons had broken the lane's dirt surface and, because the track ran gently downhill toward open ground, the rains had washed the debris away so that year after year, generation by generation, the lane had sunk ever deeper beneath the farmland's surface so that by now a man on foot could not see over the lane's sloping banks. The Yankees did not know it, but they were placidly advancing over sunlit pastureland toward a natural firestep that was crammed with rebels. These Confederate troops guarded the center of Lee's line and they had not fired a shot all morning, but now, at last, they pushed their rifle barrels through the long grass that grew beneath the rail fence at the bank's lip and aimed at the unsuspecting Yankees. They let those Yankees come real close, then pulled their triggers.

Starbuck heard that first slaughtering volley fired from the sunken lane. The sound told him that the battle was widening as more Yankees crossed the creek, but his fight was still in the northern part of the field where five thousand Yankees were readying themselves to continue their westward attack, unaware that Jackson was coming from their unguarded southern flank.

Swynyard's brigade advanced on the right, emerging from the trees where the woods narrowed to cross a small pasture. The Hagerstown Pike was immediately to Starbuck's right, and beyond that lay the pastureland where the rebels had resisted attack after attack from the cornfield. The pasture was rilled with bodies heaped in rows like tidelines showing where the fight had ebbed and flowed. More bodies were folded over the fences, where men had been killed as they clambered over the rails to escape the Northern advance. Starbuck's men walked past the horror in silence. They were weary and numbed, too tired to even look at the place where they had fought so long. A Yankee artillery battery stood well out of rifle range at the pasture's far side. The battery's guns were firing south, and every shot propelled a jet of flame-filled smoke that spat fifty yards from the gun's muzzle before billowing into a vaporous mist that hung in the still air. The gunners appeared not to have noticed the rebel soldiers across the turnpike, or else they had more inviting targets to the south. Starbuck watched the gunners leap aside as their huge weapons leapt back with each shot. It was, he thought, as if those gunners were fighting a quite separate battle.

The gunners were the only living Yankees in sight and it struck Starbuck as strange that so many men could be swallowed so comprehensively into so small a patch of countryside. The noise of the battle was awesome, yet here, where in a few hours thousands had died, the living seemed to have vanished.

Then, just as Starbuck was marveling at the emptiness of the landscape, a Yankee officer rode from the trees just fifty yards ahead of the brigade. He was a young man, full-bearded and straight-backed, who carried a long, shining sword blade. He curbed his horse to stare at the distant gunners, then some instinct made him look to his right and his jaw fell open as he saw the approaching rebels. He twisted in the saddle to shout a warning toward the trees, then, before calling the alarm, turned back again to make sure the Confederates were not figments of a fear-racked imagination. "Would someone please shoot that man?" Swynyard called plaintively.

The Yankee realized his danger and raked back his spurs as he hauled on the reins. His horse twisted round and leapt back toward the trees before a single rebel had time to draw a bead on the inviting target. Starbuck heard the astonished Yankee shouting a warning, then the shout was swamped by the rebel yell that, in turn, was drowned by a shattering volley of rifle fire and an eruption of screams.

"Bayonets!" Swynyard shouted, "quick, boys!"

The brigade dragged the long blades from their holsters and slotted them onto fire-blackened muzzles. The pace quickened. Colonel Swynyard was in the front now, a sword in his hand, and Starbuck felt the tiredness slough away to be replaced by a sudden and unexpected exhilaration.

"Fire!" Swynyard shouted. The Yankees had appeared. Scores of men had tumbled in disarray from the trees, only to be flanked by Swynyard's attack. "Fire!" the colonel shouted again. Rifles flamed, then the bayonets drove forward. "Don't let them stand!" Swynyard roared. "Get them moving, boys, get them moving!"

The Yankees stood no chance. They had been attacked on their open flank and the three battle lines crumpled. The Yankees nearest to the point of attack had no room to turn and face the rebels; the unlucky were driven down by vengeful Confederates while the fortunate fled to tangle with the battalions behind who were struggling to turn their companies through ninety degrees. The cumbersome maneuver was confused by the trees and by the rebel shells that tore through the high branches to explode shrapnel and leaves down into the confusion. The Yankees in the northernmost part of the wood stood the best chance, and some battalions there managed to turn their lines, but most of the regiments collided as they wheeled, officers shouted contradictory orders, fugitives jostled the nervous ranks, and always, everywhere, there sounded the vicious yelping of the rebel war cry. Panic prompted some Northern units to open fire on fellow Yankees. Shouted orders were lost in the din, and all the while the rebel attack swept on like a flood seeking the weakest parts of a crumbling dike. Some Northern units put up a fight, but one by one the defenders were outflanked and were forced to join the retreat. For a time some battalions in the northern part of the woods resisted the attack, but at last they too were outflanked and the whole division tumbled in panic from the trees to flee into the shelter of the North Woods.

The rebels pursued into the open ground and now the Yankee batteries by the Hagerstown Pike could join the fight and their case shot boomed and cracked into the gray ranks. Yankee skirmishers sheltered behind haystacks and farm buildings to lay a deadly fire on the rebel ranks, while out of the East Woods, which had seemed deserted not long before, new batteries of Northern guns appeared and, with the fuses of their shells cut perilously short, took the rebel charge in the flank.

Starbuck was kneeling beside the broken fence that edged the turnpike. His battalion, which looked scarcely bigger than a company, was strung along the road where they sheltered from the Northern artillery that fired across the cornfield. Starbuck gazed in horror at the trampled corn where the bodies lay in clumps. Here and there a cornstalk survived, but for the most part the field looked as though a herd of giant hogs had rooted up a graveyard. Except that some of the bodies still lived and once in a while, in a lull of the guns' awful sound, a weak cry for help sounded from inside the corn.

The fire of the Yankee guns stopped abruptly. Starbuck frowned, guessing the cause. One or two of his men glanced at him nervously as he gingerly stood, then as he climbed onto a wobbling patch of surviving rail fence. At first he just saw a cloud of gunsmoke, a cloud so thick that the sun was like a silver dollar in the sky, then in the lower smoke he glimpsed what he feared. There was a line of Yankees advancing out of the East Woods to take the rebels in the flank. "Back to the trees!" Starbuck shouted, "form there!" This battle, he thought, was a nightmare without end. It flowed like molten lava across the plateau and his poor battalion was being swept with the flow from one crisis to another. He paused halfway across the small pasture that separated the West Woods from the pike to cut off a dead Yankee's cartridge pouch, then he joined his men. "Take your bayonets off," he told them. "We'll just have to shoot the bastards down." He was about to send a man to find Swynyard and tell him the news, but suddenly there was no need, for a rush of rebels arrived at the tree line to add their rifles to Starbuck's shrunken battalion.

The Yankees were walking to death. They were crossing the cornfield, stepping around the bodies, advancing toward the pike with its broken fences, and, once there, they were within point-blank range of the mass of rifles waiting in the shadows. "Wait!" Starbuck called as the

Yankees reached the shattered fence on the far side of the road. There were not as many Northerners as he had first feared. He had thought a whole brigade might be crossing the cornfield, but now he could see only two Stars and Stripes and two state flags hanging limp in the still air. It was a pair of forlorn battalions thrown into horror. "Wait," he said, "let them get close."

The two Northern battalions, their careful lines disordered by the need to step around the dead and dying in the corn, crossed the remnants of the first rail fence, then Starbuck shouted at his men to fire. The opening volley stunned the Yankees, throwing them down in a new tideline of dead and dying. The rear ranks stepped forward and fired at the rebel rifle smoke, but the Yankees were firing at shadows in shadows and the rebels had flesh-and-blood targets. Starbuck pulled his trigger, crying aloud with the pain of the rifle's recoil as it pounded back into the raw bruise of his right shoulder. At this range it was impossible to miss; the Yankees were not even a hundred yards away and the rebel bullets were thumping into the shrinking lines, banging on rifle stocks, jetting blood from men who were thrown two paces back by the force of the bullets, yet somehow the enemy clung to their position and tried to return the dreadful fire.

Sergeant Case was at the right-hand end of Starbuck's line, though by now there were so many rebel units firing at the Yankees that it was hard to tell where one battalion began and another ended. The sergeant wriggled back from the firing line. He had not shot once, saving his three bullets for his own purposes, but now he worked his way north until he could see Starbuck standing beside a tree. Case edged into some brush, then raised his head and watched Starbuck fire. He saw him drop the rifle's butt to reload, and Case glanced around to make sure no one was watching him and then he brought up the Sharps rifle and aimed at Starbuck's head. He had to be quick. The rifle's leaf sight was folded flat, for he was so close to his target that the heavy half-inch bullet would not drop as much as its own width in its brief flight. He put the front leaf sight on Starbuck's head, lined the rear notch, and pulled the trigger. Smoke billowed to hide him as he scrambled out of the brush and back toward the tree line.

Starbuck had lowered his head to spit the bullet into his rifle. A bullet whipped past his skull to whack the tree beside him with the force of an ax hitting timber. Splinters of bark lodged in his hair. He cursed the Yankees, brought up the gun, primed, aimed, and fired. A Northern flag-bearer whipped about as he was hit in the shoulder and his flag rippled prettily through the smoke as it fell. Someone snatched up the banner and was immediately hit by a pair of bullets that threw him back across the broken fence. The Yankees were at last going back from the galling fire. They went reluctantly, holding their ravaged ranks as they stepped rearward so that no man would show his back to the enemy.

None of the rebels pursued. They fired as the Yankees retreated, and kept firing until the two battalions had disappeared into the smoke hanging over the cornfield. The two battalions went as mysteriously as they had arrived, their contribution to the day a row of bodies by the pike's bullet-riddled fences. There was a pause after the Yankees vanished, then the shells began to come again, crackling through the high branches, exploding leaves and twigs in showers, and spitting metal fragments down to the woods' floor.

A staff officer shouted for Swynyard's brigade to form up in the wood. Swynyard himself was talking to a grim-faced General Jackson. The colonel nodded, then ran toward his men. "The Yankees are in the church again," he explained grimly.

The brigade stumbled south through the trees, too tired to speak, too dry-mouthed to curse, going to where more Yankees waited to kill and be killed.

And it was still only morning.

Colonel Thorne watched grimly as General McClellan tried to understand the messages that arrived from across the creek. One dusty messenger spoke only of defeat, of a horde of rebels destroying General Sumner's troops in the far woods, while other aides brought urgent requests for reinforcements to exploit successful attacks. McClellan met all the messengers with the same stern face with which he had learned to hide his uncertainties.

The Young Napoleon was doing his best to understand the battle from his view across the creek. It had seemed simple enough in the dawn: His men had attacked again and again until at last the rebels had been pushed out of the nearer woods, but in the last hour everything had become confused. Like a spreading forest fire, the battle was now raging across two miles of countryside and from some places the news was all good and from others it was disastrous, and none made sense. McClellan, still fearing Lee's masterstroke that would destroy his army, was holding back his reserves, though now a sweaty, dust-covered messenger was begging him to send every man available to support General Greene, who had recaptured the Dunker church and was holding it against every counterattack. McClellan, in truth, was not too sure where the Dunker church was. General Greene's messenger was promising that a successful attack could split the rebel army in two, but McClellan doubted the optimism. He knew that General Sumner's corps was in desperate trouble to the north of the church, while to the south there was a maelstrom of fire erupting in the bare fields. That fire was sucking in every new brigade that crossed the creek. "Tell Greene he'll be supported," McClellan promised, then promptly forgot the promise as he tried to discover what was happening to the far south, where General Burnside was supposed to be across the creek by now and advancing on the rebels' single road to retreat.

But, before General Burnside could cut that retreat, he first had to cross a twelve-foot-wide stone bridge, and the bridge was guarded by rebel marksmen well dug into the steep slope on its western bank, and General Burnside's men were piling in heaps of dead as they tried to storm the crossing. Again and again they rushed the bridge, and again and again the rebel bullets turned the leading ranks into quivering heaps of bloody men who lay in the broiling sun and cried for help, for water, for any relief from their misery. "General Burnside can't get his men over the Rohrbach Bridge," a messenger admitted to General McClellan. "It's too closely defended, sir."

"Why doesn't the fool use a ford!" McClellan protested.

But no one was certain where the ford was and the general's map was no help. McClellan, in desperation, turned on Thorne. "Go, show them! Hurry, man!" That, at least, got rid of Thorne, whose baleful gaze had unsettled the general all morning. "Tell them to hurry!" he shouted after the colonel, then he looked back to the open fields across the creek where the battle had become so inexplicably fierce. A message had arrived telling of a trench-like lane that was holding up the advance, but McClellan was not at all sure why his army was even attacking the hidden obstacle. He had not ordered any such assault. He had intended for his attacks to hit hard in the north and, once that enemy flank was turned, to harry the rebels from the south before advancing to glorious victory in the center, but somehow the Northern army had become embroiled in the center long before the enemy's flanks had collapsed. Not only embroiled, but, judging from the white smoke that boiled up from the fields, the center was fighting as hard as men had ever fought.

It was hard because the rebels were in the sunken road, and from its lip they were turning the fields of newly sown winter wheat into croplands of the dead. Thousands of men, bereft of orders when they crossed the creek, marched toward that battle and one by one the brigades went forward until the rebel fire ripped their ranks apart. One Northern battalion was defeated before it even came within sight of the rebels, let alone within reach of their rifles, for, as it was marching past a spread of farm buildings, a rebel shell tore into a line of beehives and the enraged insects turned on the nearest targets. Men scattered in frantic disarray while more shells plunged blindly into their panicked ranks. Northern guns were taking up the fight, dropping shells over the heads of their infantry at the rebels in the road, while from beyond the creek the heavy Parrott guns fired at the rebel rear to smash the wagons trying to bring ammunition to the road's defenders.

It was nearing lunchtime. In the kitchen of the Pry farm the cooks readied a cold collation for the general as telegraphers sent a message to Washington. "We are in the midst of the most terrible battle of the war," McClellan reported, "perhaps of history. Thus far it looks well, but I have great odds against me. Hurry up all the troops possible." The twenty thousand men of his reserve, who could have given him victory if he had hurried them across the creek and sent them to the Dunker church, played horseshoes in the meadows. Some wrote letters, some slept. Theirs was a lazy day in hot sunlight, far from the blood and sweat and stink of the men who fought and died across the creek.

While to the south, still far to the south, the rebel Light Division marched toward the guns.

Starbuck crouched in the woods. Sweat poured down his face and stung his eyes. The remains of the Yellowlegs were back at the edge of the trees near the Dunker church and it was plain that the Yankees were also back in force about the small building, for when Potter's skirmishers had run forward they had been greeted by a withering blast of rifle fire that had spun one man down and persuaded the others to seek cover. Yankee bullets whipped through the trees as more rebel battalions were brought back to make the assault on the church. To Starbuck this fight for the church was like a private skirmish that had little connection with the storm of fire that sounded further south. If the battle did have a pattern, then he had long lost all understanding of it; instead it seemed like a series of desperate, bloody, and accidental clashes that flared, flourished, and died without meaning.

This new fight for the church also promised to be bloody for, while Starbuck waited in the trees, the Yankees brought up two guns that unlimbered just across the turnpike from the Dunker church. The horses were taken back while the gunners rammed their weapons, but instead of opening fire, the gun's commander ran toward the church. He was evidently seeking orders. The nearest gun was no more than two hundred yards away and Starbuck knew that one blast of canister would be sufficient to destroy what remained of his battalion.

The idea came to him then, but he was so befuddled and tired that it took some few seconds for him to realize that the idea could work, then more seconds while he debated whether he had the energy to make the necessary effort. The temptation was to do as little as possible. His men had fought beyond the expectations of anyone in the army and no one could blame them now for letting other men do the dying and fighting, but the appeal of the idea was irresistible. He twisted and saw Lucifer crouching with his dog. "I want the officers here," he told the boy, "all except Mister Potter."

The boy darted away through the brush while Starbuck turned back to stare at the nearest gun. It was a Napoleon, the French-designed cannon that was the workhorse for both armies. Its flared muzzle could fire a twelve-pound roundshot, canister, shell, or case shot, but it was the canister that the infantry feared most. The Napoleon might not have the range and power of the big rifled cannon, but its smoothbore barrel spat canister in a regular, killing pattern where the larger rifled guns could skew the shower of lead into strange shapes that sometimes flew safely overhead. The Napoleon, so far as the infantry was concerned, was a giant shotgun mounted on massive wheels.

The Yankee gunners were relaxed, plainly unaware that enemy infantry was close. A faded Stars and Stripes hung on the limber, which stood with its lid open. A shirtsleeved man carried ammunition and stacked it close to the gun, where another man leaned on the barrel and cleaned his fingernails with a knife. Every now and then he glanced over his right shoulder toward the east as if he expected to see reinforcements coming, but all he saw were his gun's horses cropping the pasture's bloodied grass a hundred yards away. After a time he yawned, folded the knife, and fanned his face with his hat.

Dennison and Peel joined Starbuck. These, with Potter, were his only captains. After the battle, Starbuck thought, there would needs be wholesale promotions, but that could wait. Now he told the two men what he wanted, cut short their anxieties, and sent them away. A minute later their shrunken companies came to the tree line, where Starbuck concealed the men in the shadows and thick brush. He walked behind the line of men telling them what he expected of them. "You don't fire till the gun has fired," he said, "then you kill the gunners. Then you charge. One shot up your barrel, bayonets on, don't stop to reload." An excitement touched Starbuck's voice and communicated itself to the men who, tired as they were, grinned at him. "They say we're no good, lads," Starbuck told them, "they say we're the Yellowlegs. Well, we're about to give the army a present of one gun. Maybe two. Remember, one shot only, don't fire till the cannon's fired, then charge like there was a score of naked whores serving that gun."

"Wish there were," a man said.

There was a sudden crashing in the timber behind Starbuck, who turned to see the drunken Colonel Maitland, who had somehow recovered his horse and now rode with drawn sword toward Starbuck's battalion. "I'll lead you, boys!" Maitland shouted. "Victory all the way! Up now! Get ready."

Starbuck grabbed the bridle before Maitland had a chance to roust the men to a premature attack. He dragged the horse round, pointed it toward the heart of the woods, and slapped its rump. Maitland somehow kept his seat as he rode away shouting and brandishing the sword. The noise he made was drowned by the furious sound of the fighting farther south. "Wait, lads," Starbuck calmed his men, "just wait."

Sergeant Case stared at the unsuspecting gunners. He was tempted to fire at them as soon as the attack on the Dunker church opened, and so deny Starbuck his victory by alerting the gunners to their danger, but Case only had two bullets left for his Sharps rifle and he dared not waste one. His hatred of Starbuck was being fed by what he perceived as Starbuck's unprofessionalism. Soon, Case reckoned, the battalion would be so shrunken that it would cease to exist, and what of Dennison's promise then? Case wanted to be an officer, he wanted to command the Yellowlegs, whom he planned to drill and discipline into the finest battalion in the Confederate army, but now Starbuck was threatening to thin its emaciated ranks even further. It was amateurism, the Sergeant thought, sheer bloody amateurism.

A cheer sounded in the woods, then the rebel yell erupted. Swynyard's voice shouted out of the shadows. "Go, Nate! Go!"

"Wait!" Starbuck shouted at his men. "Just wait!"

A splinter of rifle fire met the rebel charge, then a louder volley sounded as the charging rebels fired at the Yankees. The gunners had sprung to life. The barrel of the nearest gun was aimed roughly where Starbuck's skirmishers were placed and Starbuck prayed it was not charged with canister. He watched the gun captain duck aside and yank the lanyard that scraped the friction primer across the tube. The gun bucked violently back, spitting its flame and smoke toward the trees.

"Fire!" Starbuck shouted. Dimly over the crack of his rifles he heard the clatter of bullets striking the cannon. He hauled out his revolver. "Now charge!"

He ran from the trees and could see that the gunners had been hit hard. The gun captain was on his knees, holding his belly with one hand and the gun's wheel with another. Two other men were down while the rest of the crew hesitated between reloading and looking for the danger.

The Yellowlegs charged. The gun lay beyond the junction of the turnpike and the Smoketown Road and the remnants of two sets of fences lay in their path, but the men leaped the rails and stumbled on as fast as their tired legs would carry them. It was a race now between the weary infantrymen and the hard-hit gun crew, who began trying to handspike the Napoleon round to face the attack. A wounded gunner was holding a charge of canister, ready to plunge it down the barrel, then he saw the race was lost and he just dropped the charge and fled toward the east, his suspenders flapping about his legs as he limped away.

The second gun tried to save the first, but before its gunners could charge the barrel and turn the gun, the defenders of the Dunker church gave way. They had been attacked from two sides, caught in a screaming vice of vengeful gray, and the thousand Yankees under General Greene had taken enough. They scattered and fled, and the gunners of the second Napoleon simply brought up their horses, limbered up the gun, and galloped away. Starbuck's men, still screaming their challenge, pounced on the first gun, slapping its hot barrel and shouting their victory while, just yards away, the broken Yankees streamed past, pursued by rifle fire from the woods. Starbuck's men watched them go, too tired to make an effort to interfere. A wounded gunner begged for water and one of Starbuck's men knelt beside the man and tipped a canteen to his lips. "Never knew you boys were there," the gunner said. He struggled to sit up and managed at last to prop himself against his gun's wheel. "They said it only was all our boys in the trees." He sighed, then felt in his pocket to bring out a wrapped tintype of a woman that he set on his lap. He stared at the image.

"We'll find you a doctor," Starbuck promised.

The man looked up at Starbuck briefly, then stared again at the tintype. "Too late for doctors," he said. "One of you boys put a bullet in my guts. Don't hurt much, not yet, but there isn't a doctor born who can help. If I was a dog you'd have put me down by now." He gave the portrait a gentle touch. "Prettiest girl in Fitchburg," he said softly, "and we've only been married two months." He paused, closed his eyes as a spasm of pain flickered deep in his guts, then looked up at Starbuck. "Where you boys from?" he asked.

"Virginia."

"That's her name," the gunner said, "Virginia Simmons."

Starbuck crouched beside the man. "She is pretty," he said. The photograph showed a slender, fair-haired girl with an anxious face. "And I reckon you'll see her again," he added.

"Not this side of the pearly gates," the gunner said. He had grown a wispy brown beard in an evident attempt to make himself look older. He glanced at the revolver in Starbuck's hand, then up into Starbuck's eyes. "You an officer?"

"Yes."

"You reckon there's a heaven?"

Starbuck paused, struck by the intensity of the question. "Yes," he said gently, "I know there is."

"Me, too," the gunner said.

" 'I know that my Redeemer liveth,' " Starbuck quoted.

The gunner nodded, then looked back at his wife. "And I'll be waiting for you, girl," he said, "with coffee on the boil." He smiled. "She always likes her coffee scalding hot." A tear showed in his eye. "Never knew you boys were there," he said in a weaker voice.

Some of the rebels had pursued the broken Yankees out into the pastureland, but a barrage of canister drove them back. One musket ball struck the barrel of the captured cannon and Starbuck ordered his men back to the trees. He stooped to the wounded gunner to see if the man wanted to be carried back, but the man was already dead. His lap was puddled with blood, his eyes were wide open, and a fly was crawling into his mouth. Starbuck left him.

Back at the tree line some of his men put their heads on their arms and slept. Others stared sightlessly east where the gunsmoke lay like a sea-fog, while in the corn, the pastures, and the ravaged woods, the wounded cried on unheeded.

The heat of the battle had moved south, leaving the scene of the morning's fighting full of exhausted survivors too weak to fight more. Now it was the sunken road that acted like a giant meat grinder. Battalion after battalion walked into the rebel fire, and battalion after battalion died on the open ground, and still more men came from the east to add their deaths to the day's rich toll.

But the rebels were dying as well. The road might be a defender's dream, but it had one shortcoming. It ran directly eastward from the Hagerstown Pike, then bent sharply south and east so that once the Yankees had managed to place a battery on a line directly east of the road's first stretch, they were able to enfilade the stubborn Confederate defenders. Shells plunged into the sunken road and the steep banks magnified the carnage of each explosion. The fire of the defenders grew weaker, yet still they drove back one attack after another. The Irishmen of New York nearly broke through. They had been told that the Confederates were the friends of the British and that was incentive enough to drive the green flags forward. The flags had golden Irish harps embroidered on the green and the Irishmen carried the harps further forward than any flag had yet reached, but there was no bravery sufficient to carry men through the last few murderous yards of fire. One black-bearded giant of a man screamed his war cry in Gaelic and urged his compatriots on as though he could win the war and avenge his people single-handed, but a rebel's bullet put the man down, and the charge, like so many others, was finally shredded into raw and bloody tatters by the remorseless rifle fire. The Irish made a new line of bodies, closer than any others to the lane's fiery lip, while in the lane itself, where the shells plunged to tear dead bodies into mincemeat, the rebel dead thickened.

Other men died on the lower creek, where every effort to take the Rohrbach Bridge had failed. The corpses lay like a barrier on the east bank and the very sight of so many dead served as a deterrent to the waiting Yankee battalions, who knew their turn must come to assault the deadly passage. Thorne came there too, and came with the authority of his enemy McClellan. He found General Burnside on the hill overlooking the bridge. "Where the hell are the guns?" Thorne snarled.

General Burnside, astonished at being addressed in such a peremptory fashion, sounded defensive. "Waiting to cross," he explained, gesturing toward a lane behind the hill where the guns were sheltering.

"You need them up here," Thorne insisted.

"But there are no roads," an aide protested.

"Then make a road!" Thorne shouted. "Get a thousand men if you have to, but drag the damn things up here. Now! Two guns, twelve-pounders, canister and case shot only. And for Christ's sake, hurry!"

South of the Potomac, marching in swirls of dust under the merciless sun, the Light Division was also being chivvied and harried to keep moving, to keep moving, always to keep moving toward the sound of the killing.

While on the Pry house lawn General McClellan enjoyed his lunch.

Two Napoleons were fetched to the summit of the hill above the Rohrbach Bridge and their presence turned the battle for the crossing. The very first blast of canister whipped a half-dozen sharpshooters out of their hiding places in the tops of the trees on the western bank, and left others dangling lifelessly from the ropes that had held them safe to the branches. The second and third discharges of canister decimated the rebel defenders in their rifle pits.

A Pennsylvania battalion, promised a keg of whiskey if they took the bridge, charged forward. There were still enough rebels to kill the leading ranks, but the men behind leaped over their dead and stormed onto the stone roadway that arched across the creek. More Yankees followed, jostling between the balustrades as they hurried to carry their revenge to the rebels, who scrambled hurriedly out of their pits and up over the hill.

Downstream, at Snaveley's Ford, another brigade at last made the crossing to the western bank and the Yankees were finally loose in Lee's rear, but it was one thing to be across the creek and quite another to form the battalions and brigades into their columns. Guns had to be fetched over the creek, disarray had to be straightened, and the ground had to be reconnoitered. Thorne cursed McClellan for keeping the army's cavalry at headquarters where it served no purpose. If the cavalry could have been unleashed here, behind the rebel army, he could have struck panic into Lee's men, but the Northern cavalry was two miles away and General Burnside would not advance his infantry until all was ready. A handful of rebel skirmishers harried the Northerners as they laboriously marched unit after unit across the river. Thorne raged at Burnside for speed, but Burnside would not be hurried. "The day's young yet," he said, indicating the brevity of the shadows, "and there's no need for impetuosity. We shall do it properly. Besides," Burnside went on as though his next point was irrefutable, "we can't attack till the infantry is resupplied with ammunition. Their pouches are empty, Thorne, empty. Men can't fight with empty pouches."

Thorne wondered how any general could have failed to carry sufficient ammunition for a day's hard fighting, but he bit back the comment. The day was indeed young, and it needed to be, for Burnside's units were crossing the bridge at a snail's pace and, once over the river, they lingered aimlessly until staff officers arrived to direct them to their proper places. Burnside's advance, when it came, would be a slow, grinding assault instead of a lightning strike, and Thorne could only pray that Lee did not choose to retreat before the North's trap swung ponderously shut. He forced his horse up the steep hill where the rebel defenders had fought for so long and, once at the summit, he stared across an empty landscape of cornfields, shade trees, and pastureland, and, in the heat-hazed distance where it was marked by the dust kicked up by a trail of ambulances going slowly south toward the river, he could see the enemy's only route home. A rebel skirmisher fired at Thorne and the bullet whipped close beside his ear. Thorne saw the patch of smoke and reckoned the shot had been all of four hundred yards. He raised his hat in ironic salute to a well-aimed near miss, then turned his horse down from the high ground.

The sunken lane at last fell. The Yankees, capturing the road, found they could not cross the track without stepping on the bodies of its defenders, and though those defenders had failed, they had hurt their attackers so hard that the Yankees were in no fit state to advance farther.

The battle, which had burned so fierce, smoldered in the afternoon. Weary men staggered about the plateau that was hung with smoke and smothered with the foul miasma of bodies beginning to rot in the hot sun. Batteries waited for new ammunition, infantry counted their cartridges, and officers counted their men. Units that had started the day five hundred strong were less than a hundred now. The dead possessed the field, while the living searched for water and peered into the eye-stinging smoke for a sign of the enemy.

The rebels were hardest hit. There were no reserves left, not one man, and so Lee made a barrier of artillery to defend Sharpsburg and its single road, which led back to the Confederacy. The guns were just in place when a weary messenger on a tired, dust-stained, and sweat-whitened horse came up the track from the town. Hill's Light Division had reached the ford. The Confederacy's last troops were crossing the river and coming north.

The rest of Lee's army waited. They knew the mauled Yankees were making ready and that soon the blue ranks would appear over the brow of the plateau and the fighting would begin again. The dead who had been searched for ammunition were searched again and the precious cartridges shared out. There was no hot water to clean out the fouled barrels of the rifles, nor any urine, for the men were parched dry by thirst and sweat. They waited.

The spring that would drive the Yankees' trap shut was coiling itself tight as Burnside's men slowly readied themselves for the advance, but General McClellan could not shake the northern part of the battlefield from his fears. It was from that northern sector, which had been harrowed by death all morning, that he expected the great rebel counterattack that would jeopardize his army's existence. One of his generals reported imminent disaster in those northern fields, while another claimed that with one more effort the North could sweep the rebels out of the West Woods and back through Sharpsburg altogether, and so fierce was their argument that once his lunch was taken McClellan crossed the creek for the first and only time that day. He met his generals, he listened to their arguments, and then he pronounced his verdict. Caution, he declared, was best. The generals must hold their ground against the worst the rebels could throw against them, but they were to make no more attacks. The enemy, he said, must not be provoked and then, with that decided, McClellan went back to his armchair, from where he sought reassurance that his heavy reserve of men was still in place to meet the rebel attack he knew must be coming. After all, as he explained to Pinkerton, the rebels did outnumber him.

"That they do, chief, that they do," Pinkerton agreed enthusiastically. "Hordes of the scoundrels, just hordes!" The Scotsman blew his nose vigorously, then unfolded the handkerchief to inspect the result. "It's a miracle we've done as well as we have, chief," he opined, still staring at the handkerchief. "Nothing short of a miracle."

McClellan, who rather thought it was his superior generalship that had staved off disaster all day, grunted, then stooped to the telescope to watch as the troops in the center of the field at last began their advance from the sunken lane. Their job was to hold Lee's men in Sharpsburg while Burnside cut behind them. It was a grand sight, McClellan thought. Thousands of men marched beneath their flags. Wisps of smoke drifted across the telescope's lens, giving the great attack a fine romantic flavor.

It was less romantic in the ranks. There, advancing across open fields toward the massive gun line assembled on the hill above the village, the North suffered as the smoldering battle burst again into livid flame. The cannons' long range meant the infantry had no chance of replying, but could only trudge through the smoke of the explosions and across the blood of their comrades until it was their turn to be hit. Ahead of them was the skyline above the village, but that skyline was rimmed by guns that pumped tongues of flame and billows of smoke. The shells screamed and wailed and cracked and killed, while from beyond the creek the heavy Federal guns returned the fire with big shells that rumbled in the sky to flower in bloody gouts on the rebel artillery line.

Burnside's men started forward at last. There, and only there on all the battlefield, a band played as the flags were carried up the hill to begin the grand attack that would cut the retreat of the rebel army.

For at last the Northern trap was swinging shut and the long day's killing was coming to its climax.

The Yankees in the North and East Woods were quiet, but the northern flank of the federal advance on Sharpsburg was visible from the woods about the Dunker church and those men, like the larger mass that advanced from the captured sunken lane, were met by the horror of Lee's artillery line. Some of Starbuck's men fired their rifles at the distant enemy, but most were content to shelter in the trees and watch as the artillery explosions gouged the enemy. Their own gun, the Napoleon they had captured, stood fifty yards away. Potter had begun to carve a legend on the gun's trail, "A gift from the Yellowlegs," but the hardness of the wood had blunted his small pocket-knife and he had abandoned his efforts. "It's odd," he said to Starbuck now, "but one day this will all be in the history books."

"Odd?" Starbuck frowned as he tried to wrench his thoughts from his parched weariness to Potter's airy statement. "Why odd?"

"Because I guess I never thought of America as a place where history is made," Potter said, "at least, not since the Revolution. History belongs to the rest of the world. Crimea, Napoleon, Garibaldi, the Indian mutiny." He shrugged. "We came to America to escape history, isn't that right?"

"We're making it now," Starbuck said curtly.

"Then we'd better make sure we win," Potter said, "because history is written by the winners." He yawned. "Do I have permission to get drunk?"

"Not yet. This thing ain't over."

Potter grimaced, then stared at the cannon. "I've always wanted to fire a cannon," Potter said wistfully.

"Me too," Starbuck said.

"How difficult can it be?" Potter inquired. "Ain't nothing but an oversized rifle. A man don't need a college degree."

Starbuck gazed at the enemy, whose enthusiasm had been blunted by the day's carnage so that their advance now wavered under the rain of artillery shells. Maybe another gun, opening from their flank, would push them back. "We can try," he said, encouraged by the thought that the Yankees were far enough away for their skirmishers to be inaccurate. "A couple of shots, maybe."

"It is our gun," Potter said firmly. "We'd be sadly remiss not to check that it works before handing it over."

"True." Starbuck hesitated, once more gauging the distance between the Napoleon and the distant Yankees. "Let's try it," he decided.

Three of Potter's company volunteered to serve as crew, one of them the Irish saddler, John Connolly, who had a bloody bandage round his left arm but insisted he was fit enough to fight; then Lucifer insisted that he knew something of artillery, though Starbuck suspected the boy simply wanted to join in the excitement of firing a cannon.

No Yankee noticed them as they ran forward. The gun was still pointing toward the woods by the Dunker church, so Potter and his men lifted the tail and maneuvered the heavy barrel around while Starbuck rummaged in the limber that had already yielded three full canteens of water and a boiled ham wrapped in canvas for his hungry men. Now he pulled out a bag of powder, a case shot, and a package of fuses. The instructions on the packet told him to tear off the paper, then press against the small end of the fuse. "I thought this was supposed to be easy," Starbuck said. He had extracted one of the fuses, a simple paper tube filled with powder, but he could not relate the tube to the printed instructions.

"Give it me," Lucifer said, and he tore the fuse into halves and pushed one half into a drilled copper plug that formed part of the case shot. "Five seconds is too long," Lucifer said, judging the distance to the enemy. "Give it two and a half."

"How the hell do you know all this?" Starbuck asked.

"Just do," Lucifer said, once again hiding his past. His dog was tied to his belt by its leash of rifle slings that almost tangled Lucifer's legs as he carried the shell to the gun. "You have to put the powder in first," he told Starbuck.

Starbuck pushed the powder bag into the tube, then Lucifer plugged the case shot into the muzzle. A bullet whistled overhead. Starbuck guessed it was an errant shot, not deliberately aimed at his men.

Lucifer had taken charge now. He had found the friction primer and a vent pick and, once the charge had been rammed down the barrel, he leaned over the muzzle and pushed the pick hard down to pierce the canvas bag of powder. He inserted the friction primer, attached the lanyard that had been in the dead gunner's hand, then stepped back. "Ready," he said.

"What about the elevation?" Colonel Swynyard had seen the activity about the gun and come to join the makeshift crew. "Looks low to me," he added, gesturing at the wormed elevating screw.

Starbuck gave the screw a pair of turns, but it seemed to make little difference. Maybe a man did need a college degree after all. "Let's just fire the damn thing," he said, then held up a hand. "Wait." The dead gunner with his wife's picture still on his lap had fallen behind the wheel and Starbuck first dragged the body clear, then picked up the tintype. It seemed sacrilegious to throw it away, so he put the picture in his pocket, then nodded at Lucifer. "You fire it," he said.

Fifty yards behind the gun Sergeant Case took aim. He had found Lieutenant Dennison and the two men were in the brush at the wood's edge. Case had almost given up hope of finding an opportunity to kill Starbuck, but suddenly Starbuck was fifty yards away and in the open while Case and Dennison were hidden deep in brush. "Fire when the nigger pulls the string," Case told the Lieutenant. "You go for the bastard's body, I'll go for a head shot."

Dennison, dry mouthed, could not answer, so just nodded. He was desperately nervous. He was about to commit murder and his hand was shaking as he rested his rifle on a small hillock. The men about the cannon had their backs to him and he was suddenly unsure which was Starbuck, but then he recognized the revolver holster Starbuck always wore at the small of his back and he aimed a few inches above it, where the gray jacket was darkened by a smear of blood. Case, calmer than Dennison, aimed at Starbuck's black hair. "Wait till they fire," he warned Dennison.

Dennison nodded again, and the small movement was enough to dislodge the sights from his target. He hurriedly reaimed and had only just realized that he was sighting the wrong man when Lucifer ducked away from the gun and yanked the lanyard.

The Napoleon crashed back, its wheels bucking six inches up from the turf as the lunette at the end of its tail plowed hard back through the dirt. The noise was immense, a crack to hurt the ears of anyone within fifty paces. Smoke gushed ahead, writhing with flame, and under the cover of the noise, while the remnants of the Yellowlegs cheered, Case and Dennison fired.

Potter pitched violently forward onto the ground.

Starbuck was turning as the bullet hit Potter and, as he turned, a mist of blood exploded from the side of his face and then he too fell.

The shell screamed across the field. The elevation had been much too low and the smoking case shot ricocheted off a patch of dry ground to explode harmlessly behind the Yankees. It killed no one.

"It's all yours," Case said, lowering the Sharps rifle. "All yours." And soon, Case thought, it would all be his. The Virginia Fusiliers, the smartest regiment in the Confederacy.

"Thank you, Captain," Dennison managed to answer.

While to the south the great guns boomed and the Yankees closed on Sharpsburg.

Lee could only watch as disaster threatened. He stood on the low height above the town, where his guns were lined along the edge of Sharpsburg's cemetery, and he watched as a flood of Yankees filled the countryside to the east and to the south.

His men were still fighting. Their cannons were tearing huge holes in the Northern files while the gray infantry was stubbornly defending every fence, wall, and farm building, but it was the Yankees who had the advantage. There seemed so many of them. Wherever Lee looked another battalion or brigade would appear from hidden ground to join the advance on the town and toward the road that ran south toward the Confederate states. An aide checked each new appearance through a telescope and each time, just as Lee hoped that it might be one of the Light Division's battalions appearing on the flank, the aide would laconically announce, "It's Yankee, sir."

"Are you sure?" Lee asked once.

"Sir?" the aide offered the telescope.

"Can't use it," Lee said, gesturing with his bandaged hands.

The guns banged on, layering a new mist of smoke across the high ground. Some of the guns had been dismounted by the heavy Yankee counterfire, others lay canted on splintered wheels that gunners struggled to change. One of the army's few heavy Parrott guns had exploded, killing two of its crew and foully wounding another three. "Try to find out if they varnished their shells," Lee said to the aide.

"Sir?" The aide frowned in puzzlement.

"The gun crew. The Parrott," Lee explained. "Find out if they greased the shells. Not now, just when you have a moment."

"Yes, sir," the aide said and trained his telescope south again.

Belvedere Delaney climbed up through the gravestones to join the nervous band of aides who stood a few paces behind Lee. Delaney's uniform was bloody and his face sheened with sweat. Lee noted his arrival and smiled at him. "Are you wounded, Delaney?"

"Other men's blood, sir," Delaney answered. He was tired through and appalled beyond measure by what he had seen this day. He had never dreamed that such horrors could exist outside of slaughterhouses. The town was filled with wounded, and every house was sheltering dying and broken men. Yet the worst moment of the day had been when Delaney had gone down into a cellar to fetch some apples that the householder was storing for the winter and now offered to the wounded troops. As Delaney had filled a pail with the fruit he had felt liquid drip on his head. It had been blood seeping through the floorboards. He had begun to weep then, and his eyes were still red.

Lee saw that the lawyer was engulfed in horror. "Thank you for all your efforts, Delaney," he said gently.

"I did nothing, sir," Delaney said, "nothing," and he suddenly felt guilty, for it was he, surely, who had precipitated this slaughter. He suddenly resented it, fearing that the memory of blood dripping through floorboards would sour his idyllic life in some foreign capital. He shook that suspicion away, then frowned and managed to blurt out what he had been sent to say. "Colonel Chilton wonders if you should withdraw, sir."

Lee laughed. "And you were the only man brave enough to convey the message? Maybe you should abandon the law, Delaney, and take up soldiering. We need brave men. But in the meantime you can tell Chilton that we haven't lost yet." Delaney flinched as the shrapnel from a Yankee shell whipped the air overhead. Lee appeared not to notice the whirring sound of the hot metal. "We haven't lost yet," he said again with a tone of wistfulness.

"No," Delaney said, not because he believed the general, but because it was not his place to point out the obvious. The Yankees were winning. Half the Southern army lay in exhaustion and the other half was being driven remorselessly back by the vast Northern assault. Colonel Chilton had readied an ambulance to hurry Lee away from the imminent disaster, but Lee, it seemed, was not willing to go.

More troops appeared in the south. Lee glanced at them, but even at this distance it was possible to see that the new men were wearing blue. He sighed, but said nothing. The aide turned the glass on the newly arrived troops who were dangerously close to the single road south. The air was hazed by the heat and obscured by filaments of smoke and the aide stared for a long time before he spoke. "Sir?" he said.

"I know, Hudson," Lee said gently. "I've seen them. They wear blue." He sounded immensely tired as if he was suddenly realizing that it was all over. He knew he should make some effort to withdraw now, to rescue what he could of his army, but he seemed consumed by a terrible lassitude. If he did not escape then he would be captured and McClellan would have him as his guest at dinner and the humiliation of such a meal seemed unbearable.

"Re-equipped at Harper's Ferry, sir," the aide said.

"I'm sorry?" Lee asked, thinking he must have misheard the aide.

Hudson's voice rose in sudden excitement. "They're our men in Yankee coats, sir. It's our banner!"

Lee smiled. "The flags look alike when there's no wind."

"It's our banner, sir!" Hudson insisted. "It is, sir!" And suddenly the splintering sound of musketry echoed across the landscape and the far-off blue-coated troops were whitened by smoke as they fired a volley at other troops, also blue-coated. New guns were unlimbering and their fire was streaking slantwise across the attacking Yankee troops. It was the Light Division, come at last, and Lee closed his eyes as though he was at prayer. "Well done, Hill," he murmured, "well, well done." He would not have to eat McClellan's humble pie. More troops appeared to the south, these in gray, and suddenly the Yankee advance, which had reached almost to the gardens at the edge of Sharpsburg, was checked.

For the Light Division had arrived.

Lucifer, pulling the lanyard that had fired the gun, saw the two shots fired from the edge of the trees. A heartbeat later he connected the two shots with the two bodies on the gun's far side. Potter was flat on his belly, Starbuck was on his knees, but with his head on the ground spilling blood. Neither man moved until Starbuck, after a hopeless effort to straighten up, collapsed.

Lucifer shouted in anger and drew his revolver. He ran toward the patches of smoke, tugging the small dog along by its leash.

Colonel Swynyard realized a second after Lucifer that the shots had been fired from the rebel side. He started after the boy and saw one man rise up out of the brush. Lucifer had drawn his revolver and was pointing it at the man. The Colonel shouted at him. "No! No, boy! No!"

Lucifer did not care. He fired, and his bullet went wide up into the trees. He slowed to take proper aim, knowing that the man who had shot Starbuck would need twenty seconds to reload his rifle. "Murderer!" he screamed at Case and raised the revolver again.

Case dropped the trigger guard and put his last cartridge into the breech of the Sharps. He snapped the guard up and thumbed the percussion cap into place.

Lucifer fired again, but even at twenty yards a revolver was inaccurate.

"No!" Swynyard called again and ran after the boy.

Case raised the gun. He saw the look of terror dawn on Lucifer's face and that look pleased him. He was grinning as he fired.

The boy was plucked backward. The force of the heavy bullet was so great that it lifted him off the ground and tugged the small dog back with him. The dog yelped in terror as Lucifer fell back, then whined as the small body twitched. Blood was pumping out of a hole in Lucifer's skull and the twitching stopped quickly.

Swynyard stooped by the boy, but knew he was dead long before he put a hand on the small throat. He looked up at Case, who shrugged. "He was shooting at me, Colonel," Case said, "you saw him."

"Name?" Swynyard snapped, standing up.

"Case," Case said defiantly, then slung the rifle. "And there ain't no bloody law 'gainst shooting niggers, sir. Specially niggers with guns."

"There is a law, Case, about shooting your own officers," Swynyard said.

Case shook his head. "Hell, Colonel, me and the Captain were firing at a pair of bloody Yankees out in the field." He jerked his beard toward the Smoketown Road. "Out there, Colonel. I reckon they killed Starbuck. Weren't me."

A second figure stood up beside Case. Swynyard recognized Captain Dennison, who licked his lips nervously, then nodded his head to support Case's statement. "In that patch of brush, Colonel," Dennison said, pointing toward the road. "Pair of Yankee skirmishers. I reckon we killed them both."

Swynyard turned. About three hundred yards away, just beside the Smoketown Road, there was a small patch of thorns where a mess of bodies lay thick under the pall of filmy smoke that smothered the field. Not enough smoke, Swynyard reckoned, to show that a pair of Yankee skirmishers had fired from the bushes, but he felt a terrible weariness as he understood that the two men would stick by their story and it would be a hard one to disprove. He turned back to them. He would put them under arrest anyway. There had been a time, he knew, when he would have shot them down like dogs, but he obeyed a higher law now. He would do the proper thing even though he guessed it would be useless.

He opened his mouth to speak, then saw a look of utter horror show on both men's' faces. They were staring past him and Swynyard turned to see what had scared them.

Starbuck was standing. The left side of his face was a horror of blood. He staggered, then spat a great gob of thick blood and scraps of broken teeth. The bullet had gone through his open mouth, scored across his tongue, torn away four teeth from his upper jaw, then ripped out through his cheek. He walked unsteadily toward the two men, then paused beside Lucifer. He knelt by the boy and Swynyard saw the tears rolling down to mix with the blood. "Nate," Swynyard said, but Starbuck shook his head as if he did not want anything said. He stroked Lucifer's dead face with his hand, then untied the whimpering puppy from the boy's belt. He stood and walked toward Case and Dennison. He spoke to them, but the wound made his words a blood-curdled mumble. He spat again, then pointed toward the clump of bushes. "Go," he managed to say.

Swynyard understood. "Go and find the men you killed," he ordered the two.

"Hell," Case said, "there's a bunch of dead Yankees there!"

"Then bring me two warm bodies!" Swynyard snapped. "Because if they aren't warm, Captain Dennison, I'll know you're lying. And if you are lying, Captain Dennison, I'll have the two of you in front of a firing squad."

"Go!" Starbuck snarled, spitting more blood.

The two men walked east. Starbuck waited till they were gone, then turned back to the gun. Blood was pouring down his face as he heaved on the handspike to turn the trail the few feet necessary so that the barrel was pointing toward the Smoketown Road.

"No, Nate," Swynyard said. "No."

Starbuck ignored the colonel. He went to the limber and brought back a bag of powder and a canister. Two of Potter's men rammed the cannon while Connolly ran to retrieve the vent pick from Lucifer's body.

Potter rolled over. He was crying. Swynyard, who had not expected his protest to work, knelt beside him. "Is it hurting, son?"

"Stone jug of whiskey," Potter said, "best damn whiskey I ever saw. I was saving it, Colonel, and they bust it. God damn bust it. Now my back's soaked in whiskey, but it's all on the outside and I was praying so hard for it to be on the inside."

Swynyard tried not to smile, but could not help it. "You ain't hurt?" he asked.

"Had the breath knocked clean out of me," Potter said, then sat up. He took Swynyard's offered hand and hauled himself to his feet. "Had my back to them, Colonel," he said, "and I was shot in the back."

"There are proper procedures," Swynyard said lamely.

Starbuck gave his opinion of proper procedures, an opinion so muffled by blood that it came out as a splutter of gore and bone. He bent, spat again, then straightened and cupped his hands about his shattered mouth. "Case!" he roared.

Case and Dennison had been advancing cautiously into the open, almost as scared of the distant Yankees as they were of what waited for them on their return to the battalion. Then they saw there would be no return. The cannon was fifty yards from them, and aimed straight for them. Dennison shook his head, Case began to run, and Starbuck whipped the lanyard back.

The smoke of the cannon enveloped the two men, but not until the blast of canister had turned them to red ribbons of flesh.

Starbuck did not even look to see what the canister had done. He walked back to Lucifer and cradled the dead boy in his arms. He hugged him, rocking the small body, and dripping blood onto the boy's bloody face. Swynyard knelt beside him. "You need a doctor, Nate."

"It'll wait," Starbuck managed to say. "I never knew his real Christian name," he added, speaking slowly to articulate the words through the torn-up mess inside his mouth, "so what the hell can I put on his grave?"

"That he was a brave soldier," Swynyard said.

"He was," Starbuck said, "he truly was."

The guns to the south fell silent. The silence seemed unnatural, for all day long the sky had been bruised by fire, but now there was silence. Silence and a small wind that at long last stirred the smoke and carried the stench of battle east across the creek. The killing was over.

In the night the wounded cried. Some died. Flickering campfires showed where the armies rested, the small flames marking the advances the Yankees had made during the day's long fight. The North and East Woods were theirs, and all the field that lay between the creek and the high ground above the town, but the rebels had not broken, they had not fled. The Light Division, sweating from its aching march, had struck Burnside's flank and hurled his carefully composed columns back just when they had thought they had broken through to the town.

Confederate Provosts searched the town's wooden houses for men who had taken refuge from the fighting. They rousted the fugitives from cellars and attics, from cowsheds and springhouses, then marched them back to their units. A child, killed by a Yankee shell that had screamed over the ridge to plunge into Sharpsburg, lay in her best frock on a parlor table. A house burned, its stone chimney stack all that was left when the sun rose above the Red Hill on the Thursday morning. The plateau was still hung with a haze of smoke and by the stench of the dead that lay in ghastly windrows across the fire-scorched fields.

All night men had trickled back to Swynyard's Brigade so that now there were 112 men left in Faulconer's Legion and seventy eight in Starbuck's battalion. When the rising sun dazzled them they shaded their eyes and stared east from the woods close to the Dunker church and waited for the Yankees to attack. But the Yankees did not come. Instead, an hour after dawn, a man rode across the field with a white flag and sought permission from the rebels to rescue the Federal wounded, who lay crying in the bloody fields. Men who had cursed and killed the day before now joined together to disentangle the dead from the dying. Yankee and rebel worked together, filling the ambulances with broken men. The first shallow graves were dug, though it seemed that all the digging in the world would prove unequal to the task of burying the dead.

Captain Truslow decided to doctor Starbuck. There were no surgeons to spare for lightly wounded men, so Truslow used a rusty pair of long-nosed pliers to take out the scraps of tooth and bone. He lay Starbuck flat and stooped over the mangled mouth. "God in his heaven," he complained when Starbuck flinched at the pain. "Worse than a girl, you are. Just lie still, for Christ's sake. Water!"

Lieutenant Potter poured water from a bucket to swill the blood from Starbuck's open mouth. Truslow probed again, swilled out the blood once more, then kept digging and tugging until he was sure every loose scrap of bone and tooth was free. He put three crude stitches into

Starbuck's cheek. "This'll take the gloss off your good looks," Truslow said happily, knotting the cotton thread.

"Women like a scar," Potter said.

"He did enough caterwauling without a scar," Truslow growled, "so God help the ladies now." He had found a small bottle of brandy on a dead Yankee and he poured the raw spirit into Starbuck's bloody mouth. "Swill it out," he said, then gave Starbuck a pad made from a folded strip torn from the bottom of a dead man's shirt. "Bite on that till it stops bleeding," he ordered.

"Yes, doctor," Starbuck mumbled.

In the afternoon Starbuck dug Lucifer's grave beneath an elm tree while Potter carved the words "A brave soldier" into the elm's trunk. Potter went to remove the revolver from Lucifer's body before they put it in the shallow grave, but Starbuck stopped him. "Leave it with him," he said. "God knows he might need it where he's going." Potter nodded, but unbuckled the pouch to take out the remaining cartridges. Inside the pouch he found a carefully wrapped oilcloth package that he took out and showed to Starbuck. Starbuck took it, untied the string, and found the piece of paper that Caton Rothwell had shown him on the night after the fight with Case. He read the signature aloud. "Billy Blythe," he mumbled. "Son of a bitch."

"Who?"

Starbuck showed him the paper. "That was Tumlin's revolver," he said, pointing to the gun that Potter had placed in Lucifer's right hand, "and this paper belonged to Sergeant Rothwell. Jesus." He stopped, realizing that Tumlin must have killed Rothwell. "Now why the hell would Tumlin take it off Rothwell's body?"

"God knows," Potter said.

"I'd like to meet Mister Tumlin again," Starbuck said. He spat blood. "God," he went on vengefully, "but I would like that." He put the paper in his pocket, then helped lift Lucifer into his grave. They covered him with soil.

"You want to say a prayer?" Potter asked.

"I already have." Starbuck picked up Imp's lead and led the dog to the wood's edge. He bit down on the pad, almost relishing the pain as he stared at the field, which was thronged with soldiers of both sides. They were exchanging stories and swapping Northern newspapers for Southern journals. Some had cloths tied about their faces to keep away the stink of the dead.

Potter came and stood beside Starbuck. "I never did get my whiskey," he said wistfully.

Starbuck took the bloody pad from his mouth. "When we're back south," he promised, "you and I will get drunk together."

"I guess we are going back south," Potter said.

"I guess," Starbuck said, then spat a dribble of bloody spittle. Lee's army was in no state to stay, no state to fight. It had taken one hell of a beating and, though it had given one as well, it had no choice but to retreat.

Gunners limbered up the cannon that Starbuck's men had captured and towed it away toward Sharpsburg. Swynyard had insisted that the legend Potter had begun carving on the trail be finished so that the gunners would know that the despised Yellowlegs had captured the gun, and so Truslow had burned the words into the wood with the red-hot tip of a bayonet. Swynyard now crossed to Starbuck. "How's the mouth?"

"Painful, sir."

Swynyard drew Starbuck out of Potter's earshot. "Mister Maitland," the colonel said, "confessed to me that he can't abide the sight of blood."

Starbuck, despite the pain in his jaw, smiled. "He said as much to me," he said.

"He's squeamish," Swynyard shrugged. "Told me he once fainted when one of his slaves had a nosebleed. I guess he wanted a chance to overcome the fear, but it didn't work. He agrees with me that Richmond might be a more suitable place for him to work." The colonel's ravaged face split in a smile. "So the Legion's yours, Nate. What's left of it. Them and the Yellowlegs."

"Thank you, sir."

Swynyard paused, staring across the field where the living moved so slowly among the dead. "I've got some other news."

"Good, I hope."

Swynyard nodded.

"Jackson just promoted me. I'm a Brigadier General."

Starbuck smiled again, tearing at the stitches in his cheek. He ignored the pain and held out his hand. "Congratulations, General."

Swynyard had tears in his eyes. "God has been good to me, Nate, so very good. Why did I wait so long to find Him?" Starbuck made no answer and the general smiled. "I'm having a prayer meeting at sundown," he said, "but I don't suppose you'll come?"

"I don't suppose I will, General," Starbuck said.

"And after prayers," General Swynyard said, "we march."

"Home?" Starbuck asked.

"Home," Swynyard said.

Because the invasion was over.

~ HISTORICAL ~ NOTE

THE BATTLE OF ANTIETAM (SHARPSBURG, TO SOUTHERNERS) is famous for being the bloodiest day in all America's history. Close to 23,000 men died in that one day. It was, in the proper sense of the word, a shambles.

Lee was a gambler, and his decision to fight in the fields about Sharpsburg was one of his biggest wagers. He feared the political consequences of a retreat without a battle, and hoped that his opponent's natural caution would make McClellan fumble and yield the outnumbered rebels a famous victory. The gamble failed. Lee's pride demanded that his army stay in place on the day after the battle, for that, by the soldiers' terms of honor, denoted that the battle was not lost, but the campaign was nevertheless a failure. The North was spared a prolonged invasion and no European country was encouraged to join the South. By keeping his army on the field Lee could claim a technical victory, but on the Thursday night the rebel army slipped away, and by Friday evening there were no rebel soldiers left in the United States other than the dead and the prisoners.

Lee's invasion failed, but it was hardly because of George McClellan, who was presented with a marvelous chance to end the war at Antietam. If he had attacked twenty-four hours earlier, he would undoubtedly have destroyed Lee's army, which was smaller than it ever would be again until the war's very end. Yet McClellan was wracked by doubts and waited while Lee was reinforced. And if, when he did at last summon the courage to attack, McClellan had coordinated his assaults, he would have routed Lee, but instead the Northern attacks came one at a time, and Lee was able to move his shrinking forces to meet each new assault. McClellan's plan of attack had been to engage Lee's flanks, then send the killing blow through the center when the rebel reserves had been depleted, but the fight never remotely resembled that plan. Instead the battle degenerated into a series of bloody encounters over which neither side had full control. It has been called a soldier's battle, for it was the common soldier who fought it, and fought it with an extraordinary bravery. McClellan could have resumed the fight on Thursday and, with his huge reserve, which had not fired a shot, he would surely have finished the business quickly enough, but he was too frightened to try. He claimed his soldiers were tired, and Lee's army was allowed to slip away to fight again. Lee's army had suffered grievously and all it had to show for its efforts were the captured guns and supplies from Harper's Ferry.

Antietam was McClellan's last battlefield command. He himself believed he had displayed the highest military artistry, but President Lincoln had taken enough of the Young Napoleon's timidity and new generals would now take over the North's army. McClellan went on to make himself a political nuisance. He ran as the Democratic candidate for president in 1864, but, fortunately for the Union, he failed to unseat Lincoln. To his dying day the Young Napoleon would defend his appalling leadership, but the truth is that with McClellan's dismissal the rebels lost one of their strongest military assets.

The story of the Lost Order is famous. No one knows how the copy was lost, and after the war, when survivors conducted endless autopsies on their campaigns, everyone involved denied any knowledge of the order. All that we know is that the two soldiers from the 27th Indiana regiment found the order wrapped around three cigars and its discovery was enough to prod McClellan out of his customary caution. If the order had not been found, Lee would probably have reached the Susquehanna as he planned, but once his strategy had been revealed the invasion was doomed. The two soldiers who found the order, Bloss and Mitchell, were both wounded in the cornfield.

The fight in the cornfield and the battle for the sunken lane were the two bloodiest episodes in the battle, with the struggle for the Rohrbach Bridge (now named the Burnside Bridge) coming close behind. To walk the terrain today is to marvel at the bravery of men who could attack across such open country in the face of terrible fire. The battlefield is well preserved, though the East and West Woods are much shrunken from their former sizes. A road, heavily lined with regimental memorials, now runs south of the cornfield while an observation tower stands at the dogleg corner of the sunken lane. Anyone wanting to know more about the campaign and battle should read Stephen Sear's *Landscape Turned Red*, a book that was constantly by my side during the writing of *The Bloody Ground* and, to my mind, the finest book on a single Civil War battle, maybe on any nineteenth-century battle, ever written.

Antietam was indeed a ghastly affair. The North was badly led and its men's bravest efforts were wasted, but the rebel retreat afforded President Lincoln the opportunity to proclaim a victory and, in its wake, to issue his Emancipation Proclamation. The war, which had been ostensibly about states' rights, was now firmly a moral campaign to abolish slavery. But to proclaim the slaves free was one thing, to liberate them was another, and the road to Richmond would prove to be hard and long. Lee had been rebuffed at Antietam, but he was far from beaten. Starbuck will march again.

BOOKS BY BERNARD CORNWELL

THE SAXON TALES
THE LAST KINGDOM
ISBN 978-0-06-088718-6 (trade paperback) • ISBN 978-0-06-112657-4 (abridged CD)
ISBN 978-0-06-075933-9 (large print)

Set during the reign of King Alfred the Great, *The Last Kingdom* depicts a time when law and order were ripped violently apart by a pagan assault on Christian England.

THE PALE HORSEMAN: A Novel
ISBN 978-0-06-114483-7 (trade paperback) • ISBN 978-0-06-078748-6 (abridged CD)

As England is reduced to nothing but a small patch of marshland, a beguiling sorceress and fearful Danish warrior complicate Alfred's desperate plans.

LORDS OF THE NORTH: A Novel
ISBN 978-0-06-114904-7 (trade paperback) • ISBN 978-0-06-115578-9 (abridged CD)
ISBN 978-0-06-088863-3 (large print)

After achieving victory at King Alfred's side, Uhtred of Bebbanburg returns to his home in the North, finally free of his allegiance to the king—or so he believes.

SWORD SONG: The Battle for London
ISBN 978-0-06-088864-0 (hardcover) • ISBN 978-0-06-137094-6 (abridged CD)
ISBN 978-0-06-088866-4 (large print)

Alfred survived the Danish invasions, but fresh Viking ships are arriving to plunder and enslave the Saxons.

THE BURNING LAND: A Novel
ISBN 978-0-06-088876-3 (trade paperback) • ISBN 978-0-06-088875-6 (large print)

The epic story of the birth of England and the legendary king who made it possible.

DEATH OF KINGS: A Novel
ISBN 978-0-06-196965-2 (hardcover) COMING JANUARY 2012!

The sixth volume in the bestselling Saxon Tales series resumes the saga of the birth of a nation.

THE RICHARD SHARPE SERIES
SHARPE'S TIGER
Richard Sharpe and the Siege of Seringapatam, 1799
ISBN 978-0-06-093230-5 (trade paperback) • ISBN 978-0-06-101269-3 (mass market paperback)

The first of Richard Sharpe's India trilogy, in which young Private Sharpe must battle both man and beast behind enemy lines as the British army fights its way through India.

SHARPE'S TRIUMPH
Richard Sharpe and the Battle of Assaye, September 1803
ISBN 978-0-06-095197-9 (trade paperback)

Richard Sharpe must defeat the plans of a British traitor and a native Indian mercenary army in this second volume of the India trilogy.

SHARPE'S FORTRESS
Richard Sharpe and the Siege of Gawilghur, December 1803
ISBN 978-0-06-109863-5 (trade paperback)

In this explosive conclusion to the India trilogy, Sharpe and Sir Arthur Wellesley's army try to conquer an impregnable fort in a battle with stakes both personal and professional.

SHARPE'S TRAFALGAR
Richard Sharpe and the Battle of Trafalgar, October 21, 1805
ISBN 978-0-06-109862-8 (trade paperback)

Having secured a reputation as a fighting soldier in India, Ensign Richard Sharpe returns to England and gets caught up in one of the most spectacular naval battles in history.

SHARPE'S PREY
Richard Sharpe and the Expedition to Denmark, 1807
ISBN 978-0-06-008453-0 (trade paperback)

Sharpe fights once again to keep the treacherous French troops at bay in Denmark.

SHARPE'S HAVOC
Richard Sharpe and the Campaign in Northern Portugal, Spring 1809
ISBN 978-0-06-056670-8 (trade paperback)

Sharpe finds himself in Portugal, fighting the savage armies of Napoleon Bonaparte, as they try to bring the Iberian Peninsula under their control.

SHARPE'S ESCAPE
Richard Sharpe and the Bussaco Campaign, 1810
ISBN 978-0-06-056155-0 (trade paperback)

Sharpe has made enemies among the Portuguese, and when the British army falls back through Coimbra, he and Sergeant Harper are lured into a trap designed to kill them.

SHARPE'S FURY
Richard Sharpe and the Battle of Barrosa, March 1811
ISBN 978-0-06-056156-7 (trade paperback) • ISBN 978-0-06-137416-6 (abridged CD)

Richard Sharpe has been sent by Wellington on a mission to Cadiz, now the capital of Spain, to rescue the British ambassador from a spot of undiplomatic trouble.

SHARPE'S BATTLE
Richard Sharpe and the Battle of Fuentes de Oñoro, May 1811
ISBN 978-0-06-093228-2 (trade paperback)

As Napoleon threatens to crush Britain on the battlefield, Lt. Col. Richard Sharpe leads a ragtag army to exact personal revenge.

SHARPE'S DEVIL
Richard Sharpe and the Emperor, Chile 1820
ISBN 978-0-06-093229-9 (trade paperback)

An honored veteran of the Napoleonic Wars, Lt. Col. Richard Sharpe is drawn into a deadly battle, both on land and on the high seas.

THE NATHANIEL STARBUCK CHRONICLES
REBEL
The Nathaniel Starbuck Chronicles: Book One • Bull Run, 1861
ISBN 978-0-06-093461-3 (trade paperback)

When a Richmond landowner snatches young Nate Starbuck from the grip of a Yankee-hating mob, Nate turns his back forever on his life in Boston to fight against his native North in this powerful and evocative story of the Civil War's first battle and the men who fought it.

COPPERHEAD
The Nathaniel Starbuck Chronicles: Book Two • Ball's Bluff, 1862
ISBN 978-0-06-093462-0 (trade paperback)

Nate Starbuck is accused of being a Yankee spy. In order to prove his innocence and prevent the fall of Richmond, he must test his endurance and seek out the real spy.

BATTLE FLAG
The Nathaniel Starbuck Chronicles: Book Three • Second Manassas, 1862
ISBN 978-0-06-093718-8 (trade paperback)

The acclaimed Civil War series continues as Confederate Captain Nate Starbuck takes part in the war's most extraordinary scenes.

THE BLOODY GROUND

The Nathaniel Starbuck Chronicles: Book Four • The Battle of Antietam, 1862

ISBN 978-0-06-093719-5 (trade paperback)

Nate serves under General Robert E. Lee during the famous battle at Antietam Creek.

THE GRAIL QUEST SERIES
THE ARCHER'S TALE

ISBN 978-0-06-093576-4 (trade paperback)

Determined to avenge his family's honor after a band of raiders brutally pillages his village, Thomas joins the Hundred Years War and embarks on a quest for the Holy Grail.

VAGABOND

ISBN 978-0-06-093578-8 (trade paperback)

Thomas continues his quest as he weaves through the battlefields of the Hundred Years War.

HERETIC

ISBN 978-0-06-074828-9 (trade paperback)

To reclaim what's rightfully his, Thomas finds himself in a murderous race with a black rider.

THE SAILING NOVELS
SCOUNDREL
A Novel of Suspense

ISBN 978-0-06-208238-1 (trade paperback)

A relentlessly suspenseful contemporary thriller set in the lethal world of international terror.

STORMCHILD
A Novel of Suspense

ISBN 978-0-06-209265-6 (trade paperback)

A man must save his daughter from Genesis, a shadowy environmental activist group.

WILDTRACK
A Novel of Suspense

ISBN 978-0-06-146264-1 (trade paperback)

Nick Sandman dreams of sailing away from his troubled life. But to keep afloat, he strikes a devil's bargain with another sailor...

CRACKDOWN
A Novel of Suspense

ISBN 978-0-06-143837-0 (trade paperback)

After accepting a job on a yacht, Nick Breakspear is lured into a web of cocaine, cash, and cold-blooded killings.

STANDALONE NOVELS
THE FORT: A Novel of the Revolutionary War

ISBN 978-0-06-201087-2 (trade paperback)

The story of the Penobscot Expedition, ultimately the largest American naval expedition of the Revolutionary War, has largely been left untold—until now.

AGINCOURT: A Novel

ISBN 978-0-06-157890-8 (trade paperback) • ISBN 978-0-06-078096-8 (unabridged CD)
ISBN 978-0-06-171972-1 (large print)

The inspiring story of that "band of brothers" who survives devastating hunger and disease only to face the horrors of the field of Agincourt.

GALLOWS THIEF: A Novel

ISBN 978-0-06-008274-1 (trade paperback) • ISBN 978-0-06-051628-4 (mass market paperback)

A private investigator in 1820s London explores a murder case that may rescue an innocent man from the gallows.